The Mapping of the

The Mapping
of the Strait of Juan de Fuca

Jeff Schwaner

greatunpublished.com
Title No. 4
2000

The Mapping of the Strait of Juan de Fuca

for my family

Prologue

In 1675 Don Antonio de Vea set his ships along the hem of Peru's rocky skirt, in an attempt to locate and flush out an alleged colony of British buccaneers: shadow-ships had been seen traveling by moonlight, strange songs drifted in pieces through the trees from the uninhabited area of the island; the colonists were afraid of raids. But de Vea returned, "convinced, from the poverty of the land, that no settlement of Europeans could be maintained there...." However, one of the Spanish barques, with a crew of sixteen men, was wrecked with no apparent cause on the Evangelists islands. The strangest report reaching de Vea's ears concerned an old Spanish ship, seaweed hanging from every crack, as if it had been submerged for a century, seen cruising the entrance to the Strait. The closest observer, who was a slave thought to be of Tartar origin and was rowing a boat searching for survivors, exclaimed to de Vea that the ship pulled alongside him, further that it disappeared into a thin mist seconds later, and still further that as it faded the outer hull grew transparent, and the bulk of the vessel within shone in the moonlight like bones. "Bones picked clean by the sea, and flying the Spanish colors," de Vea noted briefly in his log. He later crossed it out, and still later felt the need to throw the log into the sea, perhaps because of that phrase, or perhaps for some other reason altogether, but it was recovered by a Mosquito Indian named William, who found it in a shark's stomach during the two years he was stranded and separated from the famous band of privateers led by Captain Henry Morgan, who himself would retire to a political post in Port Royal as governor of newly English-controlled Jamaica...

Yet stories shift like the tide: by the time de Vea returned to

Callao the following year, the ship of bones flying the Spanish colors had become an unidentifiable ship flying a flag on which crossed bones had been painted or sewn; somewhere in the local drinking houses the bones linked up with a skull, and from thereon Callao's streets could often be heard echoing drunken arguments as to just where the now familiar skull-and-crossbones insignia originated.

Some people seemed to have caught wind of the earlier story, though. Rumors of a ghost-ship circulated among the Spanish sailors, and on to their wives, or perhaps it went the other way, and mothers would tuck in their children with stories meant to stress the evils of remaining restless after bedtime, of the ship of dead savages who cruised the night mist snatching up children, of the black feathers growing from their hollow armpits, the cold fingers, the seed-yellow teeth smiling, "Come with us on the ship of bones…"

Part One

History makes maps, and they in turn make history.
—Greenwood

I. The First Letter

The first letter came in thunder, with the watermark of a sea-
lion—an arcane, 16th century version with fangs and bloody claws—
attacking a mermaid off the rocks of Cape Flattery. The postmark
was purple, dated 7 August The Strait of Juan de Fuca and arrived in
Jamaica three and a half weeks after Tinsel Croom last contemplated
the island's night lightning from aboard the Scottish gambling vessel
Gregorian; three and a half weeks after he last signaled to Cletis
on the shore and gave Captain Felix Mendelsohn the okay to plow
through the heavy order of tide and wreckweed and leave Jamaica
forever. The letter read:

Dear Tinsel,

How is Cletis? Last night all my jewelry turned the color of
blood & I feared for him. Are manta rays really dangerous,
Tinsel? I thought they had no teeth. I know you've been gone
only a day. Lancelot (poor dear), I fed him too much cod liver oil,
and he passed an ugly brown stone on your favorite ottoman. See
you soon, watch out for the sun!

Your loving wife, Polly.

The second, fourth, fifth and third letters arrived, in that order
and at intervals of forty-five minutes, on the morning of 15 August
at the Ottilie Orphan Asylum in Jamaica-Queens, New York. These
were kept in a moleskin pouch by their recipient the inebriate palm-
reader Edna of Beaver Road, who saw things and had maps that
changed with history. This fact, and all the others which led to the
mapping of the Strait of Juan de Fuca in 1746, were bound in a book
which could be read only under a microscope, written therein by a

strange woman in red and passed on to Tinsel Croom on the eve of his first departure, from the Mobridge, South Dakota Elementary School. The date was 6 August. The telegram, "SON CLETIS ATTACKED BY MANTA STOP DR CHARLES ANDREWS MEMORIAL HOSPITAL STOP PLEASE COME SOON STOP DR FLECK." Even then great bodies, in the ways of maps and globes, were being magnified, folded, flattened and superimposed on the corners of history conventionally reserved for deep seas. And when the thunder came, it was with the sound of maps crashing.

II. The Landing

Because the South Dakota summer had so far been overcast and mild, because he was of European and Canadian origin, because he very rarely took to the arid beaches of Ellendale, Aberdeen and Pierre by Lake Oahe—because in summary he was through-and-through a Croom—Tinsel's skin was exceptionally pale in a translucent sort of way, and like the sunset's reflection on the scratched double plexiglass stormproofed windows of the Gregorian's Bar-on-the-Fore, Tinsel's exposed forearms and neck had in a short time already assumed a pinkish glow that seemed to him to attract more bugs—the biting kind, he noted—as the ship approached Port Royal from the mainland. Water taxis scudded by, banking heavily off the fudgy wake the larger vessel gouged on the inlet's surface, some honking disapproval with rusty air horns as they cut wide hooks around the waves. Tinsel watched them, checking his notebook to re-assure himself of his hotel reservations. The new travel agent in Mobridge, Cattie Crowley, had disoriented him, her hands fluttering and disappearing under sheets she covered with—what were they?—travel agent glyphs, Tinsel figured, ancient shorthand found in scrolls copied from cave walls revealed in an earthquake in San Francisco in 1908...

"Pirates, eh-hm." Captain Mendelsohn had positioned his head a few inches from Tinsel's right ear.

"Wha. I'm sorry, Captain, I was daydreami-"

"Pirates. Port Royal here: manifestly, eh hm, the pirate *maven* ye might say." The last word sounding somewhere between sigh and see; Felix Mendelsohn, first and only Scot to captain a gambling boat in the mile of water between Kingston and the peninsula of Port Royal, seemed to have a mouth with as many accents as teeth, though those numbered barely a dozen. He glanced behind him, where he had jammed his right shoe in a spoke of the ornate oak helm, steadying the course while he poured a Hound Dog Beer into a paper drinking horn.

"Ye get Henry Morgan here. Pirates and thieves. Three-fingered Jack; the booccaneers. Gallows Point, where a many of them swoong, Mister Crum. Or his head brought beck in a boocket of rum, to preserve it, y'know, collect the reward."

"I see." Tinsel consulted his Fodors. "And then the earthquake—"

"And the earthquake of 1692, clear swallewed two-theerds of the township! It was a *great* victory for the Christians." Two more water taxis passed them, then crisscrossed each other in front of the *Gregorian*, making a funnel the ship's nose drew itself into before cutting the wakes' foam. Tinsel watched the product of it all slough off to the side in a diminished rolling. The evening tide reminded him of fins, hills that really did roll.

"Felix—may I call you Felix?"

"Aye."

"Felix, any sharks or mantas around here?"

"Aye. Sharks in the shallows and reefs, mants out further, though they on occasion do skid aboot them, yes. They like the smoother sands, I hear. Though my son Loomis, now, used to be afeard of them. Thought they'd eat yer shadow if they caught yeh. Heh!"

"Are they, uh, big around here?" Tinsel caught a large fly nibbling his arm, wedged it between his elbow and the plexiglass window.

"Big? Layrge? Oh, certayn, huge, some even say they're having teeth now, though I wouldn't go thet far, harhar. Just big enough, though, aye. *Sure*."

Something collided into the window by Tinsel's elbow. Tinsel remembered the fly—No, absurd—but Captain Mendelsohn, already removed to the open fore of the ship, the breeze waving his hair like impossible landing directions, picked a dark lump from the deck and displayed it at the window to Tinsel.

"Doctor bird." He pressed his grey lips to the plexiglass. The bird was a green-breasted but otherwise black hummingbird, the exact size of the captain's palm. He removed his lips from the window and whistled a low sounding like a foghorn. He shook his head, and his hair resumed its signaling, more frantically as the wind picked up. "Aye, doctor bird," his breath stained the glass like the residue of an old language. "Certayn and *thet's* a bad sign. Jamaica's national bird, she is."

Somewhere beneath Tinsel's elbow, the fly squeezed itself free, flew up into the Bar's purple mosquito light, and crackled as the sun touched the water beyond Port Royal and Long Bay's last nap of shore, and night began in earnest.

III. The Second Letter

Here is the text of the second letter of Polly Croom to her husband Tinsel, as received and re-organized by Edna of Beaver Road, at approximately nine p.m. the night of August 15, a night the color of Jack Daniels and the smell of porous macadam. Outside and across 158th Street in Prospect Cemetery, her half-sister stood listening for the giveaway sizzle sound the dead make as they separate themselves from the posture of their remains and prepare to walk abroad on the evening's moonless air. And just to the north, the Ottilie Orphan Asylum, where sat the hideously wrinkled woman, orphaned by her country, her century, who would be the next to see the message, instruct Edna in the ways of its interpretation to help them find at last what was rightfully theirs. Edna's ghost-fingers ached as she wrote, and when she was done she folded it the way she'd been taught and hid it in her hair:

a	doesnt		I	
Oh		shape		
act				I'm
otherwise	sick			
and		else		in
	stone			
August				injured
nuts		straight		
	focus		it	
Back		from		Its
Polly		that		
priorities	the			

```
changed    get                    jar
put                   Tinsel
           going
dear                  gotta          Lancelot
says                  Wan            What
Doctor                gravity
see                   well           with
does                                 mean
seem

           you               Yours
```

The original design of the text, as Polly considered with smoky green eyes attuned to the nuances of spelling and punctuation, read:

August 8th

Dear Tinsel,

Back from the doctors! Lancelot doesn't seem sick or otherwise injured. I put that stone in a jar, you gotta see it Tinsel. It's changed shape, or else I'm going nuts...

Oh well Doctor Wan says I should 1) get priorities straight, 2) "focus" and 3) "act with gravity." What does that mean?

Yours, Polly

IV. Mutterings

When Tinsel arrived at the Rose & Thorn Inn, where Cattie Crowley had reserved him a room, he was surprised to find that it was not a hotel at all, not an overpriced b n' b either, but a dark nightclub whose smoky environs was the result neither of steamy dancing nor mysterious, fragrant hand-rolled cigars or long, leaf-caked bone pipes but Florida-exported menthol Torietons, unreliable and especially smelly smokes because of their cool blue and green plastic filters, which were built cheaply and melted slowly while being smoked, permeating the air with the thin, high smell of fresh toys. The outer perimeter of the Inn's small front yard was guarded by high-gloss plastic reproductions of a white marble bust of General Douglas A MacArthur, the original of which, holster and loaded Buckeye Duck Control shotgun draped over his forehead, kept solitary watch on a shelf over the owner's bed. An inner perimeter of bicycle racks covered with foliage seemed to denote a next line of defense. If MacArthur doesn't scare them off—who off? Tinsel wondered—then the waitresses and dishwashers behind the barricades would... The door, opened by the host to put out the house cat, ricocheted off its high window a glimpse of the piano Tinsel could hear above the sounds of eating, and he went in.

He noticed from his perch at the bar that all the occupants in the inn were white—the diners, drinkers, wait-persons and host himself. Most notably white, however, and the closest thing to the center of attention given his relative invisibility in a cloud of noxious Torieton fume, was the entertainment, draped over his piano stool like a casino over Atlantic City, his fingers scraping occasional notes from

the piano then catching them again with his sequined cuffs, like so
many strays or a bummed cigarette, his voice smooth as the plastic
coathooks in the hall and dyed in the same pastel colors, who began
Tinsel's journey into the unknown with this crowd pleaser, sung to
the tune of "Mack the Knife," the Bobby Darin version, in half time,

Swami, King of the Riii-ii-verr!
Oh you girls had better, better watch your, step!
Just one look—hey!—sends, your thighs a-quiver!
And he deliiivers, all, over, the map!
In Cowabunga, hey in Boise, yes!
With the natives, hey, and crazy mountain folk!
In the high schools, of New Joiiizeeeyah!
They're so noisy, noisy when that Swami pokes!
And the beaches—hey, Swami knock-out, holy boy!—
He's a curlin', those groovy, tuby waves!
You know it's, uh, hey! high tide
When Swami's girlin, ho!
He's out spe-lunnn-kin! in those
Underwater caves....

Tinsel remembered the music as big band stuff, so this version,
slowed and barely apparent as a piano translation, seemed to create
huge gaps in his mind where a trombone, a trumpet, a twist of per-
cussion should punctuate the overt chord changes, intensify the cool-
ness and hip attitude by its volume and straightforwardness alone;
these gaps seemed to materialize as cloudy islands above the piano,
smoking now from the synthetic incense rising from the pedals, into
an archipelago, little clear formations in the smoky blue sea, imper-
vious to all but the largest shifts in depth, jutting out like isolated
dares. The next verse a new island, suddenly familiar:

And that Tinsel, hey! hangin like a dead (uh)
Duck! With a last cluck! on my Christmas tree!
Who's in the holly, hey! A-hockin Polly?
Why, it's....
(in quarter time now, the changes hanging like painful yawns)

Sw-aaa—meeeeee, I said it's
Sway-ay-ay-ay Meeeeeeeeee!
Hey! Youuuuuuuu
Dirrrr.....teeeeeeee
Booooooooyyyyyyyyyy Yeah!!

The last hammer fell, puncturing the remains of the song as a broken wire, having snapped into the air above the piano, swept through Tinsel's islands like a tidal wave and dropped weightlessly into the performer's lap. Tinsel leaned back against the bar to steady himself, shook his head. A bug flew out of his beer into Field's face, who had till now been arguing with the barman, an established duck hunter, about firearms. His attention thus diverted in capturing and then de-winging the fly, he dropped it back in Tinsel's beer, nudged him with his thick, flannel-ruffled elbow, "Hey, Tinsel, d'ja know the word *piano*, sides bein the instrument, is also a musical direction? Means, "a passage to be played softly." Maybe I oughta tell that slimer up there, huh?" Receiving no answer, he turned back to the barman, a Rhode Island expatriot named Healey. "Now there's no way you're gonna nail an adult pintail with a rifle-bore firearm. Those guys shoot from high grass like a greyhound from the gate, and the only way to get em is to blast from the hip at a predetermined angle that's comparable to the duck's ascension in the first five yards. You don't have near the time to aim from the shoulder..." The bar was named "The Blind," and the absence of neon beer signs compensated for by shelves of subtly underlit mallard decoys. Their restive eyes settled on Tinsel, he thought, applying a clear coat of coincidence to his sudden anxiety. He took, finally, another sip of beer, spit out the bug, and turned to listen to Field's argument. Field was one of three Americans Tinsel had met aboard the *Gregorian*, the others two nuns AWOL from the convent of the order Sisters of the Pentecostal Profusion in Miami, who vowed in their enthusiasm to never stop speaking, in tongues preferably, as a conciliatory gesture to their Lord for having put up so long with all the previous vows of silence the Catholic Church had been authorizing. At any rate, they hadn't had much to say aboard the ship, strolling serenely from the rest rooms, where they spent the choppier half of the cruise, to the slot machines where Sister Ray Schultz, guided by divine or at least blessed silver dollars, redeemed herself seven times seven the minimum ten dollar divvy Captain Mendolsohn charged for the use of the machines. After cashing out the sister with a non-transferable credit good only at the *Gregorian's* on-ship bar, the Captain shanked the vessel hard to starboard into the wake of a sizeable school of dolphin, thereby assuring the sisters would remain restroom bound for the voyage's duration.

Field had inexplicably changed his mind about pintails, and was now comparing the relative ratio of error in Springfield and Garand rifles, giving the edge to the M-1 hanging tenderly over the ale tap, and positioning his rhetoric along the lines of his beer glass, preparing the compliment—and what's the difference between a compliment and an insult, Field figured, as long as you hit the bullseye—that would once more find his cup newly foamed with sparkling Hound Dog. Suddenly he remembered Tinsel.

"I thought you said this joint was a hotel. Where you gonna sleep, Tinsel? Behind the bar? Yuk yukyuk," waving his mug in huge orbits around a low-hanging light.

"Oh, so you're the guy." The barman looked at him. "My name's Healey. I'm the manager. We do have a place, one room really, before the old owners changed careers and added on the bar. Depending how long you stay, may come a night or two you'll be sharing it with someone; your travel agent said you wouldn't mind." He paused while refilling Field's glass. "Yeah, Mister Croom, now you're the only person we've had reserving that room for twenty-two years."

Tinsel, aware for the first time in hours of his initial reason for being in Jamaica, said, "My son's that age. Twenty-two, I mean; or, he will be on the nineteenth. I'm going to see him tomorrow."

Field: "Aaargh, offspring..." he coughed into Tinsel's cup as a heavy wad of smoke pushed through the bar area; "...now that's either too brave or too stupid for me, in this world." He raised his arms involuntarily, in a gesture like a weathered spruce raised by winds into stiff mannerisms, dark green disclaimers; "Lookit this!" his head rotating to take in the bar's baleful denizens, who seemed to sprout like weeds from cracks in the floor and spread out over the surfaces of chairs, tables and stools. "I don't know about you, Tinsel, but I take a look around me, and I *can't* have children. That's why I shoot ducks!"

"Aye!" Healey filled his glass as soon as it touched the bar again.

"How much do I owe you for the room?" Tinsel asked.

"Bill's on your beer tab," Healey turning away to wipe the bar, "and you can pay *that* when your week's stay is done," barely paying attention to him anymore, hearing, somewhere in the blanket of dark beyond the arc of MacArthur busts now shining passive moonlight in a blurry signal, somewhere impenetrable in their small repeating cry, a thread of everglade kites, harassing pelicans from their sleep to disgorge their food so the kites could feed. And as Tinsel lay awake in the black box of his thoughts night lay with him, rising now and then into restless flapping around his head, hovering impatiently, he thought, like a long-dead bird returned to its nesting site, searching for its last place to land.

V. History, the Perfect Bathroom, & A Shipwreck

Edna's half-sister came back from the cemetery to find her hunched over the table, fiddling with Polly Croom's second letter to her husband. "That ghost was in the boneyard again today," she said, looking beyond Edna to the small street-side window. Dusk had shrugged into twilight.

"The squatter?" Edna asked, not looking up.

"Yeah."

Edna bent her head and squinted at the letter as her half-sister reached over her head to pick a piece of fruit from a bowl on the table.

"Make sure it's not the wax one, Em."

"Ha ha," squinting herself for a moment before taking a tentative nibble.

"August changed; Doctor doesn't focus; I'm injured—it's Lancelot; otherwise priorities seem stone; Tinsel with yours?..." She crumpled the letter in frustration.

"Which code are you trying?"

"One space-two space-three space. Phrases rising two, three, four, four, three, etcetera."

"Don't bother with Uncle Jack's codes, Edna. It's bullshit."

"Says who?"

"The ghosts." Em nodded to the dark window pane. "Just told me Uncle Jack was crazy; *cricked* is what they said; and I'm starting to believe them. And Cattie said—"

"I believe Cattie as much as I believe your squatter ghost,"

Edna interrupted.

"Yeah, well, he didn't say nothing about that tonight. He was just checking out the tombstones. But the ones that count —- and you know who they are," Em snatching the letter from Edna and rolling it into a compact tube that she inserted into her hairpin, "—- they think you're gonna need some assistance, and Uncle Jack ain't the one."

Edna turned in her chair. "And they got anyone in particular in mind?"

"They said he's already on his way." Em flicked her apple core to the floor, where it was covered almost immediately by Edna's cats.

•

A voice interrupts our wanderings.

Though we're ostensibly in Jamaica-Queens, New York, in a perpetually dank basement apartment, overseeing Edna in her meditation, a voice is breaking the silence. Though she can't hear it, though it's all the way from Brooklyn, for some reason she shakes her head as if to shoo away a fly, and a sentence finds itself at her lips' edge. If she finally releases it it's too late for us to hear; if her eyes rotate like dark globes we don't see it. In a Brooklyn apartment someone's already saying it, screaming it in fact to his computer, calling it by name to give it encouragement as its insides whir as if it's gorging itself at a feast. Skinny arms shoot towards the bulb of a head, fingers steal out and scratch the scalp. He's snatching someone's secrets, and he knows time's of the essence.

"Come on, William!" Checking his watch; scritch, scratch. "Save it, William. *Save the past…*"

•

Edna of Beaver Road, Edna Story Bearer, last of her tribal line, moves about the basement apartment. From the single shoebox window at ground level, where her cats coil and uncoil in the dust, she's just a topknot of natty hair. But below the earth's crust she's all motion, her body heavy and disorderly, but we know she eats constantly, increasing her mass for some future event only she knows of, perhaps; on her cheeks grave creases heave outwards like waves, ripple along the line of her lips. Light plays faltingly across her bosom, as if it sensed the sweaty darkness between her breasts, the uncounted hollows unseen beneath her loose clothing.

In her robes twinkle uncountable small globes: they're hidden in the folds of her longcoat, like hot watches whose accuracy is unimpeachable. They flow also from her shoeboxes and the shoes themselves, they rise to the cellar ceiling when the sewer floods the house, they adorn her plump, musselly fingers like blue baubles, they're everything that ever happened, possibly, adjusted in their spherical size and density for their point of view and relative importance on present bearings, according to the spells Edna says over them to protect them. Some are so small as to escape the eye altogether; some are too heavy to lift. Edna is taught they represent a constant sum, and inasmuch as stories continue to be told, re-invented or combined with others, each globe may gain or lose in the shifting.

Thus the story of Christopher Columbus, the one representing the apple in Queen Ysabel's eye, at least, adjusted for its generalized and favorable angles, had shrunk, been recalled by some distant cosmic engine, shrivelled to a size indistinguishably larger than the needle's eye in which it rested, carried in Edna's half-sister's hair, jammed there eternally, or maybe with the advent of one last story, the bright bloom of a new vantage, lost then, lost in kinks of flat ribbon and activator, a tiny prick of light disappearing into a wrinkling, shiny darkness.

•

Perhaps Edna's elders, realizing early on that the earth was no richer for the increasing number of stories of her conquest, humiliation, created in their planters and gatherers' wisdom a representational limit, in mass or weight, that the globes could reach. Some of the older men had heated arguments over this, and these reached Edna in leaks and whispers in the year of her indoctrination, careful tappings of cigars into leaf-plated vases, script barely legible on her uncle's shiny forehead, or a series of coughs, hinting at but never revealing the principle behind their legacy, her responsibility... Were the globes really an interdependent organism, were they an outgrowth of a singular flower, each story a seed within a great blooming that once, when the whole story could be told but hadn't happened yet, lay clumped in pollinic glory, surrounded by giant sun-petals, immense stretches of veiny time...

There was a lot that Edna, in her first year as Keeper of the Globes, had figured out for herself; a lot more about which she'd made educated guesses but for the absence of her elders had been unable to confirm; and in her dreams whole galaxies of questions rotated about her mind's eye in constellatory fashion. But sitting in her basement underneath Beaver Road, testing frequencies on her shortwave transatlantic radio, Edna knew this much with certainty about the globes: that she kept them; that there was one missing; and that Tinsel Croom, Principal of Mobridge Elementary School, was going to help her find it.

•

How did she know this? That information is a story in itself... But first: a word about Doctor Wan.

Wan, psychiatrist to Polly Croom and many more, specialist in workshops on codependency resulting from the feminist mystique, was known by a select few (and referred to himself as such when among certain acquaintances) as a secretive collector of the world's most furtive art, the Illuminated Panels of Arno Rizzoli, famous in New York as an interior designer who secretly laced his creations with trompe l'oeil panels; so that Rube Perrib of Rib's Famous New York Barber Shop opened his doors on Amsterdam Avenue for his first day of business only to find a whole fourth of his barber chairs were not really there, only painted on the far wall, corrected for perspective, along with a mural of the huge ceiling-to-floor mirror he'd just paid tens of thousands for, sketched by Rizzoli to "reflect" the intermediate phase in Rube's facial expression as he first discovered two of his chairs were missing, and then let his eyes wander up the far wall to where his reflection should have been. Both Vanity Fair and Better Homes & Garden had run cover stories on Rizzoli, one copy of each having been prepared on cardboard by the artist himself for a mural of a news-stand outside the Port Authority bus terminal;

even the use of a difficult surface, unfinished fiberboard, reflected so accurately the wet appearance the day's correctly forecasted rain gave it, that seven people were reported injuring their hands trying to give change to the two-dimensional old man behind the soggy pile of depth-less New York Times.

But nobody, not Better Homes & Gardens, not Vanity Fair, had heard of his Illuminated Panels series, considered by Dr. Wan the artist's greatest achievement, if simply for their invisibility. Wan had invited literally hundreds of the city's elite to his West End apartment, yet none had ever noticed that the sumptious blue towel hanging by the shower, the slightly out-of-the-way mirror on the stairs, the plush carpeting on two of the stairs themselves, the elaborate octopus doorknock, all were fakes, watercolor or acrylic or oil on balsa or beechwood. Although Wan often wondered what people dried their hands with when they used his bathroom, he otherwise thought most highly of his guests, and gauged their ignorance of the artifice around them as proof not only of Rizzoli's genius as a painter, but of his as an art critic and collector of unsurpassed subtlety.

•

But now rumor had it Rizzoli was holed up somewhere, working on the creation of his lifetime's education, his signal work, his final masterpiece; and if it were to be his best, chances were that Wan himself might not recognize it. It could be anything, anywhere...

And now Doctor Wan had disclosed this information to one Polly Croom, working on an unusual intuition, remembering a raven speaking to him in a dream that hatched its way through his cream night visor and sleeping pills and took wing; now he was taking Polly to meet the frantic Arno, paying her airfare from Mobridge. Four taxis waited for her at the airport; she recognized the three plywood ones almost immediately, and Wan knew this was a breakthrough method, he'd make the cover of Psychology Today—even if it was defunct: Rizzoli could make a cover for him—he'd write a reminiscence for Reader's Digest, he'd do the talk-show circuit, stoke up business... August 16, five days after Polly sent her fifth letter to Tinsel, she boarded a Remaining Forests Airline plane clutching a hand-painted ticket, tore open three paintings of sugar packets and emptied them into her coffee, and left behind her ailing dog Lancelot, all her jewelry and her life with the man she married and loved, if not forever, then for a time neither she nor Doctor Wan could guess at.

As the Boeing stooped into its landing posture, Doctor Wan, watching from the real taxi, remembered for a brief moment the raven landing on something in his dream, something dreamed or drawn he couldn't recall. The sky was a fierce blue, the buildings beyond the air-strip green through his sunglasses, and he was almost positive that it all wasn't a Rizzoli, that it was real, despite the day's cold distinction, the quiet August heat so perfect in his face he could almost see it being drawn, the distant squeak of the earth rising up meekly to meet Remaining Forests Airlines Flight 526, the grounding of all he wanted.

•

To Tinsel, the morning of August 8 tasted of tuna fish, waking as he did abruptly to find his vision obscured by cat fur, the house cat's pasty tongue mortaring his face as if ready to lay tiny bricks along his brow and reassert his claim as Master of the Household; fishier still came the breath of Port Royal, Healey reclining on a deck connected by an open window to Tinsel's room, busy with his pipe and fish-scaling, carving the white chunks as he went along into the shapes of various subfamilies of ducks before throwing them into his New England Patriots beer cooler; fishiest by far, though, was the voice of whomever Healey conversed with, laced throughout with some suspicion or lack of friendliness the tone of which might have better suited the Port Royal of a few centuries earlier, blurry contracts pressed for signature by a man with a red beard and a spare hook in his boot, certainly not the tone you'd use in a relaxed conversation at eleven in the morning. But there it was:

"If you don't agree with me, Healey, y'know it's fine. You go on carvin your damn ducks, now, and don't mind the business goin on about you; an when the Maroons come down the hills with their Indian friends to take back their land, you'll see how good your plaster MacArthur heads do ya." A dramatic pause. "Bad things're rising in the wind, barman."

"Naw, Flinch, what's rising is the temperature of an old poot whose brain is ill-filtered." Tinsel could hear the snik-snik of another duck carved and tossed into the cooler as Healey considered his rejoinder. "Wacked out. You're hooky, man. The Indians you're so afraid of don't even exist, inasmuch as you wiped 'em out a couple-three hundred years ago."

"That was the Spanish," Flinch correcting quickly, his chair scraping forward on the deck as if to add more, but Healey cut him off.

"Yup, and the Spanish brought you over, enslaved you, and then the English and the French chased the Spanish into the woods, and indentured you to express their gratitude for your assistance, and now here you are, two hundred years later, selling fake Indian pottery to the ungrateful descendants of your English saviors who were so greedy they needed a whole new continent of Indians to wipe out. Sounds to me like you're better off hating the English, or the Americans, even, than the bloody Maroons, or a tribe of slaughtered Indians who didn't survive long enough to see your great-great-great grandparents step over their bones to pull more diamonds from the ground."

A chair scraped again as Flinch stood up. Tinsel inched his way to the window and stole a glance: Flinch, banana in hand, caught in a glaring match with Healey, holding in his hand the shape of a hooded merganser in full mating display. Flinch swatted at the duck fillet with his banana and said, "You'll see. This town ain't finished sinkin. When they come back, they'll take us all, black and white. A shipwreck's where it's started, an it won't end till the whole island's under!" He threw the newspaper down at Healey's feet, like a flimsy white gauntlet, but before Healey could react a third figure materialized, rising from a seat directly below Tinsel's window and stooping to pick up the fallen paper. A golden flask of Hound Dog clanked with the change in his back pocket as he straightened up.

"Alrait, alrait, now yoore both peckin pellets." Glancing through

his overcast hair at the newspaper, Felix Mendelsohn read the following: "The oonly witness to the strange accident of the American-
owned vessel *Margin* said he believed he'd seen a large ship flying a
Spanish flag—which he took to be a boat fitted for tourists—"

"Or an escapee from Disney World's Pirate ride," offered
Healey.

"—until he'd seen the tettered condition of the ship, cross..."
the Captain feathered the paper open to the next page, "...cross the
horizon and out of sight beyond Yallahs. He said he saw the *Margin*
do the same, an heerd the explosion after it was oot of sight. Well,"
looking at Flinch, "last I knew them Maroons were layin crops on the
mountains, net saylin the high sees! Maybe," repositioning his Hound
Dog in his pouring hand, winking savagely at Flinch, "maybe it was
ackcherly Queen Isabella herself, captained by Curstofer Columbo
an a spankin new crew of eevil Arawak goat herders cruisin in a sixteenth century galleon to oosher in the next period of Great European Colonialism!" Flinch had something to say in response, but
Tinsel didn't hear it because the cat chose that moment to spring
on his shoulder and run his sandy tongue, coated thinly with something he'd just caught and eaten, across Tinsel's ear. Tinsel twitched
his head and the cat's bright nametag, WALTER MIGHTY, swung
with a small but cold authority toward Tinsel's right eye. He crashed
blindly into the bed. Outside, Mendelsohn had just finished what
sounded like a string of multilingual insults, and ended with the
simple declarative, "an to top it off, yer obnoxious too."

"You only say that because I'm black." Flinch puffing for more.

"Neh, I oonly say et because yer obnoxious; that yer black
means but thet you've hed less time to pick up sech self-reeghtious-
ness than the British and French have had, Imperially speakin, I
mean, so it oonly surprises me the more to see hoo quickly you've
risen, Mr. Flinch, from pickin rocks to pickin fights." The bells of
the Church of St. Peter, near deafening because of their proximity,
struck the first of eleven condescending blows, and Tinsel, gathering
his things and rushing out onto the deck by the tenth toll, found it
already empty, just a plastic cooler full of duck-shaped fish fillets to

lend even circumstantial evidence that he hadn't dreamed the whole thing. It was then that Tinsel, gazing past the cooler and up the weathered shingles of the wall to his window and the two pair of eyes watching him from within, one feline and one human, realized that he hadn't spent the night alone.

JEFF SCHWANER

VI. Swelter

It's midnight in Brooklyn; within a tea kettle water bubbles furiously, and hisses as two bags touch down and settle into the business of seeping.

A single windowpane flares with reflected light. Somewhere near its center a fly tracks its own invisible design, looking for the spell that will let it in. A teapot pipes huffs of something decidedly weedy-smelling into the air. Behind a pile of pizza boxes Swelter's grinding some numbers between his molars, even as his computer is readying the next course.

He starts with the noon sun on his back, squinting to see the letters on the charts, eyes adjusting with a perfect curve of dilation as the hours' light arcs away until, his whole head opened to the huge uncharted space above him, he finds himself reading in pitch darkness. He puts aside the manuals and printouts, almanacs, tide predictions, geological references dog-eared and paperclipped, picks his general area for the night's dive, and plugs William in.

"All the world's a screen, hoho," and it lights up for him: P&P Access passwords, a Map that blooms in the Brooklyn night like a huge weed in the chink of green light William emanates. Somewhere, in that world of information, an island...

Swelter sucks cold midnight air onto his new fillings, finds his bearings by the pulsing cursor, and heaves up anchor. I can work all night like this, he tells himself. I can see almost everything.

VII. A Familiar Head

Cletis Croom looked okay. Propped by several pillows, he sat reading Les Holm's new novel Head Diver, and sipping JA LOVE! JAMAICAN LEMON DRINK, a vitamin-enriched liquid breakfast, bottled and shipped by Hesbro Toy Company of East Florida, the makers of Torieton filters. The pillowcases were prints of various maps, one of the Greater Antilles (1620) and one of Jamaica (1915, produced by the Sugar Producers Geodetic Society); also, a map of the North American continent from 1640, where most of the west coast north of California was branded "unknowne territory," crushed fittingly by Cletis' elbow into the pillow beneath, bearing the same year and coordinates and entitled "the fantastical claims of de Fonte and others..."

As he shifted to turn the page, Cletis deftly buried all hope of a Northwest Passage beneath his bandaged forearm, a thousand miles of linen-wrapped bone, adjusted for scale of course, descending with the huge looming signatures of his friends over the entire fur-rich, canoe-laden country of three hundred years ago.

Cletis winced painfully just as Tinsel stepped into the room. But it wasn't from the pain of his wounds, but sympathy for Captain Wednull J. "Angry" Beaver, the hero of *Head Diver*, who had slipped through a hole in a worn fold of electronically-charged organic tissue and fallen into the landscape beneath. Beaver and his men worked in a library where all knowledge was collected in huge maps of living tissue, the depth of which was imaginary but potentially dangerous. Swimming in any part of the landscape could result in a thousand revelations, but would they be the ones Beaver was looking for? So

vast was the store of human knowledge that eventually the maps
had to be stacked, separated only by fiber-enriched wax paper, and
the most frequently travelled spots were highly worn and hazard-
ous. The state of Wyoming had been evacuated so the maps could
be placed flat, but despite the admirable work of the Army Corps
of Engineers the smallest inconsistencies at ground level, like the
movement of nocturnal desert animals, could throw the whole pile
out of plumb, thereby causing unpredictable shifts in the formatting
of information within and between maps or, in plain English, a complete and random reorganization of history.

All these things made Beaver's job more exciting, and now he
was paying the price of the first-person narrative hero, who, in order
to compensate for his relative security in finishing the story alive,
must be subjected to various harrowing but clear-eyed glimpses of
Death, the Abyss, the Ultimate Etcetera... Beaver, had he known he
was merely a character in a science fiction novel, would have realized
that his latest predicament was nothing personal at all but part of the
contract, falling through endless maps to the land of a Kwakiutl Indian's nightmare, chased through thick fir forests by the Dzoonokwa,
the wild being of the woods, the pre-colonial Pacific Northwest's
homegrown bigfoot; it was just payment coming due...

"Pop! I thought you weren't getting here until tonight."

"You look alright..." Tinsel started, relieved to see the smile.

"Yeah, it was really no big deal. I was snorkelling this reef right
in the bay, the reefs're only a hundred yards out, taking pictures of
batfish and tang, and I saw this great coral formation that looked just
like an alto-sax."

"You mean the bay with all the water taxis and boats?"

"Sure. There's plenty of diving, too, I mean. Real safe."

"So what happened? You got attacked by a manta ray? You got
bit, were you stealing eggs or something?" Tinsel could see only a
scattering of bandages on his son, none looking big enough to cover
the ghastly wounds he'd imagined inflicted by a huge swimming
kite.

"Okay, I was trying to take this picture, when all of a sudden my light is blocked out; I look up and see a ray, pretty big I guess, just sort of floating above me. I think he got spooked by some other divers, ducked around the reef to avoid them and then stopped when he ran into me." Tinsel began pacing the room, projecting on the ceiling above his son the idea of the manta, looking down in—what? surprise, maybe—at Cletis, now in his mind's eye sitting on an underwater infirmary bed, hefting the coral saxophone, removing his mouthpiece and blowing a single note, not trembly but clear and fluid... The sun, moving free of some bank of clouds miles away, reflected suddenly off the window and into Tinsel's eyes, and in the blue moment before vision returned fully the image of the manta transformed itself into a vision of a Spanish galleon, twenty guns athwart, a newly sewn banner of skull and crossbones high atop its mast, peeling the water before it back like a part as the single note held, then disappearing in a blink as Cletis' roommate, till now asleep, farted loudly and thumped his feet on the floor.

"Whoa, stinker. Sorry man," deferring to Cletis in light of not having been properly introduced, then shuffling off to the bathroom. Cletis' voice came back to Tinsel just as he regained focus.

"While I was moving to get a better picture of the ray, I got knocked by some huge wave into the reef. Cut me up pretty good, lots of blood, but nothing very deep. I made the surface okay, so several other divers would see me, and then Footlong here," motioning to the empty bed beside him, "suddenly appears in my face, screaming like a madman, plows over me with his surfboard." He gestured beneath Footlong's bed, to an oversized black painted surfboard, which Footlong referred to as his "cross country board." Almost the width of two normal boards, Footlong had built it to create a new sub-sport of surfing, gliding in and out with the tides until he had made a circuit of the entire island. The press had covered him as far as Wickie Wackie, and somewhere east of there, near Yallahs, was the last he remembered before running aground on Cletis' ribcage, back in Kingston Bay again.

When Footlong returned from the bathroom he began a long, protracted babble, scrambling his bedsheets in bunches and troughs to describe the tide changes, weaving his meticulously researched knowledge of the tide with his own version of the accident...Tinsel lost track, between the minutae of drift and drag, undertow and intuition, beneath the pounding of hammerhead waves and the buzzard hoverings of impossibly huge seagulls, was drifting in his mind back to the square dry banalities of South Dakota, the sneaky carvings of prepubescent slogans on waxy desktops and the communities of stiff gobs of gum gathered on the undersides of chairs like a board meeting of spare brains, when something of Footlong's story began to seep through. There was a wave lifting him into the air; there was a strange calm; there were two ships, freak lightning on a sunny day, a person with feathers strapped to his elbows... Tinsel glanced over at Footlong, whose arms were suspended like a seagull landing on a crabshell: "Did you say two ships?"

"Yah, two ships; and then—"

Cletis, who'd been reading *Head Diver* while waiting for Footlong to finish, patched on his own ending,

"Yeh, and then you plowed into my fuckin head!"

Footlong, extremely apologetic, "Oh, oh yeah, wicked sorry Cletis! I was lookin at the guy with the feather, and..."

Tinsel would have listened to the rest, but the intercom called him for a meeting with Dr. Fleck, a short hairy man with a birthmark just below his beard which Tinsel couldn't decide looked more like Italy or Florida.

"Eastern Florida," Fleck explained. "It's a tattoo. The Eastern Florida Plastics Conglomerate, and of course the good citizens of that section of the state, are applying for statehood. As a majority stockholder in one of those businesses, I thought it would be patriotic of me, a good example to the employees really, to make a significant statement on our position." His pocket was full of wax crayons, which he preferred over ink to mark his charts, and a vague but unwashable rainbow had developed over the years just over that pocket, caused by the doctor's confident swagger and the consequent movement of the crayons against his shirts.

Fleck explained to Tinsel that Cletis seemed fine, but that he was waiting on some x-rays to make sure he'd sustained no injuries to his ribs. "He had complained of some pain there," Fleck said. Tinsel inquired about Footlong. "Severe concussion," Fleck replied, eyes shifting to a set of x-rays on the wall of his office, which, as if having second thoughts, he quickly took down and slid into an open desk drawer. "He's on heavy painkillers now, but he'll probably have a dinger of a headache for quite a while. Shouldn't have been trying to surf above a reef anyway. He should be asleep for days." Fleck hesitated, seeming to sense some inconsistency or doubt in Tinsel's expression, then ushered him out of the office to the front doors. "Boy's been keeping your son awake, I hear, ranting in some way or another; at any rate, you can pick up your own around mid-afternoon tomorrow." He made some marks in his notebook with a black crayon. "Mmm. Nice day out there. Enjoy it, then, Mister Croom."

Tinsel stepped out into the coral afternoon, the thick but clear humidity sifting about him with cool knots of sea wind, feeling oddly submerged in the twists the summer day had taken. He was hungry, and walked slowly to the Cafe Redbeard where, standing in the shell-embedded doorway head and shoulders above the crowd of Japanese tourists waiting for a large table, he beheld his first wife, Cozetta Croom Bitfield, who noticed him a second later, and with a sweep of her arm blurred the day in a surging whirlpool: Tinsel closed in, and before he knew it he had eaten the Redbeard Lobster Surprise, two Red Snapper cocktails and had found his worn Pogo loafers slipped off by warm feet beneath the table, a slightly cooler ankle caressing his shin as they exchanged hotel numbers. They hadn't spoken yet, but just when Tinsel was about to offer to pick up the bill, Cozetta opened her black eyes fully on him, and began to speak.

•

"You look like a big bear without a stream to fish in," Cozetta said from somewhere behind her eyes. Tinsel couldn't quite focus on her broad lips, which were smoothed over with a low-gloss charcoal color, or the round ears which he knew winked back and forth when she spoke. He saw himself as the smallest of a million small creatures lost in her onyx irises, he could see miles behind him, in the flawless reflection, the sparkle of a single fish scale in the eye of a goofy-faced gannet hovering momentarily above the choppy waters just beyond some reef, invisible but present in its effect on the surface; he could see a million more years away, farther and farther out where there was nothing but warm blackness, and he could see closer in, to recent events: Cozetta and his marriage, their tiny apartment in Oahe, she painting next to the desk he corrected spelling tests on, and as he closed in, froze that frame and zoomed in on her black eyes they became flat and reflexive, filled with his own greedy face, and he realized he was only looking at himself again, failing Cozetta once more, before he'd even had a chance to re-introduce himself.

She must have seen the look of sudden fright in his eyes, and pinched him lightly with her toenail. Tinsel's right hand shot up in the air, to surrender or apologize, but he inadvertantly flagged down a waitress, who in the Redbeard Cafe were known to be especially violent, so he stuck a ten in her hand and ordered coffee, and like Wednull Beaver, saw the Abyss pass him by, spare him for another day.

"Some meal," Tinsel managed; then, tentatively, "some coincidence? or are you here to see Cletis too?" She dug in her pockets, uncrumpled a telegram identical to the one he'd received from Fleck, adding, "But I was here already, actually. I'm looking for a certain tombstone I saw on the cover of one of our books back in Oahe..."

"Oh, you mean the one on *Tim Pontoon's Only Hiding*," he said.

"...yes, that's it, and I wanted to see it for real before I start working on my next series. Sort of an "Emotional Tombstones" theme, I think; I've been going to all sorts of cemeteries peering at this name and that, this shape and that, you know, so I was already here for a few days, and the telegram got re-routed to my hotel. Good luck, I guess," she said, grimacing a bit at the joke.

"Your husband relayed the address?" Tinsel ventured.

"No, my roommate Monique," she said encouragingly. "Tom and I split last spring. But anyhow." The coffee arrived, half empty from the waitress managing to splash a few warning drops on every potential under-tipping customer in her section. Tinsel didn't bother asking for cream. Once more, before he could help it, in the dark, heavy surface of the coffee he saw Cozetta's eyes, attending to some flock of birds in the distance, and felt himself being pulled. But Cozetta bumped the table with her knee, her warm foot finally leaving his leg, and standing before him with a tourist map clenched in one fist said, "So, wanna go look for a tombstone?"

So it wasn't until close to ten that evening, eleven hours after Tinsel first saw a different pair of eyes, as Cozetta and he sipped dandelion wine from a flask with the printed logo COMPLIMENTS OF EAST FLORIDA WEED CONTROL INC. in Old English letters, that he got around to thinking about Witcover.

Witcover, the boucan man, Witcover the berry picker, Witcover, the occasional seller of dandelion root to the Rose & Thorn Inn, paid for his services with an equally occasional night in the spare room, when a particular reason for being indoors would get under the old dog's fingernails and itch him; he'd claim it was cold, or maybe frost or rain would make sleeping outside uncomfortable; but on the coldest, rainiest, stormiest nights Healey would never see him, and thus figured on some hidden agenda, hidden in one of Witcover's dusty cuffs, some sequence of reasoning that brought him into town when the rest of the year, had a hundred men slipped into the foothills of the Blue Mountains to find him, he'd be invisible and untrackable, barely a memory to the woods itself save the unlucky buck which, reacting to a sound in the leaves above, would have time only to glance at the strange, hairy apparition dropping towards it before its neck was twisted, by strong, merciful hands, to a quick darkness....

Tinsel had run back to his room that morning to find Witcover sitting on the hardwood floor, rubbing his feet in a shallow pan of small green buds and feeding tender strips of birch bark to Walter Mighty.

"Aah, Crum! Glad to met ya. Name's Witcover. I'm a, er, *buyer* fer Mister Healey." Tinsel saw at his feet a short spear, barbed at the tip like the lower case "t" in the old English logo on the wine bottle, he explained to Cozetta now, she standing by an open window doing toe exercises; Witcover had thought Tinsel was looking at his feet and the buds. "They're a strange thing, Crum," he'd whispered conspiringly, "make yer footprints disappear behind ya."

"Um," Tinsel had answered. "Nice to meet you, Witcover. Uh, would you care for some breakfast? I'm going now to grab some coffee and eggs or something. And, by the way, uh, where did you sleep last night," Tinsel attempting casual directness, leaning back against the door as if talking to an old war buddy. He reached into the Continental Breakfast Platter Healey had left at his door, came out with a slightly brown orange, tossed it in the air.

Witcover flinched at the sight of pesticide-produced fruit, batting it away. "Neh, eye'll just chewer on yer old bark here," peeling more strips with his thick yellow fingers. "And there's plenty of free and tasty bugs under these floorboards," pulling one up and granting a lone roach mercy as it scuttled across the floor, "and *that's* where I slept last night, Tortoise, rayt under..." patting the floor, "neath ya."

"That's Tinsel, actually."

"Ya roll around a lot, Tinsel. Bad dreams? Jet lag? Same thing to me, anyway, but no, thanks, I'm movin out this morning to catch some giant turtles. Gotta get there around mid-days when they get groggy. So, I'll sure see ya around."

"Will he still be there tonight?" Cozetta asked, rubbing his shoulders from behind him. Out her window he could see the faint white glow from the busts on the Rose & Thorn's front lawn. He tried to shrug, but his muscles had turned to noodle. "Um. Cozetta."

He felt Cozetta's soft eyelashes on the ridge of his ear lobe. "Tinsel. If I lick you right here, which I would do if I invite you to stay, your life would explode into a million pieces. Your soul would wander the earth forever. We'd eat each other into nothingness, and you could never go back to South Dakota. You'd melt in my mouth, Tinsel, and I'd stick to your teeth. You can't stay here..." breathing the next, and last, word into his brain, buzzing unbearably with crickets until he realized he was outside, on the way to the Rose & Thorn, then numbly curled on his bed before it finally registered, and resounded in his head, like a shot never fired, "*...tonight.*"

VIII. Flattery & Victoria

Monolithic rose the maps above the abandoned state of Wyoming, an inscrutable windowless warehouse, a huge cube of colorless matter, a shoebox for God; like a junkyard heap of giant mattresses it leans, lifts above the heady peaks of the highest of the Rockies, up through clouds, beyond the heights reached by inquisitive turkey vultures and golden eagles; one atop the other, each map uniform in area and volume, a snug fit along the Wyoming border, each stuffed with stories, conventional and unbelievable alike, the stuff of rumors and dreams, romance and dread secrets of underground movements and official documents, acts of God and animal, the statements of bodies in attendance, their insistent residue crisscrossing through a network of visions and imbedded into the charged field of the organic compound, the fiber of the maps themselves, uncountable electric connections waiting to be made, afloat in this gelatinous living substance, this pile of mattresses stuffed with currency too dear to take to the bank. But: for the heroes of Les Holm's Head Diver these mattresses offered no rest, no sleep but a constant barrage of information, history culled into neurological sensations transmittable to all who wear the Head Diver suit, to the intrepid research librarian of the future, where footnotes lay not coyly in the dusty moth-flustered shadows of a forgotten diary disintegrating in its pigskin cover, but instead lay crouched in three-dimensional, completely sensual accuracy, delivered with all the brunt of perceived bone. Every event and wisp of thought that advanced collection could drain from the zeitgeist, real or dreamed, was programmed and projected into one map or another, and Wednull J. Beaver knew his way around them like he knew the proverbial back of his hairy hand, now held up clearly before his eyes so he could see it along with the reader. This time the view being no less than the Abyss itself, the great veering of the body from its mortal cowl to the nakedness of mythos, death some would say but not Beaver, who'd seen the dead get up and explain their positions, who saw the history of the soul's departure float by him every day, who saw the many monsters and was not afraid...

What Abyss, then, facing him, like a reflection on the other side of his hand? Imagine the mammal of your nightmares; stand it on two feet, give it a name. The name the Kwakiutl Indians gave it was *Dzoonokwa*, the wild beast of the woods. Captain Beaver, speechless with surprise, is stared at by the creature with equal speechlessness and perhaps a bit more hunger. Together they pause that dramatic moment a semicolon in the novel's text might signal; then the chase will begin again.

For it actually began a few pages back; but might it end here? Captain Beaver, for all the fortitude granted him by the author, was admittedly tired. Exhausted. The Dzoonokwa had chased him through these ageless Douglas firs since the *Head Diver* had fallen, *plummeted* was the actual word in the text, through the membrane of the map above, incidentally a much calmer environment of suburban middle America c.1960, and had landed on the creature's unfinished dinner, *Pacochoerus aethiopicus*: raw wart hog. Its half-skinned ribs had embraced him as he thudded into the still-warm corpse. Beaver, awash in a soup of innards, had thought quickly, as heroes are wont to, and coiled the long intestine around the astonished beast's leg. With a deft, almost balletic motion it fell, raised its head to see Beaver free himself from the remains and jump into the darkness of the trees. There the chase had begun, Beaver running for what seemed like hours, though it was only a few paragraphs, doubling his tracks, throwing his scent to the woods with an aerosol spray specially designed for such circumstances. The careful *Head Diver* had lost the Dzoonokwa several times over, concealed his movements so utterly that he had become lost himself, not sure now, wheeling about an audience of mute mossy trunks, which direction he'd just come from; and it was then, lifting the back of his hand to his face as if to gain his bearings by examining the paths of his own blood, that between his fingers he saw the head of knotted fur part the branches before him, those eyes that undid so many wayward Kwakiutl warriors, whose teeth splintered the lightning, whose breath rocked the sleeping birds from their nests. Beaver had glanced down, seen the gnawed boar skull between his feet, seen his path turn in on itself. Back where he'd started...

Just as Beaver was about to begin an impossibly long inner monologue on death and history, repeated glimpses of the end, apocrypha etc., the ceiling of trees above him began to boil and bubble like a frame of film stuck in a movie projector.

The Dzoonokwa, unfazed by this commotion, extending his paws Beaver-wards, suddenly finds his way blocked by an imposing yellow object; crashing through the wall between maps comes the cavalry, Lieutenant Whiffle and First Gear Stallwood, driving a late 50's model Ithaca Public Works Department Snowplow. Stallwood grasps Beaver's wrist and pulls him aboard. "Nick of time, eh?" he says. Behind them, in the vaccuum created by the vehicle's force, flow into the ancient fir trees a few stray parked cars, ivy league students, fire hydrants and unleashed pets; the gravity in their map being at a higher setting, they float in the branches near the forest's ceiling.

Whiffle, smashing through a few more trees for good measure, pushing even the heavy pine air of the woods before him with the thick iron grill, lifts the Dzoonokwa bodily with the business end of the plow. "See ya later, Nature Boy!" he yells at the monster, blowing a bubble the size of his head and spitting out the gum wad, which floats to rest on the Dzoonokwa's elbow. "Juicy Fruit," Whiffle whispers to Beaver as he presses a red button; the plow ejects its cargo at rocket velocity into the air, where it punches another hole in the map as it exits.

"I didn't know snowplows could do that," Beaver deadpanned; they bore straight through the map's punctured ceiling into the light

of a suburban afternoon and the facile shapes of ranch houses as the
tear continued to stretch, unleashing more pets already trampling
the quiet forest with stupid yapping, roller skates and lawnmowers
tumbling in, a break that would take the mending crew weeks to
sew up, on through it all and farther they went, through a dozen
landscapes, two dozen, in the same manner until they found themselves out of it finally, flapping for breath on the Wyoming border,
the whole pile of maps jiggling behind and above them with unseen
activity or laughter, just one more day of work for Captain Beaver
and his men, the neon-lit signs above them blinking as it closes this
chapter of *Head Diver* with its bright red highway-style lettering:

Welcome to Wyoming!

"The Equality State"

1869 — Suffrage to Women

1925 — Nellie Taylor, World's First Woman Governor

2165 — Living Information Library-The Library of the Future!

Please leave requests with the library staff

•

Even the Armadillo's nights were too short for Swelter.

Swelter sat in an unlit corner of his room, eyes closed and turning, and sipped a cup of cold tea. Across a long table from him
perched the squat William, computer unparalleled, specially mod-
ified by Swelter for problems involving excessive number crunching. A printer beneath started up noisily, and spat out topographical
information, cross-referenced with predicted tide shift data, for the
San Juan Islands, Padilla Bay, Saratoga Sound and Puget Sound, the
Strait of Georgia and the Strait of Juan de Fuca, all the waterways and
accompanying islands in the 17,000 square mile area the U.S. Geological Survey titled *Victoria*. The map on the near wall, now supporting Swelter's leaning head, shows both the United States territory
and that of British Columbia, the looming island Vancouver with its
westernmost city Victoria and the islands north and west of Plumper
Sound and Tumbo Channel; but the history of border relations in
this region had never been so smooth as the Strait appears to illus-

trate, a soft perforation through its middle like a careful incision, a simple parting that leaves the world intact on either side. More apt an image of the region's history was apparent in its geology: the Juan de Fuca plate, a slab of ocean floor still sliding into the continent, getting beneath its skin and creating eruptions and irritations that would (and still do) develop into cliffs, mountains and other less user-friendly landscape. Some American-made maps had actually been distributed with a huge blank area in their northwest corner, an open ocean of blue, as if Vancouver Island did not exist simply because the USGS couldn't claim it as true motherland.

Swelter's wall map showed him depth readings at intervals of two hundred feet, the population of cities or villages noted by the size of their letters, airplane landing ports and seaplane anchorage on the various islands, the conditions of roadways from primary all-weather roads to hiking trails by the color and pattern of dots and dashes; landmarks, foreshore flats, intermittent or dry streams...

Ah, these maps, Swelter's eyes opening as he thought, these maps; information become so specialized it would take a year to learn all they could tell me, and then years more to learn what the things I had learned *mean*. He stood up.

Back when he had his job, Swelter had been chosen. Not that he didn't already think he was built for something special, no no; but. But until eight months ago, to be more specific, no one had given him his calling. And until quite recently, he hadn't known what he'd been given.

The Partner & Partner Firm's information arm swept far over the earth and back into the country's soily past, the long fingers branching out from the cuticles and shooting roots into the ground of a quickly expanding American empire. And when all the paperwork was too vast, the files too huge and dangerous, too easily lost or misplaced; and when the Firm decided to computerize its entire world of data, it was Swelter, meager paralegal Swelter, who meekly suggested creating a software landscape, a map, a continent of information as vast and mysterious as the one with which Partner & Partner's history was so tangled: it was Swelter who speculated on large,

entertaining "national parks" of public access, to allow anyone with
a PC and modem a glimpse at the unblemished beauty of P&P's
historical growth and conservation, likewise Swelter who had suggested hidden coves and desert retreats, dangerous jagged peaks of
pure info whose insides still broiled with secrets too hot to divulge,
secrets that, like their metaphorical counterpart, could eventually
erupt and change the landscape for good. "For the good of the Firm,
of course," subtle Swelter had suggested, and just like that he was
Vice President in charge of File Organization, leading a staff of six
hundred, a personal cadre groomed for security and a vast flow-chart
of jobs and timetables geared for swift and staggered entry of sensitive data, so that not even he knew the whole of it, or at least was
willing to avoid such knowledge. Times there were, Swelter pacing
the room now, judging the moon as it skidded slowly (but not slowly
enough) up the buildings along Queens Boulevard, and the Ottilie
Orphan Asylum beyond it, times there were indeed when Swelter
would see, from his office high above the assembled multitudes, two
co-workers criss-crossing each other over the great floor of computer terminals, each carrying a benign-in-itself (Swelter's phrase)
parcel of information to enter into a numbered file that would later
be matched with the geographic coordinates of the software map;
neither of them knowing if by chance they were to collide, say, bump
one into the other and drop their files together on the floor, some
undreamed-of evidence might make itself known...

Sure, he thought to himself as he heard the printer click off
beneath the table, sure sure, every company's got its secrets, shady
deals are made, inside advice sold and reputations built on malice,
extortion and blackmail every hour of the day, wake up and slip on
the banana, Swelter man, it's no big deal. But standing above it all
and watching the network of near-misses threading through each
other, thousands of partial truths stripped down to below the level
of human responsibility and twined in an intricate web of logaryth-
mic inexorability, Swelter had begun at last to see Pattern, and Pattern alone was power enough. At least that's what the Firm must have
thought: when Swelter arrived at work one morning he found his

paperwork and charts confiscated, his desk emptied of pencils and his Coordinator Password revoked. Maybe they had seen some furrowing of the brow, a slight change in his characteristically light way of strolling the floor of the work room, maybe the confident grin that had replaced his earlier meek smile had been tempered in its enthusiasm and openness a tooth or two. For whatever reason, and they certainly hadn't felt it necessary to come up with one, Swelter was dismissed, his position delegated to a dozen other P&P submanagers, none of whom were known by the others, so that the same thing wouldn't happen again.

Swelter had attempted to take it in stride, company's best interests and all that, he mused on his way out, although he wouldn't have been so willing to go quietly had he known his name had been put on a blacklist already, messages left in the files of personnel offices of every potential employer in town he had visited, resume in hand, during the next eight months. Only after those months had passed did he begin to take seriously the muted warnings of one Jog Thurnn, Icelandic migrant worker whom Swelter had observed on the work floor hundreds of times without really noticing his potential. Thurnn's potential being no more than his odd shape and bearing; he was in all ways as flexible as a brass bedframe, and combined with a tendency to nearsightedness his posture caused just the physical collision of data Swelter had so often imagined. Top-heavy Thurnn had fallen over while attempting to recover a dropped pencil, and in rising had upended a passer-by; their files of yet-to-be-entered data were mixed on the floor, and it wasn't until Thurnn reached his terminal and began working that he saw he had retained some of the other man's papers. With all the proper awe one might expect from someone discovering quite suddenly that the earth was not flat but round, and with the help of some technopyromaniacal programming he'd learned at the Helsinki World Secretary Institute in Jacksonville Florida, he managed a hard copy of mysterious but informative substance. From what would become a continent of case histories, written and oral agreements, minutes of meetings and classified documents, Thurnn extracted a miniscule chunk whose informative value, properly analyzed, would be rather like that of a moonrock: the entire geological history, to speak within the metaphor, of the Partner & Partner Firm could be gleaned from this smallest of information concentrate. Thurnn couldn't believe it: if the earth was a tooth, this cavity was dark and rotten to the core. Anxious to go public but aware that all P&P employees were watched closely if they even bought a newspaper, never mind contacted one, he'd considered confronting a meeting of the Trustees with his find, maybe accepting a pension of some sort to keep quiet, a small cottage in Vermont and a modest cash settlement; but Fear bought him out first. Fear, bravest and most impersonal of affronts, saved him, for certainly the Firm, like any responsible navigator moving about in difficult waters, would not let such obvious driftwood bob and float about in comfort. They would chop it into kindling, burn it and cast the ashes over all four corners of the sea.

So Jog Thurnn built an island.

Deep in the waters of one corner of the software country, farthest from where the PC tourists were bumbling about with their software field guides, that part being the Southeast with its huge Floridian amusement parks, Thurnn plotted out a small, hollow rock formation, a leftover upthrust of the continental shelf's last attempt at spewing forth new land from the sea bottom; and in this hollow golf-ball of an island he dropped his moonrock, covered the island with trees and bald eagles at first, then changed his mind and sank it, moved the tide table over just enough to keep it submerged for most of any given year. And he hid it well.

Swelter, leaving his office for the final time that strange, loopy day he was chosen, was knocked down, benignly enough it had seemed, by this same nearsighted Icelander, who while helping the dazed ex-Vice President up slipped a small note into his sleeve and whispered, among loud apologies and embarassed snorting sounds, the soft but entirely unmistakeably clear phrase, "The Beavers are flying."

•

The Cashinahua Indians, long since departed residents of the

North American continent, told a story about the night that went like this: the sun never stopped shining. The Indians, badly in need of rest and having no night of their own, borrowed the mouse's night; but it was too short and they woke tired. They borrowed then the tapir's night, but that was so long that when they next awoke the undergrowth from the hills had crept over their land, destroying their crops and houses. After searching far and wide they finally took the armadillo's night, which was just right, and they never gave it back. That is why the armadillo, deprived of his own night, sleeps in the daytime.

Swelter had become the Armadillo, and the night his most active and revelatory hours. Had he known in advance that the moment he started burrowing into this strange twilight of a country he would uncover the artifacts of covert business agreements that hyper-extended the Firm's influence back to the days of the Hudson Bay Company, the Northwest Passage Company, the Company of Farmers and the Senegal Company, who dealt in the slave trade to Columbus; had he known that such agreements would extend to the present and even the future, the East Florida Statehood Drive and the stranger designs Partner & Partner had on the Greater Antilles in the years ahead, had he known all this when he first exchanged his suit and tie for the tight-wrapped protective collar of the Armadillo, he might have had second thoughts, might have met Jog Thurnn's friend Fear a lot sooner than he did now tonight, reading and re-reading the printouts of recent activity in the Map by company researchers. Researchers! Swelter snorted, the sound almost startling in the solitude of the room. The visitors to the Map tonight were more like mercenaries, computer also-rans who were trying to earn overtime by searching for Swelter, who to them was simply a "foreign entrance" or some such informationless term. There seemed to be a lot of action in the Puget Sound area, also a good deal of anchoring by Cape Flattery, the rocky and difficult point of northwestern coast just below the mouth of the Strait of Juan de Fuca, where Swelter suspected Jog Thurnn had positioned, and then sunk, his island.

"Flattery will get them nowhere." He chuckled. He was ahead

of them, that much he knew. That they were looking for something at all out there did not bode well for Thurnn, whom Swelter had last seen that day when he'd been chosen, trusting him for some reason with a brief note about his discoveries and consequent action, and with the hint scrawled near the bottom, "48.15." He might have been afraid then, and retreated from the challenge. But now, caught up in the largeness of it, in the power of Pattern which everyday revealed one more gossamer thread of connection, sleep would not come to him, not until he had stared into the face of the Abyss and seen not Death, not the smiling faces of Partner & Partner, whoever they originally were, not hopelessness or nothingness, but the fine and terrifying confluence of all the thin threads tied together, the complex made singular and simple in shape, the Pattern.

The Pattern would free him; the Pattern would take the mask of Night off all of history, and then real Death might spring from the emptying shadows like sunlight, and all would know who is people, who is bird, and who is beast of the forest.

The moon, risen now above the local buildings of Queens, sat expectantly on Swelter's windowsill. Jog Thurnn had hidden his moonrock on an island, sunk it within a sea of information; Swelter, the armadillo with the moon on his side, awoke his keyboard with a flurry of commands, heaved up anchor and sailed, the long black wings of Night protecting him, into the Strait of Juan de Fuca.

•

"I don't get it."

Tinsel puzzled over his salami and scrod sandwich while Cletis and Cozetta waited patiently, building a french-fry house on the edge of his plate.

"Cletis, eat half of that fry so we can make windows on the western wall." Cozetta schemed how Tinsel's fish crumbs might reinforce the roof, experimenting with different samples when Tinsel was speaking.

"Okay, so I'm assuming by this point," wedging his left hand a third of the way into Cletis' copy of *Head Diver*, "I'm assuming that this stuff, it's electrical, is it electrical or neuro-whatever, right? The guy ducks into it, and what? Does he come out slimy?"

"No, Pop, it's sort of like jello, I think. So the maps, right, all piled high on one another, like this stiff jello. Then Captain Beaver goes in, and his skin, or uniform, whatever, *reacts*," a pause with Cletis assuming Beaver's persona, looking about the restaurant wide-eyed, arms tangling slowly with the hanging plants, scuba-diver-like, "with the jello, and it gives him information, or what have you."

"If he comes out with some under his fingernails though, he just took out some kind of history though, right?"

"Yeah, but that doesn't happen. Cause it's a, each map I mean, an *organic* thing, so it knows somehow. Like, if someone were to try taking a little piece of your body, you'd know, you get it?" Cozetta had transferred subtle fingers-ful of fish crumbs to the french-fry house's retaining walls and roof, and was now positioning salami strips to emulate shutters and doors around the house. It was mid-afternoon of the ninth of August, and Cozetta, Cletis and Tinsel had assumed the relaxed friendliness families may occasionally manifest when they realize they're no longer connected by bonds of social and personal responsibility but by the network of positive feeling that those earlier bonds formed and protected for so long. The sun seemed satisfied with its position, and whether it moved more slowly that day or the people beneath it lived more fully in that period of afternoon hours is arguable, but the island sat on a calm, a smooth caesura even in the marketplaces, where Flinch, in the midst of a hundred dollar sale of fake native pottery to a ninety year old woman from Utah, changed his mind inexplicably and halved the price, cursing himself later that evening; only the eastern wind from the mountains maintained its normal pace, cooling the sun and scattering showers like drinks on the tourists. Had the day not been slowed as it was, these winds and rain might have been foreboding to the folk of Port Antonio; they might have looked to the west and the range of the Blue Mountains and seen something to fear in the bushy arms of the inland. (Had they looked that way a few hours later, as the sky paused between thunder, reabsorbing its excess energy, they might have seen the landing lights of a small aircraft, the sun slide in a shaft through a cloudbreak to illuminate an image of brown fur and sharp teeth painted on the fuselage.) But not even Flinch, eternal pessimist and comptroller of invasion-from-within prophecies, scared as he was of uncivilized mountain folk and the disorder of conspiracies hatched, conspiracies of broken tongues and revenge schemes emanating from Jamaica's chilled heartland, not even Flinch could worry on this afternoon; business was good, the suckers were polite and carried cash, and he had enough extra by mid-morning to buy a box of Aye Carumba! Cigars, imported from East Florida, and suck them down to their soggy ashes as he sat by his cart, watching with a vague interest the construction of the Crooms' fragile house.

"Hey, Oklahoma!" he shouted to Tinsel's table.

"South Dakota, you mean." Tinsel half stood up, then realized Flinch didn't know him, though he knew Flinch from that morning on the porch. Flinch had a knack for guessing what state American tourists were from, and judging by the architecture of the frenchfry house thought he had a good chance. Usually if you could guess within one or two states, even, you'd get a sale out of the ensuing conversation.

Maybe Tinsel sensed this, or maybe he just wanted to stay where he was, with Cozetta and Cletis, or maybe he remembered a bit of Flinch's conversation that morning, and he sat back down. "Close, though," he smiled in Flinch's direction.

Flinch grunted something in response and disappeared behind a momentary smokescreen of blue-brown Aye Carumba! fumes. Before the wind had revealed him he wrote on the heel of his thumb, "Croom. South Dakota."

The first of the thunderstorms was still a few hours away, and Cletis, having given up for the moment his attempt to explain *Head Diver* to Tinsel, buried his own head in the book and would not come out when called. So Cozetta and Tinsel ordered beardfish cappucinos, slipped off their shoes and sat talking, bare feet hardly touching at the toes in the sand beneath the table, and experienced that almost electrical sensation small pleasure charges you with; looking at it this way, Tinsel might have better understood *Head Diver*, the whole body reacting to a touch, information and memory, desire or determination enlivening every cell, jumping synapses in daredevil gestures... but, too absorbed to know the structures he was absorbing, Tinsel sat and received, like the great sinkholes into which fall coastline houses, swimming pools and summer memories, all the feelings of family Cletis and Cozetta unconsciously transmitted. They talked about Cozetta's sculpture series, the search for the tombstone ongoing.

"Sculptures, paintings, I'm not sure which yet," Cozetta said. She sketched quickly and instinctively on her napkin, shapes surrounding her cappucino mug, a dance of flat people around the towering brown stoneware.

"Hey," Tinsel said, pointing, "what about a mixed dimensional thing? Paintings with sculptures popping up from them, maybe painted figures on the sculptures, and maybe the sculptures are figures too. Or were they going to be tombstones?"

"Hmm. Tinsel, that's not bad."

Cletis cutting in, "Sounds sorta dopey to me, Pop. Guh-huh."

"Nah, wait Cletis." Cozetta's long arm shot towards Cletis' head to cut off further criticism, her hand flowering at the last moment from a fist into slender fingers, two of which pinched his nostrils shut. "Make the dead the three-dimensional stuff, and the living people flat, that's sort of interesting, don't you think?"

"Oh, that's not what I meant," Tinsel said. "I'm not sure what I meant now, actually. Cletis is right." Cozetta looked at them both, a you-should-have-known-better glare at Cletis, whose nose she still held tightly.

"Mob, leb go ub by doze. Bleaze?" Cozetta released him. "Stick to your brain book, Cletis, and let your dad and I deal with the conceptual arts." They all tried to look mean at one another, all failed and settled into whatever individual version of the Croom shiteating grin each possessed, and in that moment anyone could identify them as a family at rest, bound more by some inner language and mannerism than by blood or loyalty; still, the type of family one's mother might comment on walking by with her own children, scolding them that if they only behaved they could be as happy-seeming, when actually the fact the kids didn't go nuts faced with such betrayal from their own mom proved they were already as happy and restive, somewhere inside that only externalizes itself in the way one of the kids elbows the other, or leaps up to his mother's hipbone like a saddle, yee-hawing and causing further beratement. When the grins subsided and the bill was paid, the Crooms stepped into the green calm of the day, the sun finally beginning to move again, for a moment passed under by a dark cloud pursuing other pressing business, or by some general darkness that dipped in to let the island know that time was starting again, although eight days later over Manhattan a similar darkness would last much longer, and seem to tell an altogether different story, that time was not fleeting, that time was not of the essence, but that time, for some, was up.

IX. The Fourth Letter

Revelation, as if anxious or impatient for recognition, would
meet Tinsel halfway, bearing up implacably before him and Cozetta
beneath the shade of a cottonwood tree and against a field of modest
placards to the dead on August the ninth, the day poised on the point
of its own inexorability, its immutable passage through the vapors
of the general summer buzz, dropping like chips off the odd shoulder only the next morning in the ringing stairway of his skull, to
the accompaniment of a cloister of curious seagulls who viewed him
unblinking in their testy hunger. But however it was for Tinsel, Revelation came for Polly Croom into a much calmer space, a day later to
be exact; Polly found herself suddenly awake (though not abruptly)
and kneeling at her bathtub, holding her hands over the pile of
jewelry she'd thrown in the tub sometime during the night, fingers
spread apart and hovering there as if to gauge a proper scale from
which she could take the whole pile in. Lancelot lay across the back
of her calves, snoring; have I been here all night, she wondered.

She dislodged Lancelot gently and stood up, stretched, thought
about breakfast. The stone Lance had passed two days earlier, now
the size of a twelve pound bowling ball, sat on the coffee table in
the living room. Since Tinsel had gone to visit his son, Polly had felt
a strange distance between herself and the house, so not even that
reddish rock shape, porous and slightly steaming since yesterday, not
even this lapse of memory and trancelike vigil at tubside, affected
her enough to make her worry. Rather, she felt as if her real life, the
physical and psychical thing that was Polly, that the earth would be
lacking if she suddenly disappeared, had been slowed down, sub-con-

tracted to an exclusive plane of residence, of concentration; Polly
had read that where to an amateur the possibilities are many, to the
expert they were few, and to her now, eyes rambling across the peaks
and dips of her tub as her mind did the same over her marriage, the
possibilities had all come to a single point, so far in the distance she
couldn't yet see it, but still insistent and fine: if the earth has music
for those who listen, and Tinsel was being bombarded with a com-
bustion of symphonies, dirges, concertos and accompaniments, all
the brass of the earth bashing its secrets in rococo signatures with
every cymbal crash of Cozetta's dulcimer eyelids, a silky thundering
lake of warm contradictions necessary for the downpour of history
to collect, then Polly was alone, and comfortably so, on the other
end of the gramophone's cone, at the small peak where the arriving
music squeezes through in the tiniest, most immutable pieces; and
before anything was amplified, hence distorted, Polly was there,
waiting, seeing in her inner distance the silence that's the prelude
to the earth's music, the sound that delivers motion to decision,
splits through seconds an eyes-only memo for the watchful, solid and
impenetrable as revelation must be, moving over some precognitive
nothingness.

Outside this huge cone of music, surrounded by Crooms, was
Elsewhere, where Polly would recognize, seven days later and in a
vast gallery half-real and half-artifice, that first complete sound she
had heard today, sidling up in the silence before the first note spilled
over the speakers' edges; where, vacillating between a sense of dread
premonition and a feeling of ecstatic justice as in a pitch sung too
high to hear, she would scribble the title of the piece that followed,
gathered from Arno Rizzoli, the actual artist or just a talking piece
of cardboard she couldn't tell, scribble the title on a scrap of toilet
paper in the women's room only to realize she'd done it seven days
ago, back here in the bathroom, and mailed the toilet paper to Tinsel
in her gas bill envelope, the texture of the ink-porous paper atractive
through the return address window of the mild yellow envelope...
what did it mean to do something twice, or to forget having done it,
to have made the same decision under different circumstances? or

were the decisions the same one, singular and unrepeating? was anything the same except the name of the soundtrack? If she'd reached
some decision with a knowable application, prepared for the consequences and accepted a new tack, she was yet to know it, still in the
space before the music began. But the letter would be its own cata-
lyst, opened in frenzy in Edna's apartment on the night of the seventeenth, Edna drunk into a fury of vengeance, her head darting about
the room like a bumblebee, Edna at the height of her powers, the
room adrift with globes and thunder localizing somewhere over the
waters off Manhattan as if it had intention, as if it knew the tune,
judgement passing as the weather; and who had Polly to judge but
herself, her own place in time? Whatever weight the word she wrote
might carry, the jury was, if not hung, then mute: all was quiet at
the Croom house, just the small movement of her tongue licking the
gum of an envelope, sealing away the score for another day. The message:

> 8/10 12:45 p.m. ...*Bolero??*

•

The quote of the day calendar page for August 17, torn from its
pad and stuck with a pushpin into the corkboard above Arno Rizzoli's desk, was attributed to Socrates and read *The way to gain a good
reputation is to endeavor to be what you desire to appear*. Roughly translated or not, it was a fake, painted in the colors of mid-day summer
as was the corkboard itself and all the messages on it; painted as
well was the June blue pushpin holding the quotation in place, and
painted was its oblique shadow on the board, as well as the shadows
cast by the strange copper blinds in the window, thick and vaguely
menacing, the greenish orange verdigris strips held almost still in the
presence of a slight breeze by the concurrent notches they'd hewn in
the pine molding. And if the light and the shadows on the wall aren't
real, Polly thought, eyes strafing the room with suspicion as Rizzoli's
manservant Wahr poured her tea, then where did the real light and
shadow go, and can the rest of the room be far behind?

Rizzoli and Dr. Wan, who had picked her up at 1:30 sharp from
the L'vacuua Hotel, were dressed both in black tweeds, Wan's being

polyester and Rizzoli's second button beneath the tie having been sketched in with pencil in case the wind should blow... but as long as things appear to be well—"and they'll always *appear*," Rizzoli had joked to Wan earlier; Wan, expectantly, "Wellll?"—well, then the money, the magazine profiles, the well-endowed but underwritten apprenticeships, and of course, the opening of the Retrospective, would keep life quite secure; but leave the shadow of a doubt that the artist is as bland as anyone, that he's made it not by guile and repartee but by some untaxable resource that can be neither divided nor invested in, let a sliver of suspicion that his work is not in partnership with the Art World, the concentric and magically dissolving rings of commodity, gallery rights, review space and column inches, the specialty canvas stretchers, cut through that thin net of connections and he'll find himself, Rizzoli bringing in his circus act metaphor, "unicycling in mid-air with Dildo the Bear on your shoulders and nothing below but an angry elephant or two. Aha ha—" now recounting that same story to Polly as the three sipped Armadillo Nights tea and talked about the funeral.

The tea bags were decorated with a transparent image of an armadillo shuffling across a barren land, foothills of tea behind him, who, as a result of chemical processes not explained on the box or in the list of ingredients, twitched his ears and wagged his tail as the tea within brewed in hot water. On one side of the tag were the words **East Florida Agribusiness**, on the other side what Polly thought was a fortune, the *Pacific boils over!*

"So the bodies," Rizzoli paused to make sure he had Polly's attention, "the bodies were atrocious! No amount of makeup could cover up the bloating of a cadaver so skinny that not even the sea weed and crabs would bother with; oh oh and Belcher—"

"Balcher," Wan corrected, head bowed in a silly smile.

"...yes, Balcher, him being so close to the explosion and all, why you'd think they would have considered a closed casket." He sipped his tea and set the cup on the desk, burped silently, one hand feathering out in apology. "Hmm. Or they could have asked my services, aha ha," his elbow knocking the desk as he and Wan turned laughing to Polly, who had noticed a quivering that seemed to travel visibly through Rizzoli's mug when he'd hit the desk. Was it too a painting? Hadn't she seen him drink from the mug a second ago? Polly looked up, saw them waiting on her for a response.

"Heh heh," she said slyly. They were in hysterics. Rizzoli and the good doctor then assuming a conversational pose well blocked in stage terms, three quarter profiles showing their mid-day stubbles, a thread on the artist's sketched button seeming to stick out from his shirt, they slapped their hands on their knees and broke out into the following song for their lost comrades:
(Balcher & Bartlett's Song)
Oh Bob Balcher and Mark Bartlett
Walked down that corridooorr
And lost their lives a-workin
For the Co. East Floridaaa!
They were scoutin out the local tribes
For the Com-p'ny did aspire
To expand their coastal statehood
To a cor-po-rate Empire!
And the natives, were so luscious
Bob and Mark had three or four
Best enjoy it while you can my lads
For the Co. East Floridaaa!
Now they're facin heavy wormin'
In the business of their rot
And their logs are sogged in a Jamaican bog...
(Here a pause, Wan and Rizzoli link arms and look first to heaven, then to their respective crotches)
Aaaaaaaaaannnnnnndd...
We'll never know what they caught!
No, we'll never know what they caught!

Polly clapped with great enthusiasm, piled it thick as makeup, and with each sweaty bow the two directed toward her she surveyed the room, trying to figure what was real, what just paint and plaster. The whole room could be empty, she thought, they could be rice-paper puppets, activated by fishing line from above or, the idea flaring and jettisoning out before she could comprehend it, from my own hands, spreading them out in front of her face. Wan and Rizzoli, mistaking this for a sign, high-fived her, then sat down with semi-embarrassed smiles.

"Oh gosh," Rizzoli re-composing himself with a nod at his calendar, "I've got an appointment half an hour hence with Partner & Partner; all those papers to sign..." looking to Polly, "They're underwriting my Retrospective. Insurance is the way to go with your art, these days, Ms. Croom, and Partner & Partner the most discrete, comprehensive coverage you're likely to get. They underwrote the whole East Florida Statehood Declaration, which by the way I've been commissioned to *overwrite*, I guess you could say, haha, once all the lawyers are satisfied, and they financed the big Beaver Dig Nuclear Survey that Balcher and Bartlett were—"

"Hrm," coughed Wan, "not yet, not all this, Arno. You forget that my Polly is a patient. Let's be patient, don't you think?" He scratched his nose. Smiled apologetically at Polly. "How do you feel here? You like the new surroundings?"

"Okay." said Polly. Rizzoli picked a pencil from his shirt pocket and scratched something out on his corkboard. They all got up to leave. Polly glanced at the pencil, rolling back and forth on Rizzoli's blotter, as Wahr came in and helped her with her coat. Little words lolled up to her:

CALF PELLETS   **for dry feeding
CALF MEAL   **for liquid feeding
VITADINE   **for quality mixing
NUTRI TABS   **for calf scours control
EAST FLORIDA AGRI-BUSINESS ASSOC. since 1970
"Things for the farm that don't grow on trees"

The stub of the pencil stared at her dully. "Let's go eat, boys," she heard herself say cheerily, and turning with a sweep of her coat discretely reached for the pencil, knowing somehow already that her hands would fall on the flat blotter and nothing else.

•

The fourth letter of the log's title was a "V," which, bobbing up and down on edge of a quiet inlet, attracted Witcover's attention as he dragged his giant turtle back into the foothills. The sun caught the letter in a jagged reflection, and Witcover, ever curious and thinking it might be some rich tourist's lost gold tooth, investigated.

Since Partner & Partner as a firm spared no expense in the collecting and safekeeping of information, the logbook was bound in water-proofed hide and stamped with gilded lettering, which to its credit had survived a night of meandering in the island's quirky southern tides without any great loss in legibility. So it was when Witcover pulled the now slightly slimy logbook from the shallows that he could read the entire title, *BEAVER DIG NUCLEAR RECON (re: East Flor. Expansion Dividend) Initial Notes & Survey Specifications*, and could also, had he then wished, have broken the waterproof casing and read all that was inside. But hunger won out, he slipped the book inside the turtle's open belly and kept going.

Witcover caught turtle with a little-known but efficient method involving the remora, a fish with a powerful suction cup on its head, mostly seen by TV viewers stuck to the undersides of great white sharks, hammerheads, etcetera; Witcover tied a strong line wound from young trees around the remora's tail, then set it into the water; if you knew the predilections of the local tides and could claim a certain native luck, the remora would attach itself to the first turtle it saw, its suction being so powerful that you'd have only to pull the rope in, collect your catch and kill it. Bad luck, of course, could result in the remora attaching itself to a great white shark. But Witcover knew the water; it's not certain whether he knew while pulling the logbook from the water that it acted as a remora in its own way, tugging all sorts of invisible connections, drawing some curious and desperate men from another island to follow his every movement, although no one would call Witcover a stupid man, or a man with his head in the sand; but it's also not certain, while leaving the emptied shell of the turtle in Tinsel's bed the next afternoon with the tastiest prize, the tail, whether Witcover remembered the book he'd stashed in it earlier in the day. But now it was there, and Tinsel, arriving in his room hours after the crack of dawn the following day, would certainly not be the first to see it.

•

The last time that anyone in New York City saw the sun on August 17 was just as the Partner & Partner employee whistle blew for break at three o' clock; never mind that the Firm's official time-piece was four and a half productive minutes slow, the time stuttering and halting to allow a few more moments of work from the laborers, never mind that the callback whistle seemed to rush them back to work only minutes after they'd begun their mid-shift coffees: Partner & Partner time, embodied by the Whistle, had become one of those signposts by which the entire neighborhood surrounding the building acclimated itself to the pace of business.

Polly Croom, Arno Rizzoli and Dr. Wan, and a few million other good citizens, were driving through the leechfield of traffic lights in Manhattan's macadam heart, and were momentarily blinded by an event no weatherman could have prepared them for. For at that instant the sun, perhaps bursting with some new energy strong enough to penetrate the carbon monoxide comforter the city lay snug beneath most of the day, or perhaps because our planet's eroding position in its wobbly orbit responded to its own weird traffic signal, or perhaps because Edna of Beaver Road and Swelter were both staring at some form of the Abyss twisting in its death throes, clutching in its hand a paper on which had been scrawled the name *Tinsel Croom*, perhaps for all those reasons and some known only to the heretofore unnoticed cloud of crows, hundreds of them, sitting atop the Citibank building, the sun chose that same mirrored construction for the start of a chain-reaction of high-glare reflection, next bouncing off the canoe-shaped glass Partner & Partner headquarters, scattering from there in a billion careful glances to every reflective surface in the city; to every storefront window, every apartment building, all the racks of sunglasses in town, no matter where they were, those thousands of pairs of eyes shooting light to all the cars on the streets, their hoods, hubcaps, wheel wells if the hubcaps had been misplaced, rear-view mirrors, etcetera. The last thing Polly saw before the windshield of Arno Rizzoli's car was suddenly crazed with blinding light was the white-lettered warning on the passenger side rear-view, "OBJECTS IN THIS MIRROR ARE CLOSER THAN THEY APPEAR."

Then everything went white. Traffic stopped; people froze, afraid to move, in mid-step. When visionfinally began to thrum its patient way back to Polly, the roofs of the highest buildings were already swallowed up by low, dark clouds. It was as if Night had come early to New York, not in its usual mask as the absence of something, but as a physical presence, strong and unharnessed and heralded by the crows, who, seeming to be everywhere, swept down upon the complacent pigeons and loose pets with carbon cries and gaping beaks, and did not hide their pleasure.

X. Blue Hole

What did Tinsel and Cozetta do next? Cletis could have guessed, watching them disappear in Cozetta's rented car. "Headed to Port Antonio!" Tinsel had yelled, though they'd already told him as much. Cletis thought it looked like a scene from a commercial, a traveller's cliche which fades into the next commercial before it becomes too comical or quaint. But there they were, not fading, just driving away slowly, his mom and dad, waving and smiling like they were advertising beer. But no logo spread itself across the scene. A few fine ribbons of cloud, a few sea birds, the sound of a single prop plane. That was all. And Cletis. And his parents.

"Sure, pop!" he yelled back, waving himself because he couldn't help it. "See ya later, pop."

He tucked his wrinkled copy of *Head Diver* into the back of his pants and headed for the Rose & Thorn. What would they do in Port Antonio, anyways? Cletis thought, not without some wonder, about his parents engaged in the carnal act. This led him to theorizing whether he would have to look like his father when he reached the same age, or if some new metabolic discovery could alter his aging, keep him in good form. Then, there was always exercise. But Cletis thought he would go to the hotel and read.

Indeed, some further clue to his nagging questions concerning his parents seemed to lay within the very pages following the dog-eared leaf marking his place. Here the reader could find Captain Beaver once again weathering the travails of the first-person narrative hero, imminent dangers readying themselves on all sides: to his left, the mutinous Lieutenant Whiffle, drugged by the natives' petchl-berry peace pipe; to his right, a band of drunk Spanish marauders, hired in a more sober state by Columbus to build a fort and begin settlement of the new island (new to the Spanish, anyway, Beaver had quipped to Whiffle); and immediately in front of him, a rebellious lot of angry Arawak Indians, who'd crashed a tribal coming-of-age ritual to gather warrior types interested in killing anything remotely Spanish. Their village looted, their women raped and beaten, they were beyond even their own leaders' control.

As for Beaver: he'd been dropped here merely to gather soil samples from the island over a range of various centuries, a quiet kind of assigment it would seem, observing the changes in flora and fauna over whole epochs. But he turned his back for a second, and suddenly he and Whiffle had become involved somehow in the coming-of-age ritual; friendly Whiffle lingering long enough to take a toke or two from the petchl pipe found himself full of disobedient thoughts, drifting slowly on the ebb of either ecstasy or rage, depending on how he breathed in the fumes; when he inhaled he saw a giant sunflower, when he exhaled he saw blood and broken bones; and thereupon inhaling deeply declared his intentions to usurp Beaver's position as top *Head Diver*.

By this, the seventh chapter, Beaver had become accustomed to the Abyss' cameo appearance near the end of each episode, and the reader had, too, knowing Beaver would be thinking between the lines and in all the white space of the margins, and would resolve the ongoing problem of being its chosen target, at least temporarily, in the first three paragraphs of the new chapter. This bent and crinkled page of *Head Diver* proved no exxception, for as all parties surrounded Beaver help blew in on the curl of a clangy sea breeze, a voice tender and off-key, passing through a weak point in some nearby or adjacent map, one whose story could have been Tinsel's, or Cozetta's, or Cletis' had he but read this far, on into the folds of the novel's present location, *1493 Antillean*; and the voice, if voices are to be heard within books, was indeed Tinsel Croom's, serenading his first wife as follows:

When the wind blows like a chimney

And the night burns like a tree
Oh Cozetta would y've kept me
After I was thirty-three?
If the dog's bark like a halo
Would enclose my head in sound
Would you like me, or regret me
Dear Cozetta
Would ya let me
Once again into your arms?
Oh you know I'll be around
Yes you know I'll let you down
 But Cozetta there's no harm's
Done, when I'm in your arms...

Lieutenant Whiffle flared his nostrils and looked around him.
A tiny irregularity in the sky flickered and waved, like a fading tour-
ist should, caught the attention of the Spaniards and Arawaks also.
Twenty feet above them it hovered like a patch in the air, warped and
wavered, a tear in the fabric between this and some unvisited land-
scape, from which came Tinsel's voice, his long vowels and blurry
consonants softly bludgeoning those 15th century ears as he contin-
ued:
The Blue Hole, or the Blue Lagoon
Cozetta call it what you will
But I'll swim with you while the turtles
Drink, and I'll kiss your breasts
By the kitchen sink
Just take a moment sweet bird to think...
Your Tinsel loves you still
Your Tinsel loves you still

A window to another world opened above them, flared like
Whiffle's nostrils, crackled at the edges and belched quite suddenly
two men in white coveralls, paint-spattered and wielding drippy
brushes, also singing as they had been when, moments earlier, they'd

been painting a sundeck in Jamaica, not Xamayaca of the fifteenth century but Jamaica of the twentieth, and they chanted a single stanza like a mantra as they fell,

> Oh sleepy women whom I adore!
> Them sleepy women in painted skin!
> You sleepy women please take me in
> And I'll show you how the fountain
> *pours...*

They hit the ground like pillows. A paintbucket followed, and half a ladder, its upper end caught on something in the middle of the air, invisible.

Whenever maps collided like this, special technicians had to be brought in to sort the information, see what may have leaked from one into the other. A little misplaced data can make history look a lot different, especially to an uninformed student using the library, or actually, to anyone not a Head Diver, who alone knew what belonged where amidst the great confusion of time passing. Beaver may have thought of these complications when the two painters fell through, but foremost on his mind, the foot in the front door of his brain, was Escape. He dived for the paintbucket, slugged Whiffle over the head with it, tossed him onto his shoulder and leaped in slow motion for the ladder.

A swarm of musketballs and arrows followed him, most dissolving around his protective Diver suit, but one feathered shaft piercing his unprotected wrist, the momentum of it in the weird air around the ladder carrying him clear through to the other side, where he found his wrist pinned by the arrow to a support beam on a newly painted sundeck. A green mass of shrubbery and trees formed a pocket around a small lagoon whose shore at one edge came directly to the bottom step of the deck.

Beaver, suspended momentarily, gritted his teeth and pulled at the arrow, sticking it back in the post once he was free. He adjusted his suit for gravity in the new environment: each map was set for a certain amount of free movement by the Head Divers, who could walk on the ground like regular folk, but also had the opportunity if necessary to swim away through the very air, or rather, the appearance of air, since the whole thing was in fact some neurological shadow show. Wasn't it? Beaver had never felt the urge to follow that line of questioning. He did his job, and he did it the best; that was real enough to him.

He checked his footing on the deck, then reached down and pulled up the ladder, which appeared to be sticking out of the air over the lagoon, the hole popping closed and disappearing with a puckering sound Beaver seemed to remember hearing in childhood cartoons back in the real world. The gravity levels were set differently in each map to make clean-up easier for Divers and technicians. The two painters, having fallen from a map with lower gravity, would be pretty much stuck to the ground when the cleanup crew arrived. Sometimes it went the other way: Beaver had heard from First Gear Stallwood that the Pacific Northwest of Precolumbian time still had a few 1950's-period dogs and lawnmowers floating up near the treetops. Though nobody was quite sure where the Dzoonokwa had ended up, there were no volunteers to go scouring those dark woods for leftover suburban garage ornaments, either.

Holding the still-weightless Whiffle in his left hand, he pulled his sleeve over his wound, and zipped his glove over it with his teeth. Then he checked his watch.

The Head Diver watch was a marvel among timepieces. It told time by the sun, it told it by the railroads, it told it with reference to the local disposition. It also accounted for one's place and time in history with several theories of universal order or disorder, the big bang, the eternal and balanced universe, etcetera. Beaver, checking one of these, saw that time was still expanding, albeit slowly. Hmm, this meant he was somewhere just south of the twenty-first century; he looked around.

One side of the sundeck faced the lagoon, vegetation huddling closely around its edges, as if calling a secret play that humans had no business hearing... but what was that rustling in the midst of the leafiness? Was it a giggle or a snake slipping through idle branches?

The other side of the deck supported a shack, presumably a shower-room or public bath, and a view of the ocean beyond.

"Especially pleasant," he murmured to his Head Diver Note-Taking Machine, keeping his voice lowered and watching the cautious movements of his own glassy reflection in the water beneath the deck. He watched a few curious bugs disintegrate against his Diver suit. Two pair of footprints led to the edge of the deck and the small, shadowed beach to its side, disappearing into the water. Beaver thought he heard a muted conversation, its soft consonant sounds, resonating from somewhere in the bushes.

"Well." Looking elsewhere. To the blue sky, so pure it was almost boring; to the darker shade of the shower room; to his watch again; to anywhere but the edge of the lagoon about thirty feet away, where the sun had caught for the briefest moment a bare leg, an arm. "Well. Still time for one more job," rifling through a few request forms he kept in his forearm pocket, "hm. *Cultural literacy project: Dallas Cowboy Cheerleaders, Texas 1976...* sounds bicentennial." A toilet flushed in the shack behind him. Collapsed lieutenant in one hand and holo-compass in the other, he neatly opened a flap in the obedient air and slipped through.

•

Footlong was late. Cletis sat around in Tinsel's room at the Rose & Thorn waiting for him. The clock on the floor next to the bed, made from plastic shells manufactured by Hesbro Industries, showed the big razor-clam on the six, the little one mid-way between the four and the five. He'd been reading *Head Diver* up to the point where Captain Beaver was confronting his supervisor, Sid "No Questions" Panting, over the legitimacy of certain request forms for a "Partner & Partner R&D Division." What was the R&D behind geological samples of Jamaican soil, anyway, he'd asked; they weren't classified as university, government agency or even citizen "right to know" class. There was no commerce docket number on the form, no authorizing signatures. Panting had declined to further enlighten him on the nature of the client, so Beaver, vowing silently to get to the bottom of it all, had dived with Lt. Whiffle into the fifteenth century, missing mark by three hundred miles and crashing headlong into a clearing populated, as we have seen, by some most unsavory characters.

This was as far as Cletis got when the bed beneath him began to tip to one side, a rusty creaking filling the room as the mattress and box-springs swung as if on a hinge. Speechless he clung to the bed-sheet, hazarded a look over the edge of the mattress: a headless monster, a green-black lump of scales, rose from a hole beneath the bed. Dry gray hair puffed up where the neck should have been, human arms dangling from the sides, a cough from somewhere deep inside culminating in the literal pop of a human head from a dark hole on top; a pair of hands reached up to pick some waxy substance out of the beard. The air seemed to dance with a heavy salt smell. Cletis watched the strange transformation with receding horror and growing curiosity: who was this stringy apparition walking about in a giant sea turtle shell, and why, most importantly, had he emerged from beneath the bed in his father's hotel room?

Blue eyeballs perused, under an avalanche of eyebrows, first the floor of the room, then the room in general, and lastly the upturned bed, where they saw the perched Cletis, apparently working out the problems of etiquette for such an encounter. The teeth seemed to be working on something, grinding and rolling under the leather cheeks and gray beard. Then the lips separated, and as the eyes met Cletis' stare it spoke to him.

"Name's Witcover, sonny. Ya like the turtle shell?"

"I'm Cletis. Are you—"

"...sharin the room with yer doo-dad. Uh huh. Would ya like some pep'mint bark?" He pulled some from the collar of his shirt, offered a piece to deferring Cletis, now on his feet. "Mmmm. Hrr, don't know what yer missin. Chewy." All the way up now, Witcover brought the bed back down to the floor and slowly disengaged himself from the shell. Skinny shoulders shot from the head hole, the elbows following, pointy and surrounded by rolled up shirt-sleeves. The smell of fresh peppermint reached Cletis, and he began to wish he'd accepted the offer. Witcover propped the shell against a wall.

"Well. I jist thought yer parents might like a Gen-U-Ine collectible from the sea. To remember their visit here." He turned to lift the bed again, then changed his mind, and walked to the door, turning back as he opened it to say, "Oh, an I left a little present for yer daddy in there. Mm, sure did," winking at Cletis. He dissolved into the hallway's dimness. Cletis heard a small collision seconds later, and the following exchange:

"Whoa-ho! Sorry, guy—oh hey, Witcover! How's the great outdoors, yeh heh."

"Aye, Footlong. Lookin mighty tan around those bandages, surfer boy. How about a kiss?"

"Yuk-uk."

"Yarhar. Give Beemus me best, boy. See yer around."

"Okay, yeh. Take it easy, Tree Man, yukuk..." entering the room and waving to Cletis. "Hey hey, Cletis man, sorry I'm late, had to get some more wrap for the ol' war injury, uh hyuk."

"Footlong, you know that guy?"

"Yeh, local moving monument that guy is. Jungle man. Lives in trees, eats bears whole, that sort of thing. He went surfing with me once, man but get it, he did the whole thing *under water*, yuk! Ain't kiddin', Cletis: we're waitin for a riser, an all of a sudden he goes to me, "Undertow!" like he's watchin the beach or something, and he ducks under, pops up again about fifty yards further out. Wacky guy, but he brings my uncle supplies and stuff, and keeps the poachers and bird-watchers off our land. I don't know which is worse, Cletis, poachers or bird-watchers. I mean, poachers, they got guns, but you give em a scare and they head off, they're mostly amateurs or don't know where they are, since our property isn't marked. But bird-watchers, they walk right in with their binoculars and cameras an shit, bumpin their zoom lenses into tree trunks, sprayin all that insect repellent and scarin everythin away but the hummingbirds, who'll suck sugar right outa your hands down here, so no one wants to see em. Can always tell when the bird-watchers are here cause all the birds head for our house and the swampy parts where those guys won't go. But try and get em off our land, man, and they show you their birdwatchers' badges or something, talk science and how they got a *right*. Okay, then we get Witcover. One look at Witcover, jumpin through the branches and howlin mad, and they're all fallin back, maybe takin a few pictures of him as he chases them, yellin and droppin lens caps all over the place as they go. We got a collection of lens caps back at Beemus' house, covers a whole cupboard door, man."

"Footlong, he came up from beneath the bed. Scared the shit out of me."

"Yah, he's alright, though." Footlong tittered. "Yukuk, right outta the bed, man! I can see you now, Cletis, sittin there, right, all quiet, and then '*AAAAA! Fuckin nightmare! AAAAAAAAAAA!*' Yukyuk."

"I didn't scream. You woulda though."

"Yeh. I woulda fuckin *AAAAAAA! Turtle monster! AAAA!* Heh heh," dissolving into laughter that wrinkled, wrestled with the salt smell in the room for dominance. An icecream truck went by somewhere near, jubilant bells doing something by Andrew Lloyd Webber. Cletis reached in the turtle shell, pulled out a plastic package covered with electrical tape. A note on it said, "The tail's the best. Boil it before cooking."

"Yuk," Cletis said.

"Best fuckin part man," said Footlong. "Slides right down your throat," making gagging noises and sticking his fingers in his mouth. "Come on, let's go. Uncle Beemus is waiting at the beach. Wants to show us his new air horns."

"Okay," said Cletis; but putting the huge shell on the bed he felt on the inside another piece of electrical tape, and pulled on it. "Huh." A book of some kind, the leather soggy but with a plastic casing over the pages. Cletis threw it in his rucksack and followed Footlong out the door.

•

South of Bull Bay and north of Yallahs, the southern coast of Jamaica turns in on itself. Follow the coast far enough and you'll find what's left of Port Royal, a slender finger of land still held up in protest against the way the Caribbean Sea sucked most of it under in 1692; behind it squats Kingston, a modern substitute for the earlier coast town and capital, filled with gamblers, thieves, the rich and poor both dependent on the tourism that floats in with the seasonal tides of water taxis and yachts. Further inland, towards Spanish Town, the Arawak Museum, housing some of the most important Arawak finds in the country, at the historical expense of the tribe itself, sits squarely between cities on an old burial site, a poor choice some like Flinch would say, given his belief in the dead's tendency to get back up periodically and make trouble with the current landowners.

On the other side of Kingston to the east the foothills of the Blue Mountains begin, Mavis Bank being the popular place for the sunrise climb to Blue Mountain Peak; at 7,402 feet above sea level it offers an inescapably dizzying view of the morning's first fingers of light creeping over the ocean's cold blue lip, spreading over, eventually, the protesting pointer of Port Royal. Some tourists, given to starting the climb before the traditional 2 a.m., have claimed to see the sun so low on the water that it cast the shadow of one of the Lesser Antilles' Leeward Islands all the way to the tip of the Peak. Others claimed the shadow was not the six hundred miles long it would have to be to substantiate the theory, but rather a mere two hundred mile shadow from a small hook of land at the southern tip of the Dominican Republic; Flinch, who had looked for the shadow but never seen it, told anyone who asked that it was actually the shadow of the first light on the remains of Port Royal, that lone finger casting a singular warning all the way around the globe, darkening even the sun as it went, touching the Blue Mountains to show how it would rise sometime soon when the sun wasn't looking, and descend like a cutlass on Kingston and all its sinful trappings.

Flinch was also xenophobic of the rest of the Antilles, Cuba, the Cayman Islands and Haiti, and had seen aerial photographs taken from space which confirmed his fears: Cuba was a long shark, Haiti and the Dominican Republic a giant king crab, closing tightly about the much smaller turtle shape of Jamaica.

But as Cletis and Footlong left Port Royal to bicycle the fifteen miles along the coast past Bull Bay to Footlong's uncle's house, his land abutting the public beaches at Yallahs Point, their talk fast and rambling of empty shells and invading birdwatchers, carefree conspiracy theories of the Baedeckers, Fodors and Petersons, Flinch was finding, in the form of an overheard telephone conversation, some live ammunition to fuel his paranoia.

•

Flinch was well aware of the manifold and cross-cultural meanings of the word *beaver*; he'd heard it on the tongues of firefighters and reporters, trappers and naturalists. But sliding from between the lips of one Doctor Fleck, outspoken shareholder of the Eastern Florida Plastics Conglomerate, it could have but one meaning, and Flinch knew this one as well.

His aural range sharpened over the years as a result of his general paranoia, Flinch had on several occasions heard Fleck using the word, always in the context of important business calls from Florida, amidst other veiled talk of future transactions. He would be visiting the office to pick up a new shipment of "Native American Pottery" that Hesbro put together with spare parts from their Lewis & Clark Action Figure Compatible Stoneware Collection, and for some reason, inevitably as Dr. Fleck was producing an invoice to be signed, the phone would ring. Flinch would wait patiently as the doctor entered his office and shut the door; he'd stand perfectly still, affecting a drug-induced stupor, imitate the proverbial walls-having-ears and pick up, through the porous plywood door of Fleck's office, a word or two, then a phrase, and at last complete conversations. Or Fleck's side anyways.

So coming in to pick up his mid-month shipment he'd again been interrupted by a business call, and listening this time became sure, if not what the word meant, then what it signified for Jamaica's future.

•

Many historians of American westward expansion would point out, enthusiastically or ironically, depending on which way their objectivity was leaning, that the furry, dam-building beaver was in a large way responsible for the rapid expansion of economic interests across the continent. The search for a Northwest Passage finishes a distant second, its only function as a discovery being to find a faster route for the fur industry to ply its trade than the land afforded.

Much of this early expansion was done by Companies given loosely-written charters by the President, or in some cases one or another of the various thrones back on the original Continent. And one of these companies, formed as an indivisible and invisible link between the officially chartered groups, was Partner & Partner. Created to give structure and maximum profit to the various companies, while preserving the fierce competition between the trappers, Partner & Partner chased the beaver to the West Coast and out into the water, grabbing careful handfuls of choice land as they went, strengthening their options through helpful legislators back East; so that Flinch began to think of the beaver as the ampersand between one Partner and the other, the missing link, or maybe just the secret one between American laissez-faire of manifest destiny on one side and the revered liberties of free enterprise on the other. The notion of P&P's specter, its maw already full and drooling with the drippings of Iroquois and Hopi, Sioux and Apache and dozens of other tribes including the immigrant working class of Industrial Age America; the notion of it turning its huge snout toward the Antilles and licking its chops... this image visited Flinch in Dr. Fleck's waiting room that afternoon as he overheard Fleck chuckling into his receiver: "Oh ho, ha; of course the loss of the log's information notwithstanding... good shape for certain, yes... I can imagine *recovery* in the next twelve hours; yes, I've seen them, briefly, and I pointed them in Croom's direction; who else would Witcover be carrying a shell to, ha... oh yes, sir, I would deign to say, present circumstances continuing, we're only months away from a desirable legal outcome... yes, the flagpoles were shipped today, so if they're not quite flying now, haha, the Beavers have certainly, um, landed..."

•

Since Fleck had never seen Flinch in good humor, he hardly

noticed this time his especially shaky countenance, terror or anger it would be tough to say, the pen he signed the invoice with cutting through the paper and into Fleck's blotter. After Flinch left, Fleck noticed it and, facing the window looking out on Port Royal's busy marketplace, held the blotter up to the clear air above, the sky peeking back at the doctor through the small blue hole.

•

"Tell me another lie."

They walked through the Nonesuch Historical Cemetery, on the outskirts of Port Antonio. Tombstone hunting: Tinsel hunkered down to a small nub of stone with no visible lettering, only a shallow carving of a skull-head with angel's wings. "This was my uncle Casmir," Tinsel said. "He worked for the Icelandic Secret Service in the seventeenth century, observing the expansion of the New World. He would record his information on huge Bear-Oak leaves, then ship them by undercover runners, disguised as Indians, up north where an Icelandic barque would pick it up."

"There are no Bear Oak trees in Jamaica, spy master," Cozetta smirking.

"Not anymore. The leaves would then be read, the observations transcribed onto huge stones and built into a government library."

"Government library? Iceland? Think harder. Why was your Icelandic uncle named Casmir? A strange religious conversion?"

"...then an inner wall was built inside the library, with a *secret access niche* behind a painting of a moose, so that top officials could go inside with a candle and read all the information." He stood up, dusted off his pants.

"What did they do with all the leaves, spy master?" Cozetta squatted down in the place Tinsel vacated, examining the skull face.

"They dug a hole. Planted them. Years later, my grandfather, Ventl Short Sword Crom—that's how they pronounced it before we came to the States—was walking around the library yard, and..." he leaned down to brush a fly away from Cozetta's hair, "...and he heard, Cozetta the fabulous, Cozetta the wondrous, he heard the trees around him *talking* to one another, whispering about the New

World. How the fruits there were strange and sweet..."

Cozetta gripped his elbow and left shoulder and flipped him over the tombstone, wrestling him to the ground. "Come on, spy master, tell the truth..." menacing him with her fingers poised over his ribs, "how'd you get the name Tinsel?" One stray kiss drifted lightly onto Tinsel's nose, Cozetta inches above him, pretending she didn't do it, "how'd you get such a name? What did the Icelanders care about the New World?" she ducking in again, her tongue tip dancing quick across his jawline.

"...whispering, Cozetta. How the seals would lie on the beach right next to you. How thousands of turtles made living islands of shells by the shore a man could walk on. How perpetually warm it was. How beautiful the native women were..."

She wrapped her long hair around his neck, pulled him up a bit. "Okay, spy master, what does this skull-face with the wings mean? Family symbol? Reminiscent of a birth-mark carried down by the generations? Need I search you for such a birthmark?"

"Wha, you don't think it looks like me?" yanking his head back to the earth, and Cozetta's open mouth fast over his lips. She reached with a free hand, her pelvis pressing him further into the dirt, pried open his grinning teeth and her tongue flowed in, caressing, flickering away before Tinsel could respond. Face still pressed against his, feeling his erection moving beneath her, she licked his lips slowly. Tinsel squinted at her. "You know, from here you're just one big eye, Cozetta."

"I'm gonna make you dance inside, Short Sword. You're gonna dance till those wings sprout right out from your hips, then I'm gonna teach you how to use 'em." As Tinsel brought his hands up to the small of her back he heard a bee zoom by. There was a flat unaffecting sound, and Tinsel and Cozetta were suddenly showered with shale and small rocks.

"Wha-?!" Tinsel started up, but Cozetta pushed him back beneath her.

"I think we just got shot at, Tinsel." She twisted her neck, tried to see past the nearer tombstones to where the parking lot was.

"Hmm—must have come from the other direction," nodding toward the woods on the cemetery's border. "I think."

"What, what do we do? Make a run for it? Jesus—" Rock flew off a tomstone at their feet, the impact a flat swatting noise, loud in their ears. They waited: heard a car door shut. Tires squealed on the road. When the sound of the motor had faded into the afternoon's hum, Cozetta raised herself up, picked up a piece of a shattered headstone. "Youch," she said. "Must have been a big bullet."

"We could take it to Healey," Tinsel said. "He'd know what it was from."

"What, take the rock? Sure, spy master;let's just get outta here for now." She squeezed his hand, pulled him to his feet. They ran at a crouch to their car, and only after they had been driving for five minutes, skirting the southeast coast back towards Port Royal, and reasonably certain they weren't being tailed, did they loosen their respective grip on the other's hand, and even then not entirely.

•

It was low tide again, and Uncle Beemus was afraid for the whales.

They stood out there, Beemus, Footlong and Cletis; the water moved loose sand between their toes and under their arches as they watched for the whales, for any signs. The telltale spout of steamy water, a fluke or a snout skimming the surface, even a large school of fish appearing suddenly in the shallows could signal that something was out there.

"What are we, like, gonna watch to make sure no whales are beached? I don't think it's that time of the year for whales to be moving around here, is it?" Cletis had asked after the second hour of silence moved into a third.

"That migration stuff don't mean nothin." Beemus had answered.

"Well, what does? How do ya know—" Beemus snorted, never taking his eyes off the water, and Footlong elbowed Cletis. "Low tide's when they get the *urge*," Footlong told him.

"To beach? I just said that, hamhead."

"Not to beach, man; just to, uh, come ashore..." Beemus had pointed suddenly about a hundred yards out. Something black and shiny popped through the surface. A small head shook, a tiny spout of seawater flew into the air, and it began moving toward the shore. Beemus walked halfway out to meet it, then turned around and came back. The snorkeler passed Cletis and Footlong, holding his rubber fins in one hand. Beemus returned, shaking his head no, looking professional but disappointed. "Nah, not one of em. I shoulda known, on account of he had a snorkel and mask. Ain't seen one yet what come in with a snorkel on."

"Uncle Beemus, but you haven't seen one yet at all," Footlong pointed out. Beemus glared at him. Pushing a stubby finger at Footlong's sternum he said, "Boy, *I* didn't have no snorkel on. That's for damn sure." Beemus paused, and his anger seemed to drain away. "Aah, Footlong, you're a real wanger. Let's go to the Shack and monoxidate."

Monoxidate was the word Beemus used when he meant "drink." He told Footlong the first time he gave him a beer that alcohol adds carbon monoxide to your system, but that it also gives you oxygen in the form of little bubbles. "Thus one passes breathing nutrients the old fashioned way," he had concluded, "like a fish drinkin water. That's why when you get yourself drunk they say you got your gills swilled."

So the three of them walked along the beach towards the Shack, Footlong picking up tide-stalled horseshoe crabs and whipping them around his head, yelling "Oh mighty David thus did pelt Goliath with his bountiful crabs," Cletis dodging the serrated shells and pointy tails as he swept chains of seaweed at Footlong's feet, "Thou dost permeate mine air with iniquitable stink!" their bellowing interrupted only when Beemus would stop and face the ocean, let out a short blast from the air horn he carried, hold still a second as if listening for a reply, then catch up with the boys.

The sun had weakened into the color of old bamboo, the weather running some interference with the normal sunset, and it folded down into dusk with all the ceremony of a beachgoer packing up her wicker mat in her station wagon and driving off. And as quickly as Jamaica's beach roads give way to the main drag and its highway signs and bug-splattered windshields, so the brief dusk gave way to impatient night, mosquitos and gnats forming clouds above their heads as they walked through a short overgrown path to the clearing where the Shack stood.

That it stood at all given its outward appearance was why Beemus referred to his house as the Shack. Inside it was clean and neat, cool with sea breeze and bugless largely due to the great number of lens caps Beemus had used to patch up holes in the screens. These Witcover had collected for him, and brought them when he arrived with his weekly delivery of picked fruit and compressed air from Port Royal. In return Beemus had given Witcover the permission to take what food he could from the existing vegetation, and the added responsibility, though Witcover considered it fun, of keeping poachers and birdwatchers off the property.

Footlong went to the fridge and got a six-pack of Nun Bubble Beer, a Kingston brew that went down as quickly and heavily as evening just had. "Don't care what it'll be tasting like, so long it's made here on the island, and not up in that East Florida monkeyhouse." Beemus opened a toolbox he'd taken from the lenscap-covered closet, extracted from it two air horns, painted steel gray; he attached cannisters of compressed air. "And you know, anyway," reaching for a Nun Bubble and draining the top half of it with the first gulp, "aaaaaaaah...ya know taste ain't the real thing after all, not the most important. What you're out for is quick monoxidation."

"What's the brown stuff sitting at the bottom of the bottle?" Cletis asked.

"Tamarind, maybe. Or pieces of leaf."

"Or beach sand, garhar," Footlong said. Beemus screwed a new cannister to the horn he'd been carrying, then gave each a test honk before lining them together neatly on the kitchen table. The first honk Cletis felt at some midpoint between his ears, as if there was a muscle in his head, unknown to him until now, that existed solely to spasm in a uniquely painful way when he heard the horn. The second honk he felt in his stomach, a stalwart sloshing of the Nun Bubble, which made Cletis think of the seasick nuns Tinsel said he'd met on the *Gregorian*. The third and final honk seemed to spread out above them a few feet, then envelop them in an umbrella-like film, pushing back the humid air before dissolving. And in the brief dry space, as monoxidation set in, Beemus began to speak.

•

It took Beemus thirty-seven years to discover who he really was. He came into the land he lived on partly by accident, and held no job whose duties could not be summarized by "clean this up, Beemus" or "empty that, willya Beemus?" He grew fruits and vegetables in a small plot on his land, picked selectively from the indigenous flora and, with Witcover's help, kept intruders from disturbing the animals and birds. Witcover would come over with a case of Nun Bubble and sit while Beemus drank, neither of them saying much. Occasionally Witcover and he would go out crocodile riding: the idea being to maneuver oneself to a squatting position just over a sleeping crocodile's back, then to settle down ever so slightly and make foolhardly gestures worthy of TV-movie cowboys. Often crocodiloing, as they called it, would not be undertaken without each player sporting a ten gallon hat to wave around once the ride had begun. Beemus, being heavy of the knees and prone to violent twitches when the night bugs flew in his eyes, did not often last long before the wary reptile would wake and slither in its confusion to a safer spot, or, in a few cases, sweep tail and teeth at Beemus in a manner suggesting the need for apologies. These times would find Witcover there in a flash, distracting the monster elsewhere. Once when the situation demanded even more aggressive action, Witcover had leaped past Beemus and stepped on the croc's snout, rubbing a hard circle with his hand on some part of its head. Whatever it did, create a primal vibration to its dinosaur-vintage brain or maybe work some other unlikely magic, the croc had played dead immediately, allowing the two ample time to retreat before it jerked awake. Witcover, perhaps because he'd invented the game and knew something Beemus didn't, was often more successful in his crocodiloing efforts.

On the night of Beemus' thirty-seventh birthday, though, Witcover hadn't shown, been off to some or another emergency, and left the usual case of Nun Bubble, with his apologies scrawled on a wide piece of birch bark, by the shack's front door. Beemus acquainted himself with eleven bottles before he lost count, and woke from a tremendous dream standing in the sea up to his eyebrows, his sinuses filled with water. Only a balding shiny pate bobbed above the calm waves. Beemus opened his eyes, thought for a moment that he would die; yet discerning around him some movement, reached out his hands and felt the first of the whales brush by him. Raising up on his toes he brought his nose above the surface and blew a strong spray of water and mucus high into the air; inhaled deeply and ducked back under.

Vision had become clearer. The sea moved around him in great, dark shapes, occasional white underbellies or bulbous foreheads sliding within a foot of his chest. What he saw was a pack of pilot whales, a dolphin-sized member of the whale family, most likely trying to decide how they'd ended up in this small harbor. Or, as Beemus told Footlong and Cletis, they could have come for him. He was caressed. He was bumped, swallowed some water, bumped again to the surface where he "blew" again, supported by bodies beneath him. "Thus did I learn the nature of breathing," Beemus told them. "You collect and dispel. It's a life-providing program. Really you can apply it to any search for truth, health, or happiness; collect all that's around you, dispel that which does not support your system."

"Whales taught you to breathe." Cletis smirked. Beemus reached patiently across the table to the airhorns; blasted a few healthy ounces at Cletis. Returned the air horn to its place and gently rolled another Nun Bubble in Cletis' direction. "It's called baleening, Cletis. Like a whale's baleen; it opens its mouth, takes in everything, then spits it back out through the baleen. Food gets caught in the baleen, and the excess water goes back out. Now, if you hadn't dispelled that sound, you'd be dead or something, Cletis; yer whole head woulda blown up. Have another beer. Monoxidation prepares the mind to take in expansive information it would normally dispel."

Cletis' fingers felt numb as he grasped the bottle, as if he hadn't dispelled quite enough of the sound, and it was thrumming still through
his veins, turning and turning like confused whales, or maybe they
were angry, themselves hurt and looking for the larger openings to
his heart, where they could vent their fury, he thought with sudden
fear, and destroy him.

And it did seem, in the moment before Beemus drew his next
breath, that Cletis was better prepared for what would follow, almost
prescient of it in the same way that Beemus had felt, back there in
an ocean writhing with lost whales, knowing somehow he was being
told something, that he was a messenger of sorts, or on a mission.
His body had floated up, broken the surface of the water like the thin
skin of sweat dreams drape over you, and the tide pushed him in,
weightless, a reluctant driftwood. He slept that night on the beach.
When he got back to the shack he saw Witcover had again stopped
by, this time leaving taped to the screen door a newspaper clipping
about UFO sightings along the east coast. This set some strange
sequence of tumblers clicking in Beemus' head: to his credit, he
did his research well, reading up on pilot whale beachings over the
last decade, from Cape Cod to Australia. A recent flurry of beachings in Florida proved the first link with a similar set of UFO sightings. Likewise the Barnstable beachings of '86 with the Woods Hole
"lights over the water" incident that most papers attributed to a federal operation to watchdog liberal marine biologists whose research
wasn't exclusive government property and could throw the Adminis-
tration's environmental policy into a bad light. When Beemus saw,
while strolling the public beach pondering all this, a pilot whale car-
cass ("hit by one of them cruise boats," a bystander had told him) and
later that evening a blue light hovering out in the harbor he couldn't
identify through the official channels, the last pieces of the mechanism his head had been building fell in sync, or else a previously
locked chamber swung smoothly open to him, and a great feeling of
empathy overwhelmed him, sent him flapping to the shallows, slash-
ing the incoming waves with his open hands.

He began thinking as if he were trapped in his human body,

a fellow mammal but not a man, a whale who found himself suddenly in human form, who'd been sent ashore to find out why, why the world was such a dangerous place for whales and humans alike, why one person's fun was another's undoing... Or perhaps there was a chamber hidden still, a door still to open in his mind, a message to the land dwellers, if only he could remember....

"So whales came from the UFO's; and your uncle Beemus came from the whales." Cletis and Footlong sat at the tide's edge, Nun Bubble drunk, listing back and forth with some mutually perceived rhythm that most beaches have; Footlong wrapped an arm around Cletis' neck, wrenched his head into the pre-dawn horizon, Beemus' lone figure standing hands-on-hips at the edge of seeing. "Yup. Fuckin extra-terrestrial mammal cousin from the South Atlantic, man." Beemus blew a long blast with his airhorn into the waves, which absorbed the sound immediately, seemed to absolve it of its silliness and leave him standing with the small absence its after-effect created. "Thinks they might send another one like him; to help him out, y'know. Help him remember. Fuh-huck," trying to stand up but washed out as Cletis was, "he's okay, Cletis. His father left him early, man, just fuckin left him with this beach, so I guess he's kinda sad. But—uuurp—yukuk, that's another story, ey?" climbing now to his feet using Cletis' head for leverage. "I gotta go puke."

Cletis sat on the shore, his own hangover clearing a bit with each new sounding Beemus blew; and thought where his own parents might be, where they had ever been, come to think of it, and stumbled into knee-high water to pee. A jellyfish floated by his calf, barely missing. Lucky, Cletis thought, close close. And he knew his parents were just as close lately, and he wondered if he'd be as lucky with them.

•

Fleck picked up the phone on the second ring. Dr. Wan always seemed to call him when someone was on the operating table, Fleck thought as he shut the office door, leaving Flinch in the reception area; or, when goddamn Flinch is here to pick up his pottery.

"My dear Dr. Fleck, they're coming your way."

"No, Wan, they're here already. Been for over a day now, too."

"Well, yes," Wan sounding a wee bit annoyed at having his surprise spoiled; "and what happened, then?"

"They were combing Cowlick Point and those marshes thereabouts. The homing piece in the log's binding got them within a hundred yards when they spotted a local man name of Witcover— a sort of mountain man, but harmless I'm sure— so they laid back to watch him. Anyhow, Witcover saw the log, apparently, somehow, and he, uh, picked it up and stuffed it into the gut of a dead turtle he was dragging into the woods."

A short silence. "Fleck. Just say you lost it. Don't fuck with me. I'm in Manhattan, everybody's *listening*, you see."

"Oh oh, but that's exactly what happened, unbelieving doctor. Suppose I told you a little more, that, ha ha, we lost this Witcover personage in the woods—"

"Did he know he was being followed?"

"Hardly, Wan, he's daft. Local yokel. Doesn't know when it's day or night, from what I can tell."

"Oh, a lost soul. I see. Didn't have to much trouble losing *your* men, though."

"Did you mean your men, hah; but we have this under control. We know his local haunts. Every yokel's got a few. Yes, picked him up the next afternoon, still carrying the shell, mister doctor, and if I may be convinced by our homing device, still carrying our logbook."

"So," Wan relaxing now, audibly grinning, "we have the logbook within our grasp, after all? Yes? I mean, our personal stakes as stockholders in the East Florida thing notwithstanding, there's a great deal of interest in keeping operational systems secure. I've been with Rizzoli the last few weeks, and he assures me we won't be disappointed, from the publicity standpoint, anyway, when his Retrospective opens seven days hence."

"Yes, oh yes Rizzoli; what was it he was to do for us?"

"Oh ho, mustn't tell, exactly; and even I know only the structure, though not exactly what the piece will look like. Let's just say, hm, that it will be fittingly Revolutionary, haha."

"Yes, well even for you, Wan, I'd have to say that picking Rizzoli was a masterstroke... one second—" peering through a crack in the door Fleck saw Flinch still standing there. And there he stood, eyes closed, rocking on his heels a bit as if asleep, seemingly unaware of his surroundings. Fleck turned back to the phone. "These locals, they're all imbalanced in one way or the other. I've got one in my waiting room now. Oh ho, but when the Beaver flag's flying over this little island, believe me, Wan, I'll be a happier man."

"Oh, here's to the Beaver State, my friend!" Wan sang, and the rest of the party line on the Manhattan end joined in, the Partner & Partner executives from their limo on 5th Avenue, the Officer-Secretary of New State Affairs from his office on the 42nd floor of the P&P building, the General-Supervisor of the Statehood Standing Army from his secret training barracks in Ithaca, New York, the Overseer of the Free Press and Public Announcement from his private cubicle in the Boston University library, all in good cheer and most in the correct key to Dr. Fleck's ears, who could not join in because he was in truth near overwhelmed with tears,

Here's to the Beaver State, my friend!
to the Partner & Partner way!
for the stole and coat and the beaver cap
for the good of the U.S.A.!
When the night is dark and the moon concerned
Well that Beaver's teeth do shine
And his tail is flat (and it's broad at that)
And his beard is brown and fine!
Here's to the Beaver State and all
That its corporate works entail!
For the working hacks on their beds of tacks
Through the snow, rain, sleet and hail!
Yes the world is fun when you're number one
And the Partners would extend
Their hand to you (for some servitude)
But... a Beaver's got no hands!
Hey!

A Beaver's got no hands!
So here's to the Beaver State my friends
to the Co. East Florida
May all stand true (and keep an eye out, too)
For the Co., East, Flo, riiii, daaaaa

Static crackled over the lines; Fleck sniffled, his ruddy stomach shuffling his crayons into intricate patterns on his shirt pocket. He blew his nose. Said, "Oh, listen."

"Yes?" a dozen voices asked.

"Witcover delivered the turtle shell to an American tourist whose son I've been treating. We're following him right now. His name is Tinsel Croom."

"Croom. Interesting," Wan said, his thoughts drifting momentarily to his dream of the night before, Polly and he on a bed of black feathers, wraithlike crows tearing at her back as she rode him..."Mm-hm, what luck, sahib, ha ho, I'm immured in therapy with his wife. I'll call her tomorrow, invite her to New York to meet Rizzoli, he'll go along I'm sure, and we can keep her close, haha, for any in-case-ofs."

"Sounds fishy." Fleck said. But good humor or good business getting the best of him, buried his suspicion beneath his crayons; "but yes, of course; well, to summarize then, I did point them in Croom's direction, and would deign to say, having met the man, that he will be easily manipulated; I can imagine recovery in the next twelve hours."

"How long till the Beaver flies?" an ecstatic Wan shouted over the worsening static, electrical storm sounds quickening in their ears somewhere between the words of Dr. Fleck's answer, "Yes, if they're not quite flying now, haha, the Beavers have certainly, um, landed..." Huge cheers from across the eastern seaboard crackled violently in Fleck's ears, and the line went dead. Fleck hung up and went back out to find Flinch. He hadn't moved an inch. Fleck touched his shoulder, nudged him off balance. "Wake up, hrm." He fished in his crayon pocket for a blank invoice.

"Miss Octawim, please go get that box of imports for Mr. Flinch." He waved Flinch into his office, offered him a pen, and laid the invoice on his desk. "It's amazing the things you can sell here," he snickered in Flinch's direction.

"Amazin what those American tourists will buy from any negro with a big smile. Yep," picking the box from Miss Octawim's arms and nodding his way out the door.

Fleck's snicker had evolved into a tight secretive smile. He closed the office door and looked down at the marketplace. Soon it will all be so different, he thought. A black hummingbird paused at his screen, the wings invisible and bluish, their dim hum annoying. He picked up the blotter, made a motion to scare it, but it didn't leave, backing off a foot or two and floating, its beak a thin funnel between him and the rest of the world, the wide end guarded, it seemed, by the two blue pinpricks of eyes.

•

Rizzoli led her into a janitor's closet on the fourth floor of the Museum. Above them hundreds of pairs of shoes scraped the floor with various interpretations of dance; drinks were plucked from trays passing smoothly through the thick streams of wood and chiffon; and the Manhattan elite celebrated their own presence at the pre-opening champagne party. It was the night of August 17th, 7:30 pm and a strange night for a party: no one had seen the sun set; it had disappeared four and a half hours ago. Even Rizzoli himself, some among the crowd were heard to say, could not paint a sun strongly enough to bring back the light.

"If only they knew," Dr. Wan mumbled to himself making his small way to the oyster table. The chandelier above was real, all right, mid-18th century Dutch, all brass, its eight main fixtures sloping down octopus-like; but the candles burning within the frosted-glass coverings were not, were meticulously stained by Rizzoli just two hours earlier as he hung from a very real piece of rope manipulated on the other side of a pulley by Wan, the two posturing themselves carefully to check all angles, make sure Rizzoli's "flicker effect" theory would pan out convincingly, both aware of the physical limitations of their arrangements, much as the dancers on the floor Wan slid by with his secret found themselves in a similar tug-of-war with gravity, attempting to create the illusion of lightness without losing their necessary footing. The consequent compromise with the earth's natural pull was no more apparent than at the next floor down, Polly hearing the rasp of heels and soles spread out above her head like a roomful of snakes as Rizzoli shut the closet door, slipped past her and began jimmying a small padlock on a door on the far wall. "What's behind door number one?" Polly giggled, extended her arms TV showcase-like first at the door, then the musty collection of mops in the adjacent corner, sprouting out like tired sunflowers from a rusted roller bucket. Rizzoli turned grinning, pulled a penknife from his sleeve and cut around the lock, extracting the canvas painting of the padlock and with an equally hammy gesture opening the door and motioning open-handed to the darkness beyond.

She squeezed by him into a longer room, the ceiling low enough for them to have to squat. Polly stretched her arms out to either side, felt the walls with the tips of her fingers. Rizzoli passed under her left arm. The door behind them swung lightly closed, and for a moment all Polly could feel were the walls against her fingertips. Blackness rushed into the rest of her body, eating up sensations. "Arno, what's—" "Shh." He touched her arm. "Sit down. Listen." And struck a match, lighting a kerosene lamp on the floor.

The sounds of the party upstairs were gone. Polly stretched her neck, looked around. The room resembled an oversized shoebox, and Polly imagined for an instant that she and Rizzoli were laid out on their sides like shoes, his head at her feet, tissue paper between them. "Hush puppies," she said, but he quieted her again. "Sh." He let a hand drop on her knee. "Gonna tell you a story." And he began.

(Yo ho, talk about nostalgic projection, Wan meanwhile thinking as he watched some guests meander around the foyer. A series of photographs and newsclippings outlining Rizzoli's illustrious history and achievements within the Art World, each one subtly lit from above like stations of the cross, ran along the walls of the foyer. Those not dancing were strolling from station to station, reading

the yellowed articles and glancing at the photos, banging their oys-
ter-and-champagne-blurred memories to bring up some recollection
of having attended any of the events pictured. Wan had been to
them all, of course, since he'd had Rizzoli paint him into each "UPI
Photo." The yellowed newspaper articles were hand-lettered on 40
lb. wrinkled Mohawk bond, but Rizzoli's fine water wash gave the
paper a thin, ink-shiny look. Wan's favorite was from 1962, the
New York Times article about Rizzoli sculpting a Korean War era
handgrenade and presenting it to Corporal Robert "Fighting Mad"
Maxwell, a first-aid specialist who'd single-handedly held off two
regiments of the enemy at Cho Sen Hill with nothing but a box
of grenades. The accompanying photograph showed Rizzoli center,
handing his work to Maxwell foreground right, the artist flanked on
either side by Polly Croom and the Doctor himself, looking young
and dashing and about the right age for thirty-some odd years ago,
while Polly looked her present age, her green eyes playful, her lips
open and interested, a sidelong glance that could be towards the Corporal, or the sculptor, or—dare he think it? even in the context of a
painting?—the young Dr. Wan. He could feel sweat trickling down
his thighs, his polyester pants refusing to absorb the slightest moisture, down to his socks which obediently collected it. Polly Croom,
Polly Croom, he whispered, the name alone enough when repeated
to raise his concern, bunch his boxer shorts around his stiffening
anxiety...

A gentleman bumped shoulders with him. "I was there," he
said, nodding at the photo.

"Ah ha. Mm. Yes," Wan said. "And a touching ceremony it was."

"No, I mean the War. Right along the Parallel, in the goddamn
worst of it." He held a half-smoked cigar to his mouth, Wan respond-
ing automatically with his lighter. Two fat puffs of damp cigar smoke
descended upon him, settling down like clouds around his ankles.
"Bad fuckin war. These artist guys, they weren't there. Shouldn't
be making fucking hand-grenade idols for little kids to worship, ya
know what I mean?" Wan was rubbing his swollen crotch through his
pants pocket, teletype in his head running Polly Croom Polly Croom

.

"Oh yeah. Well he was young then. Never did war stuff again, you see?" Polly Croom, Polly Polly, Polly Croom, gesturing at the rest of the photos along the wall. "All urban landscape stuff. News-stands, manhole covers, windows on buildings, eh?"

The gentleman nodded. "Yeah. Fucking city's a warzone, though.")

"My mother was quarter-Japanese, grandparents on her father's side. I heard this story first from her, although I've since read versions of it from sources diverse as Gibbon's *Rome* and some obscure annotation to the Knight's Tale. I'll tell it to you like my mother told me, pretty straight-forward, and we'll let the kinks wander in where they may...

Back sometime around 1240 — so goes the Japanese version, which would predate Chaucer by a century or so — when a new warrior class had taken over power from the emperor, a soldier named Sharaku received some land on Hokkaido Island to do with as he liked. Hokkaido is the northernmost of Japan's four main islands; its shape swirls with peninsulas, resembling a huge sting-ray with a forked tail, and although the inhabitants of the island had no way of seeing this, some living near the southern tail would refer to the island as "demonfish," "Devil's Body" and "demon's back." Perhaps because the mainland was full of broad flat regions of volcanic ash, the peninsulas' soil not quite right for farming, the heart of the island buried deep beneath stony mountains bristling here and there with evergreens; but a few families did manage to nurture small plots of rice, and Sharaku kept four such families on his land, which curled inside the sweeping tail of the ray in a place known as Uchiura Bay.

Now one of these families had a precious daughter whom they hid from Sharaku because they knew, once she had come of age, that he would take her from them. To insure the girl's safety they went so far as never naming her, for fear by some unconscious slip they might mention her in front of their lord, and face great punishment. So the girl grew without a name, and as years passed became a beautiful young woman.

It was decided by the family that she would seek refuge with Yonaga, a wandering philosopher. Japan had recently acquired Buddhism from travellers from the mainland, so besides Shinto and Confucianism there was now a third religion to absorb. Thus religious scholars were the thing to be, so to speak. Anyway, Yonaga, probably the first Buddhist on the island, was a man whose presence on his land Sharaku tolerated. The soldier asked no fealty of Yonaga, and probably would not feel the need to inquire about those seen travelling with the old man. So at the age of fourteen the girl set out to start her apprenticeship with Yonaga. She was to meet him at a spot about a day's walk away, and was no further than half that distance when a lone rider approached her. The man was clad in light chainmail and the usual armaments of a well-paid soldier. It was Sharaku, crossing the desolate border of his land in search of intruders. Some of the farmers had seen strangely-dressed men walking in the trees by the foothills of Ashibetsu Dake, and he feared they were spies for the landowner to the west of the mountain, whose land was larger and soil richer than Sharaku's, and who, it was rumored, was a close friend of the second shogun, who now ruled all of Japan in the name of the emperor. "What is your name?" he asked the girl. "I have none," she answered.

Sometimes the most absurd truths are the most easily believed; Sharaku, looking down at this beautiful girl wandering on the lifeless edge of his land, was immediately convinced of her honesty. He did not stop to question her further, though, and whether he thought of her in the next hour as a visiting spirit, or as a thing that sprouted from his own land, no one will know; in fact he didn't seem to be thinking at all, except when he unsheathed his sword and thrust it at the girl to scare her into submission, because he hardly removed a thread of his garments while he raped her, and when he left her unconscious on the ground her body, her external appearance, that is, was bruised and cut more by the soldier's armor than by his actual flesh. But inside she was also injured, and lay there bleeding for all of a day."

"You said your mother told you this story?" Polly interrupted.

"I heard it from her. She used to tell it to my father, when he was home from one trip or another, just before bedtime, and I just *over-heard* it, I guess." Rizzoli had found a piece of chalk on the floor, and traced in the lamp's light the outline of Hokkaido island.

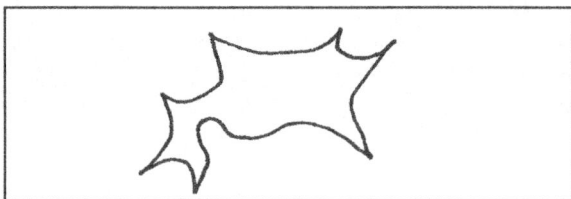

(Wan examined the skin of an oyster in the more real light of the lamps behind the refreshment tables. A curiosity overcame him suddenly, his hairpiece sliding dangerously off-part during his run to the oyster table. The shell looked correct, though not *too* correct, he reassured himself. He dropped it on the table, crushed it under the heel of his fist, and picked it up. Breaks like an oyster shell would break, he thought, smells like an oyster. The center of the shell, caved in and splintered, stared back at Wan with a droll, slimy eye. The muscles around the edges had not given way yet, so Wan pulled them apart a bit, stuck his tongue in the crack. Was that a bit of paint he tasted? What could it be? Tofu and plaster of paris? How far would Rizzoli go? The true Masterpiece could well be right here in the reception room, under everyone's nose... Wan knew it all extended somewhere beyond art, beyond the concept of perfect imitation; it also concerned function, viability and the ability to compensate for an incomplete illusion. For instance, the way these lamps had been positioned to throw light above to particular areas on the ceiling: the unprepared—or did he mean the unconsciously prepared?—observer would assume the light was reflected in the opposite direction, from the chandelier to the ceiling to the floor, but no ho, *non merci*; the mere suggestion of light would still not light a room, would not render the newsprint on the walls legible—even though the newsprint was a sham, ho ho—so some real light had to compensate for this in a way not easily suspected. Still... Wan lowered the oyster away from his face, lifted the other arm up up, up towards the top of the lampshade, where even now 5000 watts of soft light would be streaming toward the ceiling... Still, still... his fingers trembled now near the lampshade's rim. Still, could this too be an illusion, one set up carefully against my own preparations, if only for my benefit? was that possible? He hesitated: if someone observed him, saw the light reflecting off his hand then the whole chandelier gig would be ruined... would he... indecision sliced his nerves in half, inaction soldered his bones into that stiff, unnatural position, one arm raised to the ceiling, unmovable as if pointing, his muscles at the same time quivering visibly, shaking his polyester suit like it was full of moths fluttering about for a fly, an ill-stitched seam through which to escape... People began to notice, strolled in his direction casually, waiting for him to explain what he was directing their attention to, but Wan's molars were clamped in a foetal embrace, his gums singing white noise into his brain, his fingertips inches away from knowing for sure, but of course he couldn't.... He felt a hand close around his, squeeze tightly. "Hey pal, snap out of it. You okay?" His jaw suddenly working again, "Oh, sure, uh-hm, little kink in my back I was working out, yes. Thank you," everything settling back in place, a relieved giggle from the small crowd he'd gathered, and the gentleman he'd spoken with rolling an arm around his shoulders, joking about the Statue of Liberty, yukyuk... Wan glanced down to his open hand, where the oyster-eye was a bloody red, set sharply into his palm by the squeeze. "Heh heh," his own laugh compensating for something he couldn't quite place with himself alone, a humor of the room's suspicious airiness, the inevitable opening of that double door leading to the exhibit, something in the ether he could almost smell as he shuffled towards the men's room to wash out his wound.)

"The X near the bottom is Uchiura Bay, Sharaku's land. The one in the middle is the peak of Ashibetsu Dake, the second highest mountain on the island, where Yonaga will take the girl."

"What are the two lines up top?"

"They are eyes, Polly. Bloody red devil manta eyes..."

"Why you—" but she paused, the ghost-shape with slits for eyes and an X for its heart reminding her of Cletis' accident, whatever it was; she looked up at Rizzoli. Something passed between the two of them that Polly took initially for empathy, until she wondered what Rizzoli would know that he could empathise with her. Nothing, probably; the thought flicked away by the lamp's kerosene fingers. And besides, even in this darkness his eyes were too thin to contain that much warmth. "So go on," she said.

"The next morning the girl woke up and saw Yonaga sitting by her side. He'd wrapped most of her wounds with a combination of leaves and strips of cloth from his sleeves. He gave her some things to eat, never asking what had happened to her, although the girl had no doubts that he knew already. Taking her hand he led her to a well where the water was warm and sweet, and after she had drunk her fill brought her to the top of the lowlands where on a small ridge of earth backed by old toothy evergreens they looked upon the Bay. The view afforded the girl a glimpse of her family's farm. "Whose land is that?" Yonaga asked her, and the girl's answer was, "Sharaku's land." She could see the top of the thatched hut her father had built, the rice fields in which they worked. They climbed the foothills until the land began to be covered with small trees and thick curling underbrush. Walking was difficult. They found a clearing to sit in and rest, but before the girl could lay her head down Yonaga made her climb a tall tree to the very top; her arms and feet were sticky with sap, and the slightest winds swung her out over vacant spaces beyond the closest limbs. "Look back where we came. What do you see?" "I see Sharaku's land." "Now look over to where the sun sets. What do you see?" She could see another bay, similar to Uchiura Bay in size, the land around it pockmarked with cultivation. "I see a bay. I see many fields." "Who owns that land?" She did not answer, so Yonaga called her back down. "Shakotan owns that land," he said. This was when the girl first realized that she was outside Sharaku's land. Beyond his jurisdiction. Though her wounds still sang and stung as she walked, the girl felt a heaviness leave her almost immediately; but what would fill that space, now, settle inside her to stop her from floating up, away from the world? "Who owns *this* land?" she asked. "Ahaha," Yonaga picked flies and moths from the sap on the girl's arms and popped them into his mouth. "Who *do* you think owns this land? Yonaga? Shakotan? The emperor?" He spit out a bug whose taste he didn't like, poked it with his big toe. "Bug own land? You, maybe? Hah. Wait now." The short rest apparently foregone, they followed a slim, winding path that the girl thought Yonaga was making up as they went along, looking for barely discernible openings between leaves, sniffling for the scent of a fox or cupping a hand to one ear to pick up the chirp of a cricket as dusk progressed into night. Night seemed to last for days and was just hinting at the coming dawn when they reached the peak of Ashibetsu Dake, 5700 feet above sea level. A cold wind harassed them, and there were no trees to cling to. The girl beheld at first only the open blackness of night, sharp stars unmoving above the whirling winds; but then she came to see the shape of the island on all sides of her, the Sea of Japan and the North Pacific Ocean. But Yonaga pointed out into the air and asked, "Who owns this?" The girl shouted to be heard above the winds, "Nobody! Nobody owns the air. It goes where it wants to. It cannot be used for anything..." "Except to live," Yonaga said. The world began to lighten as he took her down to a quiet place, a niche in the rock sheltered by thick trees. He leaned back against a trunk wider than any doorway she'd ever seen, and rubbed his eyes. "So," he finally spoke, "you must learn to be more like the air."

"How much of this is true?" Polly asked. They were both sitting on the same side of the lamp, Polly having moved over to look at Rizzoli's drawing of the island. The far half of the room yawned big and dark, its edges undiscernible. Rizzoli had lowered the wick as day turned into night in the story he told, so now it gave out a small orange hum of light that didn't quite reach their faces. Polly studied Rizzoli as he prepared to answer her; sitting Indian style like her, his chin angled toward her in an inquisitive way, unmoving, he seemed almost an abstract of himself, a dim nod of recognition to his own existence, despite the illusions and secrecy, his physical density, the precious weight that kept him relevant: Polly reached for his hand, he at the same time breaking his pose and turning to speak, the sympathy or closeness she felt breaking down also, her hand stuck awkwardly out as if to shake his.

"I'm not sure I like the real you as much as I like the idea of what's behind you," she said. She dropped her hand in her lap.

"Hm. I'm not sure it makes a difference, as long as you know what you want. And I thought," his friendly smile returning as he fed more wick to the lamp, "you wanted an answer to your question."

"Well I do."

"Okay. Inasmuch as the story itself goes, I don't know. I'm not sure you can walk from Uchiura Bay to Ashibetsu Dake in one day. I'm not even sure you can climb to the peak. It may be all covered with snow. Then again, maybe not. Fifty seven hundred feet isn't exactly Mount Everest. As for the characters, who knows? Like I said, the story seems to come from more than one source. I've always remembered it because I wanted to be just like Yonaga—bug-eating aside, haha—"

(Wan positioned himself over the toilet, then changed his mind and faced the stall door. His hands were still wet, blood running thinly over the cracks and lines of his palm. The stalls were painted a red color acrimonious in contrast with the less-threatening feeling of the blue walls and floor, shiny tiles that seemed to promote a hazy feeling in the lavatory. Wan didn't like the way the silver spigots of the sinks seemed to compete with the blue for prominence. But in the stall, surrounded by red walls, the only silver was the toilet handle, and he didn't have to face that way, did he, oh ho, no; after checking the other stalls for occupants, convinced he was alone, he chose the one in the corner, unbuckled his pants and let his boxers fall to his knees. "Polly Croom, Polly Polly, oh Polly…" stroking fiercely before he was even erect, the slapping sound making a funny echo off the blue walls though his words, muted as they were, remained confined to the stall. When the voice spoke from behind the bright red wall to his right, he barely lost his rhythm.

"Wehll, whose she then, Polly Croob. She yer gal? Gone away an lef ya lonely?"

"Who are *you*," Wan stroking mechanically, feeling blood pouring into his penis from within, and without, the cut in his palm spreading blood over his growing erection.

"I'm Whiteleaf. I live here."

"How come I didn't see your legs under the stall door? You what, you some kinda pervert," the slapping sound bouncing between his words, "Polly, Polly…"

"Ain't got me no legs. You white people cut dem off bout two hundert years ago, know what I mean?" A pause, Whiteleaf's voice sounding a little closer and confidential. "Polly, Polly, heh heh. Why I bet she don't even want you."

"Of course..she does..Polly..wants.."

"Y'know what's beneath this moosayum? A Wanabscott burial ground. S'where I was buried; then you all came and chopped my legs off with yer big yella machines." They were both silent for a moment.

"S'why I gotta sit here. Till you all go away."

"Tell me," Wan asked, slowing his stroke just enough to think, "why did you say Wanabscott? Wasn't this island full of Manhattan indians or something before we came?" Wan heard Whiteleaf shifting on his toilet seat. It sounded like leaves scraping across a dry street.

"Now that's the thing about you Mericans. Thinkin history just starts in a place when you come on in an slaughter somebody. It just so happens we Wanabscotts were here before them Manahattins. Maybe we was callin each other somethin different. Maybe not. But we were too small, so we got moved out." He rasped out a giggle. "But not fore I got shot an arrow right in my *ear*."

Wan was not impressed. His erection pointed towards the hole in the door where the latch should have been; Wan was imagining Polly walking by mistake into the men's room, and he shooting off through the hole in the door into that empty hazy blue space, where it would land on the floor next to her high heels. And of course she'd bend down, right on the floor, he'd see her through the blue hole, and—

"Haha, I kin read yer mind. Haha," Whiteleaf breaking his concentration for a second.

"Fuck you, you legless ghost... Polly Polly, oh Polly," the image of her coming back to him now, naked and on her knees by the stall door...

"Yukyuk; she don' even want you. Does she? Haha."

"Of course she wants me. Polly wants me, she *wants* me," Wan could feel he was about to come. Whiteleaf banged against the wall, then quieted suddenly.

"Hey. Bet ya don't make it to the door."

"I'm going to go right through that door, I'm going to explode all over it, you bet I am, Pol, Polleee..." He hesitated as the wave spread through him, looked down. Semen dribbled off the head of his penis and down his knuckles.

"Didn even reach the floor." Whiteleaf's voice was fading now, and Wan's vision blurred as he looked down at himself, wilting and red. "Nah, she don' want you; ha ha. Hah..." till it was just a dry whistle of air in the pipes above him, and looking towards the hole and the floor beyond saw for a second a huge eye, its iris impossibly red, staring blankly at him. He shook his head, heard the men's room door open and several people walk in. The eye was gone. He flushed the toilet, rinsed his hands in the swirling water, wiped the back of his pants and pushed the door open.)

•

The nightcap's knee didn't jerk up into Tinsel's gut until three hours after he drank it. Sitting with Cozetta in The Body Grove, a bar a few miles east of Yallahs, the breakers of a particularly rough tide rising to the bottom of the soutward-facing bay window behind the band platform, Tinsel had felt unaffected by the alcohol. The adrenalin fear had shot into his system was ebbing, finally, like the tide outside—they'd parked the car at a restaurant half a mile down the road and walked till they'd found a noisy bar to hide in—but his mind, rising to the occasion like a tide equal and opposite the one visible outside the glass behind the band as they tuned up, had begun to rock his inner ear with an overture of all the possibilities, who what where why, the song loud and limitless in logic. Fear, wily thing that it is, remained like an undertow, shifting his incoming thoughts or cutting them short before they could empower him, pulling him beneath the surface noise to a deep vacuous silence...

Lightning overlit the ocean outside just as the band, Tequila Mockingbird, lit into their first power chord, the real thunder following as if on cue the first note from the bass, music and flashes of the oncoming storm wandering through the tables and dancing crowd and red and blue stage lights until it chafed the floor and echoed itself. A few people hooted and clapped their hands. Efrain Romero, lead singer and electric tambourine master, downed a can of Red Stripe and launched into the opening number, "Walking Translation":

Well, my Opus was erased
without the slightest trace
But my modem's still callin me
The 'lectronic messageboard says
It's in a sunken place
Down at the edge of the Electron Sea....

Cozetta came to the table with two beers. "Fatlips at the bar insisted we try this brand." She clunked them down on the table, mimicked the bartender's lisp. "You mushtht tassthtte thish to beleeeeeve it." She leaned over the table and blew lightly on his forehead. "Sweating, my little Tinsel is sweating. You must be thinking again, hon. Now you know what I've told you about that..." Tinsel snarled unconvincingly.

"You look pretty calm, considering our lives are, whatever," uncomfortable with the seriousness of the phrase, "In Danger."

"Oh yeah." Cozetta inched her chair over to his side of the table. "But I was thinking." Tinsel squinting at her quizzically, she continuing, "oh yeah, haha, I was thinking; but listen. It was probably some kids or something, ya know, out to scare the tourists or something."

"Kids're packing nice firepower these days. Silencers, too..."

"Okay, alright; but we're okay for now, there's not a reason to think it will happen again, they were probably scaring everyone who came into the graveyard, huh? And we can get Cletis tonight at Footlong's and catch an early flight out tomorrow." There followed a moment that should have been meaningful silence, the two of them left to ponder what they would do once they got back to the States, how the caring in each other's eyes might survive under the constant stare of Life Returned to Normal, but instead the precious seconds folded into a chalky feedback as the lead guitarist, who'd been playing his two-chord solo with his tongue, snapped a string with his overhanging incisors. The sound uncurled like a rattlesnake, took one big wave around the room then snapped away suddenly as a roadie shut off the amp. The bassist took the opportunity to shift into a moody solo, picked it up to a Louis Jordan swing, dropped back down to a medley of Elvis Presley ballads transformingfinally into a religious flow of flats as the lead singer whistled "Nearer My God To Thee." The guitarist plugged in a Johnnie Smith widebody and strummed patiently, nodding whenever the Deity was invoked; the girl behind the sound board lowered the volume and lights in reverence until nobody was sure the band was playing anymore, or even there at all. So Cozetta and Tinsel did get their moment of silence. They held hands there, tuned quietly to one another, as the barely discernible shapes of people moved about them in rustling skirts and jeans.

"Tinsel." Cozetta began. "I'll need a little time. Before I could say either way."

"Yeah. I knew." He whispered.

"It's not just me, Tinsel. I have to figure this out for you, too. And if I didn't, I wouldn't be here in the first place." She scratched behind his ears, kissed his nose. "Back when we were talking about gunshots, I was going to say, Look, I didn't expect to ever see you again anyway. I wouldn't have looked you up, I mean, and I don't know why you would call me. You and Polly have got on well enough, and—anyhow, I see you now, and you're the same slow, patient Tinsel. I feel the same love I felt years ago, a slow wondering thing, like you; it's not that I think you're indecisive, Tinsel. I mean, if you were decisive you wouldn't be here with me after the divorce and all; it's more like you just don't recognize the word. 'Decision' is not in your language. But now we run into each other, spend this time together, and I'm moved, Tinsel. I feel we're gliding along somewhere. I'm saying, just, I want to *enjoy* you; I want to be with you. I just don't know where it ends. Maybe I'm just dumb; maybe I'm just a deer caught in the headlights."

"Oh, I dunno," the best that Tinsel, a little defensive, could manage, "maybe you're the car and I'm the deer, Cozetta, y'ever think of it that way; and those things you think are headlights, they're just your bright reflections in my big, fat, venison-brained *eyes*." They exchanged a long sideways glance, that gradually curved into weary grins that said Okay, it was okay again to put it off for just a little longer.

"Whew. That was close." Cozetta reached for her beer.

"I'll say. You didn't know I was so aphoristic, did you?"

"Aphoristic?" she searching the table for a bottle opener.

"Yeah. Or what? Aphoristic? Synechdochal? Psycho-mythological? Intelligent, maybe?"

"What? For flipping *my* metaphor? It was a half-assed one, anyway, Tinsel."

"Yuh huh. You wanna order some shrimp?" Tinsel raised a hand for the waiter, but out of the stage mist a different form appeared before them, none other than Tequila Mockingbird guitarist Jay Valento, who introduced himself as such and, picking up Cozetta's bottle and wedging the can's lip behind his front teeth, popped it open for her. "Hey. Nun Bubble is outrageous beer. You guys have the best taste in the bar." He waved over to Romero. "Yo, Efrain. Nun Bubble enthusiasts!" and the next half hour found the four of them drinking beer and talking about the band's prospects in Jamaica. Valento wore a t-shirt, white with block letters, that said "Collect U.S. Commemoratives: They're Fun. They're History. They're America."

"Oh yeah. Ever since I was a kid I collected stamps. My favorite year, though—1974. Definitely.—Yeah, Efrain laughs, but he *knows*, man; 1974's the best. Skylab, Carl Sandburg memorial stamp, the American butterfly block of four. Fuckin *awesome* year. Everything pales before it. Other years had great single issues, but 1974, the whole *year*. Although there's always the Issue A price hike strip, for dweebs of course, or the Lincoln slave face error—"

"Wha, Lincoln Slave Face, what's that?" Tinsel asked. The bartender had run out of Nun Bubble, and Tinsel was drinking the fateful nightcap that would not affect him until the thunderstorm still building up outside had passed.

"Yeah, 1926 I think, one, maybe two-cent issue, the Lincoln profile thing. But the machinery hadn't been cleaned properly, so the plates got inked with more than one color. Now the stamp's supposed to be this dark green, but the center of each stamp, where the cross-hatching's the closest, and where Lincoln's face happened to be, came out a little browner than the edges. They must've done a few thousand sheets before the defect was noticed. Now, there's only three or four left. Just three or four single stamps! But rumor has it..." Valento looked around, put his arms around Efrain and Tinsel to increase privacy; "...rumor has it that a full sheet of the defected printing still exists intact, that some millionaire recluse—or dotty old hag, depending which rumor you're listening to—who lives here, here on this little island, has squirreled that sheet away until it's worth enough on the international market to buy—get this—the entire island!" He leaned back into his chair. "I don't hardly believe it myself, but we figured we'd come and check it out, you know. Get

a little beach time looking for the great missing slave-face sheet..."
Valento seemed to drift into his own thoughts. Efrain nudged him.
"Time we tried another song, right?"

"I don't know. That first set tired me. My teeth hurt."

"We'd love to hear you play again," Cozetta urged them away.
"Honestly. Another original number?"

"Oh sure," Efrain said. "They're all original. We make them up
out on the beach. I think I need suntan oil on to really be able to
think..." Cozetta shooed them back towards the stage. She whispered to Tinsel, "Hey you. I feel like someone's watching us all of
a sudden." Tinsel looked around the bar, craning his neck. "Who?
Somebody in particular?"

"Good job, spy master. Want to paint a target on your forehead
while you're at it?"

"Oh." Tinsel's scanning of the room had shown him no one suspicious looking. No dark blue suits, or middle-aged men with garish
flower shirts and raybans. Still, now that Cozetta mentioned it, he
did feel like their table was being watched over...

Tequila Mockingbird had taken the stage for the second set.
Efrain had armed himself with a tambourine that showered sparks
onto the dance floor when he bounced it off his hip; Valento wore
a fresh t-shirt depicting the missing Lincoln stamp on the front,
with the words on the back reading "Have You Seen These Children?" along with an expiration date and the stamp of the American
Dairy Council. He tapped his foot once, twice, nodded with a gesture appropriately rock n' roll to Tinsel and Cozetta as he led the
band into the song with a slow bar chord G, bending the strings and
then playing on up the neck through the warped note. Reverb from
the sound board made the last small cry echo and roll over on itself;
Efrain said, "This song's dedicated to those out there still interested
in a little adventure..." scattered cheers from the audience, "to those
who embark as pirates on the world and come back humbled like,
uh, that old fisherman..." appreciative claps as Efrain looked back to
respond to something his drummer was saying, "and, oh yeah, to a
girl named Groovy. One, two, one two three —" and they were off:

Now you've heard of a whale named Moby
And a wolfhound named White Fang
but on the great North American island
There was quite a more singular thing
His face was fair and furry
And no equals had his teeth
As they sank in the screaming Douglas firs
and into the ponds beneath
He'd a tail as flat as a pancake
and a mudhouse big as a Ford
Of all the creatures on the pond
Beaver Groovy was their lord—hey!
Groo-vy the King of Beavers
Groo-vy the King of Beavers
Though rain and sleet and thunder
Would knock upon his dam
His paws would never waver
As they slapped the mighty sand
All the hunters he frustrated
Cause they never could get through
Groovy dammed up all the rivers
Bit holes in their canoes
He dammed Lake Minnesota
And he dammed the Great Lakes, too
And he buried the Northwest Passage
with a mountaintop or two
But one day as he was paddling
Through the drifts of Puget Sound
He was seen by Trapper Marley
And Trapper Marley shot him down
Groo-vy the King of Beavers!
Groo-vy the King of Beavers!
Trapper Marley took old Groovy's head
and he hung it from a tree
So that all the beasts of the forest

Might fear him when they see
But one day when Marley was sleeping
Strong winds began to blow
& the body of Groovy came walking
and his head the trees let go
And it chopped Trapper Marley's head off
But Revenge won't cure all ills
Cause Groovy's headless body
Walks through the forest still—hey!
Groovy the Headless King of Beavers!
Groovy the Headless King of Beavers!
Now some say they've seen Bigfoot
Some say the missing link
But the only thing that's missing
Are Groovy's giant teeth
Now everyone likes the beaver
as it sleeps in its rivery bed
But the teeth of the greatest beaver king
Are still buried in Marley's head!
Groo-vy the King of Beavers!
Groovy the Headless King of Beavers!

"That sounds familiar," Cozetta murmured as the band members traded off solos to extend the song. Tinsel was looking up behind him. A huge mural on the wall had attracted his attention. It was a copy from a medieval manuscript: a small boat with one sail and three men aboard stood atop a green lake or sea. Beside or beneath them rolled an enormous fish, with nine fins shaped like waves, its mouth opening (or closing) on two flesh-colored fish. Tinsel thought they looked like human legs hanging from the monster's mouth; maybe the muralist hadn't known which the original intended, so he'd purposefully blurred the image. The monster's head was round and gray, eyes seeming to be looking elsewhere, to some Abstract horizon beyond the wall, pondering the question the rest of the body punctuated like a great question mark. Cozetta noticed it too. "How ruminant that face is," she said. Thunder rolled in suddenly, close. Rain began to tick on the bay window.

"Huh?"

"The face. It's almost sad, don't you think?" Tinsel squinted to re-examine the mural, but the expression of the fish had greatly changed. The flat grey eye he had remembered was gone, a shiny blue hole set deeper in the wood now reflecting a stage light—and was there a smaller, more liquid movement to it...The storm was suddenly upon them, a wave of thunder and the crashing of rain's needles on the tin roof. Lightning slipped down like a sheet over the window, and then as quickly as it came it had gone. Tinsel grabbed Cozetta's arm and stood up. "It's looking at us. Let's get out of here." Someone chose that moment to blow a fuse somewhere in the bar. It could have been the girl at the sound board, or the bartender recharging his portable mixer with his battered extension cord, or some one splashing water around in the men's room where several exposed wires ran across the ceiling, though as Cozetta would say later when these were proposed, "But." Before they could get two steps Efrain and Valento had them by the elbows, guiding them to a back door opening almost directly on the water's edge. Creeping around the building's side they saw a ladder propped against the wall, and a hole from which poured blue smoky light as the emergency generator kicked in from somewhere in the basement. The rain had let up.

"Somebody *was*..." Cozetta looking up as they passed the ladder. Efrain was counting heads, the drummer and bassist taking up the rear. "Okay, all here. Who's got The Book." He seemed to be looking at Tinsel expectantly; then Cooter, the drummer, passed over his shoulder a thick spiral bound tome. "The Ultimate Fake Book." Efrain thumbed through it as if he could read the songs in the darkness by touch alone. "Don't go on a gig without it." Everybody guffawed, Cozetta har-harred, and Tinsel was lifted into the passenger seat of a Honda Savage Fun Motor Scooter, Cozetta leaping aboard in front of him. "Hang on," she said and started the engine with the accelerator grip halfway around. They wheelied unsteadily for a few yards. Cozetta brought it down hard, and they sped off along the roadside, headlights off, the only light that of the full moon shining along the polished wheel-guards, so it was only as they hit the small animal five minutes later, in the split-second before they were tossed into the air and the bushes beyond, that they saw the eyes, and in them the moon reflected; and though the moon was blue, the eyes were the same serious grey Tinsel remembered the fish in the mural as having, and when he pulled himself shaking from the thicket, suddenly drunk and sick, calling Cozetta's name and hearing her voice a few yards away, he saw through the dirt in his eyes two grey moons in the sky stare impassively back at him. The scooter's motor ground into the dirt and died.

The fish in the mural was The Whale from the Ashmole Bestiary, a folio dated to c.1210, made perhaps in the North Midlands, which would raise the chances, depending on the time of year, that the whale the painting was modeled after was not a single whale but more likely a close swimming pack of pilot whales beginning their southward migration. Thus the many-finned monster. The animal unfortunate enough to cross Cozetta Croom Bitfield's path was the Northern Ash Mole, named after the British scientist Fontaine G. Ashe, who introduced the reticent mammal, known in America as a star-nosed mole, to Jamaica in a controlled experiment to compete with certain other mammals for territory along agricultural land and irrigation lines. The experiment was never really controlled enough; several pair of ashmoles simply dug their way out of the drop-cages in which they'd been housed, and began living fruitful, if not extravagant, lives near the dumpsites of local taverns and inns. Rizzoli could have told Polly most of this, had he but known Cozetta and Tinsel's story: but he was busy with other stories for Polly, so many that when he came out of a dream still speaking quietly he found he was alone, stripped to his underwear and bound lightly at the wrists with a pair of Polly's hose, unsure what he'd dreamt and what he'd done, how much of it had been made up in the dark. Moments later his mind registered the cause of his waking—-the sounds of a man, deeply in pain, perhaps fighting for his life with each breath, indeed the sounds of a man being beaten within an inch of his life... "Good Lord," Rizzoli whispered, throwing on his pants and shirt before chuckling unconsciously at himself for employing such a conventional expletive; he rolled the hose into his pocket and sprang to the door with renewed composure. Just outside he stopped: not that what he beheld was so complete a Spectacle that he couldn't comprehend it—on the contrary, he thought, slipping on a pair of lenses (real bifocals) to focus, this could have been expected and avoided. But, for such a conventional trope on the conventional, what a Spectacle it was still, he thought: Polly Croom, barefoot and bare-legged, her hair loosed from its knot and shimmering with quick blond light, mercilessly pummelling a wobbling Doctor Wan, face bloodied and teary-eyed, hands full of Polaroid photographs, eyes occupied somewhere behind his beaten brow, concentrating on just how ignoble his enterprise was, not even the passing thought of glancing down her sweating body, bare shoulders crossed by a thin laced bra, no blouse—and maybe it was this, Rizzoli mused as Wan conceded his knees to gravity, maybe Polly's total composure in brutalizing this eel of a man makes her most noble, makes the possible sordid aspect be raised to true Spectacle—Polly's voice also composed though exclaiming, "Blue hole! Blue hole! You shithead!" The knockout punch was a wedding band to the bridge of the nose. Wan lay finally in peace, disappearing slowly into his oversized polyester suit, sunk till only one protesting finger remained visible, as if he had at last thought of something to say in his defense.

"Hoo boy." Rizzoli leaned against the door. Polly held up her arm as if to beckon him, then opened her palm and spread the fingers, bringing the thumb and forefinger around in a tight circle, the Okay sign, a view through it to Polly's glistening breastbone; but Rizzoli looked through and saw only blue, blue.

Part Two

Who but a fool would take his left hand by his right,
and say to himself, how d'ye do?
Partners! I must have Partners!

— *Maltese sailor aboard the Pequod*

XI. Dreams Beneath the Dilatometric

Somewhere in the Abruzzi e Molise, in its bulky 5,880 square miles of southwest Italy; in a year implied but unstated within a codicil to instructions laid out to be followed in the case of the demise of a splinter-group of the Roman Catholic brotherhood Ablutionists of Absolute and Hopeless Order; somewhere in a transitive state between liquid and gas, in its chemical or molecular precision beyond common scientific reckoning, is encased within its vial what's alleged to be and what's been prayed to as the Tears of Saint Jude: the emotional made physical, the spiritual manifest of a distinct vine of belief, the reminder of pains taken to ensure miracles for the forlorn or forgotten; and, as often is the case with the ancient layers of the Catholic Church, the potentially valuable made invisible and untouchable, the cause of all rejoicing hidden, though the story of the lamp bid otherwise, the revealing concealed by dark habit.

At this point in the Abruzzi's history, with all of Italy pensive with self-disgust, straining under the smile of Mussolini, in its correlating place a small monastery stands; and in its precise center sits Brother Clifford King, visiting American late of the Sacred Heart, fasting to gain the encouragement of God; he hopes the clarity of hunger will help him redefine his faith, but what Brother King will help clarify in the next few moments, albeit obliviously, are the four definitions found in the American Heritage Dictionary of the English Language for the archaic word *misericord.*

1. Misericord: in a monastery, to have certain rules relaxed for a specific reason. Brother Clifford, his fast observed until now at the request of the rector, sits in a stall against the wall of a small chamber for monks granted such dispensation, waiting for the rector to call upon

him with an explanation of why his fast has been halted. He is aware
of being somewhat guilty of a dream which visited him just before
waking: he stood before the drawbridge of an immense medieval
castle. Floating over it was the crown of God, wrought with jewels
so beautiful yet so humble they seemed hesitant to shine. Brother
Clifford was holding a card in his hand, an invitation to a funeral.
"Who has died?" said someone behind him, and before he could stop
himself he'd answered: "It's the death of God; the death of Man; the
death of the Son of Man." The castle blanched suddenly, and the
crown plummeted to the ground, its eight jeweled points embedded
in the earth around him.

   2. The room itself is called the misericord, though Brother Clifford's
elders at the Sacred Heart in Woonsocket, Rhode Island—called by
the high school students there "the brothers of the Scared Heart"—
who take no part in fasts or other physically testing ritual, have never
informed him of this secondary definition.

   *3. Also, the word refers to a bracket on the underside of a hinged seat in
a church stall, which may be raised for the purpose of standing and leaning
against the wall.* Brother Clifford, as if to illustrate in the way of game
show models opening car doors and swivelling bucket seats, pulls up
the seat and stands, his frail shoulders square to the wall; his elbows
rest on a shallow shelf running along the dark panelling. His black
tassel swings in patient arcs from his waist, drawing past his knees
pendulum-like and passing at its end across the face of a strange
painted carving, unseen by him and unknown by anyone now alive,
dug with some skill into the underside of the lifted seat.

   The dagger had been spring-activated decades ago, so techni-
cally no one was at fault: Brother Clifford, in lifting his seat, had
merely helped to illustrate the last, and most ablutive, definition of
the misericord: *4. That ceremonial dagger used to shorten the agony of a
defeated knight as he lies grounded in the weight of his armor and the pain
of his injuries.*

   It shoots from the wall and with a whack into his spine, a great
trick of skill in reverse, cuts a neat line between the lumbar and
thoracic regions, cracking no vertebrae but splitting whatever shell

encases one's worldly essence and releasing the body in a new, lazy attitude as it slides toward the floor.

Perhaps under the weight of his spiritual armor, or perhaps due merely to gravity, the earth reaching up from under the floorboards to take back its own, Brother Clifford slumps to his knees, no longer feeling the soreness of countless hours of prayer; the brightly carved face now seems to peer intently at him as he slides unaware by it. What has it been considering, there, staring unblinking at the floor for so many years. How did it regard the darkness, the dust motes? Did it read them as the entrails of the air?

Brother Clifford, also unblinking, lets his head loll back, taking in the vaulted ceiling, the rich panelled shadows. From there, from somewhere in the unfocused above, a simple drop of blood descends and hits the bridge of his nose. His eyes search the high emptiness; does he see Him, the Christ, face stripped of His beard and clothed in the finest silver garments, looking down upon him? A hand reaches down to touch his arm... but no, there are no stigmata, no wound where the sword pierced His side as they peeled him from the cross... It is not the Christ. It is only a witness to this ending moment. Today the Knights of God lose.

"*Ametur cor Jesu*," blessed be the heart of Jesus. Were those his last words? Pastor Don Pializzi Remfallano will record them as such; but in truth before they are out—if ever those words were forthcoming—a silver hand hushes them. For fear of the commotion any sound might bring, Wednull J. Beaver, forehead bleeding from shrapnel of North Korean ordnance forged thirteen years later in time, his body stuck in a seam between maps, half in the Abruzzi and half Elsewhere, silences the dying brother with one gloved hand and with the other picks a small vial from the mouth of the carved face beneath the seat. Yes, it is the face of Saint Jude. Yes, it is the fabled vial of his tears. As Beaver lifts it to his eyes his hands begin to shake; a tremor is running through the map, the sound of an angry beast howling its way across the shadows of its unfinished story. Beaver knows it's time to leave, but some quirk in the technology's already made that decision for him, friction sliding away and his grip on whatever invisible ledge he grasps loosened. He could have said, "Here I go again," or something to the like; but Captain Beaver was no middle-century cartoon character. His lips shut like Saint Peter's Gate, reserving judgment. Moments before he is unceremoniously popped into the warm waters of the Caribbean, the vial slips from his gloved hand and shatters on the floor by the unconcerned posture of Brother Clifford King's earthly remains.

And for a few seconds, the world falls into dream.

•

These are the dreams in which ears turn to stone.

Tinsel Croom, thrown from the back of a motor-scooter driven by his ex-wife, is in that sleep far beyond recall; as if in abeyance to some rule of inverse returns he rockets through its cyclical gradations. As it was Tinsel who was most ungraciously flopped, amidst a scumble of leaves vines and small animals that edge to the side of the road at night, into unconsciousness, so Tinsel will be the first to slip athletically into the images of his nightmare, Tinsel the most composed in his slumber, Tinsel the first to dream.

Into shape and out of shapes: Tinsel feels himself distributed into a million parts as he plummets, speculated on as if by a committee outside himself, with total access to possible images from which a dream-shape might form. Who knows what it might depend on, the last TV show you watched or a distant tickle from the babysitter when you were ten, but eventually comes some pucker of acclimation, a tiniest agreement replicating in colorful fractals, spinning off an endless permutation of values until the pattern reaches a consistency, a notion almost organic. For this moment Tinsel extends new feelers everywhere, filling space about him in his new shape, the notion become awareness of what he's become.

The shape of the dreamer is octopi, or the octopus of all octopi, the curlingest most extraordinary creature dredged up from any Saturday afternoon movie he's seen. The transformation is startling, even in the void, and Tinsel is left pondering his new shape as only a cephalopod can. He thrashes his tentacles, he puckers his suction cups, spews ink until he decides it's not so bad after all, might even be a little fun with some scenery, let's see, settling finally for the compatible blue underwater scene, languid bellyfish and stern rockfish Sunday-driving along the bottom. The water is tropical, as you can imagine, although his new body can withstand temperatures much lower without discomfort. And what's this? —*yes*, it's a conveniently located shipwreck, and a relatively recent arrival to the real estate, judging by the barnacles. An octopus's dream house: Tinsel slithers in through the splintered bilge, tangles his tentacles briefly in the Jacob's ladder that's somehow drifted inside, observes the keelson and unused kudge, and slides upwards in search of baubles. A few coins in the companionway, a gold-plated watch, the usual detritus. In the cabin he experiments with his new arms, whipping soggy gobs of paper about, crumpling charts and booklets into sucker-balls he lobs through the blown-out windows... eventually he bores of the game and returns outside. Tinsel cruises along the taffrail, arriving aft and passing across the face of the vessel's moniker, *Margin*. And attempts his first joke as an octopus: "*Margin*. Well, at least they know what the bottom line is, heh heh. Gllblllghlll," regressing into gutteral cephalopod chuckles...

Does his beak twist into a grin? Does his head bubble with unbelievable juices? Before he can, before it does, something disturbs his new sensibilities, makes him pucker and unpucker his numerous suction cups. What comes across his field of vision, causes him to champ that just-formed beak in octopus consternation? What makes him strain against both the impulse to shoot out tentacles in attack and to disappear in a cloud of ink?

It shuffles toward him with lazy steps, kicking up loose plant life in a cloud of its own, leaving a strange, infuriatingly *dry* trail of whitish powder as proof of its movement, since it seems to get no closer for all its labor. A nearly human representation of frailty and age, it seems as weighed down by gravity as Tinsel-Octopus is freed of it. Its body is covered with some kind of white powder, and the head, while not hairless, bobs a little bit as it walks, stray gray strands

waffling in the current, a wrinkled-grape shape crowned with a worn
headdress of feathers; the current moving between them makes the
headdress appear now full of still crow feathers, now perhaps only
two or three white herring gull, their black tips weaving as if to aban-
don the head-band like leaves anxious to be off the tree. The thread-
bare band shows a faded, repeating pattern of faces and eyes. To
Tinsel the faces seem at first those of birds, until the beaks seem
to take on their own expression, as if faces unto themselves. In the
center of the headband is a frog with open mouth, two small hands
holding the end of the stuck-out tongue. All this obscured somewhat by the powdery substance—the bleached wrinkles at each eye's
corner, the small shafts of hair escaping the head's crown and puffed
at the top like chaff, each feature in fact seeming more hazy and less
definite as the figure gets closer.

"Hey," says Tinsel, "you're spoiling my water scene."

Ignoring the comment for the moment, "Hi. Name's Whiteleaf." It turns on its heels. "Well; come on." And then, as it begins
walking back the way it came, "Ain't like this isn't *my* dream, either."

•

Whiteleaf normally occupies the same stall in the men's room
of the Museum, he explains to Tinsel. "Only suddenly I find myself
sleepwalkin. An next thing is, I find you standin underwater, heh
heh."

"Well, I'm an octopus," Tinsel says, defensive.

"Oh," says Whiteleaf," pausing to look. "I see now."

*What a cheap excuse for a ghost, Tinsel thinks. What memory could
this have come from? Scooby-Doo? Other bad made-for-TV programming?
Some old geezer covered with white face paint or clown powder...*

"Ho ho, I know what yer thinkin," Whiteleaf interrupts. "I'm
no idea of yers. Least not anymore'n yer one of mine."

Something white looms ahead. "This ain't face paint anyway. I
just sleepwalked through a bag of dry plaster mixin in the janitor's
closet. Heh heh. Now I'm all white, like you." He stops a moment.

"Oh, forgot, yer an ocktypus, hm. Well, here we are."

They look upon a cavernous coral reef, bleached pure white, a vast skeleton of whatever lush enterpise it might have once been; now it's apparently deserted. No fish swim in and out its myriad entrances, no crabs or eels scramble for their shadowy holes. Nothing moves.

"Why is it all white? I mean, what does it symbolize? Purity? The bone behind the brain?" Tinsel gamely nonchalanting it with a few Jungian brevities, reaches with a tentacle to feel the coral, breaks off a piece by mistake. "Oops."

"It's white cuz it's dead." Whiteleaf steps under an arch and into a large passageway, looks back at Tinsel. "Them coral creatures; they're all dead now." He leans into a wall and it breaks with a powdery boom, his shape disappearing into the new milkiness and shadow. "Yeh, an all the algae that make the color, they died first." Tinsel peering around a corner sees an empty chamber. Whiteleaf's voice drifts to him from somewhere deeper in. "You wanna know why?"

"Yes, I want to know." Tinsel trying to get the hang of moving like an octopus, knocking his head—*was* it a head?—against the low ceiling.

"Because," Whiteleaf's voice goes on, further within, "the water got too warm, so them coral creatures ex-pelled what algaes they'd got, and... there goes the color, Mister Ocktypus... dead, dead, dead, just like me, heh heh. Now ain't that somethin. You folks start buildin things agin, an everythin else starts dyin agin. Makes a guy like you wonder, I bet."

"What are you talking about?"

"I didn say nothin. I ain't even got legs." The voice fades out completely. Tinsel thinks about it, floating there with his tentacles swarming about him, and can't remember actually seeing Whiteleaf's legs. All he can remember is the frog on the headband...

"Of course you have legs!" he shouts. He's lost, no idea which direction to go, not sure from where he came. "Of course you have legs! You just brought me here, didn't you? Now come back!"

"Nah." The voice drifts in for a second. It's conspiratorial; it's close. "You people started buildin, an I lost my legs. That's all I 'member..." and then it's nothing again, Tinsel alone in his new body and environment, and for a second he feels dangerously close to some permanence in this position, like he'll never have two arms and legs again, never see Cozetta and Cletis, nothing but mounds of coral corpses and no food fit for an octopus... But now he's changing once more, as if the shape has served its moment, slowly approximating his waking self, human Tinsel; and again it begins to feel too close to the real thing: his human feet fill human shoes, which fill with water; his eyes lose their protective film, the huge optic nerves shrinking in the space before his brain, his beak opens into lips and teeth that can't hold back the now brackish water flooding down his throat...

Drowning, Tinsel makes a fleeting attempt to veto these images, re-think his dream world into another phase, but he's already blacked out.

•

Pastor Don Pializzi Remfallano flushes the toilet in his private bath and brushes fig-bar crumbs off his habit. He crosses the hall at a brisk pace, past his private study, the Pastor's library, and the long row of doors leading to the guest rooms. Ever since Bishop Gelano ordered the old bug-infested doors to be replaced, the slight difference in stain on the new doors has given Pastor Remfallano the impression in passing by them that he's caught inside a giant accordion, which will at any moment contract violently and squeeze out his very soul.

His mother Angela had tried to indoctrinate him in the playing of that most unholy of instruments, and it was only in turning to God that he escaped the horrifying vocation. Long lists of polka chords still chimed in his head passing through this part of the hallway, his mother standing sternly by him, his father slapping hammy thighs to keep time, but also as a warning...

Entering the *misericord* he sees the slumped Brother Clifford and knows immediately he's dead—the body lay in such natural confusion, ungraceful but inoffensive in its bone-casual, pre-stiffened state that he takes some seconds admiring it, envying it almost its peacefulness; but then alarm for a fallen Catholic moves him quickly to the body, leaning close to the blue lips to feel for any breath.

"Aye Carumba!" The strange exclamation slips evenly and perfectly pronounced from the Pastor's own lips as he rolls Brother Clifford over and sees the ornate hilt standing perpendicular to the point at which it enters the back. The Spanish language, its authority and intonation, has been the pastor's secret love for decades, and minutes earlier he was reading through a book of Spanish verbs, which he hides on a small shelf behind the toilet, marvelling at the ease and fluidity of the grammar, how much nicer it feels on his tongue than his native Italian, even given the obvious similarities. He tries to pull the blade out but it is wedged firmly in the bone, his efforts producing only a low grinding sound that trembles up his arm and stills him.

His eyes wander up the wall to a piece of hinged panelling, dangling from a rusty spring mechanism over two feet long in its relaxed state. Yes, that would do it, he thinks...

Travelling back down the wall to the underside of Brother Clifford's raised seat, his eyes meet a pair staring back at him, staring him down. Behind those wooden eyes an entire face lurks in relief, painted to a lively expressiveness, the mouth open and the lips pulled back from the teeth, as if to champ a bit. Pastor Remfallano fits his finger between the two white rows, then pulls it back... did he imagine it, the slightest bit of pressure on his finger, or were the wooden teeth actually closing down on him, biting as the blush-painted skin slid slowly over the cheekbones, the eyes watery and bright...

"Madre de Dios." He snaps himself out of it. Whoever this face represents, it's no one Pastor Remfallano has ever seen, in manuscripts or on stained glass windows. And why was it carved on the underside of a seat, where people might only find it by mistake, and what had it to do with the consequences suffered by Brother Clifford for becoming its discoverer?

"Surely it is the face of the Devil." And saying so he pulls off his left shoe, scattering with his robes the unseen remnants of a broken vial, grips the shoe by the toe and smashes the hard heel into that graven image, bludgeoning the ancient features until they splinter and are unrecognizable. But the face is etched into his eyelids, it seems, and floats in the reddish darkness as he blows out the room's only candle and crosses himself.

•

How can we leave a man to drown in the depths of his own reflection? Tinsel Croom, floating in the hollows of that abandoned reef, that dead sea skull, deserves better. But even now, as far in the air above Bull Bay's surface as Tinsel is below it, over and out beyond the beach where Cletis and Footlong lay sleeping, slung out like seaweed, riding out their hangovers, the sky begins to pucker and quiver; even now a visible object is expelled.

The clear Caribbean morning receives the plummeting form of Captain Beaver, yanked so recently from the snowy mountains of Italy, like a mollusk receives a grain of sand, that small imperfection around which it may create a pearl. And what's a drowning man compared to this gem?

As he falls; as he whistles like an arrow toward the sea, as if it were a creature to be targeted so; his mind is, for the brief moment, clear. Speed has gutted it; pure propulsion, something more than gravity, has left it smooth as polished limestone; though we can imagine that a distance covered over time will encourage thought, the Head Diver derives nothing from the experience. He resides out of time, or through it; perhaps the language can't acquire the space he's found! In a word, he *sleeps*. And in his sleep accelerates, as bodies falling are wont to, and smashes through the ocean's skin and into its puddingy depths.

Up for air, some semi-conscious node of nerves signalling the need to swim, creating new necessities in that improvisorial way living tissue tends to delight in doing, he bobs disinterestedly. His hand is grasped; he is lifted from the water. A face forms before him as some inner set of eyes open against slumber's foam. A mouth opens in a smile, revealing teeth.

For a moment he sees the face of the Patron, of Saint Jude as he stared from his place beneath the seat in the *Abruzzi*, vial still held sweetly in his teeth. But in an abrupt transmogrification those teeth grow long and sharp, a dank breath issues, fur fills the fleshy spaces and the eyes grow ember red. Between canine and molar a sprig of pigflesh is wedged; the Dzoonokwa bites down on the vial, spraying the sacred tears into Beaver's eyes. Through his closed eyes he scrambles into the next chamber of dream, pinning his hopes against nightmares, as out in the world of the waking he clamps his hand around an unseen arm and hauls himself up into the boat, to be steadied there as he heaves for breath by the two astonished faces watching him.

•

Les Holm, author of *Head Diver*, wakes up in a cold sweat. The men in black suits had visited him again. But this time there was something different.

He'd heard of them years ago, maybe after the Gulf Coast sightings: strange men visiting neighborhoods and knocking on doors, asking if this or that person present might have seen the flying saucer. Everybody knew they were Fed, of course; collecting information, as well as names, maybe planting bugs, discouraging witnesses from speaking freely about what they'd seen. The government was as intimate with aliens as Nixon had been with the Democratic Party headquarters in the seventies; then again, he guessed, everybody also knew the men in black were the aliens themselves. They covered their faces with hats and scarves, spoke haltingly, or forgetting which continent they were on, spoke the wrong language, only to change from fluent Serbo-Croatian to downeast Mainer in less than a breath. They didn't sweat; they fell oddly silent for minutes at a time, as if listening to messages on another wavelength; they forgot to wear shoes sometimes; they refused any offers of food or drink; and they kidnapped the uncooperative.

But what did they want with a semi-successful science fiction novelist? Holm had never seen a UFO. On the other hand, he'd never seen the men in black, either. They came to him in his dreams.

Badgering him, as usual, about his book.

"This...Beaver..." one of them had said, moving its elbows in a shrug that reminded him eerily of Shaggy from the Scooby Doo cartoon; "this...*muhmuhmuhmuhmuh*...Beaver," going on as if nothing weird had happened, "is excitability, hm?" Was that a smile? A lead-in for him to respond? Their eyes, most of their faces in fact, lurked in the shadows of huge wraparound sunglasses. They stood in his living room just inside the front door, though in his dream he couldn't remember whether he'd opened it or whether they'd merely been there as the scene began.

"Oh, ha ha, I don't know," he'd tried. *"Mm, ha ha,"* one had immediately imitated him. The other two repeated it mechanically, striking the poses of relaxed department store dummies. *"MM Ha Ha,"* they said. *"Mm Ha Ha."*

"Beaver's a stand-up fellow—" Holm had started to argue, feeling sweat gathering beneath his overwrought moustache. At that point the three fell into the freakish silence previously described. Holm weaved a bit on the balls of his feet as they stood there frozen, as if they were shapes deserted by their spirits. As he was beginning to inch to the side enough to get a look behind the rim of the sunglasses, the one closest to him perked up, re-animated... no, no, just his imagination; but enough to keep him glued there. Eventually Holm sensed a change in the room, realizing with a start that perhaps they weren't off listening to some foreign broadcast at all, not extending outward but inward, listening in fact to *him*, probing, suggesting...

He'd woken up at this point, as usual, but sensed immediately the difference. He was not tangled in the same knot of sheets, sweat broken out on him like a new skin. "Stand up fellow," he had murmured to himself, unaware until this present moment, as his eyes open fully, that he's been sitting at his terminal, the electric ebb and flow of the screen lulling him like a nightlight; unaware that he's been recasting the eighth chapter of *Head Diver* as he's slept, repeating his defense of his main character like a mantra; unaware until this very moment, as his nostrils quiver and the sweat begins to weave its way out from under his feverish pate and run in rivulets like tears past his eyes, that he's taken his stand-up fellow Captain Beaver, knocked him unconscious and sent him to hell.

•

Why does one man, of all the men women and children in the world at this moment of ubiquitous dreamtime, hold yet his brown eyes open?

For a second ago he was snoring, signalling through subtle twitches running the length of his faded bedsheet a certain self-satisfaction with his inner activity. At night he re-imagines the day coming, revises the day previous; in the revision he sells all his pottery, and the breasts of the whore on Promenade are fuller, more like his ex-wife's, but as if she remembers nothing about the time they were lifted bodily from the Sleepy Rose because he'd lost his roll of bills. She calls him Rock while she's running her nails down his chest, calls him Baby when they've shed everything but her tissue-like bra and laid them on the dumpster in the alley, calls him every syllable in the city as they touch and lock there, half-reclined against a plastic garbage can, calls him everything but his name; *Flinch, Flinch,* he says, hoping she might repeat it. But as soon as he tells her she looks away, and he wakes up.

"Inevitable Greece." Wide awake, it's hard not to think of that other handful of islands and gods that watched and did nothing as their queen played coy to the hundred suitors. And what was Greece now if not a whore who couldn't give up her finality, time raping her slowly as progress inched its way in? Not that the Antilles weren't far ahead of her; but Ithaca saw him recasting his wife's image by a rocky

shore. Here, by a cave somehow connected historically to Odysseus'
return, he'd learned that she hadn't waited for him, that she couldn't
even remember when she'd first given herself up. So a half mile from
the cave of the nymphs where Odysseus hid his treasure, Flinch had
taken his own; when she'd turned back to him before rolling into the
surf to wash herself, afterward, he'd seen that love had fled from that
stare like the hundred suitors from the sudden hail of arrows, the
storm a precise act of the gods from which none had escaped.

Flinch, alone now in his bed, was not so lucky. He survived,
an unlucky Ishmael, but with no tale of consequence to tell. He'd
searched out the biggest thing and found it malignant. Love might
be an invention, but it was still a monster, an infernal engine, too
fast and too deep-diving to follow. And if it spat him out like Jonah,
he'd no cataclysm to preach. The gods, those leeches, bled you slowly.
Flinch doesn't fall back to sleep, because he knows if he does his
whore will turn in his arms into a crayfish, a shark, an octopus. He
lets his eyes go watery instead, the geography of the body fading
into the shapes of islands, unfillable bodies of water between them.
Anyone could see the fate of his land in the fate of their hearts.
Flinch didn't have to look twice.

But he does: above his head, unblinking and huge, the visage of
inevitability floats. And its face is huge, and white.

•

The Gods, Again, the Gods: Abutting the relatively open crown of
Cho-Sen Hill is a deep escarpment, gouged over the years by erosion,
glacial movement or continental stress, perhaps, no two geologists
have ever agreed exactly; but the steep nature of the sides, and the
flat terrace well over tree-level, its suddenness to those approaching
from the ground, make it an ideal point from which to command an
armed unit hoping to hold the high road in a low-lands kind of war.

And holding, "Holding, holding, holding," as Lt. Robert "Fighting Mad" Maxwell has told his company more than twice, "is how
the poop always seems to droop here in Korea, hwaaagh, hwaaagh."

His laugh scrapes across his tongue like slow-motion twin chainsaws dancing a duet. Maxwell calls the hill, which has no name, number or elevation on his map, Korea, because nobody's quite sure anymore whether they're in North Korea or South Korea. So it's Korea; it will be called Cho-Sen Hill in the history books, when a journalist asks Maxwell where he was when it all went down, and an enthusiastic English- major-turned-translator interprets the remark as metaphoric, cutting the country's name and its meaning, "the chosen," in two arbitrarily even pieces. It's a joke Maxwell wouldn't laugh at.

"Where are we, men?" he croaks in the morning's cold call to duty.

"Korea!" they answer.

"Hwaaagh, hwaaagh, hwaaagh."

•

Private Lentil Coopsman is sure they're past the Parallel, even though no U.N. troops should be there. It's October 4, 1950, and the platoon has had no contact with the enemy—or with the U.N.

forces, for that matter—for sixteen days. The Blue Unit, known among the lesser payscales as the Doorstops, has been that long without radio contact, since Maxwell kicked it inside-out with his left foot when he started hearing orders that didn't compliment his intuition. The Doorstops, renowned for holding the proverbial line, having missed an anticipated skirmish with the enemy and having nothing better to do until rations ran out, have found the most natural point from which to defend themselves and settled in for a long stay. Whether they're facing north or south, defending the hill from the North Koreans or the UN forces, doesn't seem to matter to Maxwell, though the irony certainly isn't lost on him.

"You don't know who you're fightin for anyway, hwaaagh, hwaaagh, hwaaagh, anymore'n I know there's a difference between the Koreans we're shootin and the Koreans we're savin."

"Or between the Koreans and the Japs," platoon sergeant Skean volunteers.

Wherever they go, whomever they're fighting, they listen to Maxwell. Maxwell snorts, spits against a tree, peels the bark off and tastes the green skin, waves his hand in the air a bit and lights a stogie, blowing the match out with breath through his left nostril, the right one filled with an emergency wad of chewing tobacco and a small pill, should he ever be against a wall not of his choosing, guaranteed to deliver its lethal dose scant moments after that first pleasurable chew sets on the tastebuds.

"Gonna rain," he says.

And it does, with a thunderclap to herald the heavy downpour. The enemy offensive begins seconds later, perforating the trees with gunfire. Four soldiers drop dead immediately, probably convinced it was the weather that got them. Platoon sergeant Skean is winged in the shoulder blade as the rest of the company head for their positions, and with the first pause in fire his high whine is the only thing that can be heard. The forest below is quiet as a Christmas tree.

"Fuckin Japs. Ohhh, fuckin Japs busted my shoulder." He's lying close to the middle of the open crown; Maxwell lets him stay put. "Don't get em. Wait." Nobody moves. Skean's agony threads through the trees, hanging from their branches like lights, twinkling with promise to the rest of them.

"Hwaaagh, outnumbered I bet." Maxwell lies face down as close to the edge of the escarpment as possible given his solid beer belly. Below him...

"Whadda ya see?" to Private Stephens.

"Nothin but trees. Sir."

"You heard, though, hwaaagh. Big guns."

"Sounded like one of ours. They can't be that close. But you can't tell with the trees, sir."

"Guess we better get ridda some of them trees then." Maxwell carries no gun or knife; beside him always is a box of grenades, and strung about his body in webs, each one with his initials scratched near the ring release. Barely looking, he lofts half a dozen over the edge. Explosions; a few screams; the sound of people moving. Things being carried. It's always like this, Maxwell thinks. A dozen more and they'll be backing into that little flat area we mined, and it'll serve em right too.

"How'd they get one of our guns?" Stephens scratches his helmet. In the distance, like balloons popping, the mines are being detonated.

Behind them Sergeant Skean whimpers softly, waiting for night.

•

It took longer than Maxwell thought for the ammo to run low, but he'd had the matter settled in his mind for two days.

"Go back and get more," he says.

"But Lieutenant, we don't know where we are." Maxwell lifts a finger for silence, pulls a pin from a grenade, counts two and hooks it outward, going by ear; six seconds later a brief scream punctuates the explosion.

"Tryin to get sneaky," Maxwell shouts to the forest. Then turning back to Private Stephens, and pulling another pin as he says it, "Go that way."

They move out at nightfall. Maxwell alone, cradling his last box of grenades in his lap, seems to meditate, dirt and trees exploding around him. He taunts them all night, shouting the few Korean obscenities he's learned from the farmers whose land they'd cut through. By evening he knows there's something large afoot here, and his hunch is that the charlies below aren't the same NK troops that ran crying like babies from the first American forces; there's been a patient and confident air to their advance, assuming of course that they thought the hill was being defended by more than one soldier. Perhaps they haven't had to see a retreat yet, perhaps because they were travelling in large numbers as yet undetected by the US F-51s and F-80s. By which he means, of course, they're the Chinese. Any soldier on the ground could feel them coming, anyone with his nose to the grindstone knew that the commies wouldn't send a two-bit army up against the United Nations without something up their sleeve. But apparently MacArthur had his nose elsewhere.

Slowly and humorlessly, an attack begins. This time it's the storm that follows close behind; freakish winds bend the trees to the ground, cold rain stings the ground like bees. Maxwell sees more men than he can count struggling to hold their positions beneath him as the undergrowth blows away, or becomes uprooted in the torrents running down the hill.

"Time, time. Let it rain, hwaagh." He attacks indiscriminately, tossing grenades with both hands, catching both the retreating and the advancing soldiers. A lone climber has reached a point a few feet beneath the cliff when the rain gives him away. Maxwell shoots an arm down to him, leaves a grenade in the falling man's grasp. The face is briefly desperate, but then it's too dark to see the descent. But the cap, blown off, lands on an outhang of twig, and when lightning strikes Maxwell sees the single red star on it.

"Nice try." Time to move: his niche in the cliff has become a runoff stream, and it's when he's reaching into his crate to gather up what's left that he sees the pin hanging on his finger, his initials sparkling in the rain. He looks down to his feet. Something rolls into the dark puddles there.

"Shit. I knew that was gonna happen someday." Captain Wednull J. Beaver arrives at the moment of the explosion, dropped again without warning, and receives a quarter-inch scrap of metal casing just above his right eyebrow. The blast propels him onto a floor of moving mud. The echo, its iron booming, dies away, and silence comes into focus, the silence of rain on an open hill.

•

He tilts his head to look at his watch. Blood runs into his left eye, the same blood that will drop like a sacrament on Brother Clifford King, that already has, in a sense, ten years earlier; but Head Divers were used to seeing things out of their timely order. And Beaver knew, anyway, that time *was* relative, it had to be to be kept, that some stories happened in it and some happened with no time referent at all. And those were the most dangerous, the stories people wanted burned, the gods they wanted torn down before they became apparent...

"Ech." His Head Diver Compass giving him no clear reading,

he signals for Catalogue Override—a voice comes from somewhere in the air around him, synthetic and calm, almost visible as comic-book squiggly lines above his head, the fabric of the map's imaging wrinkled by the force of the transmission—

"Override. Carol speaking."

"This is Beaver. I just diverted from—well, I'm not sure where I just diverted from. You guys haven't been too gentle lately with the landings. Ended up patching in here at the tail-end of an explosion. Minor injury, but it's the equipment I'm more worried about. Like, why isn't working, folks? I keep losing my bearings."

"So?" the voice sounding telephone-operator bored.

"So where am I? I've had no control over my destinations lately. All these strange requests... "P&P Classified"... what's classified to me, anyway? I'm in charge of the whole Research Division!... just give me my proper coordinates; and *don't* try to drop me off someplace that's not on my docket. I seem to be on the top of this hill, tropical storm, guns on the ground..." noticing some movement, "wait, some-one else near me."

It took only a quick look to see that Maxwell was dead, that a brown stream of mud had moved his arm a lifelike few inches. The whole body would probably be washed over the edge in a few hours. Beaver crawls over to him. His dog-tags have been blown up into his mouth by the explosion, and Beaver pries them from his teeth. Does a sense of *deja vu* spill over him? Or does the feeling only come when you sense you're trapped, unlike Beaver, into looking at your life as an unbroken line bordered by times and dates? Is he aware of it, or is he comfortable with it, this being the type of thing that happens in the mind all the time; Les Holm, under the influence of that malignant sleep.... a feeling does sweep over Beaver, like a dark tide carrying in something foreign to the beach, but he blinks more blood out of his eyes and it disappears.

"Robert Maxwell," he reads. "Fighting Mad. Blue Unit."

"Well there you go, Captain Beaver," the voice says. "You're in the Korean War conflict, October 6, 1950. Imaging has you sur-rounded by hostile North Korean and Chinese troops advancing up the escarpment before you; also flanking the crown to your left. Better get moving, Captain. I've got some new coordinates fed into your equipment—"

"Nuh uh." Beaver's suddenly suspicious, and any faithful reader of *Head Diver* could sympathize. Something's been different about this chapter, something disturbing; as if you'd been introduced to a great guy by a person whose opinion you trusted, only to find that opinions change, that some people can't be trusted... what turned the color of Chapter Eight yellow? Beaver's got his ideas. He's been kept pre-occupied with self-preservation too much to notice the type of information he's been dredging up lately. And for whom? Somebody needed some hard-to-get info bad, they needed the best Head Diver to get it, and they needed him otherwise out of the way. "Mmm..."

"Captain, please transfer position now. Conflict approaching."

Voices call out somewhere over the hill. The storm's been broken over the back of the sun, its last few fragments drizzling and dissolving high above the ground. Suddenly Beaver recalls the name on the tags he's holding.

"Maxwell. Maxwell didn't die. He was a decorated hero."

"What's that, Captain?" the squiggles above him query. "Time to go; we're ready to process your new position." Noise around him grows, machine gun fire sprays the trees behind him.

Beaver checks his suit, locates the Comptroller Access switch. A single ball-in-socket joint of wires connects him to Outside Recall, the emergency override to the outside world. It can be activated by the Head Diver himself, or in circumstances of extreme danger, by the Comptroller's office.

"It's history, Captain," the disembodied voice stresses. It's now been changed to a male voice, an authoritative father figure speaking in admonishing tones. "Please don't get involved. Your transfer—"

Beaver pulls the Comptroller Access Switch, disconnects Outside Recall. The air goes blank. "It's not history the way I see it," he said. A few sparks streak across the sky. There's plenty of time to set things right, if you know how. First things first.

Gun sings out in sudden chorus. Leading the movement. Beaver crouches, looks around him. A few feet from the near corpse something shines. Maxwell's grenades.

•

Tinsel Croom learned about the Korean War from two distinct sources. As an eleventh grader he skimmed J.B. Lippincott's American History text to pass the Thursday afternoon quiz in Mr. Boisvert's social studies class. From his studies he produced the essay that follows: "There was North Korea and South Korea. Both were run by guys who weren't elected. They seemed to be crazy. Before that the Russians tried to win Korea, and the Japanese tried, too. Once an English ship got chased off the coast. All they wanted was to set up trade. The Koreans made interesting crafts. Then the North Koreans invaded the South Koreans, and Americans helped the United Nations get it back. This was known as the Korean War. In the end neither side got any extra land, and to this day they do not correspond."

Ten years later Tinsel bought a boxful of old comic books at a neighbor's yard sale, and came across his second source.

Sgt. Fury and his Howling Commandos, although known to have fought primarily in the Second World War, or at least the Marvel Comics version of it, had jumped in a more recent issue into the Korean War in a special team-up issue with Captain America. In the story the fictional Nick Fury met the historical Robert Maxwell, who at the time of the comic's printing was retired from his military service and instructing Webeloes for Cub Scout Pack #1 of Rhode Island: Maxwell's hand-grenading talent was elevated now to the level of the Green Arrow's bowmanship, and twice in the twenty-eight page storyline he saved Captain America from an ambush. Captain America later returned the favor: in the climactic battle with the Red Skull and the Sandman, who had somehow leapt twenty years back in time from fighting Spiderman and the Fantastic Four to working undercover for the Chinese, Captain America deflected a bullet with Maxwell's name written all over it by throwing his titanium red white and blue shield. The bullet ricocheted into the Sandman's eye, giving Sgt. Fury the opportunity to water him down and cover him with a specially designed tarpaulin. The Red Skull, as usual, got away.

So when Tinsel, sputtering in the midst of his dream oceanscape a last drowning breath, suddenly finds his sea perforated with air, then the air perforated with the last vestiges of a thunderstorm, then his still-human (but still dream-agile) form hurtling down through it, towards an approaching gauntlet of tree tops, crashing through leaf and limb, through retreating shreds of shadow; when he finally hits the ground in an eruption of mud and uniformed corpses, makes his way to his knees and finds himself uninjured, stands up and observes a single larger-than-life figure, fallen enemies strewn at his feet or the lucky ones streaming into the woods beyond in retreat, Tinsel has a brief feeling of collaboration with history, of witnessing something he knows has already happened, and the rest seems to fall in place as if he's remembering it; he knows without looking that the corpses around him are North Korean troops, but that also included among them are bodies that bear evidence to the as-yet-unacknowledged involvement of the Red Army, he knows that he stands closer to the Yalu River than any American or U.N. troops have been authorized to pursue the retreating North Korean troops, and he knows that the man walking towards him now, holding his last grenade, which is no longer needed, and approaching him with a calm and self-assurance that one could only expect from a comic book hero, Sgt. Fury or his Howling Commandos, for instance, the men of S.H.I.E.L.D., is someone about whom he must've read, either in eleventh grade or in still-crisp four color tones ten years later, someone who changed the course of the war before anyone knew it was going sour in the first place, someone whose name is in fact on the tip of his muddy Croom tongue, but all that comes out of this grand revelation as the man steadies Tinsel with a strong hand on his shoulder is the comic-book-like, "Wh-who *are* you?"

"Why," and the man pauses for a second, "I'm Robert Maxwell."

•

Dr. Fleck wakes up, to the sound of retreating footsoldiers.

He's sitting at his kitchen table in front of a large bowl filled with cereal. The bowl he'd taken from one of Flinch's shipments of Hesbro "Native Jamaican Pottery", and the cereal was Hesbro's Fruit Flavored Sugar Fish, a product of such complete artificiality that its chemical makeup had to be protected in "Seven Unique Patents Pending!" Inorganic imitation oats compound molded into the shapes of various fish, its artificial sweetener and flavors grafted on under high temperature, Sugar Fish were 100% nutritionally complete, and even secreted a small coloring when placed in skim milk that gave it a green, briny tint.

Just above the milk line a ring of figures dances before Doctor Fleck's waking eyes. The style is more Mexican than Jamaican, but Hesbro never paid that much attention to it, and neither did the tourists. Between two solid lines of undulating charcoal waves an octopus pursues a slender fish carrying on its head a golden scroll. The octopus is pursued by an Indian ghost, who has three feathers atop his head and whose skull shows beneath its skin. Behind the Indian a small island breaks in half from a lightning bolt, and behind that the fish with the scroll completes the circuit.

He's always had funny dreams when he eats cereal before bed. But this time he hadn't even made it to the bedroom, but had fallen asleep, spoon in his hand twitching tentatively, as if waiting for grace to end. Now he pours milk in, eats another bowlful of the stuff. "What the heck."

Fleck rises from the chair, head groggy, and listens to messages on his answering machine. Ah, one from his mother; he's missed her birthday again. Fleck settles back into the chair. He thinks of his mother Martha showing him his first x-ray at the hospital, when he'd broken a rib wrestling with Marty Gaughin, who'd called him Fatty Fleck, Fleck the Wreck; she had taken the x-ray from the doctor's hands, drawn a slash across it with a white crayon and presented it to him at bedside, saying, "See, you evil thing, you've broken my heart." Fleck had decided then to become a surgeon. Nobody would draw a claim against him again; he'd have control over those blue gray worlds inside every person ever hurt, be it by car, husband, or mother.

Fleck's residency after med school was at the Eastern Florida Plastics Conglomerate and Industrial Park Emergency Treatment building, where he had begun his practice of marking his patients' organs with wax crayons. No one had ever seen the progress (and deterioration) of their own interiors, so Fleck felt he could lay claim to that vision. A gentle blue mark across the outer stomach lining, orange along the little-understood liver, or bumping xylophone-green down one side of the ribcage, Fleck would delineate his territory, then close its discovery from the rest of the world with graceful stitches. The only part of the body Fleck had had the opportunity to mark but hadn't was the heart. He swore he'd never claim anyone's heart, as his mother had so early in his life.

Some nights he thought he could feel the white slash laying heavy on his chest, complicating his breathing, and dreamed of performing an operation on himself to remove it. Remembering this makes Fleck chuckle. He scratches his tattoo absentmindedly, dips his spoon into the cereal and stirs it. As milk sweeps over the bowl's edge, the Indian ghost disappears, materializing over the kitchen table with a surgeon's mask and smock. Fleck looks down at the bowl. Gone too is the octopus, and the air around him seems thick with tentacles. There's a heavy smell of seaweed and slime in the room. One last look: the fish with the scroll is crawling over the rim of the bowl, struggling to grow legs and lungs before it suffocates; and the island is now a broken heart.

Fleck notices that his eyes are closed. A voice near his head whispers, "We'll have it out in no time, doctor. Ah, nurse—" A needle pierces his forearm just below the elbow.

The phone rings loudly, and Doctor Fleck, as if on cue, falls face first into his bowl of cereal, fast asleep.

•

But something goes awfully wrong.

He knows it even before he sees the poster on the far wall

of the operating room proclaiming *NEVER TRUST A NOCTUR-NAL, MARINE MOLLUSK TO DO A MAN'S JOB.* He knows it even before he sees the EKG machine next to his cot tottering back and forth as if about to fall on him. He knows it before he realizes he's been strapped in his repose, before he feels the cot bouncing beneath him on its wheels, before he comes to the understanding that some foreign presence is swimming inside his body, connected to the EKG machine with fat yellow hemp, which the octopus with the surgeon's mask is paying out hastily to keep a healthy slack. He knows it even before he hears the octopus mutter through pursed beak, "My, something's gone awfully wrong."

He knows it as soon as he opens his eyes and sees the Indian ghost peering down at him. The face is lined with deep creases the likes of which Fleck's not seen even on large intestines, and the creases are clogged with some kind of white powder. Other parts of his body are similarly caked. His dry mouth opens on blackened gums.

"Wehll, wehll," he says.

Fleck makes as if to speak, but the Indian immediately plugs a red snapper between his lips. He pushes it down to the gagging point, and Fleck can feel the fish's bubbling mouth opening and closing against the back of his tongue. His nostrils fill with the smell of rotting scales. He overhears the octopus: "Heck, that's a lot of rope. He shoulda got there by now."

"That fish is always losin his way, heheh." The Indian props a bucket full of water on the table by Fleck's thigh. "Why, I'll just bet ya two more a these sqirmy eels that he'll just go on swimmin in there long as he like." He waved them over Fleck's head for effect. "Just gotta wait, like always."

Something bumps against his ribcage; from the inside, the doctor thinks, *from inside me!* "Hm. You're right, Nurse Whiteleaf. We're just about out of line. Guess I better cut him loose—"

The Indian carefully places an oarfish on Fleck's throat. The doctor feels gills pulse against his neck, a flat eye look blindly into the hollow of his throat.

"No, wait. He's got it..."

Octopus and Indian look intently at Fleck. A sudden cold sweeps over his stomach, as if swept by icy scales. Music begins somewhere, the first longings of a flute.

Something tugs at his heart. Literally.

•

Somewhere in the course of the night's travels and in the ears of the sleeping Cletis and Footlong the persistent sound of Beemus' airhorn grew distant and decreased into a tone or texture, like fog or the crash of the surf, in becoming familiar to us, lose their distinction and become part of the palate of our dreams .

So it was that the ocean was still before them, the drizzle still damp on their clothes, sand clinging to their sides where they'd lain, and Beemus still out at the tide-line, soft in the fog as a forgotten totem, when they woke up simultaneously with the sound of a new bar clear in their heads, neither sand nor beer-induced; in what key it began they couldn't tell, what note it produced they couldn't read, but they got up, breathed in the air of the hollow night, and waded into the woods after it .

In the palimpsest of toe-paths they scrabbled over embankments, brushed leaves and sand-fleas out of their eyes, drew mud into their sneakers with one step and squished it out with the next, became thoroughly lost. At one point something large and slow loomed before them, a white curving mass blocking the path. "Uh oh," Footlong threw an arm out to stop Cletis.

"What? What is it," Cletis said.

"Shhh." Footlong didn't turn to look at Cletis. "Hold still." For a long moment they stood there. Then with a swift snap it was gone, the trail ahead of them clear, and the sounds of human voices gaining over the silence .

"You know what that was," Footlong took Cletis by the shoulders to convey the import of what he was about to reveal.

"Nuh uh."

"Cletis man; that was Big Mama."

"No way, Footlong—"

"Not kiddin, Cletis."

"—whadda ya think, I hatched out of an egg this morning? "

"No, man; but a hundred years ago, in some swampy place forgotten to mankind, *she* did. "

Cletis and Footlong had argued earlier over the improbability of crocodile riding. "I'm not kidding," Beemus had told Cletis, "an if I were I wouldn't have *this*," taking his fishing cap from a wooden peg. From between layers of the cardboard visor he removed a battered Polaroid.

"Some people call her Peter Pan, on account of the book I guess. But I call her Big Mama. Probly the only croc this side of Florida that Witcover hasn't ridden. *Won't* ride. "

"Is he scared of her?"

"No. He just respects her too much." He flipped the Polaroid onto the table. Cletis examined it, squinting .

"I guess you took this shot on the run, huh?" Footlong said .

"We're talkin a real moving picture, now boys."

"Hyuk. Uncle Beemus, yer funny as a tree, man."

"Right."

"What do you mean by Witcover respecting her too much?" Cletis said .

"He won't ride her cause he don't wanna pay the price. "

"Yeah, I told you; he's scared."

"No. What I mean is, if you're gonna try an ride Big Mama, ya gotta offer her something for her trouble. Do ya see them sparkly things on her fingers there?" They all looked closely at the photo. At various points along the throat and underbelly of what could possibly have been a large, white and out-of-focus crocodile, it did appear as if some shiny gems had been imbedded into the mottled skin. The short arms held the body forward and off the ground as if they had just finished a final pushup; the mouth was open in a tired but satisfied display of teeth .

"Ya see, Big Mama likes jewelry; rings in particular, but... "

"Gimme that photo." Footlong squinted at it.

"...if ya lose ya gotta give her some jewelry; she pins ya down,

right, with one big mitt, all that weight on yer heart-box an those
rings sparkling in yer face... "

"You mean you've tried to ride her?" Cletis asked .

Beemus belched. "Say Footlong, when's the last time you saw
Granny Bernie's engagement rock? "

"Uh, four, five years ago."

"Yep, about that long since I tried."

The ground where it had been seemed to hold some residue of
its passing, glowing slightly, as they bent down to look for tracks.
"Hey, hey, look at this," Footlong pointing between his feet. "Is that a
huge foot or what?" Whether it was a footprint or not was debatable,
but equally undebatable was the fresh furrow something had made
dragging—its own stomach, perhaps?—across the path.

Voices grew louder around them. People were coming down the
path. The moon came out above them. Something sparkled at Cletis'
feet. They both leaned over to pick it up, bumping heads. When they
rose, a blue jewel in Cletis' palm glowing aquamarine in the moonlight, they were already surrounded by the angry mob, which began
to part before them at the sound of a certain note they'd heard earlier, all heads turning as an aisle was created for the lady in red.

•

They were led along a series of switching paths, herded one
moment by those behind them, pulled to the side the next by those
in front of them to clear the way for a faster-moving contingent
coming up from the rear. At times small groups of three and four
would break off, slide silently onto a forking path only to rejoin the
primary group at a later time. Cletis tried to fix his gaze on one
or another of them but in the dark there was little he could see.
Most of them appeared to be young, his age or a few years older;
at some points he thought he'd heard a smaller child's voice. Their
clothes seemed sewn into the night: dark, unfantastic, unseparable
from their bodies and the general speed of the group's movement.

Ahead of them always went the lady in red.

"Cletis, man, are we gonna be boiled in oil or what?" Footlong
trotted at his side.

"I dunno. Do you think these people speak English?"

"Probably, but all they've done so far is push and cough." They were threading through the line now, picking up speed, passing up the spine of the entourage. "No one's even said *Hello* or *You're our prisoner* or anything, man."

"Maybe we're not prisoners."

"Hyeah, right. We're prisoners of Zenda, man." Footlong shook his head. It was then that they reached the front of the line, which had actually stopped to let them by, babbling as they were, to where Cletis happened to look up from his feet in time to stop Footlong inches from the lady, her red dress whispering over the tops of their sneakers, who had turned to face them, a finger to her lips to silence them.

They were near a shore, but Footlong, who ought to have known, did not recognize its characteristics: a somewhat rocky beach, a makeshift dock that resembled a natural jetty of rocks and driftwood. The sky was clearing out around the moon, and its band of light on the water was pierced from below by the remains of a mostly submerged ship. It wasn't until Cletis had taken all of this in that he realized he was being left behind; the group had moved beyond him to his left, where most had already gathered around a stout fire.

"Footlong, was that fire there a minute ago," he said, turning.

But Footlong was gone.

•

"He's somebody's son. And he's dying."

Footlong caught Cletis halfway to the fire, coming out to meet him.

"Where?"

"Right by the fire. He's on a board, or boat or somethin, I can't get close enough to tell. He showed up a few days ago, with a little food in a leather bag and a parrot on his shoulder. Said he'd been invited by his relatives to finish something they couldn't finish themselves." Cletis tried to peer over the heads of the outer edge of the group, but couldn't see anything.

A murmuring rose among the crowd. "Come on," Cletis said, "let's see what's going on." They slid along a seam in the circle until they found themselves within a few feet of the prostrate boy. He looked no more than seventeen, laid in a thin canoe-shaped vessel whose one end covered his head like a skullcap. The woman in the red dress leaned over him, studying him; from behind her emerged a large green parrot, who hopped to the edge of the canoe and looked directly at Cletis. "God Bless The King and Queen of England," it croaked. Cletis recognized the voice as what he'd earlier thought a child's voice, but something else...

"Footlong, you recognize that parrot?" he whispered. The woman shot a hard glance at him; Footlong shook his head no. "Nuh uh."

"Is he, uhm, going to die?" Cletis addressed the woman. "Should we call an ambulance or something." The boy's eyes were closed; his face was drawn, sunken and dark. The woman ignored them.

"Maybe it's a funeral," Footlong suggested.

"Maybe we should go," Cletis began backing up. A hand gripped his shoulder and spun him around. "I don't believe you're goin nowhere, Mister Croom."

Cletis raised his arm to fend off the oncoming blow, but Field stuck a can of Red Stripe in the open hand, smiling down at him and Footlong.

"Field's the name. Friend of your pa's, from the boat. Excuse me a second, boys," leaning between them to address the woman. "Uh, I looked all over, right, but I couldn't find it nowheres. That globe thing is *gone*, far as I can see."

"Wait, hold on," Cletis' hand emerging from his pocket with the stone he'd found. He held it before the firelight; small imperfections, opaque in the glow of the stone, stood out like continents, branched into peninsulas and islands, though it was no world he'd ever seen before. "I bet this is it," tossing it to Field.

"Where'd ya find it, ya little water-rat?" Field eyeing it suspiciously.

"About ten minutes down that path, or one of those paths,

anyway," Footlong volunteered. "And you're pretty lucky Big Mama didn't find that, man, she woulda snatched it right outta your hands."

"Big Mama?" Field looked quickly at the woman in red, who appeared oblivious of them. "Boys," he pulled them close to him, so they could smell the beer and nervous sweat on him, "if you lose somethin, say a jewel, to Big Mama, you don't aim to get it back now, do ya? I mean, you're not likely to see it again, am I right?"

"Never been known to happen," Footlong professed.

"Then in that case, no, I didn't lose it to Big Mama. Never heard of her, in that case." He stepped beyond them, next to the lady in red, and placed the globe in the boy's hands. The woman whispered to the boy, "Ready to go?" Cletis couldn't tell whether the head nodded, whether the lips drew slightly thinner in the prelude to a smile, or if it was just the body's response to the first jolt as a few others stepped forward and began to push the canoe out to the water's edge, and beyond the range of the firelight.

"You boys gonna need help findin your way back to the beach, huh?" Field said. They ducked into the thicker darkness of the trees. "That woman is some piece of work, ain't she? Earlier this afternoon, saw her walking around near the dock by the *Gregorian*. So I go up to her, hello an all that stuff, an next thing I know, hyuk, I'm holdin that blue ball, harhar. So I thought we had a date tonight, all alone an all; turned out it was some party. *Par-dooo*, baby."

"What was her name? Did she tell you?" Cletis asked.

"I dunno, boys, I don't know; and I don't believe she did."

•

"Where are we now?"

Dizzy from cutting the stars from the uniforms of Chinese corpses, the rain letting off and the slow burning of the dead rising into his nose like an iron autumn, as if the war were as natural and cyclical, Tinsel leans back against a scarred tree trunk. A few empty shells sprinkle down from the branches above him.

Debris seems still to be falling, and Tinsel wonders if even now a single bullet, fired straight up by a soldier at the moment of his unwinding, could be reaching its peak high up in the blade-thin edges of the atmosphere, the arc folding back in on itself, the point re-aligning with gravity, hurtling down towards the spot of his heredi-tary balding...

"We're about forty miles north of where we were when we met, and, believe it or not, four days earlier." Tinsel notices a sparkle of silver beneath his partner's loose-fitting fatigues. Captain Beaver has not accumulated the protective beer belly Maxwell had cultivated before his undoing.

"Look. Just call me Maxwell." He glances through some trees, then back at Tinsel. "That's what you're going to have to call me in Lincoln, for the press."

"Uh huh." Shaking his head. A motor throbs in and out of hear-ing. They wait for it to appear on the unpaved road beyond the trees. A small jeep edges over the crest of a hill a few hundred yards away. "Here they come. Eyes open."

Tinsel gets his first view of live Chinese soldiers a minute later. It takes forty minutes for them to reach the bend in the road where he squats hidden, and where most of them veer onto the high road. But a smaller group takes the low road, then on command cut through the trees ten yards to Tinsel's right. "The lady or the tiger, huh?" Beaver whispers to him. Hunkering down, Tinsel watches the impassive faces, wonders what calm electric thought pattern keeps them so cool, unflinching. Three platoons pass like a whisper. Tinsel looks up to Beaver.

"Yeah, I know." Beaver says in a flat voice, barely audible. "They all look the same to you."

•

Only as the last platoon glides past them does Tinsel notice some difference. "There they are," Beaver pointing them out although Tinsel already knows now, a tight smile stretched unvigorously across his teeth. "The lapels."

On the chest of those soldiers is a bare space where a patch should be, the clean fabric glowing the shape of a star. Tinsel looks down to his hand, the People's Republic stars still clenched in his fist.

"The ones who got Maxwell," Beaver says.

"Then who–"

"Never mind. Look alive–" Beaver says, standing up. He crosses his fingers, blows through them. It's a musical sound, low and unexpected, then rising for a moment as if to fly away. The patch-less troops turn around as if under a spell, heads down now, creeping towards them.

Beaver lets the sound die out, kneels beside Tinsel. "Did you grab a gun or anything back at the Hill?"

"No."

"Me neither." And stands up to his full height, just a few feet between him and the nearest of the footsoldiers, who've fanned out as they made their approach. "Hei-" is the only sound from the closest's lips; then the liquid click of metal sliding through the air as all rifles turn in at Beaver. The fan closes in on itself; Tinsel can see his partner's undoing even through his closed eyelids, squinched shut as light and sound melt around him and the smell of metal goes sour in his nose. But when he opens his eyes Beaver is somehow behind them all, appearing himself almost translucent, a crackle of light arriving. He reaches up and tears the air in front of him like a curtain.

Behind the tree he clings to, Tinsel sees, beyond, the tint of a blue sky, the peak of a mountain. "What the?"

The soldiers are sucked in, no time for triggers or breath. When things seem to make sense again to Tinsel, Beaver is running his hand down a wrinkly seam of air while holding in a headlock a struggling Chinese soldier.

"This guy," he grunts, turning him around so Tinsel can see the red star on his chest, "doesn't belong." Everything is quiet again; the only proof that anyone was ever here beside Beaver and Tinsel is the young man quivering under Beaver's hold. "And he won't remember anything," Beaver looks down into his eyes, and Tinsel can almost see the vector of suggestion, shiny as steel, dissolve into the boy's wide pupils, "will he?"

•

"Where'd you send them?" Tinsel asks. They're looking down a steep muddy bank on the Imjin River. Clouds drawl out long thunder-stories to each other.

"I'm not sure." He's watching the clouds, listening to the low murmurs rising in volume. The sky's a gray sidewalk of sound. "But history only happens once, and here it's already happened." He holds up a hand to cut off Tinsel's question. "There's no leeway, no room for undoing. Nothing is that forgivable if it's happened; or necessary if it hasn't. Someone's been messing with the stories, Tinsel, the ones you know, and some you don't yet. Nothing we can't fix, though." Beaver's grin is hard and proper, as if already seeing. Tinsel drops the star patches into the river. They disappear in the green foam with little resistance.

"What about those guys?"

"They'll find their way to the right place. Technicians may have to come in, but they won't be hard to trace…" Lightning streams down across the river, its reflection cracking along the surface like ice, raising birds from the undergrowth. "The thing is, *those guys* really *weren't* there in the first place. They crashed Maxwell's party. You've read the comic books, Tinsel; four days from now, Robert Maxwell becomes a hero.

"And heroes don't die."

Somewhere above, before its story can be told, a discharge of current rattles down from a cloud, and its answering current swerves up from the ground, enveloping two figures in solid light. When the thunder speaks a second and a half later, no one is there to listen; one could say, then, the earth was as silent as it's ever been.

•

Where is Tinsel now, that nothing will wake him? Inches deep in a ditch of swollen, rotted leaves, fronds damp with dew bending underneath him. A swamp toad perches on his breastbone. Dry sticks above him cast strange explanations in moonlight relief across his forehead.

Cars pass in their iron casings, throwing their own light on the road ahead, as if to explain what they can't see before they're upon it.

But is it already too late for them, as it was for Tinsel? Does it matter if you know what you're being thrown by?

•

"Tinsel, hit the deck!"

He's on his back, mud thrown up from the passing truck evenly distributed over his body, Beaver squinting down at him. They're decades ahead of their former selves, dressed in pinstripe suits, disguised as undercover cops disguising as local contacts for a transfer of anti-tank missiles from Miami, where they were bought from the Cubans, to their eventual destination in Ithaca, New York. The strategic mid-point being Central Falls, Rhode Island, where the trucks—three of them, paint-rubbed U-Hauls featuring fading cowboys, dinosaurs and a lighthouse from Cape Fear whose ocean and jetty had dissolved entirely in the sun—stop for a ten kilo pickup of cocaine from the converted pump-well beneath DiNoble's Garage on Smithfield Avenue. They just see their contact, Donald Drycleaner, round the corner in his brown '74 Ford LTD when Tinsel goes into his trance, losing a notch or two of consciousness. What sends him off is the roar of an approaching truck; what takes him back is Beaver's hand pulling him out of the road as the truck bears down on him, invisible to the driver because in a way he's no longer there, his attention pulled to another time or place. Beaver's seen this a million times. Every rookie Head Diver goes through it at least once, a sort of sensory overload, a matching of memory catalogues, the personal grafting onto whatever time referent the environment offers. A persistent temptation to relax, and remember.

Without any training Tinsel is especially susceptible. His pinstripes flicker as he begins to fade, far away, but physically still too much here, on the street...

Then Beaver's voice, "Hit the deck!" and a helping hand, and Tinsel, dizzy, re-appearing in full pinstripes and road soup. Beaver yanks him to his feet. Points to a patch of sidewalk. "Right there."

"Yeah, okay." Tinsel obedient.

"I mean it. Stand. Don't move. I'll be back," already walking over to Donald Drycleaner's parked car and the four lean fingers adjusting the rear-view mirror. The thumb, he explains, "got lost in a heavy dice accident." Beaver leans in the open window. Cigarette ash seems to hang in the closed air like constellations, rotating slowly around Drycleaner's yellow right eye. The left one concealed by a paisley silk patch, though Beaver's information says it's just an affectation; and Beaver, watching the way the smuggler's right eye moves, can guess that this is probably true. The pupil's too lazy, and so's its lateral movement, to be a loner.

"Ten years ago today," Drycleaner's saying, scratching the patch with a tobacco-stained fingernail, "she flew *right* out of my head. Now, I will wear *this* patch, until I can a*venge* myself. And then I will pull out the bastard's own eye—*eemph!*" making a plucking motion, "—and put it *right*, here," he smiles, pointing back at the patch.

"Novel idea," says Beaver.

"You have said a handful," says Drycleaner.

•

Beaver retrieves Tinsel, who is introduced to Drycleaner as Mario Milk, but who Drycleaner will remember to his dying day as Detective Tovil Compton, Tinsel's second alias and a moniker he made up himself while listening to Beaver's plan. "Crompton," Drycleaner would say, after they had flashed their badges and interrogated him inside one of the trucks, the gleam of metal sweating in the shadows, "Crompton, when I next see you, we will *both*, re*gret* it."

Even though Tinsel had played good cop to Beaver's bad, it was he who decided to remove Drycleaner's eyepatch. Drycleaner had been tough up till then, acting as if he really were someone who'd lost an eye in the line of work; but when Tinsel pulled the paisley patch down so it hung like an albatross around his neck, Drycleaner was drained of any remaining bravado. Now he sits, tied to a chair, the eyepatch stuck to his sweating forehead like a mystic eye, gathering some real anger equal in parts to his despair.

"Crompton, I swear, under *most*, of the circumstances I can ima*g*ine, I will avenge this humiliation. I will *cause* you, *great*, sorrow." Tinsel peers unlistening out the front window of the truck.

"Hey, Maxwell, what year is this?"

"Mid-1990, give or take a year. Did you know, Tinsel, this town's only a mile square, but it's *the* hot-spot for smuggling on the eastern seaboard. Will be for two decades more, too." Beaver checks the schedule Drycleaner gave him. "Why do you ask?"

"I live just a few years from here," Tinsel says.

•

Donald Drycleaner is impressed but suspicious when Beaver tells him that he will be set free within an hour, if only he signs a statement attesting to the details of his involvement in the weapons shipment. Beaver shows him the envelope; it's an address Drycleaner doesn't recognize.

"I'll seal it before your eyes, and drop it in a mailbox on the corner. You can watch me. The point is, *you* will never be caught or questioned, and we won't interfere with your job from here on in. I just need the facts for later."

"But for *how, much* later?"

Beaver leans into his shadow, waves the stamp end of the envelope in his face.

"Recognize this commemorative?"

"No."

"That's because it hasn't been printed yet. First the Postal Service will have to raise the price several times."

"And how, given my *un*availa*bil*ity," Drycleaner waxing rhetorical, "how is this letter to be given its, legiti*mal*ity?"

"It so happens that the previous owner of this jacket," Tinsel says, producing inkpad and stamp,

"was a Notary Public."

•

"Signed, sealed, and soon to be delivered," Beaver says. "Wait," Tinsel says, pulling out a gob of color from his pocket. "Easter Seals!" He flattens them out atop a crate; "I got em from a weird lady passing em out at my travel agent's office. I guess she was from the Easter Seals Foundation or something. Dressed like Mrs.

Santa Claus. Anyway, let's see, flowers, small animals, nativity, more flowers...*here* we go." He separates it from the others at its perforated edges and hands it to Beaver, who licks the back and sticks it on the envelope. "I think I preferred the flowers," Beaver comments. The illustration is of an old leather tome, medieval looking, peeling cover. A hasp lock secures the book shut, and an envelope leans against the spine, sealed with a spot of red wax and ribbon pinned with a gold anchor.

"It's festive in its own way, I think," Tinsel mumbles as they climb out the driver's side of the cab. When he hears the door shut, Donald Drycleaner jerks his head around viciously, looking for a sharp corner he can edge the chair up to and cut his ropes. At some point his momentum tips him backwards. He hits his head on the floor. When he wakes up he's two minutes late for the pick-up; lying in a sweat on the floor of the truck. On all the walls and in racks, metal gleams with dull afternoon light. His eyepatch is in its proper place.

The driver he hired for the haul is knocking at the window. "Hey One Eye! Let me in!"

•

As early as 11:30 a.m. and no later than 12:05 p.m. every weekday and Saturdays, Sandy McQuenchler, an offical individual filament at the slender tip of the tangled branch of the local reach of the Federal Government commonly known as the Postal Service, unlocks the mailbox at the corner of Smithfield and Mineral Spring Avenues and removes from it those envelopes and packages and postcards that have gathered over the past evening. But the day after Beaver drops his envelope in the same box, as Sandy empties its contents and stuffs them into his pouch, one envelope remains, unseen, wedged perhaps in the metal creasing of the mailbox's dark iron corner. Or maybe not: maybe the letter is invisible, or evasive. For the next day, Sandy McQuenchler misses the same piece of mail again; and the next day, and the next. It is not until some time later, when Donald Drycleaner has expired in the arms of one Madame Ipswich of Pine Street, when Tinsel Croom wakes on a beach empty but for him and the bewitching Cozetta Croom Bitfield, it is not until that day that Sandy McQuenchler, now sporting a snowy beard and a new pair of Postal Service shorts, reaches into the mailbox on the corner of Smithfield and Mineral Spring for the one-thousand-four-hundred-and-ninety-second time, indeed for the last time in his career as a mail carrier, that he finally takes out the letter which has for so long eluded him, and sends it on its way. The address is:

Blackning Church Brooklyn, NY 100 —

•

On October 21, 1921 Al Jolson premiered his newest extravaganza, *Bombo*; he played Gus, a young explorer's cook, who, transported back to 1492, becomes Bombo, the servant of Christopher Columbus who convinces Queen Ferdinand to finance the voyage across the ocean. Bombo is instrumental in the purchase of Manhattan from the Indians, which he manages for twenty-four dollars worth of trinkets.

"And if you give us Brooklyn," Bombo confides to the chief, "we'll throw in a pair of rusty scissors."

Bombo was notable for its debut of Jolson's newest song, "Mammy," which the black-faced Gus/Bombo would sing on one bent knee, arms outstretched to the crowd:

The sun shines East
The sun shines West
But I know where
The sun shines best...

•

The Jeep is American and abandoned, the radiator perforated with ordnance, but it still seats two in the front, three in back with room for the Backseat Driver, the name X Corps had given the customized Percy howitzer which, too heavy and awkward to be turned around completely, slid on a hollow, greased fourteen-inch blade giving it a range of 165 degrees. Its rusted Schnauzer nose points due West, so the 200 degrees it couldn't possibly defend itself against fairly represents the range of Tinsel's vision.

Dawn creeps in a red and gold smear across the frost on the Jeep's windshield, its preparatory light on the Sea of Japan, the flickering variances of olive, gray, white, blue-green and bone: one minute the surface is the color of raw cowhide, like the inside of a baseball glove. The next second it's sparkling a sharp green that seems almost too dark to be seen at all. Beneath the surface must live such old and coiling serpents, Tinsel thinks, things that have been rolling around since before there were shapes, so old they've forgotten what they are, what color they were, what were their original names; and when the islands and first continents began spreading over the surface of their sea, they took themselves and all the colors that hadn't been seen or claimed by other creatures and descended to the world's dark bottom. But once in a while the ocean itself remembers them, and the memory flickers briefly on the surface before the flat, blank sun finds its sea legs and gets up.

The war's gone by in a wave, but it feels like only the first of three concentric rings in a new kind of circus. And if I can't even figure a sunrise, Tinsel thinks, how can I get a grip on this war, what I'm doing here at all? It has occurred to Tinsel that he's dreaming; but the air feels a little too full of salt and its own orders for him to dare call its bluff, try to slip back into the simpler rhythms of his hangover, and wakefulness.

But what bothers him is exactly that: it's his dream and yet its boundaries are beyond him. That to some extent they've already abandoned him, that this might be his final, eternal pose; that while he pondered something outside its farthest ring, the stakes were pulled up, the show moved, and he left behind, like a poster to be picked up by one arriving late, the dust from the trucks still hanging in the air over the hilly road to the next town.

•

Jolson played the Apollo Theater in Chicago on Tuesday September 19, 1922; *Bombo*'s second season. During the show Jolson smelled smoke, and saw a fire blazing in one of the footlights. Shuffling his feet in time to the music, he stamped out the fire to calm the restless crowd as the band, following the hurried rhythm of his feet, played a sped-up version of "Mammy":

I'se a comin'
Sorry that I made you wait
I'se a comin'
Hope an' pray I'm not too late
My little Mammy
Maaaa-mmmy

•

On October 2, 1950, stopping in San Francisco on his way home from a visit to American troops in Korea, where he'd contracted pneumonia, Jolson found himself joking with a couple of doctors in his hotel room.

"I guess I'm an important guy," he said.

"Yes, you are," they answered, assuming he was referring to the fact he had two doctors paying him a visit at the same time.

"No, I'm a real important guy," he said. "Truman had only one hour with MacArthur. I had two." He looked about the room, then reached for his pulse.

"Oh, I'm going," he said, and closed his eyes.

•

Tinsel sits there shivering. Even the sun won't warm him.

It's December in Korea; the temperatures can freefall to forty-below before you can drop your pants to urinate and pull them back up again. The simplest tasks become difficult, as even the Army discovers, digging ditches in a topsoil deep ten feet with permafrost, soldiers' hands freezing to the barrels and grips of their rifles; and it is in this weather that the Peoples Republic Army, with its hastily assembled "volunteer" corps and no air-power or reliable firearms, have been by the force of sheer numbers spearheading through the United Nations forces on all fronts. Here on the foothills of the Tae-baek range, and despite all the best efforts of General Walker, the Eighth Army has been hastily repairing southward.

Tinsel could sit and watch the indifferent sun. He could listen to the smug silence of the ocean. But then the music starts again:

I'd walk a million miles
For one of your smiles
Ma-aa-aaammy

The Chinese, somewhere north of Tinsel behind one of the identically bare hills, begin playing Jolson for the thousandth time. Eerie scraps float in and out of the wind. For the British troops it's "If You Were The Only Girl in the World," but for the Americans it's Jolson, whose last show was heard over the sound of sniper fire and attended by MacArthur himself.

At some point they'll come again, drowning the music with the pounding of their feet, howling like banshees just in case you couldn't hear the earth groaning and snapping beneath their feet, though the noise, even in this empty repetitive landscape, can't prepare you for the sight of the Chinese troops streaming over a ragged hilltop, flooding down the slope then up the next rise, running through their own covering fire, so eager they seem for death, anyone's death, Tinsel thinks. Or perhaps it's not that easy. Perhaps it's as inscrutable a motion as those first notions of light on the Sea of Japan. They came yesterday and they'll come today, though the hill will be different and the soldiers different, so many left behind... Today's sun is now fully feathered, and the ocean glistens listlessly beneath it. Beaver taps him on the arm.

"Tinsel. Time to go cause some trouble."

Tinsel: "Yup."

•

(from Doktor Hans-Karin Van Damm, *Prelude to an Intercourse with Reason*)

(Swelter's notes in bold)

We live in a society where inasmuch as every person or institution holds closely guarded secrets every secret has within it further closely guarded institutions. Secrets are never self-revelations to those who hold them; they are only remarkable to those for whom a proper context is unfamiliar. Thus we see the secret of secrets, that they have no inside: only their outside, that is their context, is remarkable. What is remarkable is that the secret itself is the outermost layer of the institution. Institutions — and people — are not built around secrets, but to the contrary secrets are built around institutions and people, like a hard, clear shell. Thus do the most guarded secrets become the most visible: by bearing the shape and stature of the thing for which the secret holds its existence, the institution itself. The institution guards a secret which guards the institution. It guards itself from revealing that it is on guard. **(Auf Wache???)** *The secret is rarely seen because it is not looked for where it can be seen; the secret is rarely heard because it is not listened for where it can be heard. To sum then: to find a secret one must never look within. Find those things that lay at points tangential to the institution and any bordering forces defined as external: there lies the shape of the soul. Like a halo, there is the secret.*

1) On the shapes: To the extent that I sub-divide or compart-mentalize myself, I am an institution. Thus may the words 'person' and 'institution' be seen to be only stylistic devices in Van Damm, and thus interchangeable for this discourse.

2) On the context: That I am trying to guard my search from the institution is not remarkable. That the institution tries to guard the object of my search from me without knowing yet the context of the subject is not.

— —The phone rings. Swelter snaps up from his dream like a pen leaving a notepad.

Lifting the phone from its cradle, he begins to say his name. But he notices the late hour and tries to cover up, just in case...

"Fred's All Anchovy. We deliver."

Silence on the other end. The sound of rain drumming on a distant phone booth.

"Day or night, soft drinks free—"

The thick nordic accent. "It's Jog Thurnn."

•

Swelter packs his notebooks and a few printouts in a tan canvas bag. "At 2:43 a.m." Thurnn had told him.

Breggy's Diner was only five minutes away, and he had half an hour. He sits on the edge of the bed. Thurnn's unfinished translation of the Van Damm essay looks back at him from the night table. He'd plucked it from the Employee Files in what was to be his last day of work; Thurnn had handed it in with his resume to show his versatility with language-based models. Swelter had managed to procure a copy of the German from a local bookseller specializing in 19th century philosophy.

It turned out that Thurnn's translation was pretty good, though Swelter thought maybe a bit on the inventive side. Substituting a transliteration of *auf Wache* for what appeared in the original text to be *vor bewachen*—*to guard against* becoming the colloquial *on guard* in the process—did give the sentence a more obedient grammar but took from it the sense of brinksmanship in Van Damm that Swelter admired: it made his mathematical reason curl at the end, giving it not only a sense of flourish but also of threat, a sweeping danger inherent in taking something past its discernible end to where things became thin and chaotic...

At the diner he doodles long spirals twisting around one another on the paper napkin. It is 2:30. A waitress materializes by his side.

"Minimum's three-fifty after midnight. New rule, okay?" She wasn't chewing gum, but he had the impression that she should be.

"What's the special tonight?" Swelter waving his menu in surrender.

"Elbow sandwich. Ever had it?"

"No."

"Nelson in the back, he loves them. Chef's favorite. It comes with coffee, but if you order one refill that'll put you over three-fifty, and you'll be okay."

"Sounds like I'll have the elbow sandwich," pulling the coffee across the table. Swelter takes out the Van Damm manuscript and places it beside the cup. He yawns. Squidges some sleep out of his eye. Looks up. The waitress still standing there.

"You want your sauce hot or cold?"

"Huh?"

"Your tomato sauce. Hot or cold?"

"Hot, please." Again the implacable feeling that she should be chewing gum. "Thank you." She is gone in a snap of starch.

Swelter thinks as he waits, and waits as he pauses between thoughts, holding the space open for revelation. But none comes. Perhaps night seems to ready to spill the beans precisely because it's so empty. He's returned without knowing to the doodle, placing a box in the middle of the napkin and marking it with inchoate runes, designs and a broad keyhole in its middle. Above the swirling lines he draws a clockface, changes his mind and leaves out the hands, just a hollow nob in the middle of the sphere, a radius with space at its center. He puts a black dot in the middle. How many circles of secrecy will he intersect on his way to Jog Thurnn's little moonrock? How many islands are already out there, with secrets of their own growing mossy above them with trees and undergrowth, how many will he have to wade about, peeking in dark holes of data, plumbing the depth of ones and zeros beyond William's glowing screen in the positive-negative night of Brooklyn, its only quiet and empty hours, to find nothing so simple or evil as he'd expected, but the wrong center out of context, maybe a red herring placed by Thurnn himself or maybe the complex nest of something actual, its shape deceiving as in a stupid seabird, bufflehead or something else that courts in the salt shallows, the egg of the institution of an entire species unknown, ingrained in that shallow shell of self-interest and preservation, continuity a ubiquitous calling, the truth so unconcealable and easily cracked...

Down comes the green ceramic plate; up rises the peppery scent of hot spaghetti sauce. Elbows peek from beneath the bread like eyesockets, squirm as if for a better view of his mouth as he picks it up.

Swelter remembers when he lived with his sister on President Street in Brooklyn, at the edge of the newly gentrified neighborhoods. Bread smells floated on warm ribbons of air from every corner store, and middle-aged men thick as the doorways in which they sat stayed out past midnight on summer nights to make sure the local teenagers didn't hassle anyone. His first week there he'd needed to ask directions eight times, and had always been pointed on his way as carefully and politely as he'd inquired. Jill had just been released from the hospital where she had been treated for bulemia. During her stay she'd picked up some of the habits of other patients, things they did to pass the time or keep their minds thinking constructively; Swelter was never sure what she'd been told to do by the nurses and what she did in self-defense, but Jill spent her more anxious hours carving animal figures out of Dove soap bars. At any particular trip to the bathroom Swelter could encounter a pod of pink dolphin floating in the sink, a bay green frog squatting on the tissue dispenser, or an adult African elephant playing with its baby. Swelter never figured out how she had entwined their two trunks. One day he'd woken up around four in the morning with his bladder jammed against a book he'd been reading, and groped his way through the dark to the bathroom. She'd been up all night, by the looks of it: he counted seventy two slender arms, laying scattered across the yellow and white floor tiles. They were all broken at the thicker end, some with clean lines like they were cut off by mistake, others showing rough chalky stubs, as if they had fallen off of their own weight. Swelter had stepped gingerly over them to the toilet, was pulling his pants down when he saw the heads, all nine of them, sharp and delicately cut, huge eyes unblinking and beaks gaping from their bottoms, bobbing in the blue toilet bowl. Perfectly carved octopus heads, perfectly carved octopus tentacles: sometimes the desired form won't hold, no matter how strong the will is. He found her in the hallway, curled against the wall. He'd walked right by her in the dark.

Sometimes secrets can't hold onto their exclusivity, and the form doesn't even have to come to such a point of stress for it to be visible... Swelter feels the first dozen or so elbows slide down his esophagus, tries to count them as they descend to the acids below. Four, five, six more weeks in the clinic, visiting Jill after that night. She became obsessed with the octopus, so he brought her books, Jacques Cousteau, The Domain of the Octopus, videotapes of reruns of Mutual of Omaha's Wild Kingdom, biology manuals on its makeup, how it differed from other mollusks more easily carved in soap; the last day he'd visited she was reading the closing chapter of Imagining the Octopus: An Historical View. She shut the book with a clap and smiled at him. "Thank goodness," she'd said, "I'mfinally done." Then they left together, he carrying her two bags while she dropped off the library books. She'd had a job offer in Pennsylvania, and left the next afternoon. Swelter moved to his current apartment a month later.

He doodles aimlessly, blindly, as he waits. Now a stab at the watch, uh oh, 3:15 and no sign of Thurnn, but the waitress coming on strong with her final refill. Swelter notices for the first time the bill, coffee-stained and dashed with tomato sauce, on the table between some stray elbows, wonders how long it's been there.

"Waiting for the arms race to end?" she asks, leaning a little into the table.

"Um." He falters a bit under the assault, her physical closeness. "Actually, I was just waiting for a friend. Did you see anyone come in the last half-hour or so?"

"Nobody's been here since *you* came in. But everyone's got their cross to bear, I guess," drawing a cruciform across the sauce on his plate with a long chartreuse fingernail. She gives him a cold wink and heads back to the kitchen.

Swelter fishes in his pocket, drops a five on the table and stands up to look around. Sure enough, the diner's empty except for him. No nordic-looking men, nobody at all. Then it hits him like a cold shower, how dumb was he, anyway, to think Thurnn would risk blowing both of their covers? Most likely Swelter's phone was tapped, Thurnn knew that. So what did he want to say? Swelter wipes his mouth with his napkin, and as he's about to drop it on the table he sees the numbers scrawled in pen on the side he'd left unmarked:

2' 43"

and Swelter knows what it means. It wasn't a time designation, though the notation was in minutes and seconds; it was a direction. A hint that he was that close. So Thurnn must have been tracking him, saw that he was close, or that time was running out, and decided to help him along. But why, Swelter thinks, unless the Company is close to catching him? Or me. Suddenly the lights in the diner seem too bright, the blackness beyond the windows too full of dark faces.

Swelter stuffs the napkin in his pocket, moves on a hunch to the next table, lifts the napkin there and looks on the other side:

2' 43"

and on the next table and the next after that. Thurnn was taking no chances.

"You wanna keep all those napkins?" The waitress back at his table, picking up the money. No shame, Swelter thinks. But he's lightheaded now. "No no, think I'll just leave them right here," dropping them in a bowl of unfinished *soup du jour* on an unbussed table, picking up his coffee mug as he passes to grab a last sip.

Something solid slips between his teeth as he's drinking. He knows before spitting it out on the table that it's a wad of chewing gum. "Haha, very classy," he says, but the waitress is out of hearing, up by the front door, talking to two men in raincoats. Swelter can see the dark suits beneath them. As he scrambles out the fire exit, sounds flaring all about him and idle taxis closing in like vultures, he squeezes his napkin in his fist to make sure it's there. Halfway home he smooths the wrinkles against his thighs, and through the strobe-light succession of intersections sees for the first time that he's drawn an octopus, its tentacles coiled around a treasure chest.

"Do you know where the Partner & Partner building is?" he asks the cabbie.

"Do I know how to piss?" the cabbie replies, turning the car around and a block away before Swelter regains his balance in the back seat.

•

The Partner & Partner building shines in the gray New York night like a windowpane reflected on the warped curve of the eye. It seems to bend, out of its own depth, to a final image of flatness. From directly below, it looms like a gargantuan thumb. From the Bronx it sticks out of Manhattan's skyline like the pointy end of a nail clipper, and several accidents at the top of Mechanic Street have been blamed on the harsh mid-day reflection; from Ellis Island and the crown of the Statue of Liberty, it appears as if the City's giving the poor huddled masses the finger, although some immigrants newly arrived and approved are convinced they see the space shuttle, ready to blast off in an explosion that would leave half of Manhattan's sky-scrapers, built as they are on sand and dead leaves, laying in an unceremonious heap; in the dawn light it looks to the traffic reporters in their helicoptors like a shimmering banana; from Brooklyn it's just annoying; and from the forty-first floor of the Dies & Drear Building downtown it looks exactly as the planners envisaged it, indeed as they were commanded to execute its construction, an arc of utter control sliding into the sky in the shape of a seventy-two story glass canoe.

The canoe: it could be said to be the elemental shape behind American history, second perhaps only to the shape of the beaver. But you can't appreciate the architect behind the beaver without stepping into swampy metaphysical ground, no, so it's easier to stick with the canoe: the beaver went across the country, the canoe took after it, and all of America followed the canoe.

It was the canoe that explored obscure waterways, was carried so often over land when no water could be found, cradled Lewis and Clark, dribbled through the corners of the North and Southwest and went as far as the beaver would go; one is carved from the trunk of a single tree, one a light frame covered with birch bark, its seams glued with thick sap; what is it but the shape at the heart of a continent, the shape of its messengers and warriors, explorers and hunters? It's carried flags and writs, hearts of phlegm and cold stony intentions; it's carried doctors to babies and diseases to villages. It rode in the cold clear blood of the country, when the shape of the messenger was made to follow the natural movements of the land, its mountains and lakes. Then an important area may have been one that could be reached at all, and on the land's terms, literally, as in a set period of time, an epoch in which movement in the specific area might be possible. Land went about its changes with little fanfare, but never stopped to admire itself, having been blessed as a body with no head or brain, or more to the point, no ego. But canoes could cover its breadth gracefully, and so egos were piled in it and sent upstream; and when the squaring of the land began, when the dotted lines dropped down to where men could see them and mark them with their fences and defend them with their own lives, as the land was already being re-shaped and its importance and history re-defined, so the shape of the messenger changed, as well as the roads it followed.

A latticework of defiance was laid over it, vectors of power that matched or complemented in no way those of the earth and the water beneath. Imagine how you might feel if enlightened cells suddenly discovered your body, peered around from the top of one of your teeth for a second or two and then said, "We'll fix everything," then getting to work, dropping straight lines across your surface, a grid partitioning your organs and extremities; they'll pull out the hairs from your arms and back to burn for fuel, and they'll dam up the heart and make it flow through new outlets at intervals of their convenience, based on a mean table of approximate times created not to reflect the changing of the seasons and the passing of the days but mostly to quell any confusion about what time the trains would arrive. Sometimes the skin will dry out from misuse, and they'll move on to another area; eventually of course someone will find the navel, and they'll drill deep down, surprised to find nothing. What use could it have had? In the end they'll fill it with waste, and when the legs have been cut down to the bone, harvested in square patches and drained of marrow, when the new veins begin to malfunction or clog with white blood cells who don't understand the simple shape of territory, one of them will find the almost invisible trail of hair that runs down the belly, and they'll all follow it, with their squares and maps and flags, already arguing on how to divide the final frontier...

Maybe the continent didn't feel like that. But it's worth mentioning that the canoe has no right angles; as the curves and natural lines of the country were tested and found wanting, so the shape of the canoe faded into its present triviality. The argument may be made that new fiberglass canoes are safer, less likely to leak and, with styrofoam sponsons hanging over each edge, virtually unsinkable. But it can also be said that the birch bark canoe is a vehicle unsinkable to those who respect its unique shape in equal parts to their respect for the land they'll use it in, the terms on which their passage depends, and that it's made to fade respectfully back into the landscape from which it came. But these observations, as anyone could tell you glancing down 95 or 1 or 17, any of the various turnpikes thruways or toll arteries, these observations are neither here nor there; the canoe's triviality lies in its new uses. Where it used to carry doctors and explorers it now carries tackle-boxes full of lures, styrofoam coolers filled with Budweiser and ice bought at the roadside filling station. It's more often found in backyards and on the roofs of cars than in the water.

So the *Partner & Partner* building stands as the pinnacle, prize tribute to the shape's triviality: a 72-story, immobile, unwater-worthy set of static curves, as obtrusive among the tall square structures of skyscrapers as those buildings' predecessors, the flat straight roads and square log-cabin houses, were to the original shapes of the island, birch and beaver, pelt tent and canoe, on which they now all stand.

•

Swelter considers the body metaphor as he's diverting the alarm system with his manager's password. When he'd been fired he knew his entry coordinates could be abolished, but it wasn't hard to find the algorithm for creating new passwords, placed as it was in the Executive Main Menu. Swelter'd memorized it the first day he got his promotion, more as a curiosity than with the designs of one intent on espionage; but now he's thankful for his curiosity.

"Thank you, thank you," he says to the doors as they open for him, "thank you" to the guard who sits snoring by the first floor elevator. Swelter knew in advance that guards would not be a problem even if awake, since the Company hired only work-study students for night-guard duty, and as a rule fired them every seven weeks, before they could get a feel for the place and its people.

"Thank you, thank you," Swelter says to the padded carpet on the stairs, skipping over the electronic eye-beams whose locations he'd also memorized out of curiosity when given a blueprint of the building's security devices. Swelter thank-yous his way up to the third floor and the Victoria Room, the knobless doors adorned with a

Kwakiutl style mural of two figures, Raven and Thunderbird. Inside Raven's wings are the shapes of smaller creatures, a conglomerate of abstract parts representing specific animals and monsters, one of which caught Swelter's eye the first time he was taken to the Victoria Room. Rent Nestleworth, systems analyst for Victoria operations, told him that all the faces he saw were parts of the same being. "The Dzoonokwa; the Indian version of *Yeti*," he told Swelter.

"I thought that was Sasquatch."

"You're thinking of the Eskimos. Right? Anyway, it varies from tribe to tribe. All depended on where they lived, what they thought was out there, you know? Not like today. A Dzoonokwa, he sees everything that goes on in his woods, even if he's not there."

"So he's got all these eyes? All these eyes are his?"

"No. Not his. That's a fish you're looking at there. And that's a beaver. He doesn't have all the eyes, Swelter. He just sees through them."

Starting at the ovoid of the Dzoonokwa's left eye, Swelter counts four of the Raven's feathers down, one across, and presses the dark pupil of a doorknob hidden there. The doors slide open. "Thank you, thank you," Swelter says.

What's wrong with the land-body metaphor, he thinks as he turns on the main terminal and projection screens, is not the sentiment but the actual problem of unity. To what extent is the human body a mass of smaller organisms whom accident has inspired to live together? What glue holds them in, creates the illusion of wholeness? He knows it's partly the illusion of conscious control over the body, which persists psychologically even though we've known for years how little our conscious thoughts have to do with the most important bodily functions, such as healing, adrenalin response, breathing...

The map lights up. Swelter gets to work. In a few minutes he changes the time in the main terminal so that the files will have this evening's activity occur officially seven hours later, around ten o'clock in the morning. Then he runs an enquiry on P&P Executive passwords, their recent movements, signified on the screen as yachts;

who's been in the Strait of Juan de Fuca lately, and how close are they to him? Seven gold yachts appear, and Swelter is a little concerned to see they form a rough circle around an area he remembers searching just a few days ago.

"Closer than I thought." Well there are ways to fix that; Swelter accesses the polar axis screen, opens the program for a look-see, and makes a minor adjustment. "There." The original map appears again. What it doesn't show is that Swelter has in effect shifted the entire continent one degree, without correcting surface imaging; the notations in the movement logs match the screen, but at some point the compasses will start pointing in different directions. "Blame it on the navigators," Swelter suggests.

For extra security he deposits a drift command into the Eyes Only file of each yacht's automatic search program, which will instruct the "navigator"—whichever byte or chip or blink of current that might be—to disregard the calculations on hourly tidal drift.

"Now for the real fun."

He calls up a new screen, glances at it, then returns to the programming. Swelter's cooking up a little surprise for his ex-employers, a wrangly nocturnal surprise for any bold yachter who gets too close to the heart of the matter... as he types he reconsiders: really the problem in his mind is cooperation, that in the human body parts must cooperate for survival. Even if the body *is* an accident of convenience, modeled after any other system of gathered life forms, how do you account for the brain? An overriding force that can do for the body so much good, so much harm: what in the entire continent, big as it is, compares to the brain, what must everything obliquely answer to? A few answers, a few syntactic compromises, tremble before him briefly, but retreat before he can scrutinize them. Tectonic plates, continental drift, accomodation of species....

"No, no, no," Swelter shakes his head to clear it. His program is finished. The technical jargon for his creation is a *worm*, a command which reacts only under certain circumstances and remains for the most part invisible, difficult and time-consuming to locate. Swelter, thinking of the Blakean Abyss, prefers to call it Leviathan; only instead of a smoking, coiling serpent his creature also partakes of the literary tradition via Jules Verne, namely a prehistoric-sized, gaping-beaked horrifically tentacled four story long organ of misinformation that appears on the Victoria's high-resolution screen as the mother of all octopi, its huge mass emerging from the water to squeeze the unfortunate yacht into irretrievable shreds of light. No angel of information could cast down a saving spell, the smartest command was flotsam in these new waves; they'd be lucky to escape at all, and if they did they'd be amnesiac captains, with no memory of where they were when the monster came...

Swelter cuts the power on the Victoria Room. As he closes the doors behind him its carved eyes once again attract him. They're not his eyes, Nestleworth had said, but he sees through them all. Somewhere in the bilge of his mind he thought he heard the forging of a single link, something primal snapping into place like fear, something clean and terrifying about land and men, but as he makes his way carefully down the stairs all he can form is a single pair of eyes, ovoids within ovoids, floating before him as if preceding him until, at the edge of the carpeting, past the snoring guard and a few feet before the marble entranceway he sees them anew; the disembodied eyes materialize on the other side of the glass door, with a dark hulking body behind them, approaching with a speed roughly equal to his. It's not his reflection, or his imagination, and only with seconds to spare does he realize that it's not the beast itself, but a body equally unfamiliar to him, in fact his first glimpse of Edna of Beaver Road, striding with a fiery certainty in her eyes, her hair loose and keening wildly in kinky black tentacles. She halts at the door's all-but-invisible edge, inches from Swelter, then lifts her arms up in the air in a motion that not only insinuates, but intends, violence. For this is when Swelter sees the sledge hammer, at the height of its arc, at the peak of its potential energy; and if there was any difference in the energy inherent in the hammer and that inherent in the arms that held it, if there was any small switch between the potential and the kinetic still to be played, Swelter could not see it.

•

So strong, so solid, are the oak heft and wrought-iron head of the sledge hammer, so strong and solid the black arm that holds it high overhead, its veins riding in sure bulges over the muscles, that the sight takes Swelter back for a moment to his Baking Soda days, that he thinks for the second of the swing's apogee that it will never come down, only remain at the height of its potentiality; at the mild age of six, when his extensive intellect was barely abuzz with wonder, when he lived in a state of relative comfort with the world, Swelter would sneak into the fridge while his mother ironed, extract a spoonful from the open baking soda box, patting the surface back down—so smart he was then, already—so it would look untouched; then, alone in the bathroom, he'd turn off the lights so just the sun leaking through the shades would make the room murky; run the cold water at an accelerated dribble, and paste the baking soda over his eyebrows, imagining himself old, pushing some of the white along his temples, like Reed Richards in the Fantastic Four, and he could see himself, no *feel* himself, getting older, absorbing the wisdom of the ages, his brain expanding even while it shrunk inside his skull, sucked feeble and dry by the eons, all of the knowledge of a roomful of grandfathers, until it was too much, he knew more than even his mother, and he'd splash his face with the cold water until he was young again, smart but not too smart to be a tiger, crawling beneath the ironing board and sinking his shiny teeth into her nurse's shoes. They tasted like the thick candy of adulthood, and as his mother yanked him up and led him to the kitchen, opening the fridge to get a piece of fruit, he'd be thankful for his rubberiness, his ability to transform himself into wild animals, thankful for his youth even then, knowing as he looked into the fridge at the arm and hammer poised there that the strength that came with getting older might be a stiffer one, however great, like a hammer that never came down.

But as this swing begins for real, he can almost taste the metal in his mouth, as if a draft preceded it, and he knows that the hammer before him has been held for ages, that far from being an isolated and unlikely strike of carthartic agony that it is a precise assault, the opening points taken to settle scores for those in graves or beyond.

Swelter knows this because he sees Edna's eyes, even through the double-strength insulate airtight yet still not hammer immune plate glass door, are so like the eyes of one who sees all that goes on in her woods, even though she be away.

But now she was back. Questions could be asked and answered later. In a moment of pure grace that might as well be homage to a returning god, Swelter pulls open the door. The hammer whistles downward, pounds through the marble floor with force enough to make the night-guard hitch in his sleep.

The handle sticks from the floor like a rudder. Edna sweeps back her cape; it glitters calmly around her body, a secret planetarium. When she speaks her voice is calm, but behind it lurks an impatient booming.

"Where's my globe?" she says.

"I'll help you find it," says Swelter.

•

Evening drifted down, sand casual, between his fingers as he held them up to the row of candles lit on the wall, the windows beyond and above them. America was a new country, they were always off dying for something; in a way it was fitting that if the sacrificial dagger should extract one more life from the mosaic of souls, it should be an American. Pastor Don Pializzi Remfallano strolls around the body as he considers the historical virtue of such reasoning. Tucked in his cassock is a smuggled copy of The Bridge of San Luis Rey. Wilder's prose was beautiful and clear, he thinks; but if only he had written in Spanish!

How much more wonderful would be the section on Dona Maria, Marquesa de Montemayer! When she crawls into the Velasquez painting to get the perfect gold chain on the neck of the Viceroy's wife! How she said to the ashamed Perichole, "I am impossible! I am impossible. I am impossible." He believed he would compose a proper translation of the novel into Spanish, possibly in verse, aided by the style of Ecclesiastes, its eloquent fatalism, its tired respect for human dignity...

Of this dignity he could find no better example than one of his parishioners from back in his missionary days in Jamaica. She was on her deathbed, her children standing by her, their hands touching the bed as if holding it up. She'd been attacked in the night just a few feet from her home. Somehow she'd made it back from the woods where she'd been dragged, and had gotten in bed to die before sending her youngest daughter to fetch Remfallano.

"I've come to take your confession," he said sweetly.

"Here; take this," handing him a tiny leather book. "It will explain everything."

The book was blank. Certain nights, maybe when it rained, maybe when he read facing the rising sun, it always seemed to vary, he thought he could make out faded words, so minute as to be illegible. He'd always kept the book with him, in the hem of his sleeve; now he removes from that sleeve a crisp handkerchief, unfolds it and opens the small, leather tome. With respect to this woman, he thinks, I will write the first notes for my Spanish translation of Wilder. He begins to write. At this moment he perceives the presence of something of significant mass directly behind him; a large, gentle hand grips the back of his skull. He's propelled face first into the rough stone wall. He dies mercifully soon, his final posture relaxed as he would have wanted, head slumped against a raised chair next to the shattered face of Saint Jude.

For its part the Dzoonokwa had made an honest mistake. Pastor Remfallano approximated Beaver both in height and general shape, at least from the back; he wore a silvery white garment, close enough to Beaver's Head Diver suit for an angry beast to strike first and, well, strike again later. Which it now does, rolling the pastor's remains from one great paw to the other, the scent of the Other still in the room. The wad of bubble gum stuck in its fur compliments of Lt. Whiffle still retained a sandy stickiness, and before rigor mortis fully sets in the pastor's clenched fist is pressed against that specific patch of hair, and from the stiffening fingers a small booklet is passed, its weathered hide cover blending in with the monster's matted carpet....

•

Tinsel waits on one knee, his face blacked with charcoal, his arms outstretched. Before him is the dark beach, its pre-dawn blackness deepened by the hull of a landing boat. From over its edge peer the eyes of Lt. Eugene Clark. He heaves a pack into Tinsel's arms.

"Got it." Beaver's beside him. The short dunes and rising cliff behind him are equally black, but this fact and the South Koreans' name for the inlet notwithstanding, its operative name is now Red Beach; and Red Beach will be the name that will stick in history's craw as part of MacArthur's plan to re-take most of South Korea with this daring pre- dawn amphibious assault. Tinsel and Clark have been here for three hours, verifying tides on the various stretches of rock and sand. Beaver called them Lewis and Clark as a joke, so now Clark refers to Tinsel as Private Lewis. When Clark jumps off the boat, Tinsel wraps one arm around his skinny shoulders and presses his tired forehead to Clark's.

"Let's get this straight. You're not even gonna remember I was here in a few hours, so for the record I'm not a friggin private. In fact at this moment I'm only a few months past breast-feeding, and I'm not even gonna start reading about this war until John F. Kennedy's dead." Clark stares at him blankly while he talks, his white eyelids above the line of his black-face camouflage giving the impression of a confused, man-sized frog. "So just call me Lewis, okay? No more of this Private shit." They trade dumb-faced stares for a moment; Tinsel flaps out his lips.

"You look like a fool nigger, Lewis," Clark says.

"Boy, this *is* the fifties," Tinsel replies. Beaver's behind them before they can break their stares, knocking their heads together with fatherly gentleness.

"Okay, boys, all the readings are fine. Only one more thing left to do. Take this pack, Clark." He turns to Tinsel. "Don't be so harsh on the boy, Lewis. He's going to be a hero."

•

Tinsel had argued that they didn't need to go to the Inchon landing. "You yourself admitted that it wasn't connected to this research stuff we're supposed to be doing."

"I don't know that I said that, exactly. History's a tricky thing; in my business, in fact, it's nothing but tricks. You can never tell how things will affect other things until it's happened."

"What's *it?*"

"Exactly. I don't know, but as far as my place goes, I'm in a particular map, and within it are the details that make up your view of history. Why you've got a map of your own is beyond my ability to judge; but I'm in this job full-time, and if you're not willing to keep your memories straight, then just tell me. Or better yet, just wake yourself up."

"Uh..."

"That's right. Since when do you control your own dreams? Even *that's* a negotiation."

"So let's make a deal."

"I'm afraid that's impossible."

"No," Tinsel said, "*you* are impossible. You are impossible," clicking his heels together for effect, "you are impossible."

And so they went to Inchon.

The attack is set to begin at ten minutes to six; hundreds of ships, loaded with men, tanks and supplies, will be launched on three different shores named Green, Blue and Red beaches. The pre-landing assault will be a barrage of carpet-bombing by Air Force F-51s and F-80s, and advance shelling by artillery boats will contribute covering fire. The timing is set to give the invading army the full advantage of the high tide. Twenty-two minutes to six finds Tinsel and Clark inching their way around the lighthouse at Red Beach's northern point. Neither of them carry arms.

"Why wouldn't this lighthouse be guarded?" Tinsel asks Clark. Clark pauses as he shrugs, answers, "Maybe the North Koreans haven't had time to find it. Charlie ain't that brilliant, you know," at which point a lone soldier, dressed in North Korean uniform, strolls around the curve of the wall whistling "California Here I Come" with better-than-average success. Right past a frozen Clark he strolls, but Tinsel he notices, because Tinsel is the one pushing him backwards, over the back of a kneeling Clark. He hits the wall hard, his head bouncing forward again as he drops unconscious.

"Real Laurel and Hardy," Tinsel says, but Clark isn't listening; he's pulling up the limp body of the soldier by his belt, yanking him into a kneeling position. He grips the back of his neck, slams his face into the wall. "Just wanted to make sure," he tells Tinsel.

"Whadda ya mean, just wanted to make sure? You bashed his face in!"

"I was just helpin the kid pick his nose—with a brick wall." Clark brings his eyes up to meet Tinsel's incredulous stare. Tinsel can feel the challenge in them like heat. The guy's got his first kill, Tinsel thinks. Clark, puffed up like a rooster, lets the stare linger a little, releases it just in time to turn into the face of a second North Korean, gun drawn.

"Ho-holee shit!" he yells, but he's already been hit in the side. Tinsel hears the bullets as they pass through Clark's ribcage and ricochet off the wall.

The soldier is watching a sinking Clark flick him the finger when Tinsel unloads his flare gun at point blank, the discharge a thick blob of light that knocks them both down before he even hears the sound of it. Tinsel's up in a second, stamping out the fire on the unconscious soldier's chest, and the words float over the empty turns of his mind, in rhythm with his boots, the sea now sounding like a crowd rocking in their seats to this police action show stopper: *The sun shines east, the sun shines west, but I know where the sun shines best...*

Before he realizes it his pants are on fire; and before he can begin screaming Beaver is behind him, cutting the fabric away with two sure strokes and flinging the pants to the ground. Clark, crouched against the wall and sitting on the body of the first soldier, holds his left hand to the entry wound and stares at the burning pants.

Tinsel turns on him, kicking the pants toward him. "Satisfied?!" Clark barely registers his inquiry.

"Come on," Beaver says. "Only ten minutes left."

•

Leonard Horsefield likes to think he's in charge. "I'm in charge of this monkey outfit," he tells everybody in the boat. They're scrambling about, adjusting position for all the boats in the upcoming attack, coordinating radar for artillery. Somewhere in the cabin coffee is brewing, but no one can locate the percolater. "I can find any spot on the map down to the last pissin' inch; now can't someone find me a cup of bloody joe?"

The land won't be visible for another hour, and by then his job will be done, the Air Force will have set the dunes on fire and the first hundred men will be ashore. As long as we hit what we're supposed to hit in the bleeding dark, Horsefield thinks. In one of those boats out there MacArthur himself sits, and though this raises morale among the troops Horsefield can't see why. "I'd rather have a rabbit's foot than that pope, boys," he says.

At eleven minutes to six the radio crackles and a senior officer tells him he can stop worrying.

"Say again?" Horsefield asks.

"I said, someone lit up the god damn lighthouse."

•

"My butt's freezing off!" Tinsel yells down to Beaver. Neither of the soldiers had keys to the lighthouse door, so Tinsel scales the slight incline of the wall to the lowest window, breaking the glass with the butt of the flare gun. He jumps inside, runs up the stairs and finds the control room. Flicks every switch he can see. Then back to the window, where Beaver gives him the okay sign. A long beam of light caresses the breakers beyond the beach. "Time," Tinsel calls down.

"Eleven till," Beaver says.

The world's well lit when he opens the door and steps back out. Planes skimming by are burning the encampments behind the lighthouse. A whole village deserted and re-filled with trenches and mines and soldiers is alive with fire and confusion. The lighthouse beam begins to reveal to Tinsel the magnitude of the project, transport ships hitting the surf, dozens of troops from Almond's X Corps jumping into the breakwater and setting down covering fire. Tinsel works his way to where Beaver sits watching the fireworks. Next to him is a sleeping Lt. Clark. Beaver puts the finishing touches on a makeshift bandage.

"Has to look sloppy so they'll believe he did it himself," Beaver says. "You ready to go?"

"Just a second," says Tinsel. He pulls his knife and makes a cut down Clark's shoelaces. Off come the boots. He severs the belt and pulls Clark's trousers off.

"A little tight, aren't they?" Beaver asks as Tinsel inches them over his hips.

"You forget, I lived through the seventies," Tinsel says. There's a roar in his ears as an F-80 coasts overhead, and then they're gone, leaving behind the half-dressed Lt. Clark where he'll be found by 10th Company, who'll help deify him as one of the battle's heros even as the jokes begin to fly about Lighthouse Eugene's Panty Raid, Stark Naked Clark, landing like shrapnel around his unofficial reputation, the sharp steely barbs that will ache him, like a lost limb, far beyond his honorable discharge ten years later.

•

Nobody would have seen the picture change, if indeed it had ever been different.

One more stop, Beaver had told Tinsel, the two whirling for a little longer than usual in some indeterminate medium between one and the next map: to Tinsel it was like travelling through the inside of a marble. Ribbons and multi-colored curls writhed in and out of potential patterns, grew enormous or shrunk back to near invisible wisps. Beaver moved them around the wriggling invitations, beneath or between or over them all, waiting motionless for some to flare before them and pass on.

"Hey Maxwell," Tinsel said as they waited out one such expansion of color, "what time is it anyway?"

"There's no time at all," Beaver said. "We're outside the cone right now, so time's ineffective. These seams are our way back into time, a *particular* time would be more accurate. A particular place. See there—" pointing to a brief starfish-shaped convergence, "—there's an opportunity to see where those different times and places coincide somehow, create an event related to the causes and effects they represent. Think of it as looking at a projection screen, except the screen is all around you. It's somehow—at least according to the guys who built it—a flexible model of perception, over time and space."

"You mean none of this is real, then, right?" Tinsel felt relief wriggling through him, a sensation a little less pleasurable than he expected: it felt more like being spread over a spider's web than caught in a safety net. "So this is a dream. Sure it's a dream. I had nothing to do with the Korean War, I was only a few months old. And if somehow any of this were real, if history got messed up, whatever, then you said those technicians would come and fix it up, right?" Beaver suddenly pulls him by the wrist, towards a pulsing octopus-shaped conglomerate of reds and blues, greens. Along the way, a ribbon slides up towards them. "Watch it," Beaver warns, but Tinsel's foot has already dipped into the shimmering surface of light, and as they pass out of its reach, Tinsel notices something's missing.

"Wha, wha, my foot's gone!" peering down his left leg to where his cuff ends abruptly as if cropped for a photograph. "Maxwell, my *foot* is *gone*," appealing to reason, "it should be on the end of this leg."

"We'll pick it up later," Beaver turning only slightly, and Tinsel sees in his eyes some unnameable color, and then they're passing through the center of the octopus, a crackling static feeling rubbing him from head to toe as they return to time, more or less intact.

•

Central Falls, Rhode Island doesn't look much different to Tinsel now that it's 1962. There are more Packards on the road, and Ramblers, and there'd be no import cars at all if it weren't for the Peugeot that the New York Times reporter and photographer drive in the lane ahead of them. The new town hall in Lincoln, where the award ceremony will be, is a single-story flat-roofed structure that also houses the Police Department. The two cars carrying the reporters and Tinsel and Beaver cruise for a space in the parking lot, which also serves as the holding area for impounded vehicles, and walk together to the front lawn, where a podium is set up beside the flag-stone path to the entrance. The seal on the podium is a growling sea-lion, which serves as a mascot for the local school system, but today a cloth draped over it for official ceremonies portrays the profile of Abraham Lincoln, left side facing, so that folks won't think the emblem was copied directly from a penny.

"Listen," Tinsel whispers to Beaver as they walk across the lawn, "if we saved Maxwell's skin by sending those extra Chinese soldiers to la-la land, then why do we have to do this stuff? Wouldn't Maxwell be doing it?"

"Not in your memory, bub."

"Oh. Huh?" Tinsel decides to change the subject. "Nice shoes," he says to the photographer.

"Nice army fatigues," the answer.

"Maxwell, this town hall looks just like the grammar school we saw down the road," Tinsel says. "And the high school."

"It was new architecture a few years ago," the reporter explains.

"Try to hide your enthusiasm," Beaver tells Tinsel.

Town Administrator Burt Baldwood greets them with meaty handshakes, introduces them to the artist. On the podium a neat package sits under midnight-blue silk wrapping.

"It's a pleasure to meet you, Corporal Maxwell, and Lieutenant, er," glancing at Tinsel's nametag, "er, Skean. Certainly a pleasure. And may I introduce—" the artist stepping forward and grasping first Beaver's, then Tinsel's, hands steadily and graciously.

"It's an honor to meet true public servants. My name is Rizzoli." His smile tempered with enough sobriety for the occasion, but hinting at some hidden enthusiasm.

"Yes, um, Mr. Rizzoli," Baldwood finishes up. Further dignitaries are introduced, coaches of the little league, the public works people, town stenographer etcetera, and the photographers place them all like hedges just out of sight of the camera's viewfinder, where they remain beaming and elbowing each other. Baldwood, whose nose will intrude from the left edge of the photograph in the unretouched proof, stands beside Tinsel. "Must have been tough over there," he mumbles confidentially to Tinsel; then, nudging at the wooden prosthetic foot sticking out of Tinsel's left pant-leg, "does it sometimes hurt, like I've read, as if it's still there?"

"I haven't missed it at all," Tinsel says.

When the photographer's hand slides up into the air like a salute, and everyone stiffens for the brief moment the flash ignites, Tinsel is glancing at a spot just past Rizzoli, where the air seems to waffle for a moment, shimmer as if a seam into another time was trying to open itself up for him. By the time Rizzoli's finished retouching and painting the photo some years later, the image of Tinsel will be looking at the spot where, at Dr. Wan's request, Polly Croom has been painted in, and from that spot any visitor to Rizzoli's retrospective who happens to gaze at the photograph could follow Polly's own gaze, and see that it is directed towards Tinsel, and that it's filled with a curiosity so deep and teasing that it could be mistaken for love.

•

Beaver had wanted to take the lighthouse at Inchon as a symbolic beachhead, a signal that his counter-attack on his as yet faceless enemy had begun. And as much as it fit his private mythology, ideas on false beacons and guideposts, as much as he did it for his own pleasure, he did it also for the discomfort, at a future date, of the Partner & Partner Company. This would take the form of a small grey notebook Beaver dropped in Lt. Clark's sack just before he had thrown it ashore to him. The notebook Beaver had pinched from the garish side pocket of Donald Drycleaner's sportcoat was the first document he'd seen with the name Partner & Partner on it, but it immediately clarified for him his own immediate danger, gave his nemesis a name; for most of his runs in the last few weeks had all been dangerous searches for obscure information filed under monikers like *P&P Research Division, PP Public Servants*, etcetera... the information desired, equally fishy, though Beaver couldn't quite figure out the context: for instance, geological samples of each of the Antilles islands, spaced a hundred years apart over a span of seven hundred years, a comprehensive graphing of tropical storm and hurricane occurence, numerous possible economic indicators, dating from the present backwards to the last full decade of the twentieth century? Was it possible that some part of Partner & Partner, maybe a faceless vestige, a lasting kernel of aggression, was trying to gather information to use at a different time, to change its own destiny? Everyone who knew history knew that Partner & Partner were dissolved by the Feds after the IRS followed a less-than-legal money trail... but had one of the Partners slipped through a crack in the sewage pipe, aging underground for a century, all the while plotting in the piss and copper stink? had it found, somewhere in the netherworld, a slot into the past, through which certain information might be conveyed like a postcard?...

Thus Drycleaner's sportscoat: the coat actually had several outer pockets, but most of them were fake, simple flaps of cloth sewn on to suggest a pocket where fashion dictated one ought to be. Though Drycleaner's hard left-hand scrawl, and the evidence of what seemed to be his habit of drooling absentmindedly while writing, made for difficult deciphering, the information that could be gathered by a patient and courageous reader was as follows:

Partner & Partner had a tacit agreement with Land Hub, Inc., to purchase a wide swathe of land along the south and southwest coast of Florida, mostly beachfront property, some supposedly government-protected land, most of which Land Hub expected to have acquired by the date of purchase, mid 1992. The actual purchaser would be a fictitious environmental group from Rhode Island, supposedly acting in the public interest. Donald Drycleaner, who would represent the company in Florida and Rhode Island, settled on the name "Save the Herons!" Acting through this front, P&P could secure a good deal of the real estate tangential to the current Eastern Florida Plastics Conglomerate and the adjoining industrial park, which would become "state land" once the East Florida charter had been legitimized. When the new state colonized the Greater Antilles, by force if necessary, but everyone was already working on the islands' political figures to cooperate, moved on the nuclear plant idea and set the Statewide Labor Executive Order into effect, P&P executives correctly assumed that heads would start rolling, first in Washington and then spreading outward like a ripple. Everyone knew the National Guard would be called in. So a buffer zone of heavily-mined and defended land and water would come in handy. How long would the people tolerate an attack by the government on one of its own states, anyway? Business, after all, was business.

But when Donald Drycleaner, watching the enchanting Madame Ipswich sway above his skinny, erect body in the Pine Street Sojourner Inn, falls victim to an unexplained respiratory failure which is not noticed by Mme. Ipswich until she comes back from the shower to get her shawl and purse, the land deal becomes, for the time being, a thing that never existed. The company sends two men down to Central Falls to burn his house, thus destroying any proof that Drycleaner might have had. As the outer clapboards begin to smoke from the fire inside, one of the arsonists steps casually over the fire department's crowd control barriers, flips a cigarette to his lips and lights it on the edge of the house. He's back before anyone can see him; and it's his stylistic signature, his coup-de-grace on the conflagration, a way to end all his jobs with satisfaction.

Sucking in his breath, and blowing a cool blue pastel smoke of Torieton into his partner's over- irritated nostrils, he says, "Another job well done."

The other one, just a kid really, first or second time out, massages his sinuses. "Fuck, how can you stand the heat this close? I think I'm gonna have another infection."

"Why did they send you with me?" He flicks his gray embers onto the underling's shoulder. "They must want you to get your experience with the very best. There is nothing left of Drycleaner or his schemes but ashes."

And the people back in New York City and down in Florida and training in the secret barracks near Ithaca, New York had no reason to believe otherwise. Until they heard from Lt. Eugene Clark's lawyer.

•

Clark, who'd retired a two-star general, was never in good spirits since assuming the civilian mantle. Not that he was a happy man
before that, what with every month going by seeing another varia-
tion of the Eugene's Inchon Panty Raid joke floating on the bathroom walls at any installation he'd been to. The military remembers
its own, and Clark doesn't cherish what he's remembered for; but
still, the very night that Donald Drycleaner breathes his last, Clark
is up late in his attic, the sound of the train passing through Boise
disturbing his bland dreams of TV characters, and he's going through
all his army souvenirs, thinking of Inchon and the blank spots where
memory abandons him right before he wakes in his underwear, a pair
of pants burning by his bare feet, hoping still that some physical item
saved from that night might provide the stimulus to jump-start his
recollection.

What he finds is a bent, gray notebook in his food satchel; and
with the strange patience of anyone up at three in the morning he
sits there and reads it. He reads it as the moon dies over Boise, fading
into a low pressure system, and as the seven-ten freight train to parts
west moans on the rails outside he's still reading, or rather, re-reading.

Most of it seems to be gibberish, fiscal stuff and company hiero-
glyphs, the secret language of business, but the thing that catches his
eye is the mention of the land acquisition on the southwest coast of
Florida. Clark's mother, getting near ninety-five but too stubborn to
die, lives in Heron Haven Elderly Estate, which squats like a brick
and stucco toad in the very middle of the plot mentioned in the
notebook. Thoughts of his faulty memory forgotten, so to speak, he
makes the obvious phone calls: nobody's going to try and sell the
land out from under the mother of a two star fucking general of the
United States Army, ma'am.

And that's exactly what he tells the District Attorney's office,
and anyone else who will listen, as two time zones away in Central
Falls, Rhode Island, a mail carrier named Sandy McQuenchler yanks
from the iron inner seams of a blue mailbox on the corner of Mineral
Spring and Smithfield Avenues a single letter, and sends it on its way.

•

In the *Abruzzi e Molise* stands a Catholic monastery at cautious peace with its snowy, mountainous surroundings. Avalanches occur often enough, the Pastor warns new acolytes, one does not even have to sin to bring down such wrath; he cautions quiet, insists on it without ever insisting too loudly, and the one group of Franciscan yodelers who came for a two month stay in 1931, Don Pializzi's first year as pastor, never returned from their first morning sojourn down the dramatic and crooked donkey path that so delicately connects the monastery to the rest of Italy.

Pastor Remfallano would look out his window every morning after first prayers, and there the peaks were, innocent as lambs and constant reminder that not only is God's plan a mystery, but it is a silent one, and a human voice in so purely a holy landscape will only bounce back to the caller the unhealthy effects of sin.

For one moment, though, there is a sound to which all the peaks and piles of snow seem to hearken; for which mountain goats hold stock-still, and snow flakes pause in the air, which becomes totally windless as a second ticks by, then two, and then, there it is, unmistakable, a rubbery rusty *twa-a-aang*, stretching over the mere fraction of a full second before coming to a hard, decisive and collisive end. For that span of a few feet through which the ceremonial dagger sails from its keep in the wall and imbeds itself between vertebrae of Brother Clifford King's spine, silence is sacred. And for the moment afterward, as if to confirm this, as the Brother slips to the floor, the gloved hands of Captain Wednull J. Beaver close over Brother Clifford's lips, extend the silence still further.

Then the goat lifts his hoof, looks at it; licks some snow off his whiskers with a snikking sound, and the peaks behind him rumble deeply, bristle with potential violence, and the air swirls in its invisible borings, and things get going again.

Inside, though, a tableau holds: at one end, the crumpled body of Brother Clifford, starting with his soft-soled shoes and travelling up his cassock to his open eyes; then the gloved hands of Beaver, one over the now silenced lips of the brother, the other holding a small clear vial of liquid. Beaver eyes it with curiosity. Then the inevitable shudder through the map, Beaver's attention diverted, and the vial dropped, a quick and effortless fall to the hard stone floor.

What the mountains don't hear, though, is that tiny smashing of glass on stone; instead, they hear the lightning-quick clicking of a zipper being unzipped, and what Brother Clifford doesn't see, eyes gazing up at the Head Diver, is a colorful seam open in the air beside him, and the torso of Captain Beaver, come back to clean up the mess he'd made, shooting through, arms outstretched and confident, catching the tiny vial in his palm mere inches from the floor and disappearing with it into a spiralling marble silence only he knows.

•

Whatever residue Tinsel might have left behind in his wake over the surface of history had not been explained to him; and when he woke up in a roadside ditch such questions were furthest from his mind. All he would remember of that drawn-out moment of dreaming sometimes floated before his eyes like colorful slivers of glass, and he'd know he was seeing the shape of a memory. What the shape signified he'd have no idea, not even of whether it was a dream-memory or the remains of a physical occasion, or whether it mattered which it was. Contrary to popular belief, the past is not behind us but before us, dancing as it does over Tinsel's irises, distorting or clarifying the oncoming, and so his tendency to say later that he often looked "beyond the past." He never could look at it, or through it.

This leaves only specific avenues of vision, of course, and if Tinsel collected one kernel of recognition to keep as the days progressed, it was that there's no such thing as a general avenue. As much as he hated to admit it, he now felt that one's direction in life was anything but general, and the place down the road from his present spot was nothing to joke at. But he did: "I'm going nowhere, but at least it's a direct flight."

Nowhere was a place that hid in the corners of Cozetta's lips when she was unhappy, a place creeping up on Cletis when he looked to his parents for guidance and found nothing palatable; was the stoic calm he felt waking to find Polly's side of the bed empty, the sound of her pacing ticking off the floorboards like a clock in an abandoned train station. Nowhere had a face, too: it was an expression of blankness where all things converged and cancelled each other out. Tinsel had felt no closer to Nowhere than in his last phase of octopus form, when he and Beaver were cruising in the matrix on their way back from Lincoln; Tinsel had suddenly metamorphosed in a convulsion of squalid shivering. And he hadn't stopped there, but had begun to expand, tentacles and suckers latching onto the colorful ribbons as they floated by. Beaver had looked back once, and with an ambivalent nod in his direction disappeared. Tinsel-Octopus kept growing, absorbing everything until he felt his almost limitless head bounce spongily against a firm surface. What was it? The limits of the marble? Had he ingested all of history? all of time? Or was he simply a cephalopod trapped in a sneaky fisherman's jar?

There was no time to formulate an answer; the horizon folded up like a road map served its purpose and drove over him the wide end of everything, octopus or not, and drowned him with its heaving ways, and when he rose more by persuasion than effort over the surface of the dilatometric, sputtering briefly into snores, he became just another thoughtless sleeping human being.

•

The moon was a snip short of full, and the planets that on earlier days in the month sat in its horn had to bob around just outside its heavy curve this night, clinging dearly to one or another aura of light that radiated in the cold down of the night's wing. Beaver could hear its black beating as he sat on a rocky island in the middle of a salt-water bay; he hadn't checked where he was. He needed just to sit and feel time as most feel it, passing through his skin while the moon shifted and shook the planets away on its path across the sky. Some nights the moon would have to stay overhead during the day, so its worshippers could use its subtle light to find berries in the underbrush, which would reflect the moon's roundness in faint fuzzy miniature at ankle-level. But on nights like this it could slide toward the sea, and Turtle, skimming the ocean surface to collect whitewater for his garden in the stillness of the deep, would hitch his great neck just far enough to the side for the moon to slip inside the shell and hide, at the sea's bottom, from the planets for the night's remainder.

The moon reflected the round face of Beaver's Head Diver Watch. He'd been reluctant to activate it since it would send out a traceable signal. On the other hand, it would come back with his exact location within seconds, and that would save him the energy of doing random, and possibly dangerous, dives to cross-reference his more instinctually-derived bearings. He knew, for instance, that about seven meters to his left, what looked like an outcropping of hard shale was actually one of the physical emergency exits from the Library, that by pushing against it he could knock himself out of it and into the empty air of Wyoming. But what would be out there, waiting for him? He had the feeling that until he got a better handle on the situation in general, he had better not trust anybody.

Clouds, running from the jaws of the great Bear, swept in front of the moon; Beaver heard the bare, wet feet creep across the rocky shore beneath him before he saw the dark outline of the young man. Unaware that he was being watched, the boy peered into the shallows, something in his hand poised just above the surf. For minutes he stood without moving; Beaver began to marvel at his patience. Then his arm shot down, the water exploded, and the air was suddenly full of the flapping of a fish thrown onto the rocks.

Beaver leaned back into a shadow. The kid was gaffing fish. This wasn't exceptional in itself; but a kid gaffing fish on a stub of rock barely big enough to be called an island *was* interesting. Did he live here alone? How much of this island will be submerged when the tide's all the way in? And what will the kid do? Beaver decided to wait around and see.

•

Nowhere had another face, that Tinsel hadn't seen or imagined; but Beaver had stared into its hollow eyes, landed on its meals, and narrowly escaped being dessert; Dr. Wan had caught a red glimpse of one iris through the hole in a restroom stall, and Swelter had twisted his neck looking at a door on which the painted likeness of its features had been distributed evenly over the space inside Raven's wing. The Dzoonokwa was finally back in its own time and place, the forest musty from trapped rain, beavers felling trees all night long, the creak of trunks in a heavy wind, the smashing of hard angry ocean on rocky coastline of an American Northwest yet to be delivered up to that portable written history that would bring with it gold and silver coins the Kwakiutl Indians would melt and fashion into bracelets with its own image engraved thereon, and with the gold would also come the imported Chinese vermillion pigment, wrapped in paper envelopes, that would replace the more rust-colored hematite and ocher-derived colors, and make its eyes in totem poles and spoons and chests and panels glow with the brighter, more rutilant fire that Wan and Beaver had seen: by these sounds and sights it recognized home.

Though it might have never found its way back on its own. It took over thirty technicians and a nerve-paralyzer net the size of a Japanese tuna boat to demobilize the wayward myth; and then nobody wanted to touch it, such was the effect its dank smell, its long, dry canines resting in the deep hair of its face, its eyelids, even though the eyes were almost fully closed as a result of the paralysis, had on the technicians. Eventually they shot him from a specialty catapult, blasted him after careful planning on a trajectory that sent the drowsy Dzoonokwa through thirty-two maps on the way to its own, where the net, and his sleepiness, dissolved slowly before its eyes like a bad dream.

Now, as it prowls the known paths of its territory, seeing everywhere signs of its dominance, something disturbs it. A familiar scent tickles its nostrils. Led to the edge of the forest, the Dzoonokwa looks past the spiky cliffs at its feet and the thrashing waves beneath it: from out over the water the smell drifted. Without pause or a moment's hesitation—and why should a myth hesitate?—the Dzoonokwa drops the countless feet to the water beneath. The blast of its belly-flop, loud as it is, barely registers in the already awesome tapestry of surging tide and rocks. A minute later the matted head pops up amid the white chaos. It drifts in the tide away from the land, paddling when it needs to correct direction, following the scent that interrupts its meals and its dreams. It is the scent of the enemy; its only enemy; it is the scent of Wednull J. Beaver, Head Diver.

•

Half an hour before the tide would be highest, Beaver sits watching the moon. He hasn't seen any sign of the boy for an hour, and is beginning to think that he must have had a skiff or canoe stowed behind a rock, when suddenly the youth appears out of a shadow not two feet away, his pointy elbow nearly tapping Beaver's head. Waves lap the soil only a few feet beneath the ledge they share, though the boy, still unaware of Beaver, seems in no hurry.

He climbs a few feet higher, to the crown of the island, and begins pushing aside a rock. Just as suddenly as he appeared he now disappears, dropping into the island itself, it seems, pulling behind him like a tail a rack of hooked flounder, their scales glistening like a rug of moons.

Beaver hears pebbles falling, and the thump of the boy's feet as he lands. A hole maybe, a hidden passageway; the island's hollow, Beaver thinks. Something grabs hold of his ankle—a crayfish swept in by the rising tide, which splashes up to his knees now. A light is struck in the hole, and Beaver peers over the edge: a small pile of driftwood smokes as the boy sets a flint to the kindling. The chamber is bone dry, and empty save for an oar, scattered fish bones, a pile of abandoned gull eggs, and the boy himself who, digging into the floor of the cave, scratches the dirt away from some treasure he's hidden. He lifts it up and marvels at it: a tiny blue globe, perhaps the size of a silver dollar, reflects silvery blue like the oil around fish eggs as he turns it around and around in the light of the fire.

Smoke pours out the island's head, making it difficult for Beaver to see down. The tide is full, levelling off, and the only part of the Head Diver still over sea level gets to wondering where he is. He unstraps the watch from his wrist, and leaning on his chest against the island's pate, brings the face of it close enough to read in the fading moonlight. He flicks the coordinate button. The reading is almost immediate:

Year: 1682 a.d. / Place Name: Vo9099: Strait of Juan de Fuca...

"Well..." Some response is lifting a lone finger in the depths of his mind, beyond triggers and training, but it doesn't have time to emerge fully, because something is tugging at his ankle again, this time not a crayfish but a hand the size of a bowling ball, and as Beaver twists around to look the red hollow eyes freeze him for a second, poking from the briny smelly coat of wet fur like the glowing chambers of a shotgun. The watch drops down the hole and into the fire, and over the ocean the moon slips in beneath the Turtle's shell and hides. In that moment of total darkness Captain Beaver reaches out for those glowing eyes as he's dragged beneath the surface.

Part Three

All this night and today I stayed waiting (to see) if the king of this place or other persons would bring gold or something else of substance; and there came many of these people, like the others of the other islands, naked and painted, some of them with white, some with red, some with black, and so on in many fashions. They brought javelins and balls of cotton to barter, which they traded here with some sailors for pieces of broken glass cups and for pieces of clay bowls. Some of them were wearing pieces of gold hanging from their noses, and they willingly gave it for a bell of the sort (put) on the foot of a sparrow hawk and for small glass beads; but it is so little that it is nothing. For it is true that any little thing given to them, as well as our coming, they considered great marvels; and they believed that we had come from the heavens.

—from the Diario of Christopher Columbus' first voyage.

XII. A Waking Version

The apron was paved and pimpled with potholes, but the Cessna clipped up and down coquetishly, smoothing itself between bounces, and rode to a stop intact. Single prop, room for two, the open mouth of a cartoonishly fanged beaver spreading over the nose up to the propeller. Under a heaving mid-day sun and between two thunderstorms it taxied and stopped. The Blue Mountains rose in every direction, a haze scheming to blot even them out.

Two men jumped out of the cockpit: we've seen them before, maybe in a dream. One strolled up to the propeller, which was still rotating lazily, and extended his arm toward it. A match flared in his hand. He lit up the Torieton menthol as the second man stumbled up behind him.

"Eew, I'm gonna be sick. What a bumpy ride."

"It is almost a pity they have once again placed us together," said the first man. "You will only be a green thorn in my side."

"Didn't I help you burn the spic's house in Rhode Island?" the second asked.

"No, you didn't." He sucked the cigarette to the filter and swallowed the smoke. "You slowed me down and impeded my grace, just as these rainstorms delayed our landing."

"Oh."

A thin blue steam rose from the first man's nostrils. "But here there will be no fires. There will be only silence and the machinery of the night. This will be all we need to procure from Croom the logbook our employers so desire."

"There's a lot of bugs here."

"Say one more word and I will shoot you," said the first, producing from his belt a silver, sleepy looking .38. It glistened in the haze. They pushed the plane into the woods and covered it with branches.

•

A white figure plummets into the ocean.

•

The American Heritage Dictionary lists 255 entries, including proper names, places, suffixes, technical and medical terms, abbreviations and symbols, and arcane variants, beginning with the letter z.

At the exact center, the 128th entry, is the word *zilch*. *Zilch* is defined as: Zero. Nothing. An insignificant person. A nonentity. Directly beneath it, the next entry, is *zillion*. The American Heritage says, Informal, an extremely large indefinite number. Used jocosely.

Between these two words the tiniest bit of white space flinches, then, as if gaining confidence, settles back into a space unquantifiable. It gives away nothing to the eye. It is both zilch and zillion.

Ignoring for the moment the smaller extremities and digits, the living thing that is Captain Wednull J. Beaver hurtles toward the sea from somewhere in the sky in the roughly consistent shape of a medieval Uncial, an early form of the z. He collides on his way downward with zillions of atoms, sub-atomic particles as he cleaves through the air like a moral judgment. Yet to anyone walking the dangerous pre-dawn streets in Kingston, or sleeping in the comfort of her hotel, or clumped up on a spit of seaweed on the beach's high-tide line, as Cletis and Footlong are, snoring through their rising hangovers, in short to anyone at all, Beaver included, who barely registers his plight, who in fact seems only connected to the event by his sheer and undeniable physical presence, his solid z-shaped bulk displacing countless invisible things, he is an insignificant person, a nonentity, zilch.

And yet here he still is, undeniable in the morning air, falling.

Just before hitting the surface his legs and arms tuck in to his chest. A shape of foam curls out of the water in his wake, and like a figure for a new language, one more interesting than a paradox of numerical value, it expends itself in a single space of sound that wakes Cletis and Footlong and directs their attention almost immediately, too late to see the splash, but with plenty of time for them to see the wake begin to spread over the calm jewelled water.

XIII. The Fifth Letter

The cable doctor Wan had wired Polly the day before she would ruminate on her marriage over a tubful of jewelry lay like a flag on the kitchen table. The yellow paper caught her eye, she'd turn away from it, a small breeze through the screen door would send it gliding like a sailboat towards her, she'd get up and look at it and put it back, she'd look out from behind the fridge door at it, she'd walk over to the table and pick it up, read it quickly so as to give it the least possible chance to mean anything, drop it on the table and herself on the chair by the phone and cross her arms. The process would begin again, and then of course the phone would ring—she knew it would, one of these times—and it would be him.

Dr. Wan had called Polly every day, twice a day actually, since Tinsel left, stepping up his pressure-therapy, his insistence that she go to New York for a few days, meet the artist friend of his, get some perspective, ad psychoanalyticum.

Not that she in fact didn't want to go; she figured it might be a way to get away from whatever *was* stifling her without admitting that something indeed was stifling her, especially without admitting it might be living in Mobridge in general, and living with Tinsel in Mobridge in particular. Not that there was anything wrong with Tinsel: he was sweet, he wasn't *un*attractive... the politics of avoidance swept in, gathered her up in merciful language and rocked her through waves of technical prepositional phrases for which she knew she'd need not find an object. Like all couples her marriage wasn't perfect, followed an easily chartable curve through romance and disillusionment, small crests and troughs, no reason though to really have to *choose*...

She'd never met Doctor Wan, found out all she knew about him through an ad in a Village Voice Tinsel had confiscated from a student in class and taken home.

"A sixth grader, Polly, reading the Village Voice! He had circled about a million of the personals; you know, GWM seeks same for R&R with BiJF and cohorts. I told the kid: if you can understand what these mean, you don't need to be sitting in this class."

"Judging from what he circled, it looked like he hadn't quite figured out his preference yet," Polly had said, laughing. Then she saw the ad: two sixteenth-page blocks in the shape of a mummy, with the words flowing across the chest: "FEELING ENCASED? Closed in, uptight, sewn up, etc. Call for personal counseling, Jungian and/or Freud plus latest in pop concepts. Open up, haha" and beneath it the phone number, squeezed in so tightly at the mummy's feet that the last number hadn't even fit. Polly had reached him on her fourth try, dialing last numbers at random.

"Of course, you just passed your first test," Wan had answered the phone on the third ring, the one statistically proven to be the most comforting for the caller. "Not too hurried in picking up the phone, not too far away to have to get there out of breath," he would explain later, "just a business-like two rings and one added for a deep breath. It inspires confidence."

Some modicum of which Polly had needed to risk the potential wrong numbers by selecting for the last digit at random—"You may have reached five or six or seven irate East Enders before you got me," he said. "It takes courage to do that. It takes smarts."

"I could have dialed directory assistance," Polly had said.

"I'm not listed."

So began their correspondence. She told Tinsel all about it, representing it as a joke, which she half-believed herself, and gave him weekly progress reports on how their marriage would improve if only Polly could learn how to decode the doctor's cryptic session-notes he'd wire her after each phone call. Wan had some deal with the phone company: his was not a 900-number, but something a little more sinister, where he represented the people who called him as the psychological profile best conditioned to long-distance telephone calling. So in exchange for a list of his clients, whom the phone company would contact with special service offers designed to fit their unique calling needs, Wan was paid a modest flat rate, plus commission on the number of hours he could keep his patients talking. It could have been that business was bad that second week in August, it could have been that Wan felt some actual need to call Polly twice a day and keep her on the phone for as long as he could; or it could have been some more subtle agenda that made him work so hard at inviting Polly to New York.

Polly knew she would go; she first realized it that moment when, sitting in the chair and looking at the phone, she felt the unrelenting urge to pull the cord from the phone's base, disconnect it for, what, an hour or two, take a bath and let her mind relax a bit. Reaching for it she suddenly caught herself in the act of choosing, deliberately acting and, by dint of such action, confessing responsibility. It was almost too much. Her hand froze inches from the phone. She counted to ten. Grabbed the base of the cord and released the catch as it rested in the socket.

The phone rang. It was him.

•

"So so, Polly, did you get it?"

"Yes." Glancing at the yellow cablegram on the table. "I didn't understand a thing about it. You don't make any sense to me, and you don't know me at all, you know."

"But that's *why*, Polly, that's exactly *why* you listen to me. If I knew something about you, anything at all, you'd find reason to discount me on the grounds that I'm misinterpreting you, emphasizing the wrong aspects of your personality, only what's salient to me and my own flawed senses. But like this, two disembodied voices, no patient history, not a scrap, I can't make such a mistake, can I? And you can stay in control without having to in effect make any risky effort at self-assertion. Take a little advice here, maybe something else I said there, like putting leftovers together, hoho."

"What do you want? We've already talked today. Let's say that I've got enough scraps from you for my next meal, psychologically speaking, okay?"

"Polly Croom. Polly."

"What?"

"Read the cable. Come to New York." And though a second later she did pull the cord from the wall, hoping it would resonate with some electronic crackle across the phone lines properly in tune with her anger, in the half-second before she broke connection, she'd heard, or thought she'd heard, anyway, the sound of Wan hanging up first. And somehow that had settled it. Even though she did take that bath she had been ready to promise herself, even though she figured she'd give herself the night to think about it, leave it open and unde-cided until the morning, she'd already sealed herself up in some small seamless case, as if packed for travel, wrapped in her bathrobe and licking the envelope addressed to Tinsel, her third letter to him just a quick hello and XO Polly written on the back of the cable-gram, which read:

8/9 a.m. Ms. Croom:

Notes:

Polly—ever procrastinating. Proliferating errors. Randomly lonesome if presented scenario limiting options (vis-a-vis essen-tials.)

Some good arrangements—reversed: like it? Contact. Feels out of time.

•

So two days later, when Polly sat at the kitchen table compos-ing her last note to her husband, when her jewelry began its second day in the tub, when she had an inkling that none of her letters would reach Tinsel anyhow, though maybe this thought gave her the only permission that would allow her to write such a letter, made it in fact a summary more succinct and straight-forward than if she had thought it was anything more than a curious dress-rehearsal of a real goodbye, her faculties seemed more numbed than ever, perhaps nec-

essarily, to the subtleties of the house surrounding her, all it stood for
and in spite of, its morning corners filled with soft chemise light, the
chimney in the den and the master bedroom well shrouded; on the
eleventh day of August, wrapped in the gauze of her irreversible and
binding decision to fly, barely aware of the facts of her household or
the fact of her dog Lancelot whining at her feet, less aware of the fact
of her hand stroking his leafy coat of fur, and oblivious to that of the
brown steaming mass growing hourly in her living room, now the size
of a couch and sporting on its side nearest the bay window a greenish
fungus, she sat and, with the ease of acknowledging a neighbor passing on the street, wrote the following:

Tinsel-

I have to leave everything. No time to really explain. Please
don't worry, you know how things were. I'll be in touch, I think.
Polly

She then reached for an envelope; addressed it and affixed the
proper postage; and hearing a rattling at the door, rose to greet the
mailman. He was not to be seen, but the day's mail stood out like
a fingerprint, proof of his passing: a phone bill, a card for Tinsel
about expanded long-distance services—Polly found it funny that
he'd insisted the bill be in his name, even though he made no long
distance calls, seemed in fact to know nobody ouside the local dialing
area—and a letter in a child's newly-learned script addressed to "Mrs.
Polly Comb."

Perhaps out of some need for order, she brought them to the
table and opened them. Conspicuously absent from the mail, she
thought as she opened the phone bill, was the yellow envelope signi-
fying a cablegram from Dr. Wan. But Wan must have known, must
have understood she was coming, even though she hadn't yet called
him to arrange the flight, hadn't contacted him since the call on the
ninth. Wan just knew.

She opened the envelope addressed to her. It was an obligatory
thank-you note from the local girl scout troop; she'd ordered a box
of cookies a few weeks ago from one of the little tentacles the troop
leader sends out to find money and latch onto it mercilessly in the

name of charity, using all the ploys and pouts a capable ten year old can muster.

> Dear Mrs. Comb,
>
> ☀ Thanks for buying those cookies. Mrs Lenahen next door wouldn't neither would Mr. Scott. Our troop-leader said she would talk about them in Church. ☺
>
>   Sincerely,
>   Maryella Collins
>
> (P.S. Because of a mistake everyone will get peanut ones this year.)

The front doorbell rang.

In suburbs like Mobridge, suburbs that are communities unto themselves and not truly sub-urban corollaries to a larger more concentrated population, most neighbors and friends learn to enter and exit a house through the side door opening into a porch or a kitchen. Dens in suburban houses, most often the front room, are more for show than for utility: they're where a family will place its heirlooms and paintings, the furniture too good to use on a day-to-day basis. The den serves as both a display and preserve for the small valuables the suburban house-dweller may amass in a family's lifetime. So it happens that the front door, equipped with both an electronic bell and often a fancy or at least functional brass door-knock, is for the most part never used. Exceptions might be religious holidays and family reunions, where the artifacts are more actively displayed, often also at times of mourning, andfinally in the case of strangers approaching the house. Nobody plays tricks with the doorbell on the much-used side door; even the local pranksters ring the front bell, then scamper behind shrubs or into the next yard to see if they have drawn the aggravated attention of someone expecting either a long-lost family member or a representative of the government, police, fire, what have you, or, in most cases, the brown bag of dogshit set on fire on the doorstep.

With this history well-ingrained in her mind, Polly strode

evenly if cautiously to the front door, and for a moment feared some complex reality might force itself upon her, burn through her gauze blinders: questions pressed on her suddenly as she reached for the door—had something happened to Tinsel? was she somehow in trouble with the law? how could she explain that huge brown rock sitting on her couch?

She opened the door. At her feet lay a box of peanut butter Girl Scout cookies. Somebody had opened them, maybe to sneak a cookie or two, had slyly cut a seam up the side of the box, but the cardboard had torn under the pressure of little fingers. Polly reached down to pick it up. Squirrels which had crept soft as snowflakes to within a few feet of the steps now watched her with sinister flinty eyes. Polly had never noticed till now how squirrels were just glorified rats, dressed up in their suburban best to match the way people arranged their houses and lives to seem removed from the visible wear of urban life. The closest one had his mouth open a bit in some unconscious expression of keen calculation and hunger. One tooth stuck out like a suggestion. Polly threw a cookie at him, missed him long by about a half-foot. The squirrel stood up on his hind legs as if to size her up, keeping his eyes all the time on the other squirrels, then dropped to all fours and flitted away with his prize. Polly closed the door.

She poured a glass of milk and sat eating cookies for a while, sufficiently engrossed in reading the lengthy roll call of ingredients, artificial and natural, on the box's torn side. The list bled onto the bottom flap, and as Polly pored over it she was so impressed by its journalistic compression that she found herself comparing it to other great lists, of the tribes and descendents of Israel in Judges, or the warships and armies of Homer; she mouthed the chemical compounds in measures of iambic pentameter, and her enjoyment almost brought her back to herself for a moment, made her pause. But not before she'd rested the cookie box over her letter to Tinsel, absentmindedly folded and sealed in the envelope instead the thank-you note from Maryella Collins, girl scout and cookie thief, and left the kitchen as it would be when Tinsel returned two weeks later, his farewell note covered with cookie pieces, tearless, the dry crumbs of her departure.

XIV. Incisions and Excisions

The shorter one sneezed as he forced the screen window. "Oh no!" he turned to Simon. "D'ya think he heard me?" Simon, ignoring his comment, planted a foot in his lower back and stepped over him into Doctor Fleck's den.

"Dear, dear doctor," entering the kitchen. Fleck dozes at the kitchen table, bowl of cereal before him and spoon-hand twitching. Simon watches him breathe, peers at the eyes skittering beneath the lids, judging the rem level. Deep sleep.

"*Mister Sandman, bring me a dream...*" Simon begins to sing softly, almost tenderly as he empties a small vial of milky fluid into Fleck's bowl, where, beading against the artificially colored chunks of chemically-altered wheat and rice, it makes its way to the bottom, invisible, awaiting milk. "...*make it a horror, make it a scream...*"

Simon's hearing may be especially acute, accustomed as it is to listening for the slightest hitch in a respiratory pattern; so the dry scrabbling he hears almost sends him back into the den. But, seeing the doctor still asleep, he tries to locate the sound's origin. It seems at first to emanate from behind Fleck's breastbone, as if something were scrambling around in there. But then he notices the crayons in Fleck's breast pocket, as if charting his dreams in disturbed technicolor, are shifting with each heave of his stomach against the plastic pocket-guard.

•

Dr. Fleck felt himself splitting into two separate beings the moment he woke up. He knew because he left one behind in his dreams, writhing beneath the manipulations and blades of a leering octopus and its shabby Indian assistant. The Fleck that rose from bed knew all his fears had been betrayed, his conscience sacked for the last time. Oh, he'd known fear and pain; fear and pain had spidered out of his miserable clucking body as they worked on him, extracting here and there maybe replacing an organ or a memory or a newly born thought. But now that part was gone, too, off to someplace safe. The thought of Venus occurred to Fleck as he opened his eyes. Why? He'd been having an emotion, just one type of emotion, the kind of emotion that one might have on Venus, he thought. Not necessarily a valid one, but definitely, nevertheless, from Venus.

An alarm sounded in his head. No, it was from the outside somewhere; he was still safe. It was harmless. He had nothing to fear now. He sat up, got out of bed, walked past the shaking alarm clock and picked up the phone.

"Hello." he said. "Hello."

"Dr. Fleck," the voice on the other end began. Like all voices from Venus, voices that must travel across a vacuum of incredible distance, it was totally silent. And Fleck began to listen.

•

"AND NOW, ladies and gentlemen, tourists and indentured servants alike, from the bowels of the Blue Mountains, far away from my air-conditioned view of Disney World but connected via satellite to Transmission Central at WEFC in the Eastern Florida Plastics Conglomerate Industrial Complex, it's your favorite and mine, pseudo-pro-populist-propaganda-pre-conditioner of the Annexation, the one and only–" a drum roll punctured by the blowing of a conch-shell horn, elephantlike, out of control— *"Phil Petrie, Talk Show Host!!!"*

Footlong's portable radio fairly vibrated with the conch-shell sound. He turned down the volume, picked out a large triton shell from the pile at the boat's fore, and blew into it, arching his back for effect. No sound: the opening was too wide to trap the air. He tossed the shell to Cletis, and then looked between them, where the man they had pulled unconscious from the water groaned and blinked his eyes.

Phil Petrie was a one man arsenal of media misinformation and twisted quotations, the Tokyo Rose for the Eastern Florida business community. Working on the idea that the Conglomerate's plans for statehood would stand a better chance if the locals could be softened up for the inevitable annexation, Partner & Partner had lured Petrie, a graduate student in white male history at Dartmouth, to plug the idea of economic expansion of the Eastern Florida business sector into the Greater Antilles. "Brothers, aren't you tired of dragging those fat luggage bags of thousand dollar cosmetic kits for sunburned, aging bloated white trash meat queens who save their pitiful income tax returns for a yearly Crimson Travel bargan bonanza to the slave-towns of Negril and Montego Bay, where you smile and yes maam and pander to the whitefolk service industry? When the Annexation comes, you can work directly for business, companies that *produce*, and produce *big*; no more cowtowing and bowing, no brother; here you'll work your eight hours with your friends, punch the clock and pick up your paychecks at the end of the week in hard American currency...

"An doncha know where I am today but the heart of the most bug-infested, monsoon-ridden, ne-an-der-thal-like holdout of Jamaican myth that's holding us all down, that's right, the near-dead ghost village of Moore Town, one of the last Maroon residencies on this island. Folks here still think they're something special, and you know the rap, magic, herb healing, voodoo curses, fierce independence, flying people—yes, you fat ugly white tourists who grew up sucking sugar daddies and watching 'Bedknobs and Broomsticks'—*flying people!!!*

"Today I will introduce you to the natives of this illustrious gas-stationless hole in the ground, show you the real thing, find no evidence whatsoever of things inhuman or supernatural save the babblings of yet another group of people held down from Economic Freedom by their own pride and pious myths!! ...then I'll be back for my late show in Eastern Florida, sipping synthetic berry soda with the recently discovered love child of Walt Disney...."

Cletis was looking out over the iron blue ocean and Footlong was humming "Whistle While You Work," his tanned forehead standing out against the blonde hair and blue eyes, and seemed distracted in his attempt to listen to Phil Petrie and take the unconscious man's pulse at the same time.

"Either he's dead, or his pulse is like a zillion-something," Footlong concluded.

"As long as you're taking my pulse with your thumb you'll be counting your own, too," he remarked as he sat up. The army fatigues, waterlogged and a size too big, covered him like a collapsed tent. Cletis could make out a jumpsuit beneath the uniform; it seemed white, but whether he was drunk or tired, he couldn't focus his eyes to tell what kind of material it was. The nametag on the uniform said "MAXWELL."

Footlong, who'd jumped back in fright and rocked the boat precipitously to port, bumped himself in the head and sat back down on a life preserver. "Blow me down! Resurrection, man! You fall out of a plane?"

"I'd prefer not to talk about it," the man grunted. He looked around. "Mmf. Jamaica."

"Got a cut on your forehead." Cletis said.

"Old war injury," the man chuckled, pulled his knees up and wrapped his arms around them.

Footlong threw him a pouch of fruit. "Ever had guineps?"

"Nope."

"The skin's tough, and don't swallow the pit. They're Jamaica's breakfast fruit, man. People eat em up." He leaned back to study the man as he bit into the guinep. "Good?" He nodded, hawking the pit over the edge of the boat. "Give a hoot! don't pollute, hyuk hyuk," Footlong said. "Hey man," turning to Cletis, "I'm still so wacked. Beemus' bug juice doesn't wear off for a day. So, the question is: are we dreaming this shit or what? I mean, is this guy really here?" He shook his head, blinked his eyes, held up his hand and counted his wiggling fingers:

One finger went to sea
Two fingers, look at me
Three fingers on the road

Four fingers catch a toad
Five fingers in a fix
Six fingers up to tricks...

"See man, I got six fingers. I'm still wacked. How about you, er–" trying to read the nametag, "Martwell, you got six fingers today too? Or maybe eight like an alien octopus come out of the water to see my uncle? Yaaah," spasming into chuckles, "yaaah man, Cletis, we're fuckin dreaming this. This guy don't look real to me. He looks like a, like a... *mass hallucination.*"

Cletis reached out to touch the man's arm. The rough pea-green sleeve was cold and wet, but with a hint of the arm's warmth beneath the fabric. But at the same moment his nerves register a second sensation: when he was six he had wanted to play a trick on Tinsel and Cozetta, and went around the house pulling all the plugs from the walls. When they came home he would tell them that Electro, the Spiderman's arch enemy, or his second-to-arch enemy, next to Doctor Octopus, anyway, had come in the house and sucked all the electricity from it. When he was pulling out a lampcord, the plug had stuck halfway out of the socket, just enough room for him to begin to poke an inquisitive finger between the prongs. The feeling that followed wasn't exactly a shock—he'd expected that to be sharp and sparky and yellow, like the mask of Electro—but a strange sensation of actually touching something physical and alive, something magnetic that he felt travel up to his teeth, some field that resisted his entrance because it would have to re-align his own energy field in order to make use of it. Touching this soggy officer now he felt the same resistance...

"I think he's real," Cletis said after pulling his hand away, "but I think I'm still pretty wacked myself."

They sat there, still for a moment, the man who had fallen to earth and the two young men who'd found him; then Footlong broke the silence.

"Well Fuckin-A!" he shouted, and threw a shell over to the man.

"Angular Triton," he said, more to himself than to Cletis and Footlong. He turned it over in his hands, felt with mild surprise a small glass vial in the folds of his sleeve, and slipped it into the shell through the wide aperture, where it wedged in the inner varice.

"Devil Fish Shell, in these parts, man," Footlong corrected him. "Long as you exist, you might as well share the language, ho hyuk."

"Friends and neighbors!" the voice of Phil Petrie yelled. "I have just knowingly inflicted injury on myself with a sterilized instrument of torture in order to test the claims of the established witch-doctor, I mean *herb*alist, in Moore Town, Miss Sassy Lassy Day. She now pats me with unnamed green leafy substance, and wraps my profusely bleeding appendage around and about with a further unidentified stalk of most unpleasant odor. Surely God in his great care never meant such a weed to be placed anywhere near human olfactory organs, but I seek *truth*, ladies and gentlemen, slaves of labor and slaves of the two week vacation, and providing I do not bleed to death on this unpaved road then truth is what I shall find, and we all know, or most of us know, anyway, that sometimes the truth just stinks..."

"Say Cletis," the man addressed him, gesturing toward the rucksack on top of the pile of shells, "whatcha got in that bag? I'm a little thirsty, I think. Maybe the guinep's making me a little ill."

Cletis reached for the bag. "I think I might have a Coke. Or a pineapple juice or something." He jiggled around the contents, heard the clink of a bottle against keys. "Aha. In here somewhere."

"Whatsa matter, man, can't you undo a double-knot?" Footlong asked. He hopped over to Cletis, upsetting both of them into the pile of shells. "Give it up, man! I'll show ya how to untie a knot, yukyuk," covering Cletis with shells. Phil Petrie's voice filled in the red cracks Cletis could see from the sun filtering through the smooth pink inner varices of the dozen tritons Footlong was burying his head with: "*Well*, Miss Sassy Lassy Day done did her damndest, dear listeners, but my bleeding is yet to be staunched. Luckily I've brought my own brand of medicine, my faithful assistant Hassan, registered nurse and ambulance driver, who is now attending to me with rational and resourceful treatments.

"Prayers and incantations, novices and novenas, my lucky listeners, fools and scholars alike, lead in the end to the miserable bonds of superstition, the aching physical and psychological pain of lame belief administered with dirty rags by totalitarian sorceress tyrants with IQs available for a quarter at most gumball machines! *If* your civilization is advanced enough to have gumball machines!!" A pause. "Boy, do I feel better now. Disinfectant and gauze. Direct pressure. That's what we need in these confusing times, natives and nuptial weekenders: a little direct pressure to bear on the wounds of this great island; a little social disinfectant to smear on the germs of our superstition and vanity, and a little gauze to wrap over the mouths of our supposed spiritual and medical leaders here in Moore Town, who do nothing but bleed our souls like leeches in the name of tradition and pride.

"Ladies and gentlemen of Moore Town, all you listeners out there mopping up the hotel mess hall or dropping hibiscus flowers in the toilets and gathering up the sheets, you folks *know* what I'm talking about. I'm talking about a little common sense. I'm talking about getting your proper due and peace of mind. I'm talking about secure jobs, independent of the volatile, and need I say *flat*, tourist industry; employment that will enable you to truly take back your own homeland! Let tourism die! Let the white meat queens freckle by their built-in pools at Stork Estates instead of along your pristine beaches, where they drop their expensive litter and release their expensive oily suntan lotions in your clear waters and drop their silk boxers and urinate on your streets in holiday drunken torpors! I'm talking the benefits of Annexation, of true American statehood, of the end of colonialism and the subtle slavery that keeps you bowing your heads and shuffling your feet and thinking there's any worth at all to the bass-ackwards tribal myths that some Englishman probably made up for you three hundred years ago! Why, I'm talking–"

But somebody had apparently had enough. Static briefly filled the airwaves, and when it cleared the sounds of a struggle could be heard.

"What the–" Cletis and Footlong stopped wrestling, sat up amid the mess of broken shells. Cletis' rucksack had come loose in the tangle, and its contents spilled over the shells and onto the floor of the boat. A new voice came over the radio: "This is Hassan. I yom Meesur Petrie's hehsistant. I will tell you this, I have seen it. Yes, with both eyes I have seen Meesur Petrie bin peek up by his neck an carree off, in de middle of em air!" A sob crackled over the static. "A flying mon have take Meesur Petrie. *Flying mon!!*"

"Footlong man, whadda ya think of." Cletis stopped the question.

"Whatwhat?" Footlong was still pulling shells out of his hair. He followed Cletis' extended arm to where it pointed: past the open rucksack, past the spilled contents, a broken bottle of apple juice, the weird logbook Cletis had found in his dad's hotel room, and the paperback copy of *Head Diver*; past it all to the place where moments earlier a near-drowned man had been sitting.

"Huh. Where'd he go?" Footlong asked. Cletis picked up a triton shell sitting in the puddle that outlined the shape of a wet body. Something glittered inside. Footlong was looking overboard. "No wake, man. That guy would have to dive like Mark Spitz to jump ship and leave no wake, dude. Cletis man, I mean this guy would have to be the Sub Mariner or some shit like that. He'd have to know how to *dive*, man!"

"Or fly," Cletis said, looking at the radio.

•

"Flying always brings me down," he was saying wistfully into the pay phone. His partner stood behind him, patting him on the shoulder.

"Simon?" The voice on the other end of the phone.

"That *is* what they write on my paycheck," Simon answered. He deftly elbowed his partner in the chin.

"It's the good doctor, Simon. He's become…"

"Unstable?"

"Unreliable, yes. Too much on his mind, it seems…"

"Hey hey, Simon…" the novice at his side again. Simon pushed the toe of his shoe into the back of the underling's knee, collapsing him immediately. He positioned his heel threateningly over the fallen one's breastbone. "Zyphoid complex," he whispered down to him, rubbing the heel in gentle cirles over the middle of his chest. "Instant death."

"So you can do it, then, Simon? We don't want it traced, don't want him to have a clue before he goes..."

"Oh, I'm afraid he's gone already; that is to say, I've anticipated this request and have recently, hm, fulfilled it..." the novice tugging at his pantleg again—would he ever give up?

"...already liquidating his stock..." Simon hung up the phone and prepared to kill his partner. "You've bothered me enough, cretin..." From the corner of his vision a speck moved into focus. A purple tattoo on the neck of a certain physician.

"That's what I was tellin you, Simon. It's *Fleck–*" looking up for forgiveness; but the boot is gone, and as he scrambles up to follow, Simon is already halfway across the street.

•

There were no tables open at the Cafe Redbeard when Fleck arrived. "But those two guys over at the table for six," the waitress pointed, "said they'd be willing to share, if you don't want to wait..."

XV. Signs and Stories

Nobody saw the posters go up, but by mid-afternoon they were everywhere.

On the sides of buildings, pasted to stop signs and streetsigns, wrapped around trashcans and telephonepoles, a letter-sized sheet of xerographic bond with the following copy:

BIGFOOT BEACH PARTY!!
at Benford Beach, sunset till ??
with music by Tequila Mockingbird
ALL INVITED

Beneath which was what appeared to be a photocopy of an article from that week's *Jamaican Jug* entitled "Bigfoot Sighted in Blue Mountains??" The article was written by Soviet scientist Valentine Sapunov, with help from *Jug* staff writer Eduardo Blum, and included a grainy thrice-reproduced photograph of what could have been a huge hairy anthropod, or a tall man running through the woods, or a close-up of a beaver standing on its hind legs, depending on which suggestion you heard first. Miss Octawim, tending to Dr. Fleck's paperwork and looking out her office window at the quiet post-lunchtime street scene, claimed she saw a yellow zygodactylic claw, that kind with two toes projecting forward and two backward, press one such poster onto a nearby lamppost; this sighting may be tempered somewhat by the observation that Miss Octawim suffered from myopia, a visual defect in which distant objects appear blurred because their images are focused in front of the retina rather than on it; Miss Octawim was also feeding Dr. Fleck's parrot Flange at the time.

Flange, whose feet were both yellow and zygodactylic, and who had been repeating a single phrase for three and a half hours, on which more will be mentioned later, had nipped Miss Octawim's finger rather unmercifully, given the fact she'd only reached into his cage to retrieve her spectacles—which she'd dropped while feeding him—amid the clutter at the bottom of his cage, old copies of the *Jamaican Jug*, scattered pieces of food and shit and wood shavings; at any rate, upon rushing to the street and reading the poster she then decided she'd seen a large *hairy* hand, revising her view perhaps to better fit the context, or, just as likely, to spite the offending parrot.

Dr. Fleck saw the poster while on his lunch hour; Cletis and Footlong, out and about the Yallahs area, raiding the many guinep stands along the travel roads, eating the fruit to cure their hangovers and spitting the pits at passing cars, spotted the poster on the side of a one such vehicle. And Footlong, a few minutes later down the road, discovered upon biting into one of his guineps that the pit seemed to be a crumpled piece of paper; and opening it and flattening it on the road he saw it was another copy of the poster.

Felix Mendolsohn found one pasted to the under-side of a toilet lid in the men's room of the *Gregorian*; Healey and Field saw one clamped in the bill of the stuffed red-breasted merganser behind the bar in the Rose & Thorn. Jay Valento and Efrain Romero, who had just bought some weed from a guy on a bicycle riding by their beach house, realized halfway through their second joint that they'd been using a copy of the poster for rolling paper; they were mildly surprised to see their band billed as the entertainment, and wondered aloud and at great length how they should dress to go see themselves play, and whether it was even worth going to see a band whose stuff they already knew so well. Cozetta, having a crawfish cappucino in the Redbeard Cafe, found her check written on a shred of the poster, and ordered four more cups in order to get the whole story. She left the Cafe at about four-thirty, the caffeine high humming in her ears like a swarm of bees, and walked towards the Rose & Thorn to call on Tinsel, unaware of the two men watching her from the shade of the Headless Stupid, a news-stand of tabloid weeklies, who put down their copies of the *Jamaican Jug* without paying the proprietor, leaving them on the curb where Flinch, passing with his cart of souvenirs, would get the pages tangled in his wheels, and turn in anger to throw a curse on them as they followed Cozetta into the dust of the afternoon traffic.

Beemus found two posters stapled to the door of the Shack; and Witcover, gathering mussels at a rocky beach on Beemus' property, picked up a poster floating in on the tide; on a quick trip to the Rose & Thorn to deliver the mussels to Healey's kitchen, Witcover stopped in Tinsel's room and laid the damp poster on Tinsel's chest as he slept. Whether it dissolved under the strange rhythms of his sleeping heart, or whether a yellow, claw-like hand reached down and snatched it from where it rested, Tinsel would wake from his nap with no more information than when he first lay down, his turtle tail in hand and cat curled by his head, his brain AWOL and idling, missing from the day and unaware even as Cozetta sidled up to him on the bed, her skin trembling from the cappucinos maybe, or who knows, reaching around him to place a hand over his heart and protect him in his absence.

•

As she lay next to him Tinsel was re-living the remainder of the previous evening in horrible film noir black and white, beginning with the moment he'd woken, disoriented, unable in the darkness even to locate the scooter whose engine, he thought, had probably entered into the earth itself to become a constant but distant sound in his ears. The night above showed no more than its square share of black continuity to him as he wandered, his face a mask of mud and worry, eyes washed out and unbelieving, re-assuring himself that Yallahs was somewhere near, a village or a bar or a bike path. But would he, covered in muck and wordlessly mouthing his relief, be mistaken for zombie or ghost, a monster or moon-crazed drunk?

But there was no moon anymore. Cozetta and he had lost one another going around opposite sides of a giant cottonwood tree; for at least a mile the vegetation between them impenetrable, catching mere slivers of each other's voices, the feeling of each step taking them farther apart, but no other way to go. Tinsel had tried, climbing into the branches, hugging the thorny darkness, falling for its little tricks, but the vegetation was devoid of sympathy, opened no avenues for him. Now he'd lost track of the time since Cozetta's last call, felt as if he were working a slow spiral outward, to the water's edge maybe, or was he only curling back around, after all, separated from the stem of his life, hung on the end of a shaving, so inconsequential to even his own story that his physical essence could be left out from here on in...

A branch whipped back Tinsel's head. He dropped his matchbook into the mud, ankle deep. Kiss it g'bye, pal. Brainy, brainy. That Tinsel's a real stand-up guy. But the sharpening of the dark that resulted clarified his sight enough to see, for a second anyway in the loping branches ahead, a real crinkle of light. He thought at first it must be himself approaching, time come around full circle, his last shaving nearing him on its own smaller winding; but then it seemed he was spared further confusion. The light had that smoky haziness one recognizes in campfires. He thought he saw the branches thin ahead, a small clearing maybe. His ears popped; he smelled the heady forest around him. And heard then the voices:

Maroons, and Tombs, and bloody Honeycombs
Mine shafts, and Pantaloons,
and no one to call us home
and no one to call us home
Us they calling woggles
Us they calling figures
Us they calling

Tinsel stumbling in and stopping the song, as if he were something consequential and elemental after all, the faces by the fire glancing up for a moment; then, as if by a mutual decision, looked back down at the books in their hands and ignored him.

In the moment of calm before the chant picked up again, Tinsel saw piles of books and pamphlets around each person seated by the fire. In one flicker of light all those faces looked similar, like acolytes of some strange faith, and in the next they seemed a conference of nations and ethnic diversity. He couldn't make up his mind so he just dropped to his knees, weary and feeling in some way welcomed or accepted, or at least safe. The chant floated through the air, coming from the trees and bushes like the chirping of crickets.

Us they calling bimbos
Us they calling senile
Us they calling wobblies
Us they calling dexter
Us they calling nigger
Us they calling xeno
Us they calling number
Us they calling legion

Legion, Legion; Tinsel walked beyond the campfire to a small cabin surrounded by low burning electrical lights. Outside the door a portable power generator hummed respectfully. Smoke seeped out the crack between the door and its upper molding, not the plastic smell of Torieton cigarettes or the car exhaust heaviness of *Aye Car-umba!* cigars, but a low register of leafiness and a tart feeling to it once the first wave passed your nose.

Two men spoke in urgent tones, one which Tinsel recognized but couldn't quite place, the other sounding more academically detached than the first, pressing his argument in a raised but unthreatening voice:

"It will take more than an adjustment of our habits," he was saying; "towns will have to die, whole counties give up their local culture, literally, as in mapmaking the word *culture* refers to the machinery of man, his bridges, underground tunnels, his factories; and indeed on these a town like Lincoln, where you're from, grows and settles and considers itself cultured." Tinsel peered in through a dusty window. The speaker, uneven teeth coiled around a pipe, had paused to re-light his tobacco. His pipe embers flared briefly, as did his nostrils, as he inhaled to catch his breath; then one by one, like the lights going out in a town seen from overhead, they blinked and were extinguished.

Tinsel rapped on the glass, then moved to the door and opened it. "Field! What the, how are, I was..." He sank into the closest chair, feeling suddenly his exhaustion. "Um, lost."

"You're okay," Field said, motioning to the other man, who went into a closet and returned with a jug. They stood silently by him as he drank.

"He must have a story to tell," the other said to Field.

"You bet I do," Tinsel hiccuped.

"No, Tinsel, he means you must be one of the folks you saw outside. They all came here with stories."

"Nobody comes to us by mistake, even if they don't mean to," the other man said. "I'm Dorfman, and this thing you've stumbled on is a regional meeting of the Polyversal History Group."

"Yeh, yeh, Tinsel, check this out. The guy Dorfman, his granddad or something started the Boy Scouts, right? But he also started another group, this Polyversal thing, where he asks the Scout kids to write down things that happen to them, their neighborhood, or the country, whatever, from their vantage point. Then they send him the stories, he keeps them, sends them another pad to fill up, and on and on it goes, huh?"

Tinsel, urgently, "Where's Cozetta? Have you seen my wife?"

"Wha, that lady's your wife? Whoa, *Tinsel*..."

"She's outside somewhere." Dorfman placed a dry hand on Tinsel's shoulder. Tinsel thought the man must be totally weightless. Hangmen would calculate a victim's weight by shaking his hand, and Tinsel, feeling no weight at all on his shoulder, wondered, Could this man be killed by hanging if he has no weight, nothing to make him subject to gravity? Was that what happened when you had all the facts and opinions of a century's worth of history? Did you become thoroughly without point of view, without gravity, unable to weigh one against the other? History had always been so heavy to Tinsel, even his personal history. He couldn't imagine it getting any lighter as you got more of it. Field took the empty glass from his hand.

"Boy, ya went through that wine fast enough."

"I thought it was water."

"Yeah, well. East Florida Chablis, same thing. Yukyuk." He turned quickly to Dorfman, as if inspired suddenly by thought, "Hey, you know I wasn't talking about revolution or anything; I was saying about, you know, how you have to live your life according to principles. I wouldn't suggest changing the world; no matter how overbearing a governing body gets, people will still form communities, trade information and gossip, make love to each other's husbands, and talk about how hard and fun it all was once they're too old to do it anymore."

Dorfman, lighting up again, "Yes, well I was not implying revolution was the necessary scale of things. I was pointing out its impracticability; even so, if it were possible, if people would sacrifice their culture, there will always be those who will see more to gain than a modicum of shared happiness. But here, without disturbing any social order, which we make and examine and justify as much as any of those in so-called Power, we can at least examine more than the commercial and official projections of order, morality, and the telling of events on a scale predetermined to glorify and necessitate government. In fact, the larger the event, in terms of scale, in terms of conventionally understood 'history,' the many more versions we have in our archives, because the number of contributors will be so high."

Field brought Tinsel a washcloth and more wine. "I met Dorfman here in the Rose & Thorn. Happy hour, right? I'm talking ducks to Healey for a free drink or three, and Dorfman next to me, he pulls out of his backpack a notebook he just got from some kid in Skaneatales, about his dad taking him duck hunting. It was wild, little boy language and stuff, but something struck me: he wrote about the motions of the brush, the duck leaving the brush, in the air, getting shot, the way it comes down, almost like a shape in the sum of the motions. So the kid says, it's like vectors, you add them up, the directions and force, whatever, the intro physics stuff he was learning in school, and the vector you make as the sum is the line of that moment in time. It shows you direction, man! Not just the duck, see, but the duck, the hunter, the brush and the bugs on the brush, all those things like one life, and the vector binds them. Pretty metaphysical, huh? But Tinsel, I thought, well maybe that's part of why I like to shot ducks, or shoot, y'know, pintails over grebes, shoot from a certain position or stance, it all adds up to a karmic thing, and then for a minute or two you're complete with the circumstances that make up the vector with you. You're happy."

"So Mr. Field is now preparing to contribute regularly to our Project." Dorfman gestured magnanimously. Tinsel noticed for the first time since he'd arrived that the entire wall behind him was actually pile upon pile of small writing tablets, dates and titles, locations and sometimes names handwritten on the spines.

"We're going to bind them together in archival bookboards," Dorfman was explaining. "Then they go to our primary location, where we distribute volumes, most at random but some upon request, to our contributing members."

"What if they don't return them?" Tinsel asked.

"They always return them."

"Fuckin weird, huh Tinsel?" Field picking from the closest pile and thumbing through it. "*They always return them…* Yukyukyuk."

"Some even send in a tablet filled only with reviews of the things they've read. They call themselves 'second opinions,' although that's a bit archaic a notion, assuming the subject complete enough through one point of view to criticize the view instead of recreating the subject. Which is what we all do, of course, whether we admit it or not. Isn't every opinion a 'first' opinion?"

"Where do you learn from, if you don't have any standard for history, or behavior or something?" Tinsel was scratching his head, starting to look at the door. Cozetta was out there somewhere, maybe reading, probably waiting for him to arrive. And he didn't want to stay too long in one place, anyway…

"Those stories are no *less* valid than these, as long as you realize they're not a word *more* valid."

"Aaah, listen to that, Tinsel." Field swigged from the wine jug. Its clay surface was dusty, and carved with at least a thousand tiny eyes. The motes of dust shifting as Field put down the jug made Tinsel think that the eyes were all moving, shifting in different directions. A thousand different versions of Tinsel Croom, those small viriations in angle? Was that what it was about? Field had cut in, "We need a standard the same way we need that culture you were talking about. It's the same thing. It's what we build and reinforce over time. We don't have to believe it, we just have to all stand there and say, Yup, we're all together, ain't we, and then go on back to our secret little lives, which we think are so epecial now because they're not the same as the 'standard' at all..."

Tinsel had rubbed his bleary eyes and slid out the door. A long piping sound from some distance away tickled his ears, like a horn of some kind playing one note over and over across the waves, which he could also hear, closer, lapping some invisible beach nearby, some meeting place for the nap of night and the shoring of certain evidence, that the sun would come up, that he'd find his wife, they'd get on a plane before anyone could catch them and sail over the clouds to a bedroom they'd never have to leave.

The chanting drifted across a warm breeze. As Tinsel walked towards the sound of the ocean, he heard other noises in the bush: herons and nightbirds moving slowly through the reeds, people rolling in their sleep over dry leaves, slapping bugs away from their skin, here and there a conversation in tones muted by intimacy, until all Tinsel could hear was the ocean, an insistent pulsing like the wind blowing through a basket, the hiss of water crashing and becoming foam and air, the swirling of immediate change; and as he felt the first wave creep through the sand beneath his feet, he saw the familiar shape of Cozetta's body, emerging from the water clean and naked; and he removed his clothes as he walked, the only things he had to prove himself, and splashed head-first in the knee high breakers, coming up for air around her thighs, nothing in the world solid but Cozetta, the uncertainty of her skin and bone, at the edge of everything leaning down to him her cool breasts, straddling him as he crouched there shivering, and he rose into her like an awareness that dawn didn't have to come, that she didn't have to leave him, but that it would, and she would stay on the edge here with him till she'd made her decision.

XVI. In Blackning Church

I. History Conciliatory

AT FIRST GLANCE, the painting did little to catch her eye. In fact she was drawn to look at it more by default; it hung on the only wall in Swelter's apartment not covered with topographical maps, meteorological data on tidal variance or yellowed pages torn from old Eldridge tide books, on a cracking piece of painted wall panelling over the dusty kitchen sink, from which Swelter refused to draw water because he didn't trust the local reservoirs. The open cupboard doors on either side of it revealed not dishes or the usual kitchen miscellany, but were stuffed instead with paperwork, printouts ringed with coffee stains, clipped newspaper articles, a pile of phone bills with red stripes along the edges of the envelopes, the doors themselves punctured with thumbtacks holding memos and suspended thoughts. A lone ceramic mug, and a wooden spoon stuck in a jar of hardening honey, provided some counterpoint; but it was natural that Edna look to the painting for further relief.

An eighteenth-century ship approached a dangerous looking iceberg. The style used was that pervading one which for the lack of a better word was often called *folk*. While the proportion, color, and minutiae of detail were well attended to, the final product had the kind of flatness, lack of depth, that made the ship's deck seem to rise from its hull like a roof, the water seem more like hair carefully laid on a pillow, the whole scene, iceberg included, the near, the far, the inbetween, eventually lay on a single flat surface that was distinguished from, though by what means Edna could not tell, the surface of the canvas.

Edna let her eyes wander down to the title, which was stamped on a thin metal sheet screwed into a maple frame:

The Island of Ice As It Appeared To Us

From The Prow Of The Thomas Mathew,

Samul Patrige, Commander, 1754

The canvas was dated July 25, 1754. Edna saw a few flecks of paint on the frame's grain. It was an original.

"I stole it from a museum in Maine." Swelter's voice sounded like a foghorn over the flotsam of crumpled paper he was sorting. Edna looked up, and he continued, his own eyes busy somewhere amidst the motions of felt-tip markers he moved with both hands across a map on his bed: "Oh, I know. But it was a college thing, initiation." He paused this time, and looked at Edna. "When I was a kid I had this dream about a ship of ice. Now, I guess when I saw that painting I decided I could settle for a ship and an island of ice." Edna realized that he was looking through her. She gave the painting another look herself; this time, perhaps caught in the vector of his stare, when she refocused on it the images seemed different. The ship's crew seemed to be attached to the deck at some indefinable point, as if they were equipment growing directly out of the planks of the deck; up in the crow's nest one waved his arms hideously as they began turned to rope. His knees were already metal bracings, his midsection melting into the mainmast. Others still appeared completely human, but seemed bolted to the deck like capstans, each face highlighted by an awful grimace. The waves beneath them now appeared to represent the movement of the iceberg towards the ship, as if preparing to board, as if it were some other-worldly vessel of water, navigating in its own substance, some phase-change communion taking place deep below, sidling up to the Thomas Mathew as it made ready to empty only-God-knew-what strange boarders or cargo onto the ship, what passengers teeming with anticipation behind the snow walls...

"Uh, uh," Edna stumbling back a step. But Swelter was still talking, "...were different, weren't they? Edna?"

Another quick glance convinced her it had been her imagination. She wheeled around casually so as not to give it another chance. "Who painted this?"

"Look on the ship," he said. "Those letters don't look like they spell out Thomas Mathew, do they? Right there—yes, your finger's almost on it. Funny, from a few feet away you could almost convince yourself that it's just the name of the ship. But look: it's mostly consonants, actually, appears to be nonsense, but it can be decoded with a traditional compass cypher by anyone who's familiar with that stuff."

"So what was his name?"

"He was," Swelter went on, "as the title implies, a passenger on the ship, though he wasn't listed in the log among crew or passenger or freight, even. I only discovered from the gentleman who lent the piece to the museum that the artist was a stowaway-with-consent, I guess you could call him: Captain Patrige had among his patrons a certain Mr. Njillson, whose fortune had come by way of, though not in knowledge of, the Catholic empire, who'd by then managed to infiltrate much of the Norse culture. I'm not saying that at some point in his young life he took the money and ran—not saying that exactly, anyhow—but he set up a surprisingly profitable agricultural community along the Sheepscot River region in Maine, or what would become Maine, and soon revealed his wider interests in his business contracts with Captain Patrige."

Swelter rummaged through a cardboard box beneath his bed. He held out a poorly-reproduced map. Edna took it, walked to the overhead light, and squinted. "This document was so light-sensitive," he explained to Edna, "that this is the best photograph I could get, no flash, you know; I made the photocopy so I could rub a highlighter over the characteristics I wanted to concentrate on. See here," pointing to an inlet labelled Ducktrap River; "somewheres about this river's mouth a boat from the Thomas Mathew would meet with a birch-bark canoe carrying two, sometimes three Indians. They were, of course, fellow conspirators in some such club, and any and all respectable settlers were more than willing to chalk up the mischief created by one secret guild or another as Indian trouble, so long as the prerequisite headband and face-paint were worn.

"One of the Indians would fall into the water and be pulled into the boat. There would then follow that sort of exchange that serves to show pretense of hostility, so any chance onlooker might think the Indian is being taken captive. Njillson was transporting something to Greenland on a pretty regular basis—Captain Patrige wrote in his own journals that he was under the impression they were dated documents, maybe taken away for security, to use for proving later land claims, mineral rights and so on. Once he caught a glimpse into a partly open bag carried by one of Njillson's men, and he swore up and down in his diary that the satchel was full of leaves." Swelter laughed, folded up the map and put it in the box.

"How it came that one of these carriers was a painter I'm not sure. Why he chose to paint that particular scene, when I would guess that close encounters with ice floes would be a regular occurence on trips North, is even less obvious. But the name of the painter: now that, thanks to a code as common to that time period as ice floes were to Greenland, that's something we can decipher."

He scratched out a diagram on a piece of paper. "If you write the letters of the alphabet around the points of a compass, like so...," scribbling, "okay, then label the compass points, you get this:

```
                    Y
                    U
                    Q
                    M
                    I
                    E
                    A
    WSOKGC                    BFJNRVZ
                    D
                    H
                    L
                    P
                    T
                    X
```

"Now write those four columns of letters along a single line according to a pre-determined sequence, let's say NSEW, or in this case, SWEN, and reference it to the alphabet below to get your cipher:

D H L P T X W S O K G C B F J N R V Z Y U Q M I E A
A B C D E F G H I J K L M N O P Q R S T U V W X Y Z

"Maybe he chose SWEN because it means *Swedish*, which might clue you in to a Northern source. At any rate, the letters on the ship in the painting which appear to be nonsense,

LDZBOV LVJB XJUV

become in translation *Casmir Crom Four*; maybe it means the fourth journey of Casmir Crom, or Casmir Crom the Fourth, which-ever you prefer."

"What's the little circle over the J?"

"Oh, that. Well, I'm afraid it might not mean anything, at least not grammatically. Though it might be a cue to number, or pronun-ciation. Names changed rather quickly at that time; English was bastardizing or simply stealing names left and right. It's likely that Njillson's associates, and Njillson himself, in order to make the name sound more continental, might have referred to our carrier-cum-painter as *Croom*."

•

Now came a paling of Edna's countenance that seemed so strong it might begin to draw Swelter's blood as well. "Where did you learn that? *How* do you know that name?"

Swelter tried his best to look nonplussed. "That? *That*? What is *that*? Let me explain something, Edna. I say nothing that does not arrive from great distances over intellectual terrain far too vast, too cruel, to survive in without reason. What comes out to you in the course of conversation, which you have so blithely referred to as *that*, is a form of such dense concentration that I can hardly begin to speak to the question of its sources without doing *more* research, without plumbing reason and language to the fringes of its emblem-atic vacuum, without in essence unravelling a suet-ball of history that's so yarny it includes your Aunt Fanny and my Uncle Genoa and

General Custer and all the popes of course, and you're asking me where did I learn *that*?" He touched an index finger pixie-like to his forehead.

"You want me to break it down for you, Swelter? I don't want the story of your life."

"Yes, yes; break it down. Names and numbers. And etcetera."

"How did you know to use that particular code? Where did you find that stuff out?" She took his mug from the cupboard, poured herself a glass of water from the kitchen sink.

"Don't do that," Swelter said. "You don't know what's in the water. Have a drink today and tomorrow you could be carrying the genes of a skunk." She emptied the glass in one gulp. "Your risk. You know there's more intelligent matter in that cup of water than in most New Yorkers. Combined." Edna's robe flickered and shimmered, reflecting a new impatience; she turned her head away from him and toward the painting above the sink. Oh ho, Swelter thought, something afoot indeed. And probably not your average size foot, either. At the same time his interest was piqued, some part of him shrugged the future off like a coat too heavy for him. He'd seen the look in Edna's eyes on others, too, that look of being so involved in connecting a few pieces of time and place, justice or injustice— take your pick, he thought, the *modus operandi*'s always the same— that they become blameless for the poverty of the rest of the puzzle. Some were martyrs, some became ghosts. None seemed to realize— and neither did he, come to think of it—from where the final sentence would descend.

For Edna, the time had come to be decisive. For her all the clocks in the world stopped as she made her mind up. For Swelter, it was a randomly repeating event, time accumulative bearing down by the zillions and departing like lost trains. They stood there.

"You have got to tell me where you got that story," she said.

"You have to tell me why I have to tell you," Swelter answered.

Then: the sharp double-rap of a fist on the door. "Who," Swelter calling loudly as he moved to the window; "Pizza. Fred's All Anchovy," and Swelter's "Yup, I'll be right there," motioning Edna out onto the fire escape, her globes musing like muffled windchimes as the two pick carefully down the rusted steps, Swelter peering one last squint through the window. As they reached the threshold over the first floor where they'd have to jump to the sidewalk, they bumped shoulders. "After you," Swelter encouraged her, and her returning stare was half mistrust, all ice and cotton, until they heard the door being kicked in. She drifted down to the street below while Swelter held still on the bottom rung for a moment, as if he had just slipped out of a fog, and seen that an island is no ship, and a ship is no island.

•

It is the night before the city is covered with crows, remember, before the black sweeps in and before the harbor is mysteriously cleared by a foghorn the size of a hand whistle... the night before Rizzoli's opening. So the evening baying out across the city can meet dawn even gently, prod awake the taxis, who've been positioned like mothballs in the corners of empty parking lots, who keep some substantial part of the city honest with dreams in other languages about new houses or dogs with wings, who'll only take you the shortest way you already know...

"Hey." From a thousand miles away a pack of hotdogs is leaping against his windshield. "Wake up, hey, open the window. Hey." He opens his eyes; the hotdogs fly apart, turn into Swelter's fingers spread over the windshield like a crack. "Will, you, let, us, *in?*" the fingers ask, tapping. The clock on the dash shows 2:35. Swelter and Edna pile in the back seat.

"Did you see anybody looking down from the window?"

"Nope. They won't come in– yet. Just check to make sure I'm scared." Swelter considers, then smiles. "I think I'm scared. But it's more because I'm curious as to how reactions, ethics, logic, all that stuff might change somehow if you're in a different state of mind. I think." Turning to the driver, "To Blackning Church."

"Black-ning Church?"

"Yes. You know the way? The shortest way, I mean?"

"Yes. The shortest way." He shifts into drive and the night goes fluid blue and follows them.

•

What can you learn about yourself on a dark taxi ride through the potholed sideroads and empty parking lots of a sleeping borough? Every building's eyelids are down, the attics' empty heads edged with indeterminate clutter; it's true that in the dark, something may squat and humble itself to its hunger, but in the end to the dust-mote gods it's all equitable.

The streetlights and the scratched rear-windows bleach out the stars. What Swelter was thinking could be whittled down variable by variable to a raw equation of mean values: he wasn't fighting enemies of the people, no side of the equation was higher than the other: but certainly one of the values was oversimplifying itself.

If Partner & Partner wanted to keep Pattern a secret that was their business, transparent as it may seem. But Swelter believed most strongly that Partner & Partner, diffused as it was, concentrating its true power on the edges, had no proper perspective from which to actually see Pattern. They were just trying to cover their tracks. He'd create an algorithm to wear them away, one permutation at a time, on any side of the equation they choose to hide and through all equal signs, until they were too small to cover up anything. The only unknown to Swelter was himself; how easy would it be for them to plot him, and if they did, would they wipe him off the face of the earth?

Three points can plot a line, curves can be identified by their tendency towards a certain equation. That would be easy enough, certainly, Swelter thought; but how do you plot a sea serpent? how do you plot an octopus?

A three pound octopus with one tentacle attached to a rock can hold a two hundred pound man underwater. Swelter, with his one arm around a submerged moonrock and a fistful of P&P short-hairs at the end of the other, could see in himself the final sign between the two values: all things being equal, he thought he'd find the weight of pure information stronger than all the best-coordinated flailings of a body out of its element.

You look like an octopus but you act like a rectangle, he told the night, the Partner & Partner building gleaming in the distance like a huge apostrophe trying to claim possession. From where he sat, thumping down Francis Bacon Street in a taxi, Swelter couldn't see possession of what; he was seeing it more as the architects had envisioned it, a ship out of water, a boat without a paddle, a fat vessel drydocked and belly-up.

•

Beneath Edna's cape things constantly moved. They corresponded to the bumps in the road, the heavy turns on the taxi's treadworn tires. The globes shifted restlessly. They shook within their spheres at yellow lights, passing patrol cars and billboards for TORIETON BRASS MONKEY FILTERED CIGARETTES. *Taste the Trace of the Ages*, the billboard commanded in three-dimensional pastel colors that glowed brightly due to a radioactive agent sprayed on them, *Grab the Brass Monkey.*

"Kiss *my* brass monkey," Edna mumbled, then turned to see if Swelter had heard. He was looking out the window, some sharp glee in his eyes, towards Manhattan and the Partner & Partner building. No monkey on that man's back, she thought as the taxi banked against a wave of oncoming traffic, she spilling nearly on top of him but he not noticing.

This morning at the Ottilie Orphan Asylum five letters had arrived at consistent intervals. The postman, recently relocated from Rhode Island, had come back every time with a new apology. The first, as simple as "Whoops, forgot this one in the truck," had stretched out to epic proportions by the fourth letter, something like "Must've fallen on the floor when I got out; then I stepped on a piece of gum in the street there—Fruit Stripe, I think—and then realized I needed to double-check the street numbers, so I jumped back into the truck and stepped on the letter, so it stuck to my shoes you know and, and errr..." handing the envelope to Edna, which was postmarked *Mobridge S.D.* and contained within it not Polly's terse farewell but Maryella Collins' insincere thank-you note, and which was indeed additionally cancelled with the gum-and-dirt impression of the recommended letter carrier walking tread. The last one Sandy McQuenchler found just after finishing his entire route; it lay on the dash languidly like it had been there all day. He offered no explanation when he approached Edna that fifth time, she reclining on a rattan chair on the Ottilie's short doorstop of a lawn. McQuenchler had never asked who Edna was, whether she might not have been the correct person to collect the orphanage's mail; it was his first day, after all, he would have believed anything. Except, maybe, that the last letter he dropped silently onto Edna's ample lap, this letter actually addressed to the Blackning Church, was one he'd missed fourteen hundred and ninety one previous times as it crouched patiently in a mailbox in Central Falls, Rhode Island, one written in the hectic hand of Donald Drycleaner and sealed perhaps by a man named Beaver in full witness of one sleeping Tinsel Croom and given eventually to Annie Aramanthra, a woman who'd received no mail for well over a hundred years and whose eyes were as large and flat as quarters.

•

Annie had been awake when Edna knocked on her door. Of course the rumors were that she never slept at all, though this wasn't true; she did take catnaps, worth about two hours a day. Her eyelids had dried into hard shutters decades ago, and their harsh unkind angle would not allow the eyes room to roll back up when she slept; so even as she dozed, pilgrims came in and sat before her, and emptied there the souls of the people they'd come to represent. Moments when her room was empty of visitors were so rare, in fact, that she never slept then, but took those minutes to look around at the walls and the ceiling, marvelling at the pure volume of emptiness. Emptiness was nothing in the vastness of space; but drape a small bit with borders, however arbitrary and however tiny the space, and emptiness became fully realized and meaningful. Such space was her most firm definition of *meaningful*, any definite volume of nothing trapped within perceived boundaries. It was her secret, her mantra, which supported her during the visits; the pilgrims, most of whom would leave after touching her cracked face or hands, went away feeling hopeful for their predicaments, felt they'd gained some strength from that touch, but in truth—another of Annie's secrets, if only for the fact that suffering pilgrims aren't too attentive to their idols—Annie was barren of empathy. She'd no moisture left at all. If you were to hold a light to her, send it hurrying down the cracks of her skin it might die somewhere within, so deep was her dryness, perhaps illuminating a bloodless bone before being extinguished. No one knows what kills light; dark seems to sneak in only in light's absence, but cannot invade or destroy it. But there was something behind those alligator eyes, constantly misting to make up for the lack of blinking, something hunkered down in the pores, crouched in her bloodstream, if she indeed still had a pulse, something in there that killed light dead.

"You're awake," Edna had said.

"I'm always awake," Annie sneered, but the communication of humor was impossible since her lips were hardened into a painful snarl, and those muscles that did twitch in response to her joke only loosened a carpet of salty drool down one cheek that seemed to be gone as soon as it had appeared, leading Edna to believe she'd hallucinated it.

"Annie Aramanthra, how are you," Edna paying the traditional respects.

"Just thinking of home," Annie answered. Nobody had ever asked her where home was. They'd all assumed it must be too painful to talk about. But Annie's childhood had been fine, her home a small farm in the Ohio River Valley. She'd had animals to pet, hard work to do, and no school. Home had been fine. When the Bambino Brothers Circus had driven their tents and animals into town, and her father had sold her for what she admitted was a healthy price to Oleo Bambino—she'd stopped growing at the age of two, and at five had already begun her strange puckering, which was at that time a moist wrinkling of her skin—she hadn't even thought *that* was bad. Oleo was good to her, she got to travel, do simple card tricks and make up horrible or fantastic futures for those who came to her seeking to learn what fate had in store for them. When she'd told a newlywed couple that in the bride's womb rested a boy who'd be killed in a house of lies surrounded by a country of broken houses, and when the woman's old slave had remembered this after Abraham Lincoln was assassinated, Annie's image in the eyes of the world had been irreversibly graven, and it was that year, 1865, that she began to dry and harden where before she had been at least as moist as a raisin. Oleo left her in a field one night as the circus was pulling up tents in a New Jersey town, after having no luck in attempting to listen against her chest for a heartbeat. She'd sat motionless for several weeks, picked at by curious crows, coons, a skunk and other scavengers, unconvinced herself that she was alive. She felt nothing of love or hate, fear or hunger, she neither took things in nor passed them back out, and when a picknicking family from Pembroke mistook her for an abandoned child ravaged by the elements she was brought to the Ottilie, where someone eventually recognized her and the visitations began.

•

The taxi ran over something solid and inert, barely avoided another object twice its size and skimmed across a puddle whose edges lapped calmly at the bottom inch of the side windows. Out on the margins of it some crows sat, dipping their beaks and shaking their heads like oil pumps.

Edna stared out the back window, watching that large shadow recede behind them. "What was that thing? Did any of you see what it was?"

"Probably one of those vans from the seventies," Swelter said. "Anyways, it's New York in the middle of the night. You never know what's out there." He was more concerned with whether the taxi had a rudder and motor in case the engine stalled in the small pond they seemed to be floating in.

"Will it stall?" Edna asked, looking at him. The taxi had slowed noticeably.

"She? No, no no," the driver, all defensive, "this is the *shortest* way." Swelter was jotting down some notes, street names and landmarks. Edna nudged him.

"Which way is the Hudson?" she asked. Swelter grimaced like it was a bad joke.

"It's beneath you. It's under all the rocks. It's in your drinking water." He poked her back. "Read your geography."

The water peaked in a resistant white curl that slid over the taxi's hood, then receded like the bulky shadow that preceded it, with a dark shrug passing over the trunk, quickly dropping below the level of the wheel wells. The dark outside seemed full of rootless business; Edna thought she saw things flapping at the edge of definition. She looked at the walls and ceiling of the cab, wondered at her sudden emptiness, lack of foresight unusual to her: what meaning would come from this odd meeting of her and Swelter? At that moment the only thing binding them were the four iron walls of the taxi, the small room they made for her loneliness, and the slim headlong vector they travelled along, winding now and then like a black creek towards some wider emptiness.

•

Annie's head had hung to one side as Edna introduced herself, and it had made her bitterness seem more quizzical or conditional. But then she summoned Edna over to massage her neck—"it's that side, yes; had an awful crick in it lately."

Edna had wondered in that moment before she touched Annie about where her home actually was, some place that made the vowels bend and shift and lengthen in a patient sort of way that made *crick* sound almost like *creek*. But when her hands touched the old woman's skin dry and deep-cracked like an ancient riverbed, she believed that Annie had never really been a child, after all, never had a home, couldn't have been born far enough back in the past to have aged so ruthlessly.

Massaging her neck was like kneading dry mud; though she couldn't see anything happening outside she felt that inside Annie's body passageways were crumbling, bones falling away and rattling down into some dusty antechamber beneath, she could feel the hairs on the neck give like brittle tree trunks after a fire.

"Alright, stop," Annie said.

Edna took off her cape and hung it inside-out over a chair. Annie looked at it admiringly.

"Nice globes," she snickered.

"I'm missing one," said Edna. She handed Annie the four letters addressed to Tinsel. "These are supposed to help me find it; but I don't know how. Show me how." Annie held up Polly's second letter to the light; played with the postage stamp, read the cancellation and smudged it with a dry thumb. *Strait of Juan de Fuca,* it read; through the smudge she could make out the frightened face of a mermaid.

"Who told you these would help you?"

"A cousin. A friend. A family connection."

"What's her name? What does she do?"

"Cattie Crowley. She's a... travel agent. That's her job. But she's the same blood as mine, Annie; we share the burden of–"

Annie wasn't listening. Holding the envelope she'd suddenly felt her wits leave her, all her words jump ship before she could stick them into a sentence. What was wrong with her? Why couldn't she think up even a simple lie to make this weirdo go away?

"Take this one," she finally said, throwing it at Edna, "and arrange the words in alphabetical order. Do it tonight, not now; then put it someplace safe." She was killing time. Her head hurt. Despair seized her, made her stupid. She moaned softly.

Edna must have figured she was in a trance, communicating with the moist spirits of the earth or ocean. Or even the desert. Even the desert was more liquid than Annie. The old woman felt gravelly suddenly, felt the earth twist against its grain, and the cape on the chair took on a passing shape or coherence, of a raven cloaking itself with a wing, revealing one steely eye which was able to look at both her eyes at once. Go away, she told it silently.

You'll be happy when I'm gone, won't you? it said. I never had help before, she told it, I don't need it now. It spread both its wings out, and in every black glint another bird roosted, and in their eyes another, and so on till the cape seemed a sieve of birds, of black beaks.

There are so many stories, it said all at once, you can't help but tell a truth this time.

Go away, she said again, and it did. The cape hung there, inert but still impressive. She noticed Edna staring at her, astonished; she must have spoken aloud.

"Come back later," she told Edna. "In an hour; two hours." Edna glared at her, suspicious. "Leave the other letters with me; take that one you're working on. Take it and come back in a few hours."

Edna gathered her robe around her and left the door behind her to slick softly shut. In the emptiness Annie listened to the faint sound of birds, of high air hissing through their feathers as they beat the wind into sudden, frightening shapes.

•

The taxi pulled up alongside a small brick church cramped between two taller apartment buildings. A black pad of water lay in the street like a welcome mat, and rolled away from the tires as if rescinding its invitation.

The front door was covered with a hardened crust of road dirt. As Swelter searched through his keys Edna tried to determine if the door was wood or metal. She pulled a dangerous-looking barette from her hair. A blade snicked out on its hinge from behind the abalone-colored shell.

"Woo! secret weapon," surprised Swelter paused in the midst of his key-ring; "very international, that. Very John Buchan."

"Who's that?" Edna asked. She stuck the knife point into the grit, jimmied a line across it at eye level. Before Swelter could answer a square-foot panel of dirt dropped from the door where Edna was chiseling. It shattered like a clay pot. The door beneath was oak, it turned out, and a sign carved in a thin sheet of pine was nailed to it:

ELDRIDGE MONTY ... VALUABLES

"I thought you said it was a church."

"Oh it is." Swelter was stuffing a key through the layer of dirt covering the key hole. It punched through with a pop of dust, and he turned it in the lock. "Look above you."

Set in a metal plate against the transom, worn down as if they'd been mercilessly patted by erasers for centuries, each letter fading like disappointed gargoyles, was the following:

BLACKNING CHURCH

"ad astra per aspera"

Swelter translated, "*To the stars through difficulties*. Haha." They went in.

•

In the foyer they stopped before two concrete statues. Swelter gestured left, right, introducing to Edna "Saint Terrence, Saint Granite. Saint Terrence founded the Blackning Church, way back in, ehr, well, nineteen-something."

"I never heard of Saint Terrence."

"Are you Catholic."

"No."

"Well, I don't think the Catholics have, either. Terrence was the leader of an inefficient Catholic labor union made mostly of Italian and Irish immigrants, most of whom did not speak English—not that it mattered, actually, since Terrence always spoke at their rallies in ancient Latin—called the Union of Absolute and Hopeless Order. Terrence's take on Scripture was that life was so precisely and beautifully—and I guess I should say *Catholically*—ordered, that labor's only job was to reinforce with Scripture its own poverty and low social ranking, and quietly go about the tasks of big business, supporting the machinations which would, Terrence thought, eventually bring about God's well-planned Apocalypse.

"Unfortunately his union members didn't understand that, and when they rose up in a spontaneous and quite *un*planned protest at Porter Bricklayers in 1924, Terrence came down to settle things and was clubbed to death by company-hired deputies.

"As for Saint Granite over here: he didn't exist at all. He was Terrence's manifestation of the individual's desire held in check by great strength, corporate strength, I guess, or maybe Divine, sort of a Pan-in-cement-shoes type of fellow. Real stand-up guy, haha."

Edna poked her knife into the dusty left eye of Saint Granite. Set deep into the concrete was a marble eye, like a playing marble, no pupil, just white swirling and dirt-smudged hints of some other colors. The right eye hole was empty. When Edna tapped her knife against the inner edges a spider scrambled out onto the blade and across her hand.

"Don't kill it," Swelter warned. "It could be loaded with toxins." He flicked it to the floor.

"From what I can tell, a few survivors fled the country and became monks or whatever you call them, holed up somewhere in the hills. LIFE profiled them when one of their members accidentally caused an avalanche yodeling; lucky guy killed two hundred fascists. And that's all I know. Anyhow, the next owner, Mr. Eldridge Monty, opened a collectibles shop which became a reliable fence for counterfeit money and imitations of artwork and old manuscripts and maps, as well as for the originals." They entered the main chamber.

Swelter flicked a switch on the wall, and a tiny yellow light cast uneasy definition over two rows of tables covered with framed paintings, cases of old coins hedged with blue velvet, piles of correspondence secured with twine, books bound in pigskin, leather, cloth and wood, locks and guns laying open to display iron chambers, plates and statuettes, reference manuals, stuffed birds with hollow bellies and wings held open with brass hinges, human bones, signed photographs and folios, all covered with a layer of dust and protective plastic of such elemental grayness that it reminded one of unconquerable landscapes, the Black Hills from an airplane or the Sahara in the last light of dusk. Almost every inch of wall space was covered by frames, photographs, felt craftwork, fabric wall hangings, certificates of authenticity, laminated calendars, college diplomas, newspaper clippings gone the way of parchment...

"Your kind of place," Edna observed.

"Oh ho," Swelter wagged his finger. "But true true." He blew dust off a black box and opened it. "Lookit this. Perfect forgeries of pages from the Ashmole Bestiary. Right down to the worm holes and nicks from the binder's thread." He lifted one sheet gently, held it to the light for Edna to see. "I believe a few of these are bluffing their lives away in the permanent collections of some of the stupidest and richest people in the country."

"How old is it?" Edna whispered. The page looked so frail; she was afraid a breath might undo it.

"About twenty, thirty years tops. But the original: where did it go?" He raised a finger to his lips. "Shhhh." He replaced the sheet in the box and examined another one. The painting was of a whale with nine or ten fins and a roundish, human head, swallowing two fish and being watched by three men in a boat. "DE BALENA," said Swelter. "The Whale. Only problem with this forgery is that artist did it for a semester project and *signed and dated* it verso," he chuckled. He flipped over the page and read, "A. Rizzoli. 1953. Rhode Island School of Design... Now you know this guy, right, he's a big name in the city these days. This is probably worth a lot of money."

"Why don't you sell it then?" Edna asked, acknowledging with her tone she was being egged on.

"Because," he said, "I like it. Ha ha," thinking for a brief moment about his own Leviathan: how close was Partner & Partner getting, right this second were they closing in, and was his creation closing in on them, inching bit by bit, haha, reaching out its electronic tentacles that would soon fill the color screen of the Victoria Room's navigation terminal with thrashing pixils, radiant fractals of destruction spreading exponentially over their pale ships and the files they represented, everything they tried to save curling up into oblivion...

"I should say, rather," he began again, "that I like this place as it is. Nobody knows I own it you see. IRS, Grandma Moses, nobody. My musty little secret, tee hee."

Any intelligent person could see that Edna had run out of patience. Her knitted brows twitched like rattlesnakes. Her nostrils flared. Her eyes sank deep into her skull and changed color. All this put Swelter in mind of his immediate situation, i.e. isolated in a dusty shop with a soul possessed of the will to affect history, one who drank from the city's water supply, no less, and it's no wonder at all that in the murky light Swelter began to visualize plagues of frogs, unsterilized hammers pounding his bones to grease, jackals licking his eyeballs, all kinds of intimations of his mortality, and faced with such finality he decided to get to the point. As best he could, that is.

Putting himself on the other side of the table from Edna, he reached for a leather-bound diary and began to read:

"From the Diary of Terrence John Wilder, unrecognized martyr of the Union of Absolute and Hopeless Order, from the twenty-sixth of May 1923: *The order of the air itself layered unto the firmaments and down to that lowest particle that passes through the bodies of insects and thus allows for their respiration—for they draw no breath but for the love of God and his System—and still further into loam and the blind runnels of worm and underground burns where the most fragile thread of water trickles among the ends of roots and through rock's hardenings all give glory to God through their need, their inclusion in his—and acceptance towards his—likely Terms! for listen! that which all need is most freely given, the air in its bounty, which nourishes all and can serve no economy and yet cannot be wasted.*

"Now don't lose your patience, Edna," Swelter said. "This is not the story of a wayward Catholic. In the end, or in the middle really, ho ho, it is the story of your mysterious painter. You asked me how I knew about him; here is how I knew." He continued.

Because I have not the ruminance to consider the complexities of the Lord's great System, nor the intellect, if such a gift be granted any man!—to translate these complexities into human terms without such faulty inflections as would reduce to gibberish the entire project, in short because I have not enough insight into His Will as would show me my own place and its eventual and glorious lapse into its elemental forms, because in essence—although it seem not my concern—that I do not know the time and the place of my death, now tonight I feel a sudden need to record some knowledge recently passed on to me which in its own manner both amazes me and stupifies yet also pleases me more greatly as an example of God's evident concern in the proper placement of souls throughout his Creation; and how the spirit is neither destitute nor powerless in facing the constrictions of time and place.

I will try to record all dates where I have them or can recall them since time seems to be the most intriguing issue in the accounts

I stand now to relate. Whosoever may find this diary, let him abridge not a word this account, nor summarize nor paraphrase, lest the pains I am taking towards exactness be taken as attitude, the exactness itelf for trivialities.

*So it happened that on the afternoon of December 19, 1923 I received at the Church a letter from one Evvie Croom-Smythe of a rather urgent nature. You may notice that this would mean I received the letter slightly under seven months **in the future**, since I write this on a lovely day in late May. And as the earth swings in its certainty around the sun and those fixed stars I can attest to having plucked the letter from my mailbox on the seventh of March 1923, two and a half months ago. But the postmark is clearly dated December of 1923, which in my absent-mindedness I did not notice until I had opened and read the letter, which was also not addressed to me at all, but to some German whose name has momentarily slipped my mind. Neither was the address ours at the Blackning Church, but rather another place altogether, which I shall try to bring up in good time; or, I should say, in the time remaining.*

I did not see the date, as I said, until I had finished reading the note, which engrossed me greatly. I include it here on this page, both envelope and letter affixed to this diary page with adhesive hinges, so that the inquisitive and cynic alike may satisfy themselves that the papers in question are whole and wholly authentic.

Swelter walked towards the center of the room, where the light was stronger. Edna followed him over, where they peered, ears touching, at a scrap of faded pink parchment; the penmanship a bit scrappy but still legible and dated at the top December 19 1923.

Of course this peaked my interest since it dated the arrival of the previous material sometime within the present month or thereabout; and thus gave me, at the time, roughly two to three months to determine just who the addressee may be, and how it came about that the letter was delivered to my Church.

But as I prepared to embark upon this mystery, the most astonishing thing yet drew my eyes to the right hand corner of the envelope. The reader of this diary may notice that the cancellation, initialled by the local postmaster, is indeed the 19th of December. More inexplicable, however, is the stamp affixed beneath it, a single two-cent stamp, from the mint year 1909, **the Abraham Lincoln birth centennial!** *Although one may believe that a postmaster may mistakenly approve delivery of a letter with insufficient postage, it would be absolutely unthinkable that an envelope like the one above would slip by any postman's eye, an envelope where the lone stamp is an unsullied example of that rarest of printing errors, the '09 Lincoln Slave Face Stamp...*

Even in the wan light Edna and Swelter had no difficulty making out the bright carmine edges of the stamp and the prototypical Lincoln profile in the middle, where the carmine had been mixed with an olive green used in printing the Benjamin Franklin issue two days earlier, the result being a milk chocolate presidential profile in high contrast to the rosey borders.

When the light went out seconds later, the carmine color still glowed in their eyes, outlining the now-invisible President, whose face nevertheless remained ingraved in the air as the color slowly lost definition in the musty darkness.

•

"No need to get frantic, now."

In the blackness three voices had spoken; two were in Edna's mind. One was the dry curdle of Annie Aramanthra; the other was Edna's own.

Annie Aramanthra: a phrase had become rhythmically attached, addended to that name in Edna's mind, a cause and effect equation that seesawed in some cerebral playground that still ranked rhythm and language above all else; it went up, it went down, but it never went beyond her ears, distributing its weight equally syllable for syllable: *Annie Aramanthra; Big Disappointment.*

What she couldn't get a grip on, to stop the crazy ride she'd been on, was either end of the seesaw. Ends were admittedly of necessity to one interested in stories, but Edna could find no ends, only middles that hinted at unblameable beginnings and that frayed off into the future. How was it that she, of all people, had been left waiting, stood up as it were, on the fulcrum, able to feel the disinterested balance more by a sense of inner ballast than the coveted facts that showed any game being played to its end... Ends eluded her. In the dark moment before Swelter struck a match her spine shook, and she knew that invisibly it continued in a vertebraic tail of ancestral bones, that her brain sprayed out beyond her to as many inconclusive thoughts as stars, that her ribcage could only balance it all, leave her motionless in the center of her own story, and the fulcrum, the unbearable point of it all, imbedded in her heart.

A candle lit up the room. In the haze she could see Annie sitting in her chair pouring over the letters, she could see herself pacing the floor; from above perhaps the footprints became interchangeable, meaningless dots on the Cartesian grid; or perhaps they could be seen to spell, unwittingly, what was dancing in her head.

For an hour they'd fortified their respective positions in Annie's room, defensive, wary of one another. Annie knew Edna expected too much, and Edna knew Annie was only looking for one last lie to lean on, but afraid she might not find one sufficient to send Edna on her way. She'd finally said, "Oh, these are in some code. I can't figure them out."

"What do you mean you can't figure them out? What *can* you do if you can't figure them out? What can you do for me?"

"Nothing then." A pause. "Alright? Nothing. Fuck it. I'm through helping anybody out. Alright? At last I'm telling the truth!" She'd tried to cackle, but only a hard short burp snuck out. She looked up at Edna. A brown film covered her eyes. "Now go away. No need to get frantic. People who need help will always find it."

Edna had left without saying a word. Every retort she'd considered had been hollowed out before reaching her lips, fallen like so many bird-bones into her throat and caught there. Now their ghosts were swooping down on Edna's head, flapping noiselessly demanding their bones back, soul-arcs of tiny anger light...

Swelter was waving two candles around her head, dangerously close to her hair. "*Woohoo*! No need to get frantic, nono; no spies on our trail, no salt on our tail. Not yet." The candles danced away into the dim squalor, Swelter's shape fading and re-appearing at the light's circumference as he negotiated a table and a pile of old newspapers.

"Over here." One of the candles hovered by a map. "Sugar Creek, Ohio, the year 1865. Just an ordinary census map, with names of the property owners next to dots representing the locations of houses. Note to the left the name S. Cornell: that's Sara Cornell, recently relieved of her abusive and drunken husband courtesy of Shiloh. Fifteen years pass just as sweet as candy, until word comes around the local drinking hole that the good Mrs. Cornell is harboring an Indian on her property.

"Now, any Indian who is neither working nor on a reservation is a no-good Indian. Sometimes it takes a while for the communal bile to rise, but by 1882 the townfolk get all the official authority they need to seize the Indian. They come into her house and face to face with the undesirable element himself, who introduces himself as William. He speaks excellent English, and Spanish as well. It's true, they're taken aback by his hospitality, by his gracious host routine, and by the fact that Mrs. Cornell seems to have left home for a few months in complete confidence William would be an apt caretaker.

"He's in his mid-twenties, it looks, and sits the mob down to tell them about his adventures on the high seas. Merchant marines? one asks. Something like that, he answers, although the idiom was most likely different back then, haha. Somewhere along the evening one of the men notices a map on the wall. It *looks* like the United States, excepting that the entire blood-and-guts center of the continent, Ohio included ma'am, are scooped out, missing. The coasts are linked by a succession of waterways branching from the east out of the Hudson Bay and from the west out of the Strait of Juan de Fuca. Sure enough, in the middle there's a dribble called Sugar Creek, but it looks a little too close to Seattle for comfort.

" 'You make that map up there?' one of the men inquires.

" "Yes," William answers, pouring him some more spiced tea.

" 'So where's Ohio?' the man asks.

" 'Ohio?' William seems confused. 'What's Ohio?' One of the men shoots the Indian in the head. They throw the body behind the woodpile outside, change their minds and drag it back inside, where they set fire to his clothes and leave the property in flames."

The candle rose and moved away, stopping further down the table. "Mrs. Cornell was away on what was to become a rather terrifying journey as her first trip for the fledgling Overland Mail Delivery Service—that's the Pony Express to you and me—carrying to the West Coast the important documents of the federal government and certain business interests from Boston."

Swelter's features disintegrated once again, reforming in a reflection on glass. Behind the transparency of teeth and arable nostrils a tapestry took shape. Swelter swung the glass door open, and his reflected face slid on angle along it and into the cabinet's dark latticework.

"Sara Cornell's travel map," Swelter said. "Kept in a moleskin pouch William gave her." Blue stitches mark waterways of the northern states, and brown stitches the paths forged and followed primarily by trappers. "She takes a route William advised, referring to a map William made from his travels. Skirting a large bay she sees a barque coming ashore. Three men are out of the boat when she realizes she's no longer wearing the beaver-fur beard William had woven onto her hat to change her appearance. She tries to disappear into the woods but they catch her. Two of the men hold her down, begin cutting pieces of her clothing off, the arms, the collar; buttons fly into the mud. The third man searches through her bags for valuables. Most of the letters were destroyed. When he looks in the moleskin pouch that has been thrown from her blouse as she struggled, he gasps, shouts for his friends to stop. He said only one word: 'William!'"

"Who were the men?" Edna asked.

"Here's where a Croom comes into the story," Swelter said. "According to the information Evvie Croom-Smythe left in her letters—which by the way arrived on April 23, 1923 at the Blackning Church, according to Terrence—our friend Casmir Crom, five generations removed from Evvie on her father's side, travelling on the Thomas Mathew in 1754, happens to be somewhere in the Hudson Bay when a violent storm hits the area. Why they were in the Bay is unclear; perhaps to pick up some more secret cargo, though the most likely reason is that Captain Patrige had some interest in the fur trade to Greenland and Iceland, and had some sweetheart deal worked out with the trappers. As long as the Companies didn't find out about this, everybody profited: the trappers got some extra trading, the Greenlanders got some lower-priced fur via the underground market, and the Companies could raise their prices on the legitimate European market if the fur harvest was not as high as the demand. After all, it was pretty much a monopoly, once you understand the dynamic between the Companies.

Unfortunately, someone on the Greenland end got greedy, tried to smuggle his take into the European market. Of course when the fur industry saw it had competition in a market where they supposedly had complete control over the raw materials, suspicions were aroused. Unfortunate for Samul Patrige, I should say; very fortunate for Casmir Crom."

Swelter moved along the wall to where a navigator's chart hung. "Look familiar?" "Hmm." "Pretty close to Ms. Cornell's little travel guide, wouldn't you say?" Along the margin was written *Notes on our Strange traveles after fynding William's friends, with drawings shewing the similarities betwen ours and the observations of de Fuca, del Fonte and others. Thomas Pepys, charter.*

"When the storm blew over about a day later, the Thomas Mathew had found itself in a dangerously narrow waterway they couldn't recognize from any charts of the area. About two miles inward travelling west they saw the grounded boat of the trappers they were apparently to meet in the Bay. The boat was punched through with holes, and the three men they recognized as their contacts were hanging by ropes from the nearby trees. In pieces.

"As the inlet was too narrow at that point to turn around, they were forced to proceed west. This brought them in twenty minutes to another small boat, and a group of seven or eight men enjoying a leisurely meal. This is the earliest record I have found, Edna, of the existence of the Partner & Partner company or any of its agents. But evidently it was by no means the first atrocity committed; the men rose from their lunch with all the extraordinary calm and patience that lifetime killers might acquire as a result of continued success, that gentlemanly attitude, haha, and they went to work. One waved a blanket or shawl in the air to attract attention. The Thomas Mathew began to lower anchor, and with the sound of the anchor hitting water another of the men had picked up his musket and with amazing marksmanship shot Samul Patrige in the left arm.

"The ship was theirs in a matter of seconds. Casmir Crom watched from his perch on the mast as the agents boarded, shot two of the crew and hacked off Patrige's left hand. 'For stealing what is not yours,' Crom overheard one say; 'and if thy hand offend thee...' As a result of his high vantage point, Crom was also first to see the glint of a cutlass in the trees along the bank; as a sword was raised to separate another of Captain Patrige's appendages from his body, a bowstring was pulled taut; an arrow shot through the branches, unseen by all save Crom until it imbedded itself to its black feathered shaft in the neck of the threatening agent. Hold on," Swelter pouring candle light over some papers on a nearby table, "oh; here it is. From the same logbook comes this account of what happened next: *Then did the murderer stop his parry towards the Captain in mid-thrust, gouting bloode from his both sides of the throat; and making unholy noises until he droppd to his knees, and strangely silent and composed then, expired.*

"Anyhow; in the next few minutes chaos, chaos; three men emerged from the woods, dark-sunburned, bare backed, hooting to one another in a mongrelized Spanish. In little more than five minutes they disarmed and disposed of the Company agents, making them look like helpless schoolboys where moments earlier they'd seemed invincible. What's more, these new characters exuded a certain joviality in their jousts, whistle while you work etcetera, speaking to one another constantly, laughing at their own indecipherable jokes as they were landing crippling blows...hm. Sorry; my language seems to be getting away from me. But they were–"

"The three trappers who attacked that woman."

"Yes." Swelter said. "Except." He wiped dust off the table edge, sat down. "You have to remember that time doesn't seem to matter in this story. The three trappers find Sara Cornell a hundred years after they slay the Partner & Partner men; but they carry with them the moleskin pouch they find on Sara. Casmir Crom sees it fall from one of their shirts and roll beneath a capstan. In all of these stories it's the map, you see; time merely being an effect of the story's range. If time's in the fabric of things, just another characteristic on this embroidery here, Edna, it can be wrapped and rolled and folded like anything else. The moleskin pouch, the map; they seem to imply that huge masses of land, like the Rocky Mountain Range and most of North America don't have to exist if they're not vital to the story being told. Is it possible? No no. Is it likely that Casmir Crom's moleskin pouch is the one referred to in documents on Sara Cornell? What we're asking here, ho ho, is, I guess not a new question; we want to know what can move mountains.

"In 1640 a Greek sailor named Apostalano Varianos, who worked under the name Juan de Fuca while sailing for the Spanish, navigated through a maze of inland seas and rivers he claimed flowed from the West coast clear through the continent. He claimed to have met another vessel that hailed from Boston, though he never identified the ship. They said they had found their way from the Hudson Bay. The record of Captain Cook's voyage thirty years later would ridicule these claims when he called what he believed to be the supposed entrance point to de Fuca's Strait *Cape Flattery*. Of course, haha, Cook was off course himself, a little south of the mark, should we say, below the belt, and then was blown past the actual entrance by a storm and saw nothing till he touched land on Vancouver Island. Now nobody believed de Fuca anyways; he was telling his story for anyone who'd buy him a drink, a down-and-out octagenarian who just happened to convince one of the more reputable cartographers of the time. Most people think he just entered the Strait beneath Vancouver, got lost in the inlets around Puget Sound, and made the rest up. Maybe he saw something that scared him. Maybe he had a vision. But the continent had already been marked with trails by trappers and hunters who would have had a good laugh over his ideas of the interior. But one thing's for sure: detail for detail, river for stream, inland for inlet, oh yes, Apostalano's map matches William's, and William's map is the centerpiece for all these stories. This map," gesturing to the wall, navigator's chart and embroidered map, "is that of history itself, in a way; stories are bound to it, bound within its boundaries, so to speak. The further we go the further we'll see the details of this place that somehow *did* move mountains."

"And how—"

"—de Fuca and William might have hitched up is another story that I haven't fit quite together yet. But." Swelter's eyes went sharp all of a sudden, and just as quickly he hooded them. "This is a funny thing you and I met. Seems like chance, doesn't it? But before I tell you anymore about what might or might not have been in that moleskin pouch, before I tell you this that or anything else, Edna, I want to know one thing: what piece of information did *you* happen upon that sent you on your single-handed assault on the Partner & Partner building this evening?"

Edna said nothing. "I know," Swelter covered the silence, "I know this has all happened fast, and that my explanation to you has been equally slow, elusive even. But I'm not an angel sent down to help you, or some spirit you've conjured. I've got my own agenda, and before I give away any free revelation I need some enlightenment myself." He pointed to her robe. "You can start right there. Tell me why your robe twinkles. Tell me anything. Just remember: it's not Edna's Glorious Triumph Over History Day. The world is not acting on your behalf; though neither is it acting against you. I'm certainly not. History won't apologize, and I'm not its apologist. But it's also not unbending. Find me a time when history—your history, Western history, Hindu Muslim Christian Jewish Napoleonic Germanic Australian Native-etcetera history—was 'pure', totally nonderivative or untainted. Now we may have a chance to inflict a little revisionism of our own into the Partner & Partner archives; but I want to know who I'm in league with. So tell me, Edna; what do you know that sent you on your search-and-destroy mission this evening?"

II. Edna Revisited

Was it really only earlier this evening? Dawn was just over a bump on the ocean, but the night was still smoky dark, filled with unseasonal chill and the sidewalks hissing steam. From beneath the city's skin gases could travel for miles before finding a vent through a random manhole. Standing over one such escape hatch Edna had been enveloped by all that stunk about life, the steam's face rising above her like a fist and closing its fingers around her in a clammy weightless grasp. She'd been wandering in anger, simply walking, past jewelry shops and rusty crosshatch gates of closed convenience stores. Between one such gate and the sunken front facade of Gil's Dodger Bistro, a black shape beckoned. It was a glob of darkness: from one end of it flared the butt of a cigarette; flared, dimmed, flared again. From another side seemed to come a cough, and from elsewhere a damp sneaker protruded. Rainwater collected in the cracks of sidewalk beneath the heel. Then from nowhere in particular came the voice:

"Hey Partner, you got some hemp? I'm as you kin see, hurtin a little, so I'm willin to negotiate." Something bristled against the cage; Edna thought she heard several voices. She had the feeling that hands were lingering in the dark near every opening.

"I'm *not* your partner, and I got nothing for you, and I am not your partner," she said, taking a few baby steps back before turning completely and walking quickly away. Behind her something slid against itself. "I've got eight big arms to hold you," it sang. Edna quickened her pace to the corner and ducked around it. Something made her stand there a second, and lean her head against the wet brick. From down the street, the noises stopped, replaced by a plaintive cry barely audible. "Waaaa," it said, as if it had learned to cry from reading comicbooks, "waaa, waaaa," sore and quiet it cried to itself, and Edna ran another two blocks before she was sure she no longer heard it, and bent down, hands on knees, panting.

Edna opened her robe and peered in. I'm not its partner, she said to the globes, I'm not its partner. *Oh but you are*, some faint voice whispered.

It would have eaten me, she said.

We'll eat you, the answer.

She turned in a circle, disoriented. A bike messenger, working into the evening, sped by her, missing her by inches. "Whoa! Sorry pardner," he called over his back to her, already half a block away. Over a moviehouse she saw a sign for *VENUS'S partS / XXX AWARD WINner*. The lowercase letters stood out, flashing a silent invitation, *part-ner; part-ner.* She went into the moviehouse and found a seat. On the screen two topless mermaids were rubbing their breasts against a skinny green elf, who was having difficulties standing up under the assault. His penis was also skinny and green, with a collar of leaves around the head. He looked to the sky and said, "Oh great Venus, which shall I ravage first? It seems there are no end of willing Partners!" From the right of the screen emerged a chorus of giant half-shells, who seemed to address the dark air above the theater seats with the following:

> From out the great hole
> Venus's parts shall rise
> Past the surface
> Of small men's lies

The elf, who had been searching in vain for the mermaids' genitalia, suddenly cried out. A furry creature appeared out of a mist and pointed towards the imp. "I am the Great Beaver of Venus! Now comes the time when you must pay for your orgiastic abuse of the Goddess's verdant springs!" One of the mermaids had caught the elf in a full-nelson; the other began sharpening a huge blade against a stone wheel. The chorus re-appeared behind the Great Beaver. "Beware," they said,

> for the wily elf
> has many great friends!
> Things can only get worse
> Before his energy's spent!

Two sea-lions charged as if on cue from the surf and a terrible fight commenced. One began tearing long strips of flesh and green

scales from the back of a mermaid; the Beaver grabbed the other by
its dripping fangs and whirled it over her head, breaking it in half on
a rock. Green bats steamed out from its body and flew in a blinding
cloud around the combatants. The elf broke free of the mermaid's
grasp and climbed on the back of a bat. He circled above them, piss-
ing at the mermaids and the Beaver, who was turning the second sea-
lion's head to snap its neck. The Beaver raised a fist to the receding
swarm above him as the chorus lamented:

Again the evil ejaculant
Escapes! But beneath his lip
He has unending promises
To hold his fright'ning Partnership.

"Ere long," the Beaver spoke up, addressing the half-shells, "I'll
sink my teeth into that failing flesh. Foul evil cannot but destroy
and break down what it please, but I, lord of dams and–" The scene
was suddenly replaced by a more conventional orgy taking place in a
penthouse with an impossible view of the Statue of Liberty. Must be
a loop of random film scenes, Edna thought. The crowd around her,
mostly raincoat types, who'd been quiet during the Venus segment,
now began wacking off with renewed enthusiasm. Edna watched for
a few minutes: women on their backs, women on their stomachs,
women on their knees, and come flying from men who would pull
out and stroke themselves to the climax as their partners held still,
mouths open or breasts squeezed together, like their world and
time itself had stopped when the men had disengaged from them.
The camera panned over them, frozen in expressions of heightened
desire, come dripping down their chests and necks. They look like
statues in parks, Edna thought. The movie broke for a commercial,
or so Edna thought; actually the entire scene was part of the commercial. The next shot was of a cigarette being lit, the camera gliding over the pastel filter to the mustacheiod lips of a rather normal
looking man, who lay in bed watching the orgy on cable while his
wife slept on the far side of the bed. His other hand was beneath
the sheets, where an exaggerated puddle had collected. "There's no

better partner after sex," the voice-over said, "than cool blue TORI-ETONS filtered cigarettes."

Venus's Parts resumed, with a tender if grotesque lovemaking scene between the Great Beaver and her husband, who were unaware of the presence of the green elf just outside their dam. "Screw this!" someone yelled, "bring back the commercial! Bring back the commercial!" The crowd picked up the chant, and Edna stood up to leave. When she got outside she realized she was in Times Square, had no idea how when she'd gotten there from the Ottilie. She didn't remember taking any train...

"Ha ha, fatty, you got yourself a partner under those robes?" a slender drag queen with an owl-face laughed at her. Edna reared back to strike him, but at the same time he pulled a stiletto from somewhere in his mink stole. The blade slid out of the handle without a sound.

"Now you know we were just havin fun, fatty," he said threateningly; then slightly more apologetic as he sheathed the blade and walked away, "Everybody's gotta protect themself. You do, too." He melted into the crowd. Edna moved into its flow herself, turning corners involuntarily and almost effortlessly, a long arrangement of right angles so that after a while she thought she was actually walking in circles, touching a huge circumference at tangents of equal distance from one another. She stopped to look at her watch. No watch. Maybe she lost it in the theater, maybe someone took it right off her as they walked beside her. Looking for a clock she saw the neon sign for THE HOUSEHOLD PARTNERS ALL NITE TOOL SHACK; crossed the street and went inside.

She bought the first thing that caught her eye. It stood propped against the wall under the sign SPECIAL: FORWARD-ACTION HEAT LAMINATED SLEDGE. (IF JOHN HENRY HAD HAD THIS DANDY, HE COULD HAVE BUILT THE TRANSCONTINENTAL IN A DAY!!) $29.95.

"If John Henry had really existed maybe 50,000 Chinese and Irish immigrants wouldn't have dropped dead building the transcontinental," a voice behind her said. She turned and sized up the man who'd spoken. Mid-fortyish, solid-looking and gray around the edges, wearing a baseball cap that said, "I visited Jamaica and all I got was this stupid hat, mon!" He stared back at her, then said, "Least that's what I read. Prob'ly in some communist magazine or something." He began to leaf through a book he was carrying, Bird Carving Basics: Bills & Beaks. "Um-hm," he said, turning a page. "I used to be a big duck hunter, you know," he told Edna. "But now I think I'm just gonna get me some wood and carve 'em, from memory or something. It's an artistic project." The back of the store was full of wood-craft merchandise, circular saws and pamphlets of stencil designs for plywood toys. Hanging from the ceiling were two carvings, a merganser in flight, and an alligator painted mustard green. A sign hung from his neck, saying "Life-sized model of last recorded alligator caught in city sewer. 1955."

"Should I buy it?" Edna looked at the sledge hammer, then at the man.

"I dunno. You got enough money?"

She dug in her pockets. "Yeah, I guess so."

"Well, get it if you want it. You, uh, going to be wor-king on the rail-road...?" he started to sing.

"When were you in Jamaica?"

"Oh, about a week ago, more or less. Hey hey, you wanna read something I wrote? About my trip and all, I mean. It's real short."

"Um."

"Oh please please, yukyuk!" He took from his back pocket a thin writing tablet. On the cover was an address. "Just seal the pages with tape and send it there when you're done," he said. "People just send stories there. You could, too." She folded it and put it in her cape. One of her globes spun out like a yo-yo.

"Hey, nice globe-thing! I saw one of them once."

"Where?" Edna, suspicious, as she picked up the sledge hammer.

"My friend found one." He grinned savagely, and laid a tentative pat on her shoulder. "It's in my story, yukyuk, I guess you'll just have to read it to find out!" He left the store. Edna began to follow, but a stocky man with a nametag reading PLOTTO intercepted her. "Ey, you wanna tek off wit the nightly special or what?" He nodded at the sledge hammer. Edna followed him back to the cash register.

"I was gonna buy it," she said.

"Sure, and Blotto sees lotsa them guys say they were gonna buy it." Plotto took her cash and cast a sideways glance at her. "But I believe you, I do. Nobody steals a sledgehammer. Ha!" He gave her the receipt. She hurried out but couldn't find the man. People on the street slid by at a uniform speed like railway cars on a greased track. She felt a corner of the writing tablet jab her stomach, took it out and held it beneath a movie marquee to read. The address on the cover was Polyversal History Group, c/o Dorfman, with a post office box number in St. Louis. She turned the first page. Hand-written in capital letters, MY OUTSTANDING VACATION IN JAMAICA and underneath that, 'Or: how my partner Tinsel Croom's son and I saved the day!!!!'

"Tinsel? Tinsel Croom?" she said out loud. She took out the letters she'd shown Annie; compared the name. Tinsel.

The rest of the title page was covered with pencil sketches of ducks, flying ducks, wading ducks, ducks leading their young, and at the bottom a duck with the notation 'pintail grebe' beneath its feet was holding its head straight up, its bill open slightly to accomodate a small globe, colored in blue crayon. The first sentence on the next page began, "It all started when we heard the story of the lady in red..." Edna hefted the sledgehammer and rested it on her shoulder, and was swept back into the sidewalk's motions as she read, never lifting her eyes as she crossed streets and rounded corners, went down stairs and boarded a train for the short subway ride which brought her above-ground one block away from the Partner & Partner building. When she finished the last sentence her mind was just beginning to assimilate it all, playing catch-up as if she were still reading the words themselves; so she didn't notice as she approached it the blue mailbox directly across the street from the Partner & Partner building, and she didn't notice as her hands secured the pages shut with a long hairpin and as she drifted past the mailbox how she opened its metal blue mouth and dropped the tablet into its dark belly. She didn't notice anything but the sober, dark curve of Partner & Partner, glinting with the light of passing cars and the last patch of moonlight the city would see before the next day when it would be shrouded in darkness; she did notice, quite suddenly, the weight of the hammer on her shoulders, the weight of her lineage hanging from her ribcage like ghost lights, and the weight of the globes jangling as she crossed the street and lifted the hammer high above her head; what she also noticed, staring at the unreflective glass of the front doors, and the high arc interrupting the sky, was that the Great Beaver was wrong, after all; evil may destroy, but it also builds.

•

III. Swelter Through The Gates of Wrath
"*YOU WHAT? You* mailed *the tablet?*"

He paced around the dark room in a jerky pattern; the candle he carried transcribed it in the air where it dissolved like invisible ink. "Wait. Don't say anything." He checked his watch. "Okay. Too late to go bust open the mailbox. Federal offense and all, hoho; it will be light out in half an hour. We'll have to intercept the mailcarrier when he does the morning pickup. At least we have a little time to plan things out, some kind of diversion maybe. It certainly would be worth the trouble of assaulting a representative of the federal government if that Croom mentioned in the writing tablet bore any relation to our Crom the painter and his Croom relatives.

"But there are two factors you should be aware of before you get too excited.

"First, the Crom/Croom line I've been telling you about ended thirty years ago. Monty got this letter from Thistle Croom's daughter-in-law back in 1961." He picked up a greeting card which had been spread open, mounted and covered with plastic shrinkwrap.

"Hmm. Now, apparently this Thistle Croom was in the information trade, like his ancestors: he was a regionally recognized horticulturist living in Utica, New York who made frequent trips to the Florida Keys. As part of an ongoing project with the Greenland Greenhouse Company he would travel three times a year to their headquarters and supply them with his studies on how tropical plants could be cultivated in colder climates. One of his associates in Florida was a Cuban national, also well-known in his corner of the world, who did landscaping for the well-to-do, both old- and new-money people throughout the state. Well, as the story goes, the Red Scare may have been softened since McCarthy, but not to a few neighbors in Palm Beach who noticed him talking softly to his plants. They shared some information themselves, and discovered that Thistle would come by on occasion to get seedlings from his friend. The neighbors suspected the plants were some kind of communication, and that there had to be a plot afoot that was more international than agricultural, haha.

"So of course they thought, given the nationality of the landscaper, that it was a Cuban-Soviet spy thing. The Palm Beach police let the Fed in on it, and Thistle hears he's under suspicion from one of his friends at Greenland Greenhouses, who hears it from an anonymous civil servant who represents his government contracts in the park service. When Thistle reads in the New York Times how his friend's been found diced into a truckload of pine-bark mulch—they identified him by his rings—Thistle was not only grief-stricken, but in fear for his own life as well. And from his own government! He couldn't believe it. He wrote a letter to the president that began, "Listen. God is very mad." He never mailed it. April 1961 saw the Bay of Pigs invasion, the incredible bungle when the anti-Castro forces weren't given any air protection, and President Kennedy going on TV and apologizing, and everything peachy, no outrage, no lasting impression on the American public. One day while his daughter-in-law was visiting, he became suddenly wordless. Here, let me read it to you:

Some part of him seemed to shut off, or maybe something quiet was turned on. He walked out of the kitchen and got his coat from the hall closet, went out in the garage and started up his car.

"A DeSoto, I believe," Swelter interrupted himself.

He put the car into reverse and never backed up. I was standing in the driveway, and I walked over to the side of the car. He was slumped over against the window, dead as a doornail. He had wanted to go somewhere...

"Indeed he was dead as a doornail, and no coroner would hazard a cause of death," Swelter handed Edna the letter. "Such an apt phrase to describe Thistle's last moments: he had seemed so fixed to do something or go somewhere, and that's what dead as a doornail means, actually, so fixed as to be immovable. But he was the last of the Crooms, I'm quite sure. I've got the whole family tree rigged up against the far wall there, all the way from Casmir up to Thistle. It was an obssession Monty had once he found those letters Evvie Croom-Smythe sent to Terrence; or actually, once he remembered those letters when he saw the painting I brought in his shop to get an, uh, estimate..."

"What about his sons? He had a daughter-in-law, so he must have had sons."

"Two of them, both dead before they could reproduce. Nathan Croom, the first son, died soon after birth; and Gentry Croom, who married Rose Tuesday in Tampa in 1958, was killed in 1959 when a five hundred pound rack of Nutty Buddies rolled off the back of his delivery truck and crushed his skull and spine. A support rim to hold the rack in place was apparently missing, although foul play was never suspected.

"Unless Thistle had a secret son, that's it for the Croom family tree. Now I know, I know, I know I know what you're going to say. Thistle had an illegitimate son. The Nutty Buddy thing was faked. A dead branch of the family tree spontaneously buds out a new Croom. I've checked them all out, Edna. I've double-checked them. I've dusted them for fingerprints. And you know what I've found? Zilch. Zero Information. Luckless me. Can't find nothin', nobody, nowhere, zilch.

"But suppose you doubt me further. There are still stories to finish that seem to wrap us all together. But as far as a current progeny in the Croom line named Tinsel: there's something you ought

to know; or rather, see." He reached across the table, towards a pile
of books, closed his eyes theatrically, picked one randomly from the
middle, and handed it to Edna.

The title?

Head Diver.

•

Annie Aramanthra was dreaming of President Lincoln again.

As with the other times, she and the President were bowling,
Annie setting up to finish her ninth frame with a tough bid for a
spare. Lincoln was drying his hands at the fan by the ball return.
"You'd need to force it into the 3-9 zone and bounce that seven," he
said.

"Keep to your own lane," Annie growled. Her approach was
a long seven steps because of her short strides. She sent the ball
straight at the three pin.

In her other dreams she'd never converted the spare; but she'd
also learned, gradually, over the decades she'd dreamt this string, the
lean of the lane's right boards. This time she'd see how far to the right
things had slipped. True to theory, the ball cut suddenly, nicked the
three pin before dropping in the gutter. The three popped across the
lane and toppled the nine, which seemed to take the seven out by
mere suggestion.

"Yes!" she screamed, pumping her fists towards the fallen pins.
"Yes!" She finished the tenth with a strike, and picked up seven more
to close.

Lincoln, who'd spared consistently with one strike in the second,
took his bowling ball from his hat. Annie sat fidgety watching him.
Lincoln's death had been the turning point in her life, though it certainly couldn't have been the only lie she'd told which came to pass;
most of her predictions at the circus had been so general that any
believer could find a way to match some event in their life to Annie's
promises. She'd just been feeling mean the day Lincoln's parents saw
her, that's all; mean and a little loose with the spirits.

"You're washed up," she told the President. "You need two
strikes to beat me." Lincoln turned his head and faced her fully; they

stared at each other for a few seconds, the cracked shrunken liar and the serious lanky Republican, a man she'd never met in life. Then he turned his attention back to the lane.

Lincoln, a southpaw, put all his action into the left channel, inside-outing the ball with a strong open-armed swing, loose at the elbow, releasing at the end of the traditional five step approach. He rode the ball hard on the right side; Edna watched it change direction halfway down and zero in on the three pin.

"No," said Edna. "No no." The one dropped the two four and seven like dominos, and the ball blasted through the three-five zone. The six pin, staggering,finally rolled obediently onto the back shoulder. A strike.

"Aaaaa. No no no no." Annie tried to cover her eyes with her fingers, but she couldn't help watching as the President removed another ball from his hat, hefted it and released.

She did close her eyes then, and when the sound had died away she opened them to see Abraham Lincoln, sixteenth President of the United States, all six-foot-four-inches and one hundred and eighty pounds of him, reaching to put on his hat. Behind him all ten pins lay like the crumbling remains of an ancient civilization.

"The union of these states is perpetual," he said.

"No no no no no no no," Edna woke up in her rocking chair. A crow was pecking at her windowsill. She rose to shoo it away but recoiled when she saw what it had in its beak. A dried apple core, animated with black ants, suggested a face with deep cheekbones and a beard running along the jawline. The lips, three ants struggling over a desired particle, twitched silently. Annie could see now that it was a red ant in between them, trying to escape. Its thorax was already half-severed. As they closed ranks on it, the black lips closed, and spoke no more.

•

Back in her dream Abe Lincoln was waiting for her, holding his bowling trophy, a painted ceramic eagle in lifelike landing posture, attached by its golden talons to a bronze bowling ball resting on a wooden base. Annie's name was engraved on the front. TV cameras

surrounded him. Keys to a car twinkled in the air. As she walked
towards him he raised the trophy to his lips and kissed it. The eagle
fell forward and shattered on the floor.

•

   "No no no no no."

   "It's all true," Swelter told her as she leafed through *Head Diver*;
"or should I have said, it's all fiction, haha. Look," grabbing another
copy of the book, "Mr. Holm even made a character based on myself,
in gratitude for the use of the unofficial Croom family archives here.
Twenty signed copies of the first edition, and my likable attributes
inscribed for the ages in a best-selling book. Not bad for an unem-
ployed computer nerd with a chip on his shoulder, hm?"

   "But but." Her body felt wrapped in uncomfortable heat, as if
the globes she'd been swathed in since youth, her people's legacy,
were heating up around her, angry coils, upset at their betrayal...
"But what about the letters?" throwing those out on the table, "what
about the booklet that man showed me in the hardware store? What
about Jamaica?"

   "Jamaica. Yes, well I admit it's all interesting enough; interesting also that you conveniently mailed the booklet that would have
given your story the strongest basis in fact–" He waved off her objec-
tions, "–no no, it's not gone yet, of course. However, as you probably
know, anybody could write a few letters to a non-existent person,
just as anybody could write a story about his adventures in Jamaica
with that nonexistent person. But I'm not saying I don't believe you.
I'm not saying something isn't funny about all this. These letters,"
looking them over quickly, "these might prove to be written in some
code. Who knows? Another Partner & Partner expatriot like myself
trying to loosen a few screws in the Company's secret toolbox? I
might not be the only one. But you might ask yourself a question
before we go on, before we try to break a few laws stealing mail,
before we go back to my apartment to consult my computer: why,
you may ask, am I still convinced enough of the integrity of your
search to give you my confidence? How do I know you're not an
agent of the Company, they who come in so many shapes and sizes,

from what I hear, from what I've read... To answer these, I'll have to continue a bit further into one of my stories.

"Well. Now we've seen how the journey of the Thomas Mathew was unfortunate for Captain Patrige, who thereafter carried his estranged hand in a leather pouch attached to his belt. When particularly drunk and angry, he would often challenge a fellow drinker to a brawl by throwing down his own hand as a gauntlet of sorts. Life of the party, haha.

"But for our man Crom: the bird's nest gave him a view sufficiently removed from the chaos below to allow him to watch all the fighting simultaneously. From that height was conveyed to him a sense of the harmony in which the three newcomers moved while sparring, and easily defeating, their more numerous opponents.

"He also saw, I think I mentioned before, a pouch, fallen from one of the engaged men, kicked in the scuffle about the deck until it came to rest in the shadow of a capstan. When the battle was over and the Captain tended to, the brigands introduced themselves as privateers in the service of the British empire, acting under the orders of one Captain Henry Morgan. Everyone on board the Thomas Mathew knew this dated them to be living in the wrong century, but no one was quite willing to quibble at this point, things being as they were. The privateers explained they were looking for a crewmate of theirs, a Mosquito Indian called by them William — I say called by them because the Mosquitos did not give themselves names; but when resisting Spanish invaders in the 17th century they found sympathy with the English buccaneers, they requested their new friends to give them names, and insisted on English names, like John, Henry, and William. These pirates, under Watling at the time, had been at anchor at Juan Fernandez island when Spanish vessels were sighted and they had to leave with great haste. There they left behind them their friend William, who had been in the woods hunting a goat.

"For two years William avoided the Spanish, who landed often on Juan Fernandez to look for him and take him captive. However, one evening William spied a group of them eating by a fire on the beach. He crept upon them easily, and actually sat just a few feet behind one of the men in the circle, stealing his belongings one by one and searching the beach sand for a good-sized stone.

"Eventually he found one, and, retreating a few yards, tossed it into the fire, where it sent up a shower of sparks and caused some confusion among the Spanish; enough for William to steal away with a landing boat and its supplies.

"Now it happens that the man whose pockets William picked was none other than Don Fernando Povo, a particularly mean-spirited man whose chief achievement was the annihilation of an unarmed village of Arawak Indians who'd formed a community with escaped Negro slaves and fled deep into the Blue Mountains.

"Povo made it a point to track them down with his own personal army. Though doubtless a few survived—and my theory is I'm speaking of your distant relatives, your great-great-great-great-etceteras—the slaughter was distressing even to the Spanish throne, who would relieve Povo of his most influential responsibilities.

"Among Povo's pockets William had found two items of interest: one was a small blue globe, a magical sort of thing..."

•

If an alarm could go off in William's head—William the computer, that is, Swelter's bloodless ally—it certainly would have. Though to be fair to those who cannot respond to criticism levied against them, the metaphor might fit more for a computer than a person. An alarm, after all, is a dispassionate thing: a metal stick wacking its shell, a battery-operated horn sounding regardless of whether the house is occupied or not. It's based on the simplest behaviorist principles, which are after all dispassionate themselves, stimuli and response. Smoke passes through a plastic grid and the horn sounds; a laser beam is broken by an unauthorized foot passing through it, and a light flashes at the night-guard's desk.

Anyways, one gets the picture. To react with alarm is to show emotion, worry, perhaps anger or despair. It might be fair to say that had Swelter seen the raw data rolling evenly from William's printer, had he picked it up and analyzed it, his face might illustrate alarm in a way befitting a 19th century psychiatric study of alarm phrenology. But he's not here, and William responds to frightening information in the only way he can, translating pure current into words and graphs. The room seems no more nor no less charged than moments ago. Still—it can be said, so let's say it!—an alarm goes off in William's head.

•

Edna had never been clear about her origins, how and what lines had been diluted along the way, who'd succeeded and who'd failed in the quest for reproduction. So faced with the beginning and end of her ancient history in the space of a single sentence she faced the issue with politic dispassion, and made the necessary, and for her most important, link.

"My globe."

"Possibly. The other object was a tiny leather volume, of whose contents I have no information other than that perhaps it served as some kind of talisman or charm against what was written by enemies' historians.

"It was upon these two objects that Casmir Crom laid his eyes when he opened that moleskin pouch two weeks later. The pirates had explained to the crew that if they kept sailing west they would hit the Strait of Juan de Fuca in a few weeks, and from there they could skirt the west coast of the continent until they found the isthmus, by which they meant California.

"Captain Patrige, hardly in a mood to be humored, decided to call their bluff, and, leaving them behind to continue their search east, headed the Thomas Mathew due west.

"From there they sailed straight into the past.

"They hit upon a strong river. The land sloped up around them until they recognized a mountain peak to the northwest of them. Not the Rockies, but Mount Olympia itself, hoho. The river emptied them into a bay of sorts which could have been Puget Sound. They cruised along the Sound until it opened into the Strait. Was this the Strait de Fuca entered, the one Cook missed?

"The Thomas Mathew anchored on the Strait's southern coast.

Casmir took a few of the crew out for a trip to see if the Indians would trade with them. They found the local tribespeople gracious, if a little cautious initially, and exploited them much as Cook's crew did, exchanging coins and small tokens for blankets, bows and in some cases women and children. We don't know exactly what those Indians made of our arrival, so it might not be so fair to indict them as uncaring or the like. If someone parked a spaceship in front of your home and made themselves out to be great travellers you might let them take your son or daughter with them too. You might even be convinced you'd met your maker, hm?

"Casmir Crom, by the way, perhaps feeling a little guilty, allowed himself to be bargained out of his shiny blue globe by a fair-skinned, light-haired native seeming intent on possessing it in exchange for a gold bracelet engraved with the face of a local celebrity. Here is in fact," Swelter going back into the dusty cabinet and coming out with a plastic bag, "the very item, or at least a good forgery of it."

"Ugh," Edna peered at it.

"So it ain't Elvis," Swelter said. "Here. Consider it a gift from the past." Edna paused ruefully before slipping it over her wrist. Unfortunately it fit perfectly, even looked a little better against her forearm. "Is it real gold?"

"Really, Edna. You'd think you believed there were Wal-Marts or something back then. Of course it is. Now listen. Two more things happened. Later that afternoon Casmir watched the strange-looking Indian row out over the Strait alone. He and a few of the crew followed behind in their own boat. They were pretty certain they weren't seen. The Indian stopped at what appeared to be a rock protruding only a few feet above the surface of the water. They had been rowing for a good hour or more, and the crew, impatient, decided to confront the boy and see what he was doing.

"By the time they got there, though, all they found was a canoe tied to an underwater plant. The water was too shallow to continue on in the dark, so they returned to the Thomas Mathew.

"The next morning Captain Patrige woke them with a great shout. They rushed to the deck to see a ship as large as theirs, decked out to fight and flying the Spanish colors. A few barques were already lowering into the water.

"Now the Thomas Mathew was only a trading ship, a messenger ship, but nevertheless it was more than capable of defending itself for short periods of time. Maybe Captain Patrige chose the right course when he set the men to hauling up anchor; maybe he just wanted to keep his other hand. As they caught the breeze the Spanish ship gave chase; but it soon became apparent that the pursuer was of an older, less wind-worthy form than the Thomas Mathew. And when the captain and crew became aware of this, and of their safety, they raised the flags of their patrons in Boston to signal their lack of respect for the Spanish flag. When the cannonballs shot a few minutes later landed well short, the crew of the Thomas Mathew let up a whooping cheer, and then went about their business, sailing eastward towards, eventually, Geenland."

Swelter held the candle to his watch. "Well. Time certainly flies when you're living in the past. Up all night and we still haven't caught up with the present. We still need answers. Like: where did that Indian boy go with your globe?

"I happen to have it on good authority that certain information dear to me in the present has been hidden for safety's sake in a computer-generated version of a map of this country. Yes yes; imagine a map, a landscape where each hill tells a story, each rise and fall of land is significant, a country consisting solely of images whose only precision is geological; to create the country as a whole, its version of history, the Company has to distort local reference—like the railroads did away with local time for the sake of their schedules—or hide that local reference away altogether. Thus some points of local interest that would be embarassing to the Company's public relations drive, things personally collated by a colleague of mine, have been dropped for safety's sake in a sunken island in the Strait of Juan de Fuca. Now I'm not saying history repeats itself, Edna. I'd never suggest that. I do think history imitates itself very consciously, however; events give themselves nuance that way, flexibility and resonance. And all the stories I've told you can be found by anyone in forgotten books in the local library—or in that gem of a map, if you know where to look.

"My confederate, whose work I supervised while still employed by Partner & Partner, had access to these stories. And I believe he used them. Of course, there's only one way to find out. But first," he said, heading towards the foyer, where he'd hung his keys around the finger of Saint Granite, "we've got to go play Post Office."

Edna began to follow, stopping to gather the letters and a copy of the book. The dustjacket of the limited-edition hardcover was a special holograph, reminiscent of 3-D baseball cards Edna'd seen on the street or on sidewalks as summer had shut down: from one angle it was a mosaic of historical events, from 20th century war scenes to cavemen fighting over a wooly mammoth, with a few natural disasters, tornado, thunder and lightning over the desert, thrown in to show off the 3-D effect; when you turned the book at an angle, the collage solidified into a single man's face, his features dulled by the helmet he wore, and on his forehead a single horizontal eye, like the ovoid Seahawk's eye on the professional football team's helmet, staring ahead with neon red intensity.

So, she thought, in here somewhere was Tinsel Croom; just a thought in someone's head. Swelter was fiddling with the lock on a wrought-iron gate behind the Saint Terrence statue. "We'll go out the side exit," he said. "I don't like people to think the building's occupied."

"Swelter?"

"Yes?" He stood, still as a statue himself, candle-light flickering off his throat and masking his face.

"*Head Diver*. Is it any good?"

He grinned apologetically. "I've never read it." Edna followed him out, taking the candle with her.

•

Four heavy industrial screws twist upward from the corners of a square bed of cement. Weather stains substitute for the crime-lab chalklines, illustrating the borders of where the mailbox once stood, had in fact stood for twelve years, before its abrupt departure.

The postman's hands hang at his sides. He can still hear, in his skull somewhere beyond his eardrums, the beating of great wings.

"What the hell happened to the mailbox?" Edna coming up on the run to the postman. Swelter trails behind. It's the time of the morning in the city before things get going, when the litter twinkles like off-off-Broadway, and everything smells faintly of wet metal. There's also ozone, like a crisp trail of leaves, which rattles in Swelter's nostrils.

"I was comin to collect the morning mail," the postman starts. He looks familiar to Edna. Edna looks familiar to him.

"Where did the fucking mailbox go??!" she shouts.

"Up. Up there." He doesn't bother to point. It's beyond seeing now.

"A what? –a helicopter?" Swelter finally arriving. "One of those military planes with the hinged wings? An Osprey? What was it?"

"Ship, I think." Edna passes her hands before his face, waves furiously at him, produces no blink.

"Is he in shock?" she asks Swelter.

"I don't know. A ship, huh? What kind of ship? A rocket ship?" They give up, start to walk away.

"We've got a lot to do. Let's go."

"What happened? Should we call the police? The ambulance?"

"Yeah. Let's get back to my apartment first."

It's the twilight of Sandy McQuenchler's career in the postal service. What was it? What was it?

"Ship, ship of. Ship of bones. I think." Sandy says it to their diminishing backs. He looks down. The screws twist up to him. He looks above him. Did something wrinkle in the air? It's the last time he'll say it.

•

They climbed up the fire escape and into Swelter's apartment just as the sun broke the horizon of tenement buildings and churches and turned the air around them the color of old newspapers. An early morning drizzle had left the streets with an oily dew. A New York Post delivery van cruised in silence through the neighborhood below them. The poster on its side announced the day's headlines:

RIZZOLI OPENING TONIGHT!! Also, BIG SURPRISE FOR
BIG APPLE BIGWIGS!!! with a photograph of the mayor wearing
a George Washington era powdered wig. The mayor, of course, was
a shareholder in Partner & Partner, and the delivery van was a sheet-
metal contraption that was motored beneath by two pedaling delivery boys who took Doctor Wan's healthy bribe and were dropping a
couple thousand copies of Rizzoli's fabricated daily. "Even more fake
than the real McCoy," Wan had confided to the delivery boys.

One of them slipped a chain switching gears as they passed
Swelter's building. The unmistakeable noise richocheted off the
brick and iron outlay of sleep, a few people hitching awake early and
not knowing why, others hearing their alarms tick in their ears and
dreading the inevitable lukewarm shower and dance into sweaty
clothes that would follow; Edna turned her head on the catwalk, half
in and half out of Swelter's world, his computer still gnawing lati-
tudes and position data, and for a moment she saw through the illusion. But it made so little sense she dismissed it before the message
made it back to her brain, and she believed what she originally had
seen was indeed the reality, a lone van on the street below.

"Ooo-wee," Swelter said from within. He was looking over some
printouts William had produced while they had been gone.

"What is it?" Edna shut the window behind her.

"Our pursuers caught up with me last night." He was helpless
to control his glee. Edna didn't bother to ask the question. She knew
he'd answer it anyway.

"Oh no, though, we're not sunk, nono, not sunk at all." He
waved her over to the screen, where seven toy-yacht shapes surrounded his blinking sloop. "The one in the middle, that's us. Those
lighter ones, P&P lackeys. Or should I call them, respectively, say, sea
urchin, abalone, uh, blue crab, uh, sea squirt?"

"What do you mean?"

"They're a bit too close, don't you think? What do you think
will happen?" He positioned a blinking cursor over one of the ships,
and pressed the Enter button. Immediately the screen zoomed into
a close up of the ship, which gained no further definition upon

its enlargement, remaining a two-dimensional toy-boat. Around it, though, blue and white fractals were squirming and churning.

"Looks like a storm," Edna commented.

"I'm sorry, your answer must be in the form of a question!" Swelter pushed a pair of 3-D glasses with paper frames onto her head. "Here now. Looklook."

Huge tentacles had twisted up from the foamy waves, squeezing the flat hull. There proceeded a dramatization of great destruction, the octopus rearing up out of the water and tiny stick figures representing megabytes of P&P documents on file jumping ship and landing in the creature's open beak...

"Crunch, crunch! Look who's come to lunch!" Swelter giggled. "This is exactly what those oafs at Partner & Partner are seeing on their high definition video screens right now, albeit with maybe a little more color; they've been up all night, Edna, trying to catch me, going for broke, and now they're sitting there with their cold coffees and their egg sandwiches, and they're watching all their files being turned to nonsense by Octopus appollyon, a creature in fact native to those very waters. Call me a teuthologist! Call me a legend in Sardenia! Call me Old Man of Poulpeville. It's almost too much for them to bear, I do believe. Crying into their styrofoam cups this moment. Ah well." Stretching spidery arms above his head, "I'd be refreshed by some coffee myself, now that I think of it. I'm going to skip down to Blimpie's. Want anything?" Edna shook her head. "I'll get you something. We've got a lot of work to do before we sleep. Promises to keep, and many miles–" he hadn't quite finished paraphrasing Frost while opening the door when he realized someone was standing directly outside it. Momentum carried him through the motion, and a tall figure waited for them in the bloodless hallway flourescence. The pizza man.

XVII. Good & Evil

"There will be no errors tonight."

The voice came from behind a pile of broken beach chairs and torm hammock netting stowed by the changing rooms at the northwest corner of the beach, where the sand turned suddenly to pine needles and feathery shade. The dusk's shadows had already started to gather there, while the sun still played glitter games with the tide and kids ran out to the surf for a last swim. Halfway down the beach Tinsel and Cletis were working on a sand sculpture, hurrying to finish before the light was gone. The sky was paling on the edges of the sea, and by the time Cozetta had returned from the travel agent and found them shoring up a two-foot high floodwall the wet sand was cast incarnadine with its lingering light. Between the two, sky and sand, the ocean was flat and dark dimpled like the skin of a giant alligator, glistening, waiting.

"You're not gonna need that," Cozetta toed at the wall. "Tide's going out." She knelt beside Tinsel, who'd returned to the sculpture. "What is it?"

"Thing is," Tinsel conspiratorial now, pulling Cletis over into the impromptu huddle, "we don't know exactly."

"Haven't reached a satisfactory conclusion yet, that is," Cletis added.

Amidst the tangle of hammock frames a match flared, and blue-black smoke rose through the netting and evaporated. "See how they're talking over there," a new voice said. "They must know something's up, huh?"

"Nonsense." Embers glowed briefly in response to the question.

"Please give me the gift of your continued silence. Croom knows nothing. He knows almost as much nothing as you; the only difference being, of course, that you are being paid for being a hindrance to me, while Croom is doing it at, shall I say, great cost to himself, hm?"

People were starting to arrive for the festivities. A motorboat ferried overnight guests from the *Gregorian*, which was anchored half a mile offshore. The party of five stepping ashore with flaming drinks in hand had just lost some indeterminate amount of money betting on reruns of old Lakers-Celtics NBA playoff games. Out into the surf they jumped and made a semi-circle around Tinsel and Cletis. Elsewhere a few roadies were hooking up sound equipment on a raised platform. Across the island car headlights were blinking on as if some pleasant circuitry had been activated, and certain confusions of the day and its glare had been replaced with these shared precisions of light. Bug-lamps on beach house decks freckled the shoreline, and as their smaller echo the five tourists standing around Tinsel held their blue-flamed drinks up against the night.

"We call them Flaming Lakers," one told Cletis. Cones of sugar rested on the rims of their wine glasses, each bearing the uniform number of an offending Los Angeles player. These were doused with alcohol and set afire, where they burned into a brownish glob that settled at the bottom of the glass. "My friends!" one said, squinting at Tinsel and Cletis' sculpture, "is this not a scale reproduction of the parquet floor of the Boston Garden? It sorta looks like that."

"I don't think so," said Tinsel. Everybody had their drinks, and the one who'd spoken ran around the sculpture's borders, a fake here and fancy-footwork there, yelling "Havlicek stole the ball! Havlicek stole the ball!" disappearing into the haze as his drink was extinguished.

"So I got the tickets straightened out," Cozetta was saying into his ear. She took time between the words to brush her lips against the cool rim of his earlobe. "We can leave around ten tomorrow morning.

"And I got a ticket for Cletis." She looked at him. "I thought maybe you might want to come to New York with us, see my studio. You know. Spend a little more time."

Cletis got up. His kneecaps were caked with wet sand. It reminded Cozetta of when he came home from his first football game. It had rained hard most of the afternoon, and the wet uniform had settled against his body, making the pads over his shoulders and knees look even more prominent. Cletis unconsciously wiped the sand from his legs, and Cozetta saw how much he'd grown, without too much help from either of us, she thought, glancing quickly at Tinsel.

"I don't think I can do it, Mom," Cletis said. He wasn't looking at her. "I've got only two more weeks before I gotta head back to school, and I've barely taken any photos for the summer credit I'm supposed to be doing. And, you know, it would just make things hectic."

Tinsel, true to form, didn't get it. "What, can't you take pictures of the city? We could drive up to Niagara Falls or the Finger Lakes, right? It could be just *like* a family outing–"

"That's what I mean, Pop," Cletis interrupted. "It would be like a family outing, but it wouldn't really be one. I've been away from home for four years now with school and all, and the only time you've both come to see me is what, when I get attacked by a manta ray? What do I have to do next time, fall off a cliff or something? I mean, it's great you two seem to be getting along fine, it really is, but on the other hand that never meant that you'd be better parents to me."

"Okay Cletis," Cozetta cut in on Tinsel's behalf; "I think your dad gets it now. Huh Tinsel?" Tinsel nodded. He looked like an abandoned snowman, arms uncomfortable, wondering how to hold back spring. "You *know* we love you, Cletis," Cozetta continued. "It's not that we didn't try. It was just time or something. So much gets in the way."

Tinsel had faded into submission. He was squinting at the sculpture, eyes hardened and moving quickly as if trying to read it, whatever answer lay hidden in the thing they'd built together without thinking, just messing around together as the sun went down.

"Yeah, okay," he said. "I never said you got your brains from my side of the family, Cletis. Come to think of it, I don't know where you got your brains." Cozetta punched him lightly.

"At least I know where I got my sense of humor," Cletis deadpanned. Cozetta reached out to the two of them and drew them in for a brief embrace. When their three faces touched, they drew away, embarrassed.

"Heh heh," Cletis said. Then he was yanked violently from behind, a hulking shadow enveloping him.

"Aaaaa! Kung Fu Beach head Sea Monster!! Waaaugh!!" Footlong, clad in a scuba suit and a giant turtle shell, spun Cletis over his head until he collapsed beneath him. Cletis rolled him over on his back and sat on the dark green belly.

"Aaa, the sun!" Footlong waved his arms and legs. "I'm frying! Someone turn me over, man! Yukyuk," as Cletis stood up. Footlong squirmed out of the turtle shell.

"Oh Dad; some guy named Witcover left this in your bedroom. With a tail, too."

"Yeah, I saw it this afternoon. Stunk up the room," Tinsel said. "That cat seemed to like it, though."

"Hey, I forgot. There was some kinda book in the shell too. It's in my backpack up with our stuff."

"Yeah yeah. With our Magic Shell," Footlong tittered. "Magic Man fell out of the sky and gave Cletis special powers."

"Huh?" Tinsel and Cozetta exchanged wary looks.

"We were both trashed on the beach this morning, and we *think* we pulled some guy out of the water."

"You saved someone's life?" Cozetta asked.

"I don't know. We were both still really drunk, and he jumped out of the boat before we got to shore. I think he might have been a mass hallucination."

"Do two people make a mass?" Footlong asked.

"Anyhow," Cletis poked at Footlong with his elbow, "he gave me some shell or something. But Footlong remembers that part better than me. Prob'ly cause he made it up."

"Uh huh." Cozetta waved it away. "Was I the only one sober last night? Enough, enough."

More could have been said, but they quieted amiably enough; further up the beach Tequila Mockingbird's drummer Cooter was beginning his sound check, and each snap of his snare drum seemed to hang low, and hover about people's heads, reluctant to fly.

•

When the pizza man had gone, and things hadfinally stopped falling and settled into a messy silence, Edna raised her head and peered about the room. Swelter had taken the worst of it, falling backwards almost immediately and taking three or four bullets with him. Edna had dropped to the ground as if she'd been shot, and then she had been, after all, catching some shrapnel off a wall or table. The pizza man had quickly turned the room inside out, upending a table over her inert body and emptying drawers and cupboards before leaving and shutting the door behind him. One thing remained on Swelter's desk, miraculously, the computer's video screen somehow unscathed, Edna's cape hung over it like a protective cloak.

On the floor in the middle of the room a disk drive was whirring, choking, whirring. Edna realized suddenly that it was Swelter. He was beneath the upturned bed, splayed out starfish-like. She knelt by him.

"Swelter? Are you okay?" She saw he wasn't, tried to dig an arm out from the open file cabinet to take his pulse.

He managed a raw whisper. "William... is William alright?"

Edna's ribs hurt. "Uh, yeah. He's alright, Swelter. The light's still on and everything."

His head turned on his neck. "Ah," he said. He gurgled something she couldn't understand, coughed a bit.

"Right," she went on, "he's just fine. I'm gonna get you some help."

"N-nuh-no." He struggled some to continue. "Puh-puh-print-out."

"Okay. Okay." She crawled over to the computer. Onscreen the octopus was dismantling the last of the Partner & Partner ships. A longitude-latitude reading was blinking in the bottom right corner. Edna looked for the PRINTSCREEN button, found it. From under a pile of books and chairs the printer revved its fan and got to work. After a few seconds of moving things, she emerged with a single piece of paper and held it high so Swelter could see it. Her ribcage was groaning against its own weight inside her. She felt the warm flow of blood down her right hip.

"Ta daaaa," the pizza man kicked open the door. "Always double-check your work!" he moved through the rubble towards her. She lifted the computer terminal and heaved it at him. He had to move to avoid it, and by the time he'd regained his balance Edna had reached the window. The first bullet dug into her left triceps. She made no sound as she threw herself through the glass and down to the street below.

•

Beemus hiked his shirtsleeves up and belched. His legs were up and his sneakers rested on the table's edge. A bug flew into his eye and he squelched it out, rubbed it on his shorts. He put down his nephew's book, bending a page back with his thumb to mark the place. He rummaged in the cupboard for another lens cap, found the hole in the screen and plugged it.

"Hawhaw," throwing a few bottles of Nun Bubble into a paper bag, "I knew that smartypants was gonna git it." He nudged the door open with his knee. People were lighting small fires on the beach ahead. A bass guitar played the intro to "Walking After Midnight".

It was going to be some party.

•

"Take this," the man at the door said.

"We-we, we didn't order a pizza," Swelter stammered.

Ignoring him, the pizza man dropped a large pepperoni into Swelter's arms. "Sorry I forgot the free colas," he said and walked away, leaving Swelter in the hallway.

"Uhm." He backed into the apartment and closed the door. Locked it. Bolted it. And placed the pizza box on the floor between Edna and him.

"What is it?" she asked. "A bomb? A clue?"

"I dunno. Heh heh. Let's open it."

They did.

•

Turned out it was a pizza.

They sat on the floor eating while William cheeped, clucked, whirred. Swelter's boat lay alone in open water, "all P&P participants having since been dispersed to Davey Jones's locker. But they'll come back with heavier equipment now that they've seen me."

"And?"

"And, they'll be eaten. But till then, we can only let William do his thing."

"What is he doing?" Edna asked.

"Narrowing our options. Scanning the depths for a submerged piece of rock. I guess there're plenty of them to go through. But he's getting closer. Every time you hear the printer run off another line, that's one more knob of mud he's disqualified. We need to find a rock that pokes its head out of the water at low tide. If we find it before then, we dive and inspect. Blow it open if necessary. Who knows."

"How long will it take?"

"I dunno. It's like a long-division problem. Every second we get a little closer, but it could be like solving for ℗. It might take all day. We might get closer and closer and never arrive. Between any two points is an infinite number of other points. You can keep dividing space in half forever."

"A video-game addict's dream."

"Ho ho. I guess you're right. Pass me the last piece."

"Nope." A bell rang. It was William's imitation of the lonely sea-buoy, clanging rustily in the salt air. Swelter had lifted it from the soundtrack of *Jaws 3-D*. Swelter jumped up, surrendering the last piece.

"Let's consult the coordinates," he said.

"If we can find this island so easily, why can't the Company?" Edna asked. "Don't they know it's there? Didn't they make this map, after all?"

"Grunts made the map, Edna. People like you and me, chained to their word processors, poured in the data, watched it settle, patted it into geological consistency, rolled out the golden fields of grain, stacked up the mountains and filled the lakes. Partner & Partner doesn't know anything about that map; it's not a consciousness, thank goodness; it's a concept, like evil is a concept. It's assembly line amorality.

"Lucky for us, if the left hand doesn't know what the right hand is doing, chances are the brain isn't doing too much itself. Maybe Partner & Partner does know the island is here, knows it in some abstract way, in some file or another, dating back years and far removed from present business; maybe in some file they found it, read William's notebook before they burned it; maybe they found it and didn't understand, didn't *remember* why they even had it; so they left it there, and made a note to the powers-that-be in the USGS to keep the island off the map..."

"Which island are you talking about? Which map?"

"Both. Those local yokels who killed our historical friend William: do you think they were organized to hunt down and murder him by some spontaneous indignation? They might not have been Partner & Partner themselves, but I'm sure they were encouraged. That's what evil does. It's in the confidence business. William stole something from Partner & Partner, even if it wasn't theirs to begin with. I'm certain, though of course there is no proof, and what better proof is that, haha, that when Sara Cornell's house was burnt down William's maps and notes were taken by P&P men in Ohio. I'm equally certain that they have that map, Edna, but never did anything with it; maybe by the time they caught William, a hundred years in the future, remember, they had no idea why they were chasing him and what he had stolen from them, of what value if any it was to continued business operations. But Partner & Partner never throw things away—they built the country on unrecyclable garbage. Believe me, I helped plan the whole thing out, it's immense. It's no ordinary take-a-stroll-with-your-modem amusement. It has depth, it has nooks and crannies filled with dangerous animals. If you just look at the surface you're just, well, looking at the surface." He examined the information on the screen. "Aha! Here's a little lump of rock right near the international border. A convenient location, no? Hm. Let us send a diver down to investigate." He looked at Edna. "I will call this diver Edna. Down, Edna, down!" A few digits of light slipped over the boat's stern and dropped into the water. Edna came over to watch.

"Until the tide comes up we can search this baby for anything resembling an opening. If Diver Edna finds no sign of this below, it will remain for us to wait the tide out and then determine a point of entry."

On the screen the diver surfaced and opened its mouth into a pulsing "o" as if coming up for breath.

"Can't you give me an oxygen mask or something?"

"Oh no, it wouldn't be fun then. Besides, most likely we'll have to sit here until the tide goes out anyway. No use getting ahead of ourselves. Thurnn may have rigged the island. There might be some trick to getting in. There might be–" pausing suddenly as if hearing something at the door; they looked around.

Silence. "There might be," he whispered, "some timing mechanism controlling the island's hatch. Because of course, this island's made only of electricity, unlike yours; who knows what Thurnn may have–" Another small sound, like a snicker of shoelaces along the wall, something that soft and clarifying. Swelter gestured Edna behind his desk, turned a dial beneath William's VDT to darken the screen, and crept towards the door, making a wide circuit so as not to approach it directly.

The small hitch of a toe snagged on the uneven carpet; a quick breath and the rustle of a coat; the flat clink of something metallic against a button; and then the unmistakable sound of a body crumpling into itself, the heavy thump on the hallway carpet. A small groan issued in a new silence.

•

Swelter knew that he shouldn't, he was sure he wouldn't, he was afraid he couldn't, but he did, against his better judgement, reach for the doorknob, his hand steady and about the only part of him not quivering, and turn it till it clicked. He pushed the door outwards.

It would not move. He put his shoulder into it, and it gave a few inches. A man lay half-conscious across his doorway, spittle on his mouth, and his eyes glazed sleepily, matching the expression of the silver gun muzzle poking out from beneath his windbreaker.

"Goodness," Swelter said.

"What? What?" Edna could stand no more. She rushed out from behind the desk, Swelter removing himself from her path, and lowered a shoulder into the door. It swung open with a chorus of groans metal and human.

Behind the door, clutching his ribs, lay a pizza man.

•

Not the pizza man they'd seen before, smaller in stature, carrying a revolver and a leather satchel around his shoulder. Beside him, equally crushed, a large empty pizza box.

"What happened to you?" Swelter turned him onto his back. He felt bones tumble like dominos.

"An unfortunate encounter," the reply barely audible. The pizza man looked as if he'd been squeezed in half. His clothing was torn and wet, and though he appeared not to be bleeding his whole ribcage seemed repositioned. A few feet down the hall was an area where it seemed a struggle had taken place: one of his shoes lay there, and a small pile of fur, which Swelter noticed he also had a handful of.

"I think his back is broken," Edna said.

"Yes, well, I imagine it's pretty ugly from where you are," the man croaked. "Internal injuries and all. Still, you must die. It's in the gameplan–" his gunhand turning on the wrist, the click of the pistol action working, but Swelter kicked it away as it went off, a bright black flower blooming on the far wall and the sound of fingers snapping under Swelter's heel.

"Fair enough," the pizza man said. "I think now that I shall expire."

•

"Don't touch him."

"He's Partner & Partner. He's dead. We've got to get out of here. He's not the only one." Swelter went through his pockets: a book of matches, a pack of cigarettes, a 3x5 card with Swelter's address and apartment number. As he folded the card to fit it into his pocket he noticed the name written on the other side. *Tinsel Croom. Rose & Thorn.* Hm. "Say, Edna," he began. "What?" He hesitated; better not to, now that he thought of it... "I'm going to get all the print-outs together. Then we're going to take the computer to your apart-ment. Nobody could possibly know who you are, Edna. You're the wildcard, hm?" He got up and walked past Edna into the apartment. She hesitated, then knelt by the body. The .38 lay gleaming lazily a few feet from her, a slender strand of smoke curling towards her, or was she just imagining it, inviting in a way, asking to be held once more. The man was on his back with his windbreaker wide open. Edna reached down and swivelled the satchel until it was resting on his chest. She popped the single snap and looked inside. The first thing she saw were the gilded letters *BEAVER DIG*. She yanked the book out and read the rest:

BEAVER DIG NUCLEAR RECON
(re East Florida Expansion Dividend)
Initial Notes & Survey Specifications
and beneath it,
     P & P

She broke the waterproof seal and opened to the title page.
BEAVER DIG. INITIAL SPECS AND GEO. SURVEY
by Balcher and Bartlett.

"Uh, Swelter."

"What time is it?" he yelled back.

"Swelter, get over here," she said.

"If you help we can be out of here by–" the book bounced off the back of his head. "Ouch." He looked down. His face got serious. "Well well."

"This is looking pretty nasty," Edna said.

"It's only the tip of the iceberg," Swelter said. "But at least we see the tip, and that's how you avoid the collision, right? Must be lucky. Perhaps good behavior puts you on the right side of luck, hm?"

"I'm not going to feel very lucky if we're not far from this apartment in five minutes," Edna said.

Swelter threw her a knapsack, and pointed to a boxful of papers. "You get those. I've got the computer," grunting as he hoisted two carry cases containing William. "If we catch a taxi, assuming haha that it's not the same one we had last night, we should—hey, Edna, did you turn out the lights?"

"No. They're still on. That's—" and then they both looked out the window and saw what every other New Yorker saw, what Polly and Rizzoli and Wan in their car and what the executives of Partner & Partner on their yacht in the harbor saw also: total blackness descending, heralded by a rain of crows, one of which swooped through the open window past Edna and Swelter, and settled on the chest of the pizza man, where it watched them with a cool black eye.

•

Had Edna asked Swelter if there was anything special about the 3x5 card beside it having his name and address written on it, Swelter might have been hard-pressed to supply an answer. Or he might have thought for a few minutes and told her glibly that besides the fact that its dimensions were roughly that of a golden rectangle, no, nothing was special about it.

A golden rectangle: a shape most appealing to Greek mathematicians and architects, whose ratio of long to short sides equalled that of the sides' sums to the long side, that ratio being roughly 1.61803:1...

The ratio for 3x5s is roughly 1.6:1, and not surprisingly the ratio for 8x5 cards falls also in that area.

The same ratio controls the Fibonacci Sequence of numbers 1,1,2,3,5,8,13,21,34,55... where each term is the sum of its two predecessors. The ratio seems present in other unrelated areas, like the numbers of rabbits born in succeeding generations. Alerted to this, Swelter might have pondered whether the ratio could be used to predict the spread of good or evil behavior over generations; or, had he a bird's eye view of a certain corner of a certain beach on the night of August 11th, and had he flown over a certain pile of discarded beach chairs he might have seen standing behind it a man holding a burning cigarette in one hand and an index card with the name Tinsel Croom on it in the other; he might have, being a bird after all, waxed creative and postulated that the younger man blowing his nose and standing slightly behind the first fellow was only about 3/5 man, and that together they made about 1.6 people about to embark upon some shady behavior; this of course contingent upon the answer to the question of whether being a bird might affect Swelter's ability to recognize a certain brand of cigarettes. But what tipped the scale, what represented the ratio's other side, the lesser Fibonacci? Let's land in a low branch and see...

"There they go," the .6 fellow says. "Sh-should we get 'em now?"

"No. Please limit your speech to the minimal," the 1 fellow says. Imagine the rest of the dialogue like this:

.6 : We'll never get them alone now. God, these bugs are killing me.

1 : We'll get them in our own good time. There's no need to take them out in a crowd scene. Patience is called for. Patience and the night will assist us. *(He hears something.)* Silence!

.6 : Silence will help us, too? Isn't that a little romantic?

1 : Idiot! I meant—

He turns but it is too late. Too late for .6 anyway. Flinch has successfully knocked him out cold with a blackjack; Flinch, who has followed the two suspicious characters he noticed tailing Cozetta Croom five hours earlier; Flinch who fears they are advance scouts for some terrible assault, in which of course he is half right; Flinch, who, though it be only for the birds, represents the one good person on the other side of the ratio, but whom luck does not favor, contrary to Swelter's wishful thinking, when he chooses to swing his weapon not at the fully competent one but at the only-fractionally conscious presence beside him. Before he can turn his head he's been knocked senseless himself by a speedy blow to the back of the neck. On his way down, black crawls in at the edges like feathers covering his eyes. There our good man lays, down but not out Flinch, who had always been down but not out, it seemed. While above him stands the difference, the lone and nondivisible quantity.

Had Swelter been there to witness, to shake his beak or do as crows do, he might have thought some more about Fibonacci, he might have thought some more about good and evil and where luck falls and who luck favors; he might have wondered what makes a man hide behind broken chairs, and what makes him lay broken outside your door. Except.

Except it didn't quite happen that way.

XVIII. The Other Foot

October 12, 1492, two hours after midnight, Rodrigo de Triana is the first man aboard Admiral Christobal Colon's ship to sight land. The Spanish Crown has promised a yearly pension of 10,000 mara-vedis for life to the lucky one; but Rodrigo hesitates. As he turns to inform his shipmates his eye is caught by the inexplicable sight of a single shoe, dangling precariously on top of the square-rigger's main-mast.

Moments later Pero Guiterrez, steward of the king's dais, cries out "Land! Land! The moon on a crystal beach!" Rodrigo has lost his claim to the pension.

But no matter: the Admiral insists he'd noticed a light earlier in the evening, and he will receive the reward.

•

Haiti, 1495. Columbus, back on his second voyage, and desper-ate to produce promised riches for his investors, orders all natives fourteen years of age and older to collect a specific quantity of gold for quarterly payment. In exchange they're given a copper token to wear around the neck as a receipt. Those found without tokens have their hands cut off and bleed to death.

A young Indian, whose offering is fractionally short of the requirement, is chased into the woods. He knows this island well, and entertains thoughts of escape. He chances a look backward, sees nothing. Suddenly he falls to the ground. Beside his broken ankle is a shoe, heel sticking out of the ground, the toe buried as if it had fallen from a great height.

Unable to stand, he hunches down in the undergrowth and listens to his pursuers pass by.

•

1909, New York. Twenty thousand women spontaneously strike to protest working conditions at the Triangle Shirtwaist Company. The International Ladies Garment Workers Union is born. In three hundred shops workers win their demands for fewer hours and cleaner facilities.

In 1911 a fire at Triangle Shirtwaist Company beginning in a rag bin spreads across the 8th, 9th and 10th floors. Doors, illegally locked to prevent employee theft, offer no route of escape. Women break windows, leap, arms linked, to the street below. One hundred and forty six will burn to death at their worktables.

A few lucky ones find a closet with an open laundry chute. The door had been held ajar by a man's shoe.

•

In 1917 Socialist Kate Richards O'Hare is arrested and sentenced to five years in prison for telling a public gathering *"the women of the United States were nothing more nor less than brood sows, to raise children to get into the army and be made into fertilizer."*

In the Missouri State Penitentiary she's taken forcibly from her cell by guards after leading a protest over the lack of air. The window above the cell block is shut and locked.

While being led away, she throws her prison-wardrobe slipper at a window, which shatters. A fresh breeze flows in. Outside, puzzled guards find only an old brown shoe.

•

At the Saint Escobille dump outside Paris, among the hundreds of thousands of corpses, dogs left behind by the fleeing French and subsequently shot by the Nazis, a single shoe lays between the teeth of a shattered jaw.

•

1988. Washington. Nobody sees it, nobody smells it, but an aide to the Senator from Illinois begins to spread the rumor, and most who hear it agree, that the prominent judge testifying testily on behalf of his nomination to the Supreme Court is repeatedly putting an invisible foot in his mouth.

The nominee is not recommended by the Judiciary Committee, and the nomination fails in the full Senate vote.

1991. The spectre seems to plague the Judiciary Committee. In the same chamber. Questions of a haunting are raised. Perhaps the foot has grown, or perhaps the judge's mouth is smaller, but its effect now is that the nominee seems unable to say anything at all.

•

1240. A young girl with no name walks carefully along the rocky black earth, leaving her home to become student to a wandering philosopher. As she walks she sets her eyes on a speck of dust on the edge of a distant line of trees. Soon the speck grows legs, four of them, then two heads, one long and hairy and one covered with metal. As it alters its course along the forest's edge and comes toward her it becomes a warrior on a horse. He stops in a cloud of black dust, reigns the horse to block her path broad-side.

"What is your name?" he asks her.

"I have no name," she replies.

Suddenly the trees explode with an alien sound. A small army of 20th century Chinese soldiers emerge from the brush, guns blazing.

Whatever the firesticks are supposed to do, they don't scare Sharaku. He knows they're about to run into the trap he'd set this morning, when he first received a warning from one of his tenants that intruders were on his land. As they crest a small rise of dirt, a hundred barbed yew spikes shoot from the dirt, and the soldiers collapse almost immediately, screaming in agony. Sharaku stirs his mount, urges her into a frenzy. He will ride over them, crush them with hooves and cut their arms off before he kills them. Then he will collect their firesticks.

From where the girl stands she sees only the horse stumbling surprised to its knees, throwing Sharaku with a spasm of its hind legs. He does not fall spectacularly, but he does fall heavily, due to his armor, and the sound of his neck breaking is a crisp snap in the empty morning air.

She walks toward the horse, which stumbles upright and tests its legs for injuries. Just behind it is a strange brown shoe, unlike any her family has ever worn, a totally alien shape sticking out of the ground toe-up. She picks it up; swinging it by the laces in time to her steps, she continues upland to where she'll meet Yonaga. She hopes she can convince him to take her to the top of the mountain. From some cliff or crag near the peak, she'll dangle the shoe by its laces over the abyss, and release it.

•

Even the ideas of the missing, or what the missing leave behind, have consequences.

And these leave only their trail of effects out of which a context must be built.

The other shoe drops into a warm twilit ether. Below it, still a mile away, are sounds of festivity: music, voices scattered on the wind, the surf combing it all into a new order. Out beyond the breakwater, lights on a boat twinkle. Directly above them an object hurtles its leisurely way downwards, its laces cracking like whips, its grommets accomodating a slight, thin whistle.

XIX. Thirteen Ways of Looking at an Octopus

I. Confession

THE DOCTOR HAD *taken a long lunch after meeting with the two* men at the cafeteria, walking in the open air, sunlight careening off his crayons and back into the blue void above; he couldn't remember how long he'd been walking, unfamiliar now with the neighborhood. The streets were thin and dusty. Few cars passed. Once he thought he heard the sound of the sea breaking over the dunes; another time he heard a buzzing in his ears, and turned to see a black humming-bird hovering just above his head. The green breast flickered and was gone.

"Doctor bird." A boy was standing next to him. He smiled and held his hand out to Fleck, waiting for his reward. "Ha ha, doctor bird." Fleck gave him the change in his pocket and moved away from the laugh.

Buildings leaned conspiratorially into one another, the thin uneven alleys between them the hemlines of some pattern of dark confidence. From one such alley a tiny shack protruded, barely as wide as its door, impossible to tell how deep it was, and above the door a gold planet painted against a starless night: Venus.

Someone came out, tucking his shirt into his pants. Ah, a water closet. Feeling the sudden urge to urinate, Fleck crossed the street and went in, closing the door behind him.

He was in darkness. One hand groped along the wall for the lightswitch while he pulled down the zipper of his pants. The swishing sound as a partition was opened in the blank air before him, and the vague hint of candle-light and a bowed human head through a heavy screen, the voice remote but direct through the fine layers of its cathecism:

"Confess your sins."

Fleck taken aback, reeling for balance on one leg and zipping up the fly, simultaneously crossing himself and delivering a blasphemous expletive or two, finally managed "I'm sorry. Thought this was a–" better not to say it, "excuse me. Very sorry."

"Of course you are." The voice unfazed. "Confess your sins."

The space around him swirled with glue-gray splotches, residue images on his corneas of x-rays: broken ribs, a femur or collarbone with compound fractures, hairline slivers of bone orbitting the wrist in its fragile belt, the junction of muscle and tendon at the top of the foot... "No, no," Fleck whispered, staggering back against the door. His crayons glowed like flares, incriminating, corroborating: *"nothing better than a green line on the lungers, eh Fleck," "here's where I marked the Brown boy's liver,"* ...He hazarded a glance at the screen. The priest-head was unmoved. Behind it he saw countless supplicants, praying on their knees and advancing step by step up a wide stair of bone, winding out of sight into a mine shaft framed with skulls whose teeth glittered with traces of gold.

"Their families have invited you," the voice said. "They've been praying for your passage."

Fleck's elbow shot out; behind him the door slapped open, he falling out to the ground, tripping on his own feet. A few people stopped to look. A young boy separated from his family and came to stand beside Fleck as he got up and brushed himself off. "Didja miss the step sir?"

"Oh I'm okay." He looked inside: a pale toilet seat and a roll of paper hanging on a nail. On the small mirror over the toilet was a lightbulb, half covered with flies. He looked around the back of the outhouse. A worm fence divided the alley into two tapering walkways. A piece of rusted fire escape blocked one route.

"You'll be on your way soon, eh?" the boy asked. His teeth were even and yellow. For a second Fleck thought he had seen them through the boy's closed lips, as if he'd spoken without opening his mouth. He was skipping away, kicking up dust from the road.

Fleck leaned against the outhouse and looked down the dirt road. A half-mile down the trees began to infringe on the neighborhood, then the land slanted up into the woods. A man walked by, naked and dark, dragging a tree limb spiked with bleeding fish. Some of them still worked their gills in sporadic bursts; the flat eyes regarded him uncuriously. Fleck looked behind him. The building was gone—all the buildings. A dirty sheep was sniffling his leather bag. The man had stopped, his back to Fleck, began to turn his head around, sweat glistening on his neck, the whites of his eyes just beginning to show...

Fleck blinked. The street was paved. A man on a cart, no legs, was tugging his trousers.

"Eh," Fleck jumping a bit.

"I said," the man not releasing him, "d'ya have somethin to spare for an old Indian?"

•

II. Thirteen Ways of Looking at an Octopus

Swelter sat at the kitchen table in Edna's basement apartment. Through a small window just below the ceiling he could look out on the continuing darkness, the streetlights' uncertain glow barely enough to see obscuring edges of concrete, shadows of metal fences or the hollow iron eyes of parked cars. From time to time one of Edna's cats, which had been harrassed by crows ever since the sky went black, would come and paw at the outside of the window; but Edna wouldn't let them in.

"They live outside," she said. "They should be grateful."

Swelter made use of every outlet in the apartment to plug in his computer. He'd forgotten his power strip back in Brooklyn. Edna had to unplug her refrigerator—"Nothing in it but vegetables anyway," she'd said, putting apples, lettuce, celery and carrots in a large bowl at the kitchen table, the bowl Swelter now picked from and looked over to see the video display as they waited for the tide to drop in the Strait of Juan de Fuca. The printer was plugged into an outlet in the bathroom wall; it spat out periodic charts that looked to Edna like weather maps. Swelter had explained, munching on an apple, "It *is* like a weather map, in a way; it shows the movement of electronic activity in our area of the map. Where it's cloudy there's a lot of action. You can still see the mistiness over at this point, where our friends from the Company met the monster of their dreams. That's because there's a lot of unorganized, and I should say unorganizable data, that won't fit into any of the landscape. So it's a disturbance of sorts, like a thundershower."

Edna had lit candles throughout the room, since no outlets were available for lamps. She did find an extension cord that allowed her to listen to her transatlantic radio. It was an old black box, with seven or eight different frequencies, shortwave, AM, FM, some she'd never tried; she could listen to Japanese television gameshows, truckers spinning dirty stories to one another on a late night run through Kansas, an International Farsi Poets Competition, old reruns of *The Shadow*, country preachers, city talk shows, the Elvis station, Radio Moscow, CNN, a live bandit broadcast of a first-run musical called *King of the River*, and, she'd sworn on several occasions, the voices of the dead. "Drowned sailors, mostly, it seems," she'd told Swelter matter-of-factly.

"By the way, any news on *this* weather?" Swelter asked.

"Satellite photos don't show any clouds, they're saying, but ground radar can't penetrate it at all. One of the weathermen said it reminded him of those readings that nuclear submarines get miles below the surface, they think are huge schools of giant squid or something."

"Oh ho," said Swelter. "Flying squid, this time, I guess."

"Anyway, they can't keep track of the planes in the air. Three accidents already at the airport."

"Oh no," Swelter, like most people, perking up for bad news. "Lots of people die?"

"No. It was one big accident, actually. Three cargo planes from Eastern Florida Imports collided in mid-air. There were conflicting reports — crows in the turbines, a big explosion, I don't know — but police are finding stuff on the ground that makes it look like it's been raining military hardware. The government says it's very interested in knowing what's going on."

"Oh I bet they are. It's not every day a renegade county in Florida tries to move arms up and down the east coast from a secret barracks in New York State, you think?" From the bathroom came sounds of William's printer.

Swelter sat down at the table and opened one of Polly's letters. He unfolded the one written on Dr. Wan's memo and flattened it out with his hands.

"Okay, while William's still printing I'm going to give this stuff a shot. Assuming that *someone* wrote these letters, we can be pretty sure they've read *Head Diver*; or maybe know about my connection to the author somehow."

"But how'd they know that I'd get the letters? Or that I'd be in contact with you?"

"Details, details... I'm kidding of course. This is the big mystery, but it's also, to my mind, pretty unanswerable. All we know for certain is that we *did* meet, we *do* have the letters, and that Tinsel Croom constitutes for us a connection tied to purpose. We don't really have the time to unwind the whole ball of wax."

"And why not? What's the hurry?"

"I've learned to love my life, Edna. I'm being hunted down by a huge monster of a corporation; in *two different landscapes,* no less. We've both got lots to gain and lots to lose here, and time is going to play a defining role in the outcome. So while we're waiting to find a way inside that island, while we're waiting for the tide to go down, while we're waiting for all I know for more P&P warships to greet us, or for another pizza man to show up outside your door, I figure we can take a look at these letters. Of course I'm curious to know how they got here, but I don't think we'll ever know if they're genuine or not, or who was behind them; and I'm not sure that it would matter, as long as they tell us something. Or even nothing..."

"Okay, okay, gimme a break," Edna raising her arms. "But I

think it's bullshit now. I'm going to listen to my radio."

"Okay. I'm sorry, Edna. I'm sorry they don't have the magical answers; but we're going to pinpoint the location of your lost globe any minute now anyway, no matter what these letters do or don't say."

"Yup." Edna was tuning in to a live concert at Central Park, which despite the darkness had not been cancelled. Organizers had asked those attending to bring their own candles, and now well over ten thousand music lovers had spread their blankets on the grass and lit candles, kerosene lamps and here and there set off firecrackers and sparkler sticks, and the conductor had signalled to the crowd, who were attentive and relatively well-behaved, and they understood that the orchestra was about to begin.

Swelter meanwhile had flipped Polly's note over and was writing the first letter of each word in Dr. Wan's memo. "A very simple code to begin with, but who knows what might turn up?" Edna grunted something in reply. "Let's see now: *Polly: every procrastinating. Proliferating errors...*" he scribbled away for a second as he worked down the short paragraph, then looked at the result:

pepperlipslovesgarlicfoot

"Nah," he said.

"What what?" Edna's attention momentarily diverted by the tone of perplexity.

"Oh, nothing. It seems you can make anything of anything sometimes." He opened another envelope, this one colored yellow with a clear plastic window, like the kind used to return phone or utility bills. Inside was a piece of toilet paper, a single word scribbled on it.

"*Bolero? Bolero?*" He scratched his head. "*Bolero?*"

"Stop grumbling," Edna said. "I'm trying to listen to *Bolero* on the radio."

Swelter jerked to his feet, upending the chair. Edna was at him in a flash, grabbing him by the collar and lifting him into the air. "Do *not* disturb me when I am listening to the Symphony! Do whatever you want with those goddamn letters, but do it quietly. If you miss a minute of this piece, you've missed the whole thing!" inching Swelter slowly above her head, like a clean-and-jerk in slow motion.

Swelter, red-faced and cheeks puffing, twitched his nose and blinked his eyes towards the tabletop. "Look," he croaked, "don't throw me for heaven's sake. Just look." As Edna turned her head a single clarinet established itself above the military-like counterpoint of tympan. She rolled her eye downward to the piece of toilet paper on the table, rolled them slowly upwards again to Swelter, and like a patient hydraulic gently lowered him to the floor. Woodwinds rose at the edge of hearing, small dissonances emerging from nowhere generating a sensual static. The smell of candles and melting wax, grass and the sound of feathers outside the window, all pulsed in compliment to the music, its build-up.

"How long?" Swelter asked.

"I dunno, seventeen minutes, eighteen."

"And low tide comes..." rummaging through William's latest statistics, "...hm, I don't know. It might coincide. It might not."

"What does it mean, Swelter?"

Swelter was at the bathroom door, tearing off the newest sheet from the printer. "Uh oh."

"Is it Partner & Partner?" Edna asked.

"Nope." Swelter held the chart so Edna could see it. Even from across the room the dark swirling was evident, and a space in its center like a hurricane.

"Eye of the storm?" she said.

"Nuh-uh. That's a beak. It's a huge octopus, Edna. My octopus. And it's eating everything in its path, or squeezing it to unusable bits of information. It's destroying the map. And it's heading our way."

"How long do we have? Does this mean we might not get inside that island in time?"

"Yes. And we've got..." hurrying over to William and punching the keys, "...we've got—about sixteen minutes; no, fifteen minutes, as of...now."

Strings took up the leading phrase, the bass behind them booming up as in thunder, and the rain began outside, a colorless and directionless explosion of water, spattering the street with crows dropped to the ground by the force of it, dousing ten thousand candles at once, ending all sound except for the symphony in the park, which played on, sheet music flying over the heads of the drenched citizenry, shooting out between skyscrapers and flying over the ocean, where the thunder waited its turn and the waves conducted their own music in their own measure.

•

Captain Beaver had heard enough.

His helmet torn open, eyes squeezed like shutters against the salt water, his resolve had not weakened as his breath gave out. Struggling underwater in the all-encompassing grip of the Dzoonokwa, the resident myth of the Kwakiutls whose totems marked their territories along the Strait's southern coast, Beaver'd been, to his credit, granted some empathic access to the creature that was now drowning him. Long loping stories of the wood, of lives lost, fevers, occasional skirmishes, calamities blamed on it, chasing a white-haired boy to the edge of the water, all streamed into Beaver faster than the seawater flooded his throat and lungs. Why, granted this gift, was he to go down anyways, what score was being settled? Beaver remembered landing on the monster's meal that first time, and it dawned on him why monsters, gods, are in the end so fragile: they kill what would hold them dear. There's no limit to the narrowness of drive, the simplicity of hunger...

As his eyelids began to loosen, water blinding him, the back of his head feeling cold and dull like nickel, Beaver attempted to entertain last thoughts of his own life. And quite suddenly there was nothing: did he have a wife, kids, hobbies, anything outside of drowning in the arms of a bigfoot? The loss of access to his own memory enraged him. A last bubble of air shot from his lungs. He reached with his hands and pushed his thumbs through the creature's open red eyes.

He felt the membrane give way. Then searing pain as it looked at him through his bones.

Suddenly the water thrashed with unexpected force. They were thrown away from the island. Vision came back to Beaver as they broke the water for a few seconds and air forced its way down his throat. Back in the ocean a huge glowing mantle moved towards them, orange with rage. A tentacle shot out, two four all. The Dzoonokwa was torn from his grasp. Before it was hurled into the dark air above the roiling waves Beaver could already see the monster's fur exploding into threads of light. Then it was gone. The huge octopus looked at through beyond him. All behind it was nonsense, fragments of wave, fish and earth. The water, retreating itself before it, slammed Beaver back against the island. He scrambled up to the rock's crown and turned around. The octopus had surfaced, revolved itself in a long ripple, displaying its beak. All around its body water was shooting in green and purple sparks, exploding, changing to pure unorganized energy.

Beaver opened the seam in the rock and dived.

•

An editorial cartoon in a December 1775 edition of the *Malden Cormorant* shows Great Britain, depicted as an octopus, reaching across the Atlantic Ocean with its eight arms. Each arm is named for a British policy whose institution in the Colonies has helped the Empire retain its grip on the Americas: the Stamp Act, the Tea Tax, and so on. One of the arms was labelled *Slavery*, and in a statement created in a town meeting and sent on to the Massachusetts House of Representatives to declare their intention to support the independence movement, they said: *we therefore renounce with disdain our connexion with a kingdom of slaves; we bid adieu to Britain.*

Of the other of the thirteen states to declare independence, Rhode Island was more interested in religious freedom; South Carolina could not lend its militia to the coming revolution, because they needed all their troops to keep their slaves from successfully rebelling.

Pennsylvania officials were already preparing their defense against charges of mutiny as their citizens organized against the impressment of seamen into the revolutionary army.

All about the thirteen states, 'perfidious Albion' was rejected.

But to unify them sufficiently to withstand the stifling hold of the
King-faced octopus, they had to rally round a new group of self-evi-
dent truths, and if ever a sleeping giant was awakened in the country's history, it was not with the explosion of bombs in Pearl Harbor;
but rather any and every moment when a citizen would chance to
read the words Jefferson wrote concerning inalienable rights—then
a real monster would hitch or blink in its sleep, dreams of escape
invading its ever-thinner slumber.

•

"Tell me one more time that it's not a conspiracy."

"It's not a conspiracy!"

Phil Petrie, Talk Show Host, was not as afraid as he'd first been
when he was swept into the air by a flying Flash Gordon look-alike
with army-surplus duds and carried deep into the woods that curled
around the Blue Mountains like a comforter. With his feet on firm
ground again, he was—being one himself—a match for any ideo-
logue.

"Mister, don't you read the god-damn newspapers? This statehood drive is no conspiracy—it's a movement. It's publicity-driven,
for crying out loud. Why, I was hired for–"

"I know exactly why you were hired. What I'd be more interested in hearing is why you haven't mentioned the new State Militia
or the weapons your state plans on using to protect its sovereignty."

"Weapons? Are you kidding? I don't know anything about it."

"Of course you don't." Beaver was getting tired of trying to talk
to Phil Petrie. Petrie, he might have known, knew only as much as he
needed to know. He just colored in between the lines so things would
look brighter.

"Let me ask you something," Petrie was saying; "Just who the
hell do *you* represent?"

"Freedom of Information," Captain Beaver said. "And self-evi-
dent truths."

He flew away.

•

Gilpatrick, author of *The Compleat Goggler*, once brought home an octopus he'd caught, and put it in his aquarium. Some time later he was awakened by a loud noise. Running downstairs he found the lid of his aquarium had been forced, and moments later discovered the octopus going through his library, book by book, turning the pages with its arms.

•

It was his encounter with the pizza man that convinced Captain Beaver he should retire.

He hadn't been hard to track down. Beaver knew his name—Simon Salmon—loathe though he'd been in his trade to give it freely, enough people knew it, or signed his paycheck. And the pizza deliverer Simon'd killed he'd stuffed in the dumpster closest to Swelter's apartment building; if the body's warm, Beaver thought as he checked for a pulse, then so am I.

Beaver saw him creeping up to Swelter's door. Amazingly, Salmon had heard Beaver coming, and got the drop on him.

"Say cheese," Salmon deadpanned, levelling the .38 at Beaver's face.

The *Head Diver* dissolved before Simon's eyes, appearing a quarter-second earlier, while "cheese" was still on his tongue, with one strong hand around Salmon's right wrist and another over his mouth.

"Don't say it again, Salm," Beaver joked.

He led Salmon around the corner and tied him up, left him to deliver the pizza to Swelter and Edna. To Salmon's credit, he'd freed himself of the gag and ties around his wrist and ankles before Beaver returned. Unfortunately, something else was waiting for him. It stepped from a hole in the wall, grabbing him precisely the way Beaver had, and drew him in.

When Beaver came back he was gone. Although he'd played up the moment, Beaver realized that he came close to underestimating the reaction speed of his mark. This Beaver *could* remember his wife and family. He just didn't want to need any reminders again.

When he rematerialized on the library's borders he gave the mountain of information one last look. Then he went into DeBrief to hand in his uniform.

"You pick a fine time to retire," Leadfellow told him. "Trustees been tryin to figger out how to git you outta there for six hours."

"What was the big deal?"

"Nothin you did, mind; you're John Wayne around here to us. Sure you got those switchboard transferees up in arms an all, but everyone knows you're ok." He folded up Beaver's uniform and laid it in the Ionizer for processing and cleaning. "You're lucky to get outta there alive is the thing. I hear say there's some networking problem, a worm in the program that's eatin all the information up, knockin down walls and so on. Fer a minute we had you radio-pegged right where it was crunchin around, an we were sure you'd had it."

"Well," Beaver said, stretching into his civvies, "I'm sure John Wayne wouldna minded fightin his last fight in old Wyoming." He checked his mini-calendar function on his watch. "But he didn't have to coach Little League."

"Know what you mean," Leadfellow confided, shaking his hand. "I sure do."

•

Flinch stirred beneath a pile of chairs. "That'll teach you for clubbing me from behind," our .6 told him after covering him with as much hammock netting and beach chair frames as he could manage, having first tied his arms and legs with hammock line. He ran off into the woods.

Had luck been consistent in its treatment of the good and evil, as Swelter postulated, perhaps Flinch might have been the first to his feet, and things would have been different. But Simon Salmon had knocked Flinch out first, hearing him sneak up on them from about twenty feet away; and then for good measure he'd clubbed his companion, our six-tenths of a man, with a forearm that was, speaking in terms relative to the shot he gave Flinch, but a love tap. He knew his companion would wake first; he only hoped he'd get the situation under control, and then get lost, and let Simon Salmon, the best of the best after all, conduct business with Mister Croom.

So, according to plan, Flinch was the last to wake up; and

according to plan, six-tenths ran helplessly into the woods, and got lost, running blindly and less sensibly until he encountered an object of equal size and comparable speed in what can only be called an unfortunate collision.

Dr. Fleck, whose narcotic mania had sent him on a breathless meander along trails on the foothills of the Blue Mountains, into the backyards of religious families and the cow pastures of the indignant Maroons, into a bus full of tourists returning from a sightseeing jaunt back to their beachside hotels, where he disembarked with them and disappeared into the underbrush amidst dusk's curlicues and doubts. From high overhead, at the height of helicopters and flying saucers, where something may or may not have been observing, the collision was inevitable. Any twig or root could have provided grace for either of the two, but their paths were free of detritus. They skimmed along the earth and into each other's arms, then sat a few feet away from each other, rubbing heads, trying to regain consciousness enough to determine what had happened.

At this point something large and wet dropped from the sky at an alarming velocity. Tree limbs snapped in warning as it passed downwards through them, thunder complained as if having had to belch it out from above, and the object of its gravitational attraction, the earth, met it with all the expected heartiness.

Flinch and six-tenths crawl over to the smoking crater a mere three yards from them, and peer over the edge. Something hairy is getting to its feet down there, scratching his head. Something that smells like the sea. It looks up to Fleck, puts its huge paws on its chest, and peels the fur and flesh back to show its wildly beating heart, pounding within its cage of ribs. Though of course six-tenths doesn't get it, Fleck sees and knows: the creature's heart is marked with a white X.

Twenty yards away, Flinch was working his own painful way to his knees, tugging at his bonds and trying to squirm out from under the pile of beach chairs. In his semi-conscious state he could hear the crunching of bone and the sound of unwanted appendages hitting the ground with a plop, but he never understood, nor would he have believed had he understood, how directly we are fed to the creatures of our imagination, how hungry they are, how lucky those are without sufficient faith to believe in monsters.

•

Water seemed to come from everywhere. It poured in through the window; it seeped up through the carpet; it spewed from the walls in springs as gouts of panelling and insulation exploded outward under the pressure. It was ankle level when the tip of land appeared out of the water on William's screen. Swelter pounded in commands at the terminal as a chink of light crept out once more from the boat and onto the island, searching, searching, turning over rocks, looking for a seal to break, an entrance.

"How can you keep track of that and know where that octopus is at the same time?" Edna yelled over the sounds of water and the music still blaring from her transatlantic.

"I was of three minds," Swelter recited, *"like an aquarium in which there are three octopuses!"* The little figure disappears into a hole in the island. "Look, Edna! Look!" A close-up of the hole, the rocky entrance ringed with barnacles, each barnacle another bit of data, and then, like a turtle's beak emerging from its shell, an approximation of a smiling Edna head appeared on the screen, holding a sparkling piece of gold rock.

"What does it say?" Edna screamed, barely audible over the last three minutes of *Bolero*. A thunderhead rolls in over them, scraping the cowlicks of skyscrapers; the air goes electric.

Swelter feels the water run over the hightops of his sneakers. "No time to read it now. Let's store it!" Swelter's belt buckle is an external hard drive; he plugs it into William. More buttons, beeps and glicks from William, who seems to resent the intrusion of a parasite. "Just do it, William. You've been real swell about this." The room is filled with a heavy whir, like a chainsaw, as William begins the transfer. "This will take, unfortunately, a few minutes." His luck has held so far; he'd plugged the computer into the highest wall outlet. He looked down. "My printer!" It glistened attractively beneath an inch of water.

The ceiling seemed to rain down on them. Swelter covered his equipment with his coat as they stood clinging to one another on the kitchen table.

A man and a woman
Are one.
A man and a woman and an octopus
Are one.

"What are you saying Swelter?" Edna shook him. Swelter handed her a piece of paper. "The coordinates. Exactly. Down to the centimeter." She rolled it up and stuck it in her hair. "It'll be the last thing to go under," she said to him. Swelter intoned,

He rode over the Strait
In a glass barque.
Once, a fear pierced him
In that he mistook
The shadow of his equipage
For an octopus.

"Just another minute," Swelter holding William up against his collarbone. The screen was tracking the movement of his octopus. It was now within striking distance to the island, but seemed to be stalled. Swelter knew he saw it, but would never be sure enough of it to confide to someone else: a small white figure, crawling out of the water at the island's edge, running up to its height and disappearing into it.

The window shattered.

Half a dozen dead crows dropped from the sill into the water. A face peeked in.

"Swelter." Jog Thurnn.

William quieted abruptly. "Done! Done! Got it!" tossing the hard drive frisbee-like to Thurnn. He shut off William and lay him gently into the water where, after seeming to entertain notions of floating, it sank silently to the floor.

"Good-bye my friend," Swelter said. And turned then to Edna. "And good luck to you!–" clambering, with Jog Thurnn's help and without a look back, out the window.

•

Edna reached for the phone.

"Dial tone, dial tone. Yes." She punched in 911.

Deep and distant, a ring could be heard, then two. Someone picked up the phone: "Yes. What happened?"

"What? What?" Edna shouted, but the transatlantic, sputtering its last sound with the final note of *Bolero*, fell from Edna's grasp, the plug pulling from the wall as it hit the water.

Edna's cape, which had been hanging on the coat rack, floated by like an ambivalent manta ray, followed by a few dozen loose globes, twinkling and rolling like they were at home in this new ether. The last thing Edna saw was that tiniest globe, the one representing a gloomy day in the fall of the year when three ships sailed into her sea like returning gods, invisible except for the fact it floated only inches from her wide-open eyes as the water lapped at her flaring nostrils. Just before a wave covered her head completely, she thought she saw that sorry orb swell as if struggling itself against the tides of history, and disappear.

III. Penanced

DOCTOR WAN APPEARED *out of the rain and mist like a floating* yellow fire hydrant as his motorboat pulled up to the yacht's stern.

"It's Wan!" he yelled into the wind. "Let me up!" A rope ladder uncurled and snapped as it reached its end, dangling near him at eye level. He threw up a line to secure his boat. Unseen hands caught it, and he climbed up.

They sat around a wide, semi-circular table in a splendidly decked out chamber amidships. Below-decks an engine hummed, making the floor vibrate. Air conditioning flew from hidden vents. A heron-like bird with slaty plumage, long black legs and a stubby neck stood in a tall cage. *Balaeniceps rex*, a plaque read. Shoe-bill.

"These," Wan pointing, making small talk, "they are native to tropical Africa, no? I didn't know they could survive in captivity."

"They can't," one of the Partners answered. "We get a new one each month or so."

Wan glanced once more around the room, then took a seat. Refrigerator, HDTV, the latest from the stock market: everything they needed was here. A few drinks sat neatly on paper coasters adorned with a map of *EASTERN FLORIDA — Our Newest, Most Innovative State!* Dried stain rings circled the new state like a bullseye. Nobody was smoking. Everyone seemed too calm; even Wan knew this meant they were nervous as hell. The doctor placed his palms flat on the table, both to assume a firm-looking posture and to support himself as he rose. Rainwater trembled down his sleeves and formed puddles between his fingers like melted rings.

"Rizzoli has betrayed us," he said.

On the wall to Wan's right was a framed page of an old nursery rhyme book. The main character was a fool named Simple Simon, who represented to the Company the gullibility of Everyman. This page had Simon standing near a tree, his right leg caught in the metal jaws of an animal trap. The verse read,

Simple Simon went a poaching
For to shoot some game
A mantrap caught him by the leg
Which gave poor Simon pain.

In the background a deer stood nibbling flowers, and from a cornfield behind him flew a crow with a corncob stuffed in his beak.

For the first time Wan wondered what he may have stepped into himself, here in the predators' den. The light was low and at table-level, effectively masking the faces of those seated around it. They could be centuries old, he thought, with little patience for post-modern psychoanalysis... then one of them reached for his drink, and betrayed a small tremble lifting it. Somebody else swallowed dryly. Just human after all, city slickers all of them. Wan breathed deeply. One of them finally spoke.

"Well, Doctor, we should hold you responsible, since this artist was your idea to begin with. But then again, we never trust artists to represent business anyway, even with the contract we had with Rizzoli."

"And it's that written contract he can use against us now," Wan warned.

"No, he won't, Wan. It's too vague to incriminate us. He wanted it that way, I'm sure, as much for his own purposes as for ours. At any rate: this trip you made was thoughtful, Doctor, especially on a night like this, but unnecessary. He was just icing on the cake. A trump card. Don't worry about him. He would have given the statehood drive appreciated celebrity-support with his name value; as for the Declaration, we assumed this might happen, so we've already taken precautions to insure–"

The phone rang. "That's probably them now. Excuse me." He pulled the phone across the table and picked up the receiver on the second ring. *Third ring,* thought Wan, you should have waited for the third ring.

"Yes. What happened?" he said. A horribly distorted static, audible to all in the room, hissed from the earpiece. Some large sound that could not be contained, some Leviathan a line as thin as telephone cable could not hope to hold, roared across space. The partners looked around at each other. The one holding the phone put the receiver gently on the table. Another loud noise greeted them, this one from outside the ship. "Whoa there, starboard!" a crew member yelled. One of the partners stood. "Sounds like they dropped a safe into the water, for Christ's sake!"

Not a safe: an anchor.

At first all they could see, as they gathered by the ship's side, was a thick rusty metal chain appearing out of the mist above their heads and continuing downward into the water. It was still paying out, link by link. As the mist fell away, a large shape began to present itself to them, a hulking row of cannons leaning out from a hull of rotted boards and seaweed. Barnacles and shells clung to any available crevice. A clinking noise like that of milk bottles knocking together drifted around them.

"What the hell is this?" someone asked. The galleon drew slowly alongside the yacht. A knotted rope ladder dropped lazily over the edge and hit the deck by Wan's feet with a moist splat.

"Hey, this is like something I saw at Disney," one of the partners tried to joke. His chuckle died in the mist.

"Come aboard." The voice was broken and flat, dry as if spoken through vocal cords made of pipe cleaners, or old reeds. The air above them whistled and clicked.

"Come aboard."

"Who the hell are you? Who sent you?" Wan shouted. The yacht's crew were approaching the rotted hull, toting semi-automatics. The mouths of the cannons dripped rainwater onto the deck where the partners stood.

"Your relatives... we've come to take you. A... a nice..." A bare arm, black with feathers strapped to the elbow, reached out with open hand. The crew opened fire in its direction. The galleon swung softly with a swell, and shifting seemed momentarily transparent, glowing with yellow-white supports behind the facade...

"Bones!" Wan yelled as it moved back into the yacht; a tremor shot across the boat's deck, knocking them to their knees. The sky cleared its throat in the dark above them. "Bones! Bones! Bones!"

XX. Where The Sun Shines Best

Night had fallen.

Jay Valento was holding court with a small group of vacationing teenagers when he saw Tinsel and Cozetta.

"Hey, Adventure Couple!" he yelled, waved them over. "How'd you guys make out last night? click your heels together and scooter into the sunset? Listen," confidentially, "I want you both to meet a real weird guy, though don't tell him I told you that. He's the one who put up the posters for the party tonight." Valento pointed to a gathering on his left. Beemus, Dorfman from the Polyversal, and a thirty-ish thin-haired man in twenties style beach attire were conversing in heated tones. "Hey! Marty! Quiet down over there, huh huh! C'mere man, some people I want you to meet!" The man separated himself from the group and walked with careful steps towards them.

Valento elbowed Tinsel. "See, the guy wears those flappers on his feet, rubber sandals, so he has to walk like a penguin to keep his balance." He made his best penguin face until the approaching guest was nearly upon them, at which time it immediately shifted back into the slightly-drunk-and-glazed look Tinsel remembered him exhibiting in the bar the previous night. "Tinsel and Cozetta, I would like you to meet Marty "Glass Ears" Chabot, host for tonight's festivities and documented tracker of UFO aural trails."

Marty extended his hands to Tinsel and Cozetta.

"Did you say Oral Trails?" Cozetta asked.

"Hardly," Marty began, "but Mr. Valento's usual condition during performance makes enunciation seem a miracle at times, doesn't it?" Valento guffawed. "I track aural trails—that's *a-u-r-a-*

l—of flying objects whose origin has not yet been determined."

"UFOs man! Fuckin *say* it, Marty, *YOOOOOOOO, EFFFFFFFF, OHHS.*" Valento made another, more obscene, penguin face behind Chabot's back.

"Yes, well, I didn't want to prejudice the good couple prematurely. You see, having worked at a department store near a rural mall which is in turn near a commercial airport and a military base, my ears have become attuned to the sounds of every known aircraft currently manufactured on the surface of the earth."

"What about one manufactured, *beneath*, the surface of the earth?" asked Valento. Tinsel shot him a glance, then addressed Marty, who'd ignored the question.

"What did you do at the department store?"

"Now that's irrelevant, don't you think?" Chabot said. "I will tell you, however, because it is a source of great pride for both me and the store. I kept a steady and aesthetically pleasing supply of tulle in all the various departments for use with visual displays. You'd be surprised how pervasive tulle is as an unconscious symbol of our hope for the future, wishes for a safety net, the collective unconscious. Need I go on?"

"I'm convinced," said Cozetta. "You must work for Spetious, right? We have one of your stores in Mobridge."

"It's pronounced like 'spacious,' actually. But yes that's right, we do have a branch store in Mobridge. I even consulted for a Christmas display there once, oh I would say about five years ago or so. Not that I'm afraid of betraying my age."

"The baby Jesus in the manger of blue tulle?" Tinsel asked incredulously.

"Yes! You actually remember it, do you?" Marty swelled with pride.

"Yeah, it was huge, Jay, you should have seen it. Baby Jesus was about ten feet tall, and it was like the shepherds were being swallowed alive by this amorphous tulle monster!"

"Or that they were overcome with the miracle of their own faith," Cozetta translated for Marty.

"Yes, that's it exactly. Now to pick back up the thread of my story—no pun intended, of course—I began to notice certain sonic booms the tone or timbre of which I'd never heard before. I questioned local air traffic controllers about what planes were aloft during the times I remembered hearing them.

Well, I was told flat out that there were no aircraft travelling over Spatious at that exact time. Of course I might have been mistaken, so I began keeping a logbook of my observations. None of them would match up with the flight schedules for the days on which they occurred."

"So they're UFOs, right?" Valento bust in, and began singing

UFOs they're all around
Leaving awesome trails of sound
From Cassee-oh-pia to the edge of time
UFOs they blow my mind

"My only explanation for this repeating phenomenon was that the sounds were the trails of planes or airships travelling so much faster than the speed of sound that it took some time for the sound to actually reach human ears, even ones as sensitive as mine," Marty continued. "Still, there was no radar that could document any of my claims, which led me to believe that these sounds are the sonic trails of airships travelling above the altitudes of normal aircraft, or travelling below the altitudes susceptible to radar, or that they perhaps are actually newfangled spaceships of some sort." Marty waited a second for sarcastic comments or disagreements, but Tinsel and Cozetta were game for more. "Of course I haven't discussed the possibility of government secret missions; but if my campaign to publicize my findings reaches enough ears, any governments involved will feel pressure to answer to the public, if only to calm hysteria over possible flying saucers."

"What do you think it really is?" Cozetta asked.

"I do have a theory; I believe, I *feel*, that the sounds are encoded messages from beyond; since I can't translate them, I don't know exactly from where they originate, but it sure as heck doesn't seem to be Disney World. Whether the transmitter is an airplane or a space-ship is anybody's guess. But whenever I hear such traces, when I pick up those faintest vibrations in the air, my ears fairly quiver with some strange empathy, and my heart literally starts pounding. I may have even had a heart attack once or twice, for all I know. But you know what they say, inner strength and so on." Marty smiled broadly and patted Valento on the back. "In my attempt to awaken the general public, I've decided to publicize the issue from all its possible angles. I heard that there was some new wave of Christian rock n roll, so I've hired Jay here to perform some songs I've written especially for that cross-section of society. I believe many of the tourist youths here are from middle American backgrounds and will relate to the Christian tradition behind the new messages in the music."

Valento tapped him on the shoulder, pointed over to Beemus and Dorfman, who were waving for him to come back. "If you'll excuse me," Marty said, "I have to speak with the other sponsors of tonight's get-together." He began walking carefully back to the group.

"Wanna go over there and listen to some more?" Cozetta asked.

"Sure," said Tinsel. "Do you think he's nuts?"

"There's lotsa different kind of nuts is the problem, you big lunkhead," Cozetta taking his arm. Her forearm was cool and pleas-ant against his own spotty sunburn and the scratches he'd gathered stumbling around in the forest the night before. "What kind of nut am I, Cozetta? Hazelnut? Macadamia? Walnut?"

"Try lug-nut," she said. "But you know how I love lugnuts."

"Ladies and Gentlemen!" Valento's voice boomed from the speakers, then squealed and peeled into distortion as he got too close to the mike. The teenage girls around the edge of the stage began taking off their tennis shoes as if a conspiracy was afoot, and throw-ing them at the lead singer. "Hey! Ha ha, I don't get it. Good evening, good evening, and thanks for attending. You may notice tables filled with refreshments and volatile mixtures of serious brew, home-made by the island's own inn-keeper, Mister P.H. Healey." Hearty applause.

"Thank you, way to go. Anyhow, we're here tonight, with the exception of our drummer Cooter who told me he don't really care either way, to warn you of the disastrous consequences of our current way of life! To alert the wise among you that there are messages of great import travelling over the clouds, yay even over the hard-set ozone layer! And that not only that, but you can get down and party to em! Yah, hit it—"

(Marty's Song)
I saw it at Orion's hip
The Good Lord in his rocketship
Twirling that almighty eye
Said you'll get up here when you die!
His lights they sparkled red and green
Such roundness have I never seen
As on the globes alight therein
The Lord in Space invites us in!
And when it landed by and by
It steamed as if a rhubarb pie
The Virgin weeping at the helm
Good Jesus guides us to His realm!
From golden windows now shine through
God's holy light from Them to you
Two winged angels at the prow
As Paul and John observe us now
O heav'nly spaceship we adore
The wingless wings you stretch before
Your robes of lasers do implore
To lift us up to Heaven's door!
Those starry gates that Peter guards
That lead to Jesus' well-kept yard
Are laced with planets' silver rings
That shine their light o'er everything!
(Jay and Efrain trade relatively brief guitar licks)
To go with you I'll leave my dog
To wife and children—trust the Lord

That in His spaceship they may see
Twixt Son and Father, waving me!...

"Too new age!" someone yelled to Jay. Some of the teenage girls began taking back their sneakers.

"Wait!" Efrain shouted. "The next number's called *Immaculate Drinking Song!*" A new flood of cheers and sneakers hit them. Jay launched into a Rawhide-style riff, righted the twang and piled on layers of fuzz until all chord-changes were buried beneath the distortion and his two front teeth, with which he re-tuned some individual strings while playing as if to create some messages not even Marty could hear. By the time Efrain started singing there were at least seven different factions in the audience arguing over exactly what song he was playing. None of them were listening anymore, but a couple of dozen people were dancing anyway.

Tinsel and Cozetta joined Marty, who was listening to Beemus and Dorfman argue with a newcomer to the group. He seemed to be patient as Dorfman outlined the future of America to him, though at one level he looked to Tinsel even less substantial than Dorfman had felt to him in the shack last night. What Cozetta saw in the newcomer, on the other hand, was as equally frightening to her: a man who was all too much there and attentive to those things projected least consciously. Dorfman was on a roll, rounding off his sentences with incomprehensible hand gestures, as if he were trying to translate in another language made only of three or four finger movements.

"Of course it's idealistic *now*," he said, "but in the future it will be obvious; there'll be fewer cars on the road, because transportation outside the immediate community will no longer be necessary, or economical for businesses. There may even be laws against it. Information unleashed, think of it; most everyone will be self-employed, and by that I mean employed in the work of a) the community and b) the processing of information for a variety of communities. The personal aspect of commerce will be played down on all but the local level, you see, where it will count most. Not counting the inevitable import/export of certain foodstuffs, food will be provided within the shire for that particular shire's needs. Here's where diversity flourishes. Differences in environment, in agriculture, in food, will draw people to experiment living in different shires, but things will always balance out naturally. Imagine, sprawling over the entire continent, a network of local culture, bolstered by free and unlimited access to information via databases in every home..."

"Sounds like the American dream, extended to all, becomes one huge nightmare of ranch houses, solar panels, backyard gardens, rain collectors and home offices," the new person had cut in.

"And what's the matter with that?" Dorfman responded. But the newcomer had just noticed Tinsel and Cozetta. Cozetta saw the extra second his eyes lingered over Tinsel, slipped down over him as if searching for something specific, before turning his head back to Dorfman, who was finishing with something like, "as long as they don't encroach on the National Parks System."

"Hm, yes. Well, all in all and despite my trepidation at your personal and rather giddy view of the future, I do find the idea of a 'polyversal' historical archive itself fascinating. Yes, I wonder if you can leave me with the address."

"The address of the library? You've got to be kidding. The library has no address. Each story is in constant circulation." Cozetta noticed with some relief that she wasn't the only one who didn't trust the man. Dorfman was taking no chances.

"Oh well. I thought I might contribute my own life-story to the archives. Everyone thinks they've something exciting to relate to the rest of the world, am I right?" laughing amiably enough. To Cozetta it seemed too calculated, a bit too self-effacing.

"Yes, fine with me," Dorfman handed him a card with an address. "That's the idea, after all." Tinsel leaned over to Cozetta and whispered in her ear, "That's not the address I saw Dorfman give Field last night."

"Mm," she mumbled, then flashed her teeth so gaudily at the group, who were now staring at her and Tinsel, that even the stranger had to smile back at the simple intensity of her expression.

"My husband was just saying how you all look like Andrew Lloyd Webber," she said.

"Did not!" Tinsel protested; but since both Marty and Dorfman resembled slightly the aforementioned circus publicist and composer of daytime television musicals, nobody took his protest seriously. The stranger extended a hand to Tinsel, saying, "I'm afraid we haven't been introduced, Mister—?"

"Croom," Tinsel said, Cozetta jabbing him in the back a half-second too late; but it might have been drowned out by the sudden shout from the crowd and the equally loud exhortation by Efrain Romero for everyone to come to the shoreline.

"Paddleboat race to the *Gregorian*!" he shouted. "First three finishers receive unheard of prizes and fantastic stuff!"

A line of silver paddleboats, some in the shapes of killer whales, seals and walruses, lined the shore like fresh donuts. A green beacon burned at the stern of the *Gregorian*, where Captain Felix Mendelsohn stood holding a checkered flag.

Tequila Mockingbird launched into 'Let Me Go, Rock & Roll' and the race began, people choosing for partners whoever climbed into the paddleboat with them. Cozetta kept tight by Tinsel's side in the rush to the surf. "Don't let go," she said to him. "Mysterious Stranger is very close to us. I don't want to get isolated on a paddleboat with Mr. Creepy."

In all the chaos that ensued they managed to stay together, and boarded a paddleboat with the streamlined head of a giant squid. Behind them a lone man paddled a mute swan boat into the tide, when another figure suddenly launched itself out of the water and into the vacant seat.

"Name's Witcover, stranger," he shouted over the general commotion to Simon; "and I don't suppose you could pedal a little faster, do ya?"

•

In the space of twenty minutes the ride would be over. Out beyond the *Gregorian*'s green light a school of uncountable size was in session, a square mile of squid rising to the surface to feed on an equally large field of shrimp, who themselves rise on nights like this to feed beneath the full moon.

•

In the time it takes fifty paddleboats to scramble over a relatively calm quarter mile of water and converge on an oversized commercial fishing-vessel-turned-casino, Tequila Mockingbird had tired of ecclesiastical minstrelling, and instead invited the crowd remaining on the shore to sit and listen as Efrain Romero hefted a saxophone and ticked precious seconds on his fingers to the drummer, who laid a quiet but firm foundation with his brushes. The people sat quietly, lulled into its heartbeat rhythm, felt their own pulses through the sand where they sat, and when Efrain's earthy sax line swung out over the beach it reached Tinsel and Cozetta helping one another up the rope ladder. Twenty such ladders had been thrown over the stern to assist in the boarding of the racers, and they hung now like damp hair on a sea dog.

"Tinsel," Cozetta said, hoisting herself onto the deck, "what's that song they're playing."

"Beats me," Tinsel said. "Doesn't sound like rock and roll anymore."

"Sounds to my ear," said a female voice behind them, "like *Bolero*." It was the waitress from the Redbeard Cafe, still in uniform, paying out line from a sizable fishing rod. A sign on deck said *Night Fishing Dinner Special. Eat All You Can Catch. See the Captain for Details.*

"Everyone grab a rod!" Mendelsohn was bellowing. "Sure an it's only a buck to try yer skill with the finned fishies, the scaly ones, harhar." Cletis came stumbling over with three rods and tackle. "Watch out for the hooks," he said, setting the poles in their sockets on the swivelling chairs.

"Strap yerselves in fer the ride of yer lives!" Mendelsohn howled. Somewhere below deck an engine growled its displeasure. The wooden boards beneath the Captain's feet groaned in agreement as the *Gregorian* pushed its way out to sea.

•

Tinsel felt a tug on his line at some point; before he knew it he'd reeled in a monster. Cletis and Footlong helped pull it up, and people gathered around with mild curiosity as it flopped on the deck, eyes pivoting in its green accordion sockets, and tried to identify it.

"It's a Red Snapper!" Marty Chabot said.

"No, it's a flounder," said the waitress.

"It's too dang dark to tell *what* it is," somebody said. That was Field. Field has swum to the *Gregorian*, late arrival that he was, when he ended up odd man out, no boats left to paddle, "up on the beach without a surfboard," he would explain later when Footlong spotted him and threw him a life preserver, hauling him up with Cletis' help, like apostles pulling in a net of the saved. Newly redeemed Field, having quickly ingratiated himself unto the Captain, proceeded to the Bar-on-the-Fore, where after the downing of three Nun Bubbles he conceived the world salubrious and plundered the cramped under-compartments of Felix Mendelsohn's private stock, emerging covered with a dark green lifeboat tarp, a single turtle-like lamella, and slid silently along the starboard side until, arms full of bottles, green clinking muffled beneath his shell, happened to ram at full sneaking-speed into the chair supporting the un-named Gentleman whom we've identified, with the help of the preceding pages, as Mr. Simon Salmon, a man for hire in the prime of his life, still a full week before his pizza days, and thus despite his later misfortune still a threatening figure to certain unwitting fellows...

"Where's yer rod, fella?" Field's turtle shell sliding once again into oblivious tarp as he stood erect, transformed into a man hiding half a dozen wine bottles in his chalky white arms, speaking nonetheless with an air of some superiority to his new friend; "can't fish without a god-damn rod, now can you?"

The man snickered vaguely. Observing Croom from this seat had been no problem until this starch-eyed vestige of neanderthal rose from some primordial puddle below deck. "Mm, yes, actually I was enjoying the calm of the ocean, my friend. Perhaps you'd rather..." beginning to vacate, "...use the seat for its more conventional purpose?"

At once he knew he'd underestimated the situation. In seconds the jovially buzzed Field had strapped him in the chair, nestled a rod between his legs, and begun to instruct him in the grosser aspects of casting. "It's too bad, freend, that yer arms are caught beneath yer seatbelt. Otherwise castin would be a mite easier, yukuk."

"Yes, certainly," Simon not one to lose his cool; "though you *have* strapped me a little tight..."

"Don't want to lose anyone overboard," Field countered. "Especially someone so grammatically correct." He sloshed into a nearby seat. "Soon as you feel a little nibble, you just let me know," Field said. "Meanwhile, I'll keep an eye on you."

•

Tender-eared Marty Chabot, who was inciting a minor riot by expounding Beemus' theory of the UFO/whale connection, asserting by insinuation that Tinsel had in all probability hooked a messenger from another planet, was blinded into silence by the floodlights the Captain turned on at Field's request. Beemus leant down and smooched the fish. "Does this look like anyone to you?" he asked Cozetta.

"John Wayne?" she ventured.

"Herbert Hoover!" offered Footlong.

"Nee, ne, Cristofer Columbo!" rang in Felix Mendelsohn, and the company present was split as to whether he was referring to the famous 1595 Theodore de Bry painting of the well-known Admiral and navigator or the equally well-known and renowned TV character, the private detective played by American actor Peter Falk.

"Actually, it looks like this lady we met today," Cletis told Footlong.

"Holy shit, the mumbo jumbo lady, Cletis!" Footlong looked warily at Tinsel and Cozetta, gauging their willingness to hear another unbelievable story. "Huh. Na no, actually it was nothin, huh Cletis."

"Yeah, that's right, just some more stuff that must not have happened, huh?"

The awkward silence broke as the waitress served notice that she'd hooked a big one; it was a fighter, and the next five minutes saw some of the worst fishing advice ever given for free urged onto the valiant woman as she reeled it patiently in.

•

   It doesn't take long for a professional escape-artist to free himself of a single leather strap holding him fast to a fishing stool. But Simon Salmon was not an escape-artist. He was an arsonist, thief and part-time hitman, and despite being a completely competent agent, he needed a full eight minutes before he'd worked his arms free. In a sense he was lucky to have taken so long, since the delay would only quicken his departure from the boat in the event that followed. But everyone's got to get off at some point. Sliding between the railing and the row of seats he suddenly spied the waitress, who, yanking on a gaffe with unaffectionate vigor, swivelled in her stool as she pulled in her catch. The Red Snapper caught him across the jaw and collarbone, knocking him into the worried water from which it had just emerged.

   A life-preserver was thrown down; ropes were flung into the ocean. But for all this the man flutter-kicked his way to the other side of the now-idle ship, whereon climbing onto a rabbit-faced paddleboat the *Gregorian* had dragged out to sea, he began the short journey back to shore.

•

   "Nivver seen nuthin like *thet*." The Captain scratched his nose. "Moost be bed luck. We're headin beck."

   The Captain retreated to start up the engine. Back on shore *Bolero* seemed to be winding tighter towards its climax, a bluesy crescendo lifting the spirits of the disappointed on deck, who leaned over starboard, their elbows on the railing, watching the lights and beach fires flicker across the wet air.

   But a siren sounded; the lights on deck blinked and went out. "Electricity's all off!" they heard the Captain yell from inside. "Keep calm! The generator'll swing on in a jiffy." The emergency lighting was activated a few seconds later.

   "Water pump's shut down!" a crew member called up. "Ballast is gonna be way screwed!"

"Aye aye aye," Mendelsohn mumbling to himself as he came outside. "Someone's got to go out an git whatever it is cloogin the intake unclooged."

"Hey Captain! Off stern!"

Where before the water had been calm as a sleeping baby's belly, as it still was off starboard, the view from stern was an ocean boiling in the moonlight, a frenzy of motion as far as they could see.

The Captain hit the floodlights. Millions of creatures, writhing, squirming, darting on the surface and as far beneath it as the lights could penetrate.

"It's a god-damn kettle of squid!" the Captain shouted. One of the crew was lowered to clean the intake screen for the pumps. Tinsel and Cozetta watched him pull handfuls of gelatinous bodies, toss them behind him.

"As soon as I get this cleaned, they just clog it up again," he said when he'd been pulled back on deck.

"We'll drift till we sink," the Captain said. The lights seemed to attract even more squid. The ship was surrounded on all sides.

"Are they feeding?" the waitress asked the Captain.

"Neh. Not anymore. They're *matin* is what they're doin, sweetie. With no regard for nothin at all they're matin; and they won't stop for seventy-two hours, makin little squid love till they die and drift to the bottom."

The males were identifiable by their color. They turned purple, their heads and tentacles became striped with red and maroon. The females shimmered translucent golds, diaphanous whites. Some swam in pairs, tentacles interwined. Others engaged in five and six-way connections, breaking off, propelling themselves like tiny jets to another group, darting at random in and out of the water's churning surface. They were dancing, face to face; they were searching for partners.

The *Gregorian* began to tilt. A thin layer of panic spread over the deck; all of a sudden people were losing their grips on the railing, lurching awkwardly across the deck for their lifejackets, slipping on the wet planks. Tinsel helped one of the crew members calm them.

"At least you can swim," he joked, imitating his true-to-life dog paddle. "I can't!" somebody yelled. Tinsel turned to one of the passengers, whom he recognized as a nun from his first trip on the ship. "Can you swim?" he asked her.

"I don't know," she said.

"Isn't the boat supposed to stay afloat? Don't you have a backup generator?" Cozetta was asking Felix Mendelsohn.

"Afraid not. We're usin the generator's juice jest to keep the lights on. Aye, she's not long for it," he sighed through his nostrils. "She's a-gooin *down*."

Tinsel was untangling the lines to the paddle boats. The *Gregorian* had two life-boats; as they were being lowered somebody noticed the first of the sharks, cutting an alleyway through the mass of squid, jaws wide open to allow the most food in; it paused a moment, shook its head and twisted in the water to speed up the swallowing, then began again. Soon a few others were visible. A few people tried to climb from the lifeboats back onto the ship.

"Sink or swim!" the Captain yelled at them. He cut the lines, and the boats drifted away from the ship.

Tinsel was the last non-crew member on board. Cozetta waited below in the mute-swan paddleboat. "You gonna grab one of the paddle boats?" he asked the Captain.

"Neh. Doon with his ship an all. Good-bye Crum."

"Whawha. But–" Mendelsohn backed Tinsel against the rail, drew the slack rope over his wrist. "Been nice knowin ya now, Crum. Wouldn't want to make yer wife wait aloon by the sharks wouldya..."

The last Tinsel saw of Captain Felix Mendelsohn that evening was his silhouette, through the half-submerged plexiglass windows of the Bar-on-the-Fore, lighting up his pipe. Then he turned and walked down into the tilting ship's belly. As Tinsel and Cozetta paddled away, he thought he'd heard the Captain's voice, muffled but still deep, giving an order to his crew that sounded like "Man the Sea Pig!" but his attention was quickly renegotiated along the lines of a seven foot blue shark cruising toward the paddleboat and swerving smoothly off to his side. Tinsel could see down its throat in the last light from the *Gregorian*: mounds of squid were streaming around, bouncing off the inner walls of its mouth, still copulating, propelling themselves at each other in blurry bursts of color, even as they were squeezed into the blackness of the belly beyond where Tinsel could not see.

•

Squid were popping up from the pedals, flipping into their laps, squirming around their ankles. The sea was dark now; they could make out the dull shapes of the other paddle boats, and the larger shadows of the life boats against the lights on the beach ahead. There was no sign behind them of the *Gregorian*.

Cozetta was re-assuring Tinsel of Cletis' safety. "I saw him on the lifeboat. The first one down. You were busy talking to the Captain."

"Okay, I'm sure he's alright. I'll just be happy to see him when we get to shore." The small fleet of boats had escaped the squid without incident. One minute was like paddling through grass, the squishy bodies flying into the air in the revolving paddles; the next minute the sea was calm again, the thrashing diminished to a pattering sound, like a brief and violent rainstorm passed through.

Back on land, a call had gone out to all available musicians, and a line of vans had driven out to the surf line and hooked up. By the time *Bolero*'s final minute began, Jay thought he saw from his elevated position on stage a dozen dozen guitars joining in, seven times seven drum kits, and then he saw, way above it all as he lifted the sax to his chapped lips, a spark ride across the sky. Nobody got the final note right, not a one, but it didn't matter; it was pure unfettered noise, it was a physical thing, a solid block of sound, a true monster, and it plunged the entire island into as profound a darkness as was the silence that accompanied it. Far away and over the low hills beyond the beach, Efrain saw the blackout spread across the island until there was no light left to see except the moon out over the sea. Efrain clapped his hand on Jay's shoulder. Jay sighed; bleary-eyed, he let his sax hang quietly against his breast. Then they looked up.

•

The island, though it was not what it once was, lay beneath the darkness and silence as if it had never changed. Most of the party-goers on the beach, or guitarists on the roofs of their vans, or the others sitting in the puddles of their seats on the lifeboats, could imagine that the moment could have been from anytime before time started ticking on the island, before gold mines and the Catholic Church, any moment in that eternal space that shot into the past. It was dark. It was quiet.

Onstage, the members of Tequila Mockingbird were gathered in a tired huddle, arms draped over one another, as if to bow to the invisible audience before them. Cooter, sniffling the air, broke the silence. "Geez, this band stinks."

Efrain chuckled. He held a butane lighter over his head. "Imagine," he said, and flicked it on.

Then things went to hell again.

•

Efrain and Jay claimed not to have seen anything. Those watching from the beach who saw mostly talked about a ring of lights, or a chandelier; one person described it as a giant silver wagon-wheel, with dozens more lights dangling from it, as if countless miners, the lights in their helmets still on, hung from myriad nooses, rotating in counterpoint to the direction of the larger wheel's spin.

Tinsel and Cozetta heard a commotion ahead of them, but saw nothing.

Cletis thought he heard the muffled sound of helicopter blades overhead, but saw no light.

The waitress, who was in the lifeboat closest to Marty Chabot's rubber-duckie paddleboat, said it was a flying saucer, no doubt about it, and that Marty was caught in a beam of light and lifted gently up through a hatch in the spacecraft's bottom. She said he had a peace-ful smile on his face.

But Footlong, who was in the same boat, testified that it was a plane that had the ability to hover soundlessly, that it had no lights, and that an iron ladder swung down behind Marty, who seemed to be looking elsewhere in the sky, and a man climbed down the ladder and, with one hand steadying himself hooked Marty in his other arm as if he were just a baby, and climbed into darkness. "Definitely human," Footlong said, "scuba diver human, for sure."

Nobody seemed to agree on what happened that night, but in the morning the remains were evident: one mile from shore, twenty million squid were still mating, and half a mile closer, a rubber-duckie paddleboat floated in the waves where it had been abandoned, held to that spot in the calm water as if by a strange gravity.

•

Wan regained consciousness to find himself alone on a deserted ship. There'd been the anchor, and then that voice, calling... terror had struck everyone dumb for a moment, but then he'd heard the awful wailing; all about him it seemed the men, the Partners and the crew, had begun melting into the deck, assuming grotesque postures as the wood or metal bracings crept up, into, their bodies. The bone ship had begun to move through the yacht, cutting it like butter, absorbing it...

Then there'd been a high, shrill whistle and before it had ended they'd all disappeared: the men, the bone ship, the anchor; he was left on his knees amidst a strangely calm and quiet ocean. Only the whistling sound, which ended itself exactly as a brown leather shoe, size 10, had smashed into the back of his near-bald pate.

Now, awake, the shoe crouched innocuously beside him, he allowed himself to breathe deeply, relax. Somehow he'd been meant to survive, chosen to stay behind. Nothing worse could happen now. He got to his feet. "It's finally over."

"No, sir." A strong hand dropped on his shoulder, swivelled him around. Wan looked into the opaque onyx visor of the Coast Guard nearest him. There were five of them, and each wore dark sunglasses and inscrutable expressions.

"No, sir, I think it's just beginning."

•

Sometime after Marty Chabot disappeared without a trace, Cozetta and Tinsel became aware of a large moving presence in the water beneath their feet. Huge bubbles, some a foot in diameter, rose to the surface in front of their paddleboat.

"Is it a whale? a porpoise?" Tinsel strained to see. Suddenly the paddleboat was lifted on a swell of foamy water.

"It's breaching!" Cozetta yelled.

From beneath them it rose, snout first, a metallic blinking eye, the arching fleshy back streaming water over its sides, andfinally the coiled pink tail, twisting back and forth like a rudder. The *Sea Pig*.

A furry hatch opened within the near ear. Captain Felix Mendelsohn poked his head and arm out, handed them a bottle of Hound Dog beer. "Meet me at seven sharrp tomorrow mornin," he said. The fuzzy ear closed with a clink, and the grinning swine sank once more, with a thrashing of bubbles about its hindquarters, into the dark sea.

•

"I saw him from the stage, but there's no way I coulda got there in time."

Efrain explained to Tinsel how he'd seen a man crawl from the water and make his way towards the towel where Tinsel and Cozetta and Cletis had left their bags.

"He went through each one. I think he mighta took something, but it looked more like a datebook or something, not a wallet or purse. I just figgered I'd tell ya so if something was missing, ya know..."

"Thanks Efrain," Cozetta said.

"Oh man, my shell's broken," Cletis pulled chunks of the triton shell from his rucksack. His finger came out bloody. Tiny shards of glass covered his hand like magic dust. "Musta been something in here I forgot about," Cletis scratching his head. "Everything's all wet and slimy."

"Oh Cletis man! The dude was goin through your stuff right at the end of the number. He was shakin your bag like this–" making appropriate movements, "—and then the song ended and the power blew and, you know, the whole island went under."

•

The next morning they met Captain Mendelsohn on the beach, and Cletis and Tinsel made plans to help with the salvage operation. Cozetta had to leave later in the morning: her one woman show at the Palm's End gallery couldn't wait. Some reporters from the *Times* had promised to show, and she'd be mentioned in the Sunday Arts section in the article previewing Arno Rizzoli's upcoming show.

•

Four days after the party Captain Mendelsohn took Tinsel out in a glass-bottomed boat.

"Ye shoulda been here yesterday when we took the little pieces away," he was saying. The salvage crew had gotten most of the *Gregorian* afloat the morning after, flanking it with huge ballasts as if it were going in dry dock and floating it to the surface. "Then there were pilot whales, porpoises, salmon and swordfish. Moonfish. Later in the day we saw flukes out yonder: a coupla sperm whales checkin to see what was left, heh heh." Birds of all kind had hovered over the surface, dipping carefully to avoid the sharks. Auks, terns: ground and air and water creatures, all feeding on love.

"Now ya see all thet *hwight* stuff down there."

"Sorta." Tinsel squinted.

"Corpses o' the poor squiddies. Fucked themselves dead, or died tryin, harhar. And beneath it all: aboot five or six billion squid embryos, gittin lahrgeer by the minute."

Mendelsohn told him how twenty percent of the embryos would die before hatching due to environmental changes, and fifty percent more would be devoured during the first week of life. "Thet's a lot of *deeath* for a little bit of life, eh. But squid you'll find in *every* ocean, in *every* sea. Aye. Everything alive will go eat a squiddie; but the squiddie's alive everywhere yeh look. Must be worth the sacrifice. Hm."

Just before the Captain had started the motor to take them in, Tinsel saw a large gray ray skimming the ocean floor, avoiding the eggs, which by now had been covered with a protective algae whose taste discouraged nibblers, but devouring the corpses, sweeping over the settlement like an angel of death.

•

"There were a ton if there were a pound of em."

The Captain was entertaining his guests for the cruise that would leave them at the airport. "Aye, quidged in eevery crevice of the boot." The lunch specials this week at the Bar-on-the-Fore were squid a l'espagnola, squid alla bolognese, squid alla Romana, and squid a la casserole. Tinsel sat back in a cushioned seat that could have been his couch at home, and nodded off to sleep.

"An you can be sure an it's more than a rumor," Felix Mendelsohn said as he removed his cap and scratched his head beneath his frazzled gray locks, "thet a diet of *fresh squiddies* is knoown by the ancients to make yer hair grow like Samson."

•

"*THE FREEMAN'S OATH.* Reverend John Glover did it in 1639; wrote and printed it, I mean. The first document printed in English in North America." Polly and Rizzoli stood over a glass case in the exhibit room. To their eyes were presented two identical pieces of paper, yellowed and brittle.

"It wasn't kept well. Three hundred years is not a long time for paper. At least, not until the Century of Progress, aha. Now the books you see in stores today will be dust in fifty years. Acid-free paper just another casualty of industrial development, mass production. But of course, of course, progress dictated it. Easier to provide, you know. So now you can read Danielle Steel in a million billion homes. But how many of those homes have a copy of the Constitution? Oh yes, haha."

Rizzoli droned on, aware that he was providing background noise for Polly as she examined the two *Oaths*. "And anyways, my word, what information that we get today do you think will be any *less* worthless fifty years hence than, say, an early twentieth century school primer? Maybe it makes sense."

"Okay, which is the genuine?" she asked.

"Ooh, do you mean the genuine Rizzoli, or the historical genuine?"

"C'mon buster."

"Well..." he pretended to peer at them, a smile disabling him now and then. "You see the one on the left: what do you think of that wormhole. Real?"

"There's a wormhole in the other one too."

"Yes well. Worms are everywhere, aren't they."

"Hm." Polly bent a few inches closer, shadowed her eyes with her hands. Two images looked up at her, as complementary as her own two eyes, as identical as two copies of the same text might remain over time. But which was playing possum?

"Okay." A smile tantamount to an apology. "Well, they're both mine, actually. Little trick, hm."

"Rattlesnake." Polly swung out at him, fully expecting her arm to be blocked, but Rizzoli let it follow its course to a halfhearted slap across his face.

"Ooh! I didn't mean it," she reaching now to caress his cheek.

"Well I think so. It was just an expression, after all. Like this one," acknowledging her touch. "Anyway, the sting is on the surface, and that's where it's to be appreciated." She brought her hand away.

"Yes, so. These two were practice pieces I did about twenty years ago, as a student. Sophomoric in their own way, though they'd fool most people. But my latest work... well, later for the latest, aha ha. Now you may have wondered as to this relationship Doctor Wan was fostering between me and the Partner & Partner company..."

"You forged documents?"

"Well, no. Not yet. But this was to be the agreement, I believe. New documents, that is twentieth century, industrial age and so on, are all too easy to forge. It's more like learning a secret cryptology; know when to put the rubber stamps, what specific typographical errors to put in top secret memos; this placement and these 'errors'— they're too easy, almost. It's a matter of getting correct materials, placing elements correctly. It's all *correct* work, you see; no *art* in it. That's not to say there's not craft. But it's the craft of assembly-line automobiles. It's the art that's fled the entire century, Polly. To duplicate a hand-written document, you have to duplicate an individual's style. In essence you have to find the key to a cryptography whose rules are unknown even by the one setting the code! Duplicating the effects of time is not difficult; there are a million pounds of paper in circulation that are exactly as old as the *Freeman's Oath*. Time is the easiest thing to do."

"You make it sound too easy." Rizzoli drew her over to a larger display case, draped over with a heavy purple velvet cover.

"How old is the velvet?" he asked. Polly gave it an inquisitive look. "Hm. Well it's easy to make a fabric look old. All you have to do is beat it up."

Rizzoli bunched a corner of the drapery in his fist. It crinkled loudly. "See? Brown paper bags. Vision's the first fool."

"But time exists is my point, Arno. Time passes, and it shows on things, on all of us, even you."

"Oh does it? And how old am I?"

"You said you were a student twenty years ago. That would make you..."

"Oh I said, I said. I may have lied. And did I tell you how old I was when I was a student? Go on, Polly, what do you really know about my age? We've been pretty close, you should know, hm? And what *do* you *know*, Polly, about time but how it affects you?" He paused a moment. "To look older or younger, I don't have to duplicate internal events, DNA, genetic coding. I just have to produce an outer surface that shows a certain typical wear. It's the same with documents. The only thing we know about aging is that things break down. Time is just a measurement of some further obscurity. Why if time weren't good for business it would be dismissed as irrelevant, another science in a vacuum."

"But science—"

"Exactly. But science. I feel the same way. It's the frontier of both human bravery and cowardice, and furthermore handles the paradox without so much as a blink, not even an obscene wink. It's ugly and dead-eyed as a toad, isn't it? But science. It's always limited to its equipment, this century's science. A pure product of its epoch. But art, on the other hand—"

"Exactly what I think, Rizzoli. But art." Polly mimicking, ready to say more. But Rizzoli seemed lost, stuck at a synapse on the verge of a brilliant leap or a crash back to earth. His features drew back for a moment, giving way, like minor characters on a stage, to an empty center, and for a moment some true expression lay close against his skull. Whatever it was, sorrow or joy, she couldn't tell. Maybe it was neither; maybe it was just Rizzoli.

"Arno?"

"Yes. Polly."

"You're okay, right?"

"Oh yes. Ah well. Let's take a look at the masterpiece."

He rolled up the cover, flicked a switch that lit the casing's interior.

Polly caught her breath. "Now one of these," he said, opening the glass door, "*is* genuine. The other is mine."

"The Declaration of Independence."

"That's what it says."

"How'd you get the original?"

"It's on loan from the Government. There are FBI men behind every curtain, Polly, and I'm not kidding. Real G-Man types." He pulled a pen from his pocket, threw it at the nearest curtain. From behind its stirring a head poked out, inquisitive.

"See, dark glasses and everything. Haha." To the agent, head floating along the curtain's edge as if disembodied, "Just checking. Sir. Thank you." The head disappeared. "And," Rizzoli aiming another pen and throwing it. It hit the curtain with a sharp clack and bounced back. "Oh. *My* plywood curtain. Nobody behind that. Ha."

He reached into the case and gently removed the document on the right side.

"Is that the real one?" Polly asked.

"Oh no. I'd be shot if I tried to actually touch it, you know. Look there. See: the genuine is in a sealed container, vacuum-packed etcetera, very fool-proof if you know what I mean; only a fool couldn't figure out how to get into it, aha. This was Partner & Partner's hope, anyway?"

"What? Some kind of mix-up?"

"See what lewd value we place on time? What's the difference between these documents? The words are the same. They're both brittle and ready to fall apart. And nobody reads either of them anymore.

"Realize, at least, that this document is nothing short of a declaration of war. Historically that's all it really means."

"That's not what it says. It's proof that people felt a need to document grievances, to give a rationale for independence."

"You're confusing the point of the article with the etiquette of it. The point was: you're either free or you're not, Polly. I think Malcolm X might have phrased it a bit differently. You're free when you start acting free. The colonies were free, more importantly, because they had all they needed; they no longer needed the support of the Continent. But this is all moot, is it not? The fat lady finished singing a few hundred years ago.

"At any rate, in a country obssessed with time as a validator of its legitimacy, a baby streaking its hair gray, what better trump card for a breakaway community of business interests interested in statehood to hold but a time honored document that attests to the need for a willingness to go to war to back up a mere memo of irreconcilable differences?"

"I'm not sure I get it."

"It's okay. They won't be happy back at the Company anyway. Because, unfortunately, there is nothing written on the back of the Declaration of Independence. However, on this," and he turned the parchment over, with an air of expectancy that seemed half-practiced itself and half true wonder, and together they stared down at the transformed paper.

•

The map was four hundred years old.

"What is it?"

"It's my version of a signature, hah. You know the story of a Greek sailor who chased his tail in the bays and rivers around Seattle and was convinced he'd found the Northwest Passage? This is the map of his travels." Polly gaped. The map *did* look over a century older than the Declaration on the other side. "It's such a politically compressed view of the country—a Northwest Passage was needed, so it was found—that I thought I'd reproduce it on the verso of the Declaration of Independence–"

"Your copy of the Declaration, you mean," Polly said.

"Obviously. Or, is it so obvious?" His voice lowered to a whisper. "I confess that I was left unguarded with both Declarations, before I sketched the map, you know, for the space of about fifteen seconds when the fed guarding me turned to receive a cup of coffee from his assistant. Of course he wasn't allowed within ten feet of the document, glass case or no glass case. Only some incredibly high connections convinced the Government to let me get that close to it. I was even allowed to handle it, for about five seconds, gloves on my hands and all, just to get some idea as to texture, etcetera. Anyway: I got up to get a cup of coffee myself, and when I sat back down, I couldn't for the life of me remember which was which, whether I'd made the switch yet or not.

"Somewhere inside me, Polly, I know; but it may be my only secret from myself that I can't truly be sure whether or not I actually drew this map on the back of the genuine Declaration of Independence." He lifted it to the light, gingerly fingered its edges. "Here. Hold it, why don't you."

Polly drew back, as if afraid to touch it. But curiosity overcame her fear, and she found herself holding the almost weightlessness of it, thinner than she could imagne, more fragile than anything so important should be, the visible imprint of quill pen grooves on the parchment's weave, the stains of ages of hands and fingers, the ink drops near the signatures...

She felt the sudden urge to crinkle the sheet in her hands. Why not? It wouldn't change the law, it wasn't the only copy of the text; the country wouldn't crumple into dust if she did it, even if it was the real one. Maybe by doing it she could determine if Arno was perpetrating one last trick, or if not, then if ideas were, as she thought she believed, independent of time, things of themselves.

"Turn it back over now, Polly. Look at my map. It's a treasure map you know." She carefully rotated the paper on her left hand. A thick *X* marked a heart-shaped island in the Strait. Beneath it, barely legible and almost obscured due to impressions from the text on the other side, were the words *Inwich Isl.* ...

"What's the treasure?"

"Ha ha. Ho ho. What's a map without a treasure? The island I added myself; it's not really there. That's the treasure. No one will ever be able to claim it."

"Are you still going to give this to Doctor Wan?"

"Sure. He wanted it."

"So what did he mean earlier when he stormed out of here saying you'd betrayed him?"

"Oh, that. Well, as you can guess, I tired of the idea of forging mass-production documents. Not my thing. He was sure the Eastern Florida thing would sink without a clean copy of the Declaration, but I doubt it will be *my* fault that things go wrong as... well, as they often do."

"Eastern Florida thing? What Eastern Florida thing?"

"Polly, it's in all the papers. Just about all that I know anyway. Thing is, you have to put it together yourself, and the facts are scattered. It's the ol' divide and conquer in the age of information. But in my mind that division might be the movement's own self-betrayal."

Betrayal, betrayal; in the moments before Polly had commenced her walloping of Wan, she'd felt that sense of betrayal. Wan showing her some colored Polaroids of Tinsel and another woman, a beautiful brunette as Wan told her, the pictures were a little fuzzy and shot from obscure angles of equally strange places, behind a gravestone, the roof of a shack by a swimming hole, all equally untenable. It was like snapshots of UFOs, she'd told him. Wan said the woman was Tinsel's ex-wife. Again, how could she be sure? All she felt certain enough about was that Tinsel was probably the man in the photos. What he was doing in each shot was unclear. But for a second she'd felt betrayed, and known in her heart she'd already left her husband to his own devices, to an empty house with only a small note in the mail promising some vague future contact, nothing beyond that, and that further she'd left him for no solid reason other than life had been almost too comfortable to be real, too uneventful to be comfortable, and ultimately too depressing to be uneventful. Dramas are created offstage, they are rehearsed endlessly offstage, and when they finally show themselves under the gaze of the audience the deck is loaded in their favor by fliers, favorable previews and word-of-mouth publicity by every family member of every person involved in the most remote way with the production; still, what the eye actually sees are the reaction of character, some compression of events in that harshly lit vacuum that merely alludes to real events. But Polly, projecting upon this all her own thumbs-up or thumbs-down, like a film of a critic describing a move based on a play, like a commentary of her own life two lives removed from the bare-bones script, could look down upon her character, its mood changes and decisions and find there was an obvious gap in interpretation. They should have given somebody else the part, she reasoned. What made her leave Tinsel? Nothing. What would make her return to him, gather him up once more in her arms as he slept? Nothing. Nothing sat on both sides of the equation, a line devoid of value but delivered intact to the world in full confidence, with all the appropriate projection and makeup and blocking, nought for nought; somehow the photos hadn't mattered. But their delivery had, and her sense of betrayal had turned over onto Doctor Wan with violent precision. She'd given up on believing in remote circumstances before she boarded the Remaining Airlines flight that dropped her into a city now turned dark. She looked out a window over Rizzoli's shoulder as he drew back the curtain, momentarily distracted, to see three ravens hovering over the short ledge, their legs dangling beneath them, landing gear, hanging aloft like oversized wasps, their expressions calm and hysterical at the same time. What was Rizzoli to her now that they'd spent that evening together? What had remained from those moments beside a change in mannerism? Only whatever secrets sleep may have brought their own two temples, touching as they had dozed in a sheet of mutual sweat, dust on his flank from the floor below, his upper arm crooked lightly over and across her ribs, as if keeping a distance more than protecting her own fragile space; whatever napped with them beneath the tent of his elbow.

She opened her eyes, realizing she'd closed them to ward off distractions while on that inner avenue. Rizzoli was talking a few feet away to one of the agents, who was watching his assistants as they made last-second adjustments to the alarm device on the case. Another brought Rizzoli a wooden box with a glass pane and some framing materials.

"Time's running down, running up," Rizzoli snapped his fingers. "I've got to set up my masterpiece, put it in place."

"They won't let you keep it in the display with the Declaration?"

"No. Security stuff. They want to seal the case up for good. Etcetera. Haha."

He was beside her now, digging into the box, two of his fingers pulling the map gently from her hand. "Five minutes to move the world. Give me a fulcrum and I'll. I have a dream. Excuse me," turning his back and getting busy with the matting. Polly realized suddenly that if the Declaration in the case was Rizzoli's, if the one he was matting now was the genuine, and if he chose to display the map and not the Declaration, he would have successfully buried history, buried it and imitated its remains.

However time normally moved for Polly it abandoned her there, maybe at a new crossroad or maybe just in the middle of the web, waiting for the great mother of time, hourglass on her back, to spin her into her place on the century's edge. It seemed like seconds, but it could have been five minutes, then Rizzoli was there. Behind him the frame reflected light obliquely. The glare made her avert her eyes.

"Which one is there?" she said. "Which side is up?"

"I don't know," he said. "I closed my eyes while I was doing it. More important to get some other stuff done right now. Polly," leaning close in an unconsciously friendly manner, "where will you go now? I've got money if you need it."

"I'll take it," she said. "And I don't know exactly whether it makes a difference where I go. I think maybe to Jamaica. I've got a stepson there."

"You'll go, too." He pressed an envelope into her hand. She didn't look down. "I know. You don't have to look. If you need anything, there's a number in there. I probably oughtn't to give you more money, but I've always got time for you, Polly. Time's just for the making if you know the style it's made in." A woman in a crimson taffeta dress with a museum nametag tapped him on the shoulder. "Ready to go?"

"Oh yes. Yes." He moved a step away from Polly, then turned back towards her and smiled. She smiled back immediately, felt some cold glow in her eyes settle as he adjusted his tie, then walked with the woman to the closed oak double doors, behind which the crowd was waiting, and they opened them, disappearing behind either door as people spilled in to see the Declaration of Independence, and the mapping of the Strait of Juan de Fuca.

XXI. Further Reading

She was a long way from home.

The man she'd hired, hidden somewhere between a camo-mile-and-mauve flannel and a Wrightsville Beach fishing hat stuck through with popsicle stick voodoo dolls, scratched at a fading tattoo between the regular intervals of re-starting the boat's engine or redirecting the craft after getting swept off course by the drift. In his other hand he held a small painted piece of wood, spat on a movable dial, held it at the sun and puzzled over it a moment.

"Oohwee, gettin close now," he said, then went back to picking at his tattoo. It depicted a snowman, who looked more like an ameoba with a chip on its shoulder, stabbing a sperm whale with a bloody harpoon. The artist had filled in some of the spaces with the obligatory shade of rusted copper. "Tryin to git it off," he'd explained earlier of his itching, which he further illustrated with the following song:

> Stovepipe the Snowman
> Was an evil whiteface soul
> And the children say when he came to play
> That he'd try to steal their legs
> Stovepipe the Snowman
> Had a cane made out of lead
> And he'd yank kids' hair and he'd bite their arms
> And he'd smash them on the head
> There must have been some magic
> In that stovepipe hat he skimmed
> For when the kids came home from school

He tried to grab their limbs! Oh
Stovepipe the Snowman
Had two eyes made out of snakes

"Enough, enough," Edna had interrupted him.

"I gotta sing it. It's a curse."

"Well. Are we there yet?" She looked out on the Strait. It was huger than she'd imagined, and Vancouver Island rose in the north like a giant porcupine, the smaller islands nestling like offspring around it.

"We're just about there; see them shallows. Hey," eyeing her now, "what are you, anyway, an old sea hag? Gonna put the curse on me?"

"You gonna find me that island?"

"Oh man. I tode you it's not there. Just shallows. Another friggin curse." The engine sputtered and died. He yanked disconsolately at it. "Eck! Squid in the propeller." Flipped the broken body back into the water.

"Just tell me when."

Five minutes passed like a schoolbus.

"When."

She looked around her. "Which side of the boat?"

"Well, you didn say nothin bout *which side of the boat*; we're right over it, fer cripe's sake."

"Move the boat over then! Now! Just a few feet..."

They looked into the water off the boat's stern. She poked a walking stick in, felt around. Dipped her arm in to the elbow. And stopped there.

"Is something..." She put on a pair of goggles and flopped overboard. The bar rose to within seven feet of the surface. Lying on it was the broken hull of a canoe. She moved over it, pushed it aside, strained the sand beneath it with her fingers, dug with her hands into the soft mound till the blood hammered in her head and her chest threatened to burst. She surfaced.

"Nothing..." she grabbed the edge of the boat, tipping it precariously to stern.

"Watchit hag! I can't swim, man; come on."

"Just... just soft... soft sand." Breath sawed in and out of her, threatening to take away her tongue. "No rocks or doors..."

"Come back up here. I told ya that," he said softly. He helped her back up, where she sat wet, panting for breath, her eyes like steel hornets in the sun.

"You prob'ly got dem coordinates wrong. Hey, let's get over to Vancouver. There's a little landing the locals know about. Beer's cheaper there. I can tell you some sick stories bout pirates, real life ones too, that I met before I got cursed."

He kept talking to her, over the sputtering motor, as they worked slowly towards the sun.

•

Tinsel got home fifteen minutes to dusk. There were a few birthday cards in the mailbox for Cletis. A phone bill. Some junk mail.

Inside the house it was raining. At least in the living room; he could see the edge of the small cloud hugging the ceiling, the wisps it trailed out into the kitchen. "Wha?" He dropped his suitcase and put the mail on the table. There was a box of stale cookies and a note from Polly, some more mail. A whimper filtered through the sound of falling water, and Tinsel peered around the corner. "Hello? Polly? Hello?"

A huge chunk of rock covered most of the floorspace, including where Tinsel remembered the coffee table had been. Some variety of vegetable matter was growing along the top of the rock, which was steaming where it touched the floor. A dragonfly hovered over it like an eagle, alighted on a tall twiggish plant growing out of the surface of it. A fog ran through the room from the floor to Tinsel's armpits. Another whine. From inside...

"Huh? Hello?" He pulled a chair over, stood up and looked at the crown of moss and plants. There seemed to be a manhole-sized space in the middle, over which sat a rock that looked like a giant bowling ball covered with barnacles. Tinsel grabbed it and tried to pry it away from the hole. The edges crumbled against his fingers and the stone fell in. A loud bark pierced the heavy air. Tinsel hoisted himself up and stuck his head in the hole.

"Shit. Lancelot!" He reached down to where the dog lay, its hindquarters twisted beneath the stone. "Stupid shit, Tinsel. Probably broke your dog's leg."

He lifted her out gingerly. She weighed almost nothing. "We'll put you down right here," he said, clearing a space on the kitchen table. She seemed to be having trouble breathing.

"Come on Lance," he said, looking around. Where the hell was the phone? Just a wire sticking out of the wall. "Wha. Wha. Come on," squeezing her ribs in a last ditch effort when her eyes began to close, and her tongue spread suddenly out like a carpet. Lancelot coughed, and a blue marble the size of a golf ball shot from her throat. Tinsel watched it roll across the rug and under the couch.

"It's okay now, girl," he told the dog. "Okay now." Her breathing was less constricted, and Tinsel detected the faintest wag of her tail. "Glad to see me? I'm glad to see you too." And then he looked around, and began to see how things had changed.

ABOUT JEFF SCHWANER

Jeff Schwaner went to Cornell University and
while there founded Pathos Press,
which published books of verse and art
using an old Challenge proofers press.

After nine years in bookselling,
including Booksmith at Chestnut Hill, Massachusetts,
Bookland at Mill Creek in Portland, Maine,
The Bookery in Ithaca, New York
and Chapter Two Bookstore
in Charleston, South Carolina,
he became a full-time editor and writer, which is to say,
he became very poor and over-worked.
Then in a fit of brilliance he co-founded
greatunpublished.com.

Despite this behavior, he still believes
he is loved by his wife and many pets.

Made in the USA
Las Vegas, NV
16 April 2024